SPECIAL DELIVERY

LEESA RONALD

ALLEN&UNWIN
SYDNEY·MELBOURNE·AUCKLAND·LONDON

This is a work of fiction. Names, characters, places and incidents are products of the author's imagination or are used fictitiously. Any resemblance to actual events, locales or persons, living or dead, is entirely coincidental.

First published in 2024

Copyright © Leesa Ronald 2024

All rights reserved. No part of this book may be reproduced or transmitted in any form or by any means, electronic or mechanical, including photocopying, recording or by any information storage and retrieval system, without prior permission in writing from the publisher. The Australian *Copyright Act 1968* (the Act) allows a maximum of one chapter or 10 per cent of this book, whichever is the greater, to be photocopied by any educational institution for its educational purposes provided that the educational institution (or body that administers it) has given a remuneration notice to the Copyright Agency (Australia) under the Act.

Allen & Unwin
Cammeraygal Country
83 Alexander Street
Crows Nest NSW 2065
Australia
Phone: (61 2) 8425 0100
Email: info@allenandunwin.com
Web: www.allenandunwin.com

Allen & Unwin acknowledges the Traditional Owners of the Country on which we live and work. We pay our respects to all Aboriginal and Torres Strait Islander Elders, past and present.

A catalogue record for this book is available from the National Library of Australia

ISBN 978 1 76147 151 3

Set in 13/18 pt Adobe Garamond Pro by Midland Typesetters, Australia
Printed and bound in Australia by the Opus Group

10 9 8 7 6 5 4 3 2 1

MIX
Paper | Supporting responsible forestry
FSC® C001695

The paper in this book is FSC® certified. FSC® promotes environmentally responsible, socially beneficial and economically viable management of the world's forests.

*To Vivi and John, whose stories were epic,
if slightly exaggerated*

CHAPTER 1

The sweat had worked its way into new crevices. Literally. New crevices. Nine months ago Poppy couldn't fill a B cup properly and would have killed for a bit of cleavage. Now, she cursed her sticky double-Ds as a bead of sweat snaked neatly between them. And butt-crack sweat, she decided, was surely life's greatest indignity.

The lack of air-conditioning in the old LandCruiser on a thirty-seven-degree day didn't help either. With the windows down and hot air blowing into her red face, she scanned for a car park outside the Orange Base Hospital. The nurse had warned her over the phone it would be hard to find a parking space at 11 am but Poppy hadn't paid attention. It was Orange, for god's sake—not Surry Hills during Mardi Gras. Now she cursed that damn nurse for not making her point more vehemently.

Poppy rolled around the car park slowly. *Please,* she bargained with whatever power was out there, *give me a car space and I will repent all my sins.* (And there'd been a few recently, so this was a real bang-for-your-buck deal.)

Out of the corner of her eye she noticed an SUV near the hospital's entrance pull away from the kerb. She groaned with relief. *Bingo.* Revving the ailing engine, she navigated to the space and paused before pulling in. Painted on the tarmac was a clear outline of a pram and the words: PARENTS WITH PRAMS ONLY.

Her belly was straining against the steering wheel. She'd be one of those parents-with-prams in three weeks—maybe less, if this heat had any baby-dropping properties. With a foetus kicking her non-existent abs and a sweat moustache forming on her upper lip, Poppy decided to exploit this loophole. Maybe it was a sign of the new her. The new Poppy who wasn't actually a good girl and who disregarded signage even when it was painted in shouty all caps. *I'm such a badass*, she thought as she steered the LandCruiser into the car space, any twinge of anxiety quickly trumped by relief at the prospect of escaping this god-awful hotbox—if only she could unstick her thighs from the vinyl seat.

It was almost as hot outside the car as in it. Her dress—yellow with cute cap sleeves—was crumpled from the drive. As she climbed out and then bent across the driver's seat to retrieve her handbag, Poppy was vaguely conscious of her hemline fluttering up near her undies. (She wasn't sure why she was still trying to make an effort to look nice when both the elements and her increasing fleshiness were conspiring against her, but first impressions were lasting, she reasoned, and this town was small.) That was when she heard a cough. A tall man in scrubs was hovering near her tailgate, clearly diverting his eyes. Ah. He had definitely seen her undies. That was unfortunate.

He coughed again.

'Yes?' Poppy said, giving him a quick up-down. He was tall with dark blond hair, the kind her mother would describe as presidential.

'This parking space is for parents with prams only,' he told her. 'You'll have to move.'

'Oh, sorry.' Poppy beamed at him, trying to charm her way out of this. 'I just figured, you know . . .' She gestured to her stomach. There could be no misunderstanding what was going on with her belly. She was well past the 'could it be a big lunch?' phase; she was in killer-whale-about-to-have-quintuplets territory.

The man just shrugged. 'You'll still have to move. Other people need this car space more than you.'

Poppy gritted her teeth and flashed her most saccharine smile, the one reserved for priests and parking inspectors. 'I know it's for parents with prams but there were no other spaces and I'm heavily pregnant so I figured it wouldn't matter this one time.' What she actually meant was: *I am fucking pregnant and I am fucking over it, so give me a break.*

He shrugged again. 'You still have to move.'

What the hell? Poppy glared at him, all pretence at friendliness gone. 'Look, I'm sorry,' she said, 'but I'm thirty-seven weeks pregnant, I am tired, I am hot, and that car is too tall for me to keep hoisting myself in and out of. It could bring on early labour and that's not safe for my baby.' She cradled her belly to make her point.

'I can assure you there's no medical research to suggest getting into a car will incite early labour,' he retorted. 'So you can move.' He crossed his arms, glaring back at her.

Poppy felt her brain implode. Who did this guy think he was? Couldn't he see she was a tiny human with an overly large baby growing inside her? Couldn't he see the tar literally melting under their feet? Couldn't he see her sweat patches, for god's sake?

'I am *not* moving this car,' Poppy huffed, squeezing between him and the LandCruiser to the neutral territory of the footpath. 'If you want to make a complaint about me to the car park police, go right ahead.' She started towards the hospital entrance then turned. 'But let me warn you, I will mount a pretty strong counter-complaint against you, you'—she racked her brain for the perfect insult—'you goody-two-shoes!'

Ah crap. So much for being a badass.

With as much poise as she could muster, Poppy lifted her chin and marched towards the hospital. The nerve of that guy! Hopefully her aggressive stomping would make up for the goody-two-shoes catastrophe.

She was still breathless and simmering with rage when she reached the sweet respite of the air-conditioned prenatal unit. It was shabbier than the one she'd been visiting in Sydney. It had a lived-in look, weighed down by knick-knacks on the reception desk and myriad flyers on the noticeboard. Worried about diet in pregnancy? There was a flyer for that. Need to buy a chicken coop? There was a flyer for that too.

Sitting in the waiting area, Poppy held her face up to the air-conditioning vents and closed her eyes. Maybe one day she'd look back on this moment and laugh at the ridiculousness of her predicament. No partner, no job, just a big fat baby on the way. Hilarious! At the moment, though, all she could feel was exhaustion—from the heat, from the broken sleep and from lugging the extra kilos around. And the most exhausting thing of all? It was the decisions. So many of them. All whirring around in her head, a million threads that braided themselves into even bigger, scarier decisions. There were too many crossroads to consider at this point in her life, so in lieu of choosing one path, she chose none. That was how she'd wound up back at the same hospital where she'd been born three decades earlier. The irony made her stomach curdle.

The exchange in the car park had shaken her. She wasn't used to feeling so tetchy. Sure, she was as anxious as any thirty-one-year-old suffering from an oily T-zone and a mild Afterpay addiction, but she was used to hiding it. In fact, she was excellent at it. At her old marketing job they'd nicknamed her Jack Johnson—as mellow as they come. She'd loved that nickname and played up to it. If one of her team missed a deadline, she'd ask herself: what would Jack do? He wouldn't get angry. He'd drink beers around a fire, dude. If the AV cut out during a presentation? He'd hit the waves, man. It wasn't a watertight management policy but it gave her a mystique of unflappability and, crucially, her colleagues liked her for it. (And Poppy loved being liked.)

That job felt aeons away now. It had been a world of stand-up desks and floor-to-ceiling windows, running for trains and racing for promotions. She'd been the office high performer, powered by overpriced caffeine and ambition, and she'd loved it. It almost hurt to think about.

'Poppy?' called an older lady, interrupting her thoughts. 'You ready?'

The midwife had long grey hair which she tied back at the nape of her neck. 'I'm Wenda,' she said as Poppy rose to meet her. 'I'll be seeing you for the rest of your appointments. Then I'll help deliver bub.' She strode down the corridor and motioned for Poppy to follow. 'It's a shame we're only getting to know each other now. Usually I prefer for us to go through the whole journey together, but hey ho—we roll with the punches, hey.'

It was a statement, not a question, so Poppy didn't reply.

'This is us,' said Wenda, unlocking a grey door with peeling plastic letters that declared it to be Office 3.

'You've got your yellow card,' said Wenda—again, more statement than question.

'Yes, here,' said Poppy, fishing the dog-eared piece of cardboard from her handbag. She sat on the patients' chair and handed the midwife the story of her pregnancy, chronicled in neat black lines on a butter-yellow background.

'I see,' said Wenda, studying it.

Like a sucker for punishment, Poppy watched as Wenda's eyes flicked to the 'Baby's Father' section. *Not present*, it said. Two words that summarised the result of a nine-year relationship and life together.

'Fantastic.' Wenda folded the card and handed it back to her. 'You're in good health and your baby is growing well. Now, is there anything you'd like to ask me?'

Poppy had so many questions. 'No,' she replied, looking at the floor.

SPECIAL DELIVERY

The older lady scrutinised her and Poppy could feel it in her eyes: the pity. She was searching for clues but Poppy wasn't going to give her any. There were things you could share with strangers at a first encounter, and then there were stories that had to be told over days and nights, preferably over bottles of wine with Taylor Swift in the background. Stories that unfolded over years couldn't be relayed in a thirty-minute appointment. They had to be let out slowly, in drips and bursts, otherwise the torrent would drown you. Poppy didn't know much, but she knew this.

Wenda patted the raised bed against the wall, her kind eyes still searching Poppy's closed face. 'Alright,' said the midwife gently. 'Let's check when this baby is coming out.'

CHAPTER 2

Aeroplane mode was a wondrous thing. A tiny icon transporting people to a liberating time when phones weren't smart and TikTok was a *Play School* sound effect. Poppy needed aeroplane mode for her brain. During her half-hour with Wenda she'd already missed four texts.

Mum: *Dear Poppy, how did it go? Remember you are my STRONG BRAVE GIRL and this will be a WONDERFUL ADVENTURE. Lol, Mum.*

Mum: *Dear Poppy, did you receive this? I thought the appointment finished at 11.30.*

Poppy checked her watch. It was 11.36 am.

Mum: *Dear Poppy, just thinking—the appointment may run over time if they want to discuss Patrick, family health history, mental health, services for single mothers etc etc. Make sure you stay and listen to that information. IT COULD BE IMPORTANT.*

Dani: *Call me when you're done, my dear. Love you xx*

Poppy began walking and dialled her best friend.

SPECIAL DELIVERY

Dani picked up on the first ring. 'PARPEEEE!'

Poppy laughed. 'DARNEEEE!'

What had started as a stupid joke while they were travelling around Croatia after uni had morphed into a years-old ritual—one that made Poppy smile every time she spoke to her friend.

'Dude, we may need to cut that shit out soon,' Dani said. 'The other mums in the park already think I'm a weirdo because of Nella's fixation with chewing the pram wheels. They don't need any more ammo to use against me.'

Poppy laughed. 'Dan, if I didn't say your name like that you would legit think I was mad at you.'

'True,' Dani agreed. 'And for that, we have to thank old mate in Croatia for his gift of loud and shit pronunciation.'

'Such a gift,' Poppy said.

'Unlike the visual of his belly button hair.'

'And the memory of his body odour.'

'And the sex lessons.'

'STOP!' Poppy gasped, giggling as the memory of the beer-bellied restaurateur humping a plastic chair flashed behind her eyes. 'I'm actually dying! You will make this baby pop out of me.'

'Mate, that would be my gift to you,' Dani said. 'If your baby just pops out, I will be so bloody jealous. If you get anything less than an eight-hour labour, I'll be pissed. You need to know what I went through or our friendship will be missing this deep level of understanding.'

'Thanks, Dan. So selfless of you.'

'I'm the Dalai Lama in Lululemon,' deadpanned her friend. 'So how did the appointment go? Was it okay?'

'It was fine.' Poppy sighed. 'I'm walking out of the hospital now. It was the same as my appointments in Sydney. No big deal. The midwife was okay, the hospital seems normal. Literally, it'll be the same as having a baby in Sydney—just no good options for Uber Eats afterwards.'

'That's a pretty big deal-breaker, you know. You sure you don't want to have the baby here? I'll deliver RaRa Ramen to the ward and comb your hair and change nappies and stuff. I'm ace at that shiz now.'

'Um, sorry, why would you comb my hair?' asked Poppy, wincing as she stepped through the automatic doors back into the shuddering heat.

'Um, because I am maternal now, and I would look after you because I am a caring legend.'

'Well, thanks, legend, but I'll be a-okay out here in the sticks, so long as I stop yelling at vigilantes in the car park.'

'Wait, what?'

Poppy groaned, a fresh layer of perspiration building at her temples. 'I just yelled at some random dude in the car park. It was full crazy-preggers-lady mode. He rocked up and was being a douche about where I could park and I lost it.'

'LOL—actual LOLs,' Dani said, chortling. 'You actually got rowdy at some poor old guy in the car park?'

Poppy groaned again. 'He wasn't even old. He was, like, our age.'

'Was he hot, at least?'

Poppy smiled to herself. Her best friend was nothing if not predictable.

'The main takeaway from the encounter was that he was a giant douche of the douchiest kind, but I guess he wasn't terrible-looking,' she admitted, thinking back to the man's broad shoulders. 'But in a really clichéd Ken doll kind of way,' she clarified. 'Not like a Ryan Gosling Ken; more like a basic model Ken, wearing scrubs. Boring. Totally wholemeal bread.' She breathed deeply, trying to expel the heat from her throat. The back of her dress was stuck to her thighs. 'Seriously, Dan, who does that? I don't know who I am anymore. I mean, I'm fine, but—'

'Are you though?' Dani interrupted. Her friend's tone was serious now.

Poppy sighed. 'Honestly? I don't know. I'm on autopilot. If I stop to think about it, I'll get overwhelmed. It's becoming so much more real now. I have no idea whether I'll be a good mum or if I'll cope on my own. I mean, you have Sam and it's still been a whirlwind for you.'

'Pops, I cannot even imagine how crazy this must feel, but you have to trust me when I say I know you'll be okay. You're clever, you're strong, you've got your parents there. This baby is so lucky to have a mum like you. I mean that.'

It wasn't that Poppy didn't believe her friend; she knew Dani was sincere. It was just that her friend thought way too highly of her.

'Thanks, Dan.' Poppy reached into her handbag for the car keys as the LandCruiser came into view. 'I love you.'

'No worries, my dear,' replied Dani, instantly jumping out of serious mode. 'If you're ever feeling overwhelmed, just close your eyes and imagine I'm right next to you, calming you with my melodious voice.' At this point, her friend began belting out an enthusiastic rendition of 'Lean On Me'.

'Hanging up now!' yelled Poppy, pressing the red button on her iPhone. She heard Dani begin to cackle before her name vanished from her screen.

It was amazing how such terrible singing could make her feel so profoundly soothed. Her fingers drummed the tune to 'Lean On Me' all the way home to her new rental, which, in every aspect, was worlds away from her old place. Her apartment in Sydney had been on the sixth floor, which felt fancy but not nauseatingly high, and if you did suffer from vertigo-induced queasiness you could always nip downstairs and self-medicate at the twenty-four-hour pharmacy or the wine bar across the street.

Her new place was in pure suburbia—unadulterated in every sense of the word. If a wine bar opened nearby it would have to serve sherry and port in a non-ironic way, given the median age of her neighbours. Poppy suspected she was the youngest in her new suburb by about forty years. The broadband was excellent, mind you, which was probably because most of her neighbours were still on the faxing bandwagon.

Everything was beige: the bricks, the roofs, the outfits. Poppy's house looked like the house next to it, and the house next to that. The 1980s brick veneer was sun-faded and chipped, the grass was starched and prickly, and the verandah was tiled with pavers the colour of Betadine. When she'd given Dani a tour over FaceTime, her best friend had shrieked in faux delight, 'Love a poo-brown palette!' That pretty much summed it up.

Secretly, though, Poppy didn't mind it. The street was lined with sprawling oaks and, most significantly, her rental had a garden. No-one in Sydney in their early thirties could afford a garden unless they were a nepo baby or a white-collar criminal. To have grass and actual trees—plural!—felt almost Kardashian-level luxe.

Poppy walked across the dusty verandah and unlocked her front door. The view inside was starting to improve. A week ago it had been a labyrinth of cardboard boxes, so disorganised that on her first night she couldn't find the cutlery so had eaten her takeaway with her bare hands. Seven days later—put it down to the prenatal nesting or a desperate instinct for self-preservation—the boxes had all been unpacked, flattened and deposited in the recycling bin. The gaping lack of furniture was a stark reminder of her new-found aloneness and everything left behind in Sydney, but slowly she was cobbling together a neat, if sparse, functional three-bedroom home. *Ready for a family*, she thought grimly. Of sorts.

Her phone buzzed in her pocket. Mum.

'Darling, I just saw two-for-one summer dresses at Rockmans!' her mother announced by way of greeting.

Poppy rolled her eyes. Her mum was an avid bargain hunter and prone to excitement at very mundane things. Weed killer, umbrellas, a well-boiled egg. 'That's great, Mum,' she replied. 'You should treat yourself.'

'Not for me, darling—for you! Lots of snazzy prints. They'd go very nicely with the baby bump. And some of them are that stretchy fabric you could yank down for breastfeeding!'

'Mum, I don't think I'm the target market for Rockmans.'

'What do you mean, darling?' Chrissie McKellar still thought she and her daughter shared the same taste in fashion despite a clear divergence at age nine, when Poppy had asked

Santa for a Roxy bikini and board shorts combo (still an iconic look) but ended up with a paisley-print Cancer Council rashie instead. It was pathetic that two decades on she still didn't know how to admit she hated paisley without hurting her mum's feelings. Poppy sighed. 'Thanks, Mum. I'll take a look tomorrow.'

'Excellent!' said her mother. 'Now, how did the appointment go? Was there much discussion about *your situation?*'

Her mother always said 'your situation' in a loud stage whisper, clearly intending to spark intrigue, which Poppy knew it definitely did among her mum's golf friends.

'No, Mum, we did not discuss my situation. It's the twenty-first century. I am not the first woman to become a single mum.'

'I know,' her mother replied, 'but I thought they might encourage you to reconnect with Patrick. Or invite him to the birth?'

'Mum! Why would they do that? I saw a midwife, not a relationship counsellor!'

'Yes, but you know those airy-fairy job descriptions these days. Everyone does a bit of everything. I thought they might recommend it. He could just be busy with his job, you know. He was always working such late nights. Have you tried to—'

'Mum,' warned Poppy.

Thwarted, her mother relented. 'I'm just trying to help.'

'I know,' Poppy said. 'But trying to convince me to get back together with Patrick is not helping.'

'Wait!' cried her mother. 'I just remembered—I have more good news for you!'

SPECIAL DELIVERY

Poppy groaned. 'Better than the Rockmans sale?'

'Yes!' said her mother, oblivious to the joke. 'Henry Marshall has moved home!'

Poppy felt her throat constrict. 'Mum! Stop this right now! I am thirty-seven weeks pregnant. I am looking for breast pads and nipple gel and one-size-fits-all undies that don't strain my vagina! I am not looking for a man!'

'Darling, don't yell "vagina". You sound a bit crass.'

Poppy almost screeched with exasperation. Her mother, who loved to tell her friends she had read the *Kama Sutra* ('a fascinating read—quite intellectually stimulating') could also be a real pearl-clutcher. Her contrariness routinely drove Poppy insane.

'Mum, I don't care that Henry has moved home. I don't care that Patrick has no interest in being a dad. I literally just care about getting through the next few days without wetting my pants. Now, I am going to go and try to put together a flat-pack cot, so I am saying goodbye and I will speak to you later.'

Her mother was quiet at the other end.

'Mum?'

'I was just trying to—'

Poppy softened. 'I know, Mum.'

'But, darling . . .'

'What?' asked Poppy cautiously.

'Darling, if you want some help with the flat pack, call me and I'll drag your father away from the sports channel and send him over with the drill.'

Poppy smiled. 'Thanks, Mum. I love you.'

LEESA RONALD

Poppy's phone dimmed to black and she considered the flat-pack box in the corner. Frankly, she'd never intended to put it together without her father's help, so she unlocked her phone again. Opening Facebook, she typed two words into the search bar: *Henry Marshall*.

CHAPTER 3

The expected cool change had not materialised, so Poppy once again found herself driving with her arms in chicken wing stance to reduce the chance of underarm sweat. While she was grateful to her parents for lending her the old Land-Cruiser, the lack of air-conditioning meant that she was permanently slicked in perspiration. It brought new meaning to the term 'pregnancy glow'.

Poppy pulled up at the supermarket and killed the engine. Sliding down from the driver's seat, she readjusted her sundress. Today's plan was simple. Buy enough food to stock a pantry, then cook and freeze, ad nauseum.

The cool air of the supermarket prickled the back of her neck as she grabbed a trolley and manoeuvred it down the aisles. After the sauna of the car and the radiating heat of the car park, the temperature inside was magnificent—almost orgasmic. Poppy bit her lip to stop from laughing at the idea of an aircongasm (an airgasm?) when she realised she was staring at a guy stacking the shelves. He gave her an awkward wave. *Oh crap!* What was his name? He'd been in her year at school. Big into *Dungeons & Dragons*. Gosh, she'd need to control the accidental sex faces in this town. Who knew who else she'd run into? Poppy gave him a double eyebrow raise, intended to translate as a casual *whassup*. D&D Guy smiled and wandered off. She couldn't for the life of her remember his name. Was it Martin? He looked like a Martin.

Before moving back to Orange, Poppy had done a granular social media deep dive on as many former classmates as possible. Turned out she wasn't the only one who'd resolved to get the hell out of town post-graduation. Of the fifty or so people in her year, there were only a handful left in Orange. A few guys were working in the mines, the vice-captain had taken over his family farm, one guy was an accountant. As far as she could tell, none of her female classmates were still in town. They'd all moved on to much cooler locales, which objectively made Poppy the biggest loser of their cohort.

She was pondering this depressing reality when the front right trolley wheel caught on a sticky part of the linoleum floor. Before she knew it, the trolley had careened into a shelf, sending bottles of pasta sauce flying.

'Fuck,' she whispered, looking around. Three bottles had smashed and red passata was everywhere. A giant red splotch had landed on her dress, smack bang on her groin. *Fuckity-fuck.*

She glanced around. There was no-one to help. She looked back to the puddle of sauce at her feet and realised dolefully that she could definitely not do a runner. The pasta sauce footprints would give her away.

'Are you going to get that cleaned up?'

Poppy swivelled and baulked. *What. Were. The chances?* Ken-doll-in-scrubs (literally, he was wearing scrubs again) was walking down the aisle, gesturing to the chaos at her feet. 'You can't leave it like that,' he said. 'You should tell someone.'

Poppy glared at him. 'Of course I was going to clean it up,' she snapped, turning back to the shelf to inspect the damage.

Ken doll was behind her now. 'I didn't mean you personally should clean it up; I just meant you can't leave this mess here and not tell anyone. It's a safety hazard.'

'Oh my god, *go away*!' cried Poppy, squatting to pick the shards of glass from the red paste. As she started placing them uselessly in a pile, she could sense him shifting uncomfortably behind her.

'Okay, I guess if you've got this under control, I can . . .' He reached over Poppy to pluck a jar of pesto from the top shelf. He was so close she could smell the laundry powder scent of his scrubs. His knees were probably two inches from her head. A raging heat rose up her neck. *I could swing my head back and smash this guy.* His knees would buckle and he'd go flying. She could watch him squirm. The image of Ken doll covered in pasta sauce was an enticing one.

'Right.' He cleared his throat. 'I'll be going then.'

'Yeah, you can fuck off,' Poppy muttered, still picking glass out of the sauce.

'Excuse me?' he said, turning around.

Poppy fixed him with a hostile stare. 'I said goodbye!'

★

As soon as she'd loaded the groceries into the boot of the LandCruiser, Poppy put her AirPods in and dialled Dani.

'PARPEEE!' her friend cried.

'DARNEE!' cried Poppy in return, reversing the LandCruiser out of the parking space. 'Thank the lord you picked up. I was going to bust a lid if you didn't. You would not believe what I have just been through.'

'Oh my god!' cried Dani. 'Is there a baby?! Tell me everything! WASTE NO WORDS!'

Poppy flicked her indicator on and laughed. 'No baby, my friend. Just a giant shit sandwich in the supermarket. Not literally, obviously, but I almost killed someone.'

'Whoa, lady, tell me more.'

'Dude, you wouldn't guess who was there.'

'No, I wouldn't,' Dani said impatiently, 'so spill already.'

Poppy paused dramatically. 'The guy from the car park.'

'Who?'

'The guy from the hospital car park—the douche. I told you about him.'

'The Ken doll in scrubs?'

'Yes, none other than hospital douche Ken. Buy one and get a free Barbie caravan bumper sticker that says *I'm a douche, and I'll be a douche about it*.'

Dani chuckled. 'So what happened?'

As she drove home, Poppy recounted the whole incident: the trolley, the broken glass, the sauce, his annoying holier-than-thou-ness, his hovering in her personal space. 'And then,' she concluded with a satisfied smirk, 'I told him to fuck off.'

'You didn't!'

'I did.'

'What are you becoming, woman?' Dani cried gleefully. 'Dropping f-bombs in public. Man, I would pay to see that. Imagine what your old workmates would pay! This is uncharted territory: fired-up Poppy. I can't wait to see her in action.'

Poppy laughed. 'Seriously, this guy is my kryptonite. I promise I am still a normal human woman. I have no intention of becoming known as the lady gangster of Orange.'

'Why not?' Dani asked. 'It might suit you. Lady gangster and baby gangster. You could make an Instagram account of all the hectic shiz you're doing around town. Breaking jars—with a baby. Parking illegally—with a baby. Shit getting real—with a baby. People would lap that up. I'm guessing at least a million followers within a month. Seriously, enjoy the dollars and thank me later.'

'Cool. Life plan sorted. So glad I've got your wisdom to guide me, Dan.'

'Here to help, amiga, here to help.'

Poppy smiled. 'I wish you actually were here, Dan. I miss your mood-lifting superpowers.'

'Ha!' barked Dani. 'You're just lucky I only charge you mates rates for my services. My next bill is in the mail, FYI. Speaking of which . . .' Dani trailed off.

'What?'

'Okay, well, not speaking of which; this topic is completely unrelated to anything. HOWEVER, it is still very, very interesting and important news, which I am very sure you will be *very* interested to learn. Which is why I intend to tell you about it at this very moment, right now.'

'Dani!' Poppy warned.

'HenryMarshallhasmovedbacktoOrange.' It came out as one terrifyingly portentous word. 'I ran into Rachel at Bondi Junction and she told me. All happened quite quickly, but he's completely packed up from Queensland. Moving home to take over the family business. Can't remember what that is, but—'

'Financial planning,' Poppy interrupted, instantly embarrassed for remembering.

'Yeah, that. *And*'—Dani paused and took a deep breath—'he's engaged.'

The LandCruiser suddenly lurched across the double lines. 'Shit!'

'Poppy?!'

'Sorry, some bloke just swerved into me,' Poppy lied. 'That's, um, interesting. Mum actually mentioned the other day that he had moved back.'

'You already knew? Why didn't you tell me?'

'Forgot, I guess,' Poppy said—another lie. She was thankful this conversation was not happening in person; her face would surely betray her. Dani knew better than anyone the special place Poppy kept in her heart for Henry. They'd broken up amicably after high school and had become the archetype of best-friend-exes. He went to uni in Brisbane, she went to Sydney, and when either of them visited each other's city they'd always crash at each other's place. Poppy loved the weekends when Henry would fly down to see his grandmother or watch the rugby with his mates and they'd seamlessly fall back into step as if no time had passed. He'd sleep on her couch and the next morning they'd go out for breakfast, each knowing exactly what the other would order.

Sure, there were times when they forgot they were just friends and succumbed to that lingering attraction neither of them could shake, but that was normal with exes, right? And truth be told, she loved those visits when they'd fall into bed and wake up wrapped in each other's arms, giggling about how drunk they'd been. In her mind, those mornings were perfect.

'How long since you've seen him?' asked Dani.

Poppy cringed, the decade-old memory still startlingly fresh. 'Not since . . . that night.'

Dani grunted sympathetically. 'Say no more, my friend. Say no more.'

CHAPTER 4

Poppy's mother had been talking nonstop for six minutes. Poppy had answered the phone and said an (unheard) hello as her mother launched into a monologue on topics that ranged from her neighbours, the finalists on *The Voice*, the price of blueberries at the moment ('outrageous!'—in a good way) and the recent New Year's Day escapades of a prime-time breakfast show host ('outrageous!'—in a bad way).

Chrissie McKellar was one of those country mums who considered a chunky pair of red-framed spectacles the height of sophistication. That her glasses matched her favourite golf skirt was a mind-boggling bonus, worthy of mentioning at least thrice-yearly.

Today she was calling to discuss the weather—specifically, the storms that were predicted to hit later that afternoon, bringing sixty-kilometre winds and forty mils of rain. The whole town was buzzing with anticipation and Poppy had found herself swept up in it too. She even had a thought to nip to Bunnings to buy flowers to plant in the soon-to-be rain-soaked soil. Such wholesomeness had never occurred to her in Sydney.

'And I told Martha,' her mother continued, 'that she better put the new Volvo in the garage overnight because we all know Peter should have had that tree cut down ages ago but of course he didn't, so now the poor Volvo is a sitting duck waiting to be crushed by that stupid old tree.'

She paused momentarily (so, so momentarily) before drawing breath. 'And then I told her that she could cut down the tree herself with one of those lady-sized chainsaws that they sell in the gift shops these days. They have pink and floral-patterned ones and they're quite lovely actually; I was thinking of buying one for myself. Or, she could just use that young fellow Cheryl told us about—the one who was playing football in Sydney but who's now doing landscape gardening in town. I've been told he's very attractive-looking and he often takes his shirt off while he's working. Not that I'm interested in that, of course. I've just heard he's very effective at his job.'

At that moment, a large crack of thunder sounded in the distance.

'Good golly!' her mother yelped. 'Did you hear that? It must be close now. Oh, I hope Martha has moved that car into the garage—it'll be such a waste of money if it gets a branch skewered through the roof. Well, darling, I'd better go and get the washing off the line—I can't have my undies blowing into the neighbours' gardens. They would die with fright. Or they may use them as tents for the grandchildren. Either way, I would die of embarrassment. Oh, what's that Paul? The sports channel has cut out? No, that's a shame.'

Her mother's voice switched to a loud whisper. 'What am I supposed to do to amuse your father now? This bloody storm!' Converting back to full volume, she continued, 'Darling, I must go. I'm sorry I've no time to chat, but it's been lovely to hear from you. You make sure to let me know how your appointment goes, too—and don't forget to go buy those newborn singlets. The Bonds sale ends today!'

The phone went silent and Poppy stared at it. Nine minutes. Nine full minutes and her mother hadn't realised that Poppy had said not one single word. It had to be a record. Honestly, her mother should be put in a museum and studied.

Poppy looked at her watch. Her appointment with Wenda wasn't for another forty minutes but looking out the window she could see dark purple clouds steamrolling towards town. She didn't fancy taking the car out in the peak of the storm, so she grabbed her keys and headed for the door.

The first raindrops had started to fall in giant, solid plops by the time she arrived at the hospital. Congratulating herself on her choice of clothing (a button-up denim pinafore, no chance of going see-through), she pulled her handbag over her arm and jumped out of the car. The fat raindrops were inescapable. They splashed into her hairline and slipped down her dress and into the curve of her Birkenstocks. The petrichor smell of wet earth filled her nostrils and the moisture tickled her tongue. After weeks of suffocating heat, it was glorious.

Poppy cupped her hands under her belly in a makeshift brace and jog-shuffled to the undercover hospital portico, careful not to slip. Her chest thumped with pain. If she'd known she'd be attempting to run for the first time in months, she would have worn a sports bra.

The light inside the hospital was synthetic and bright compared to the darkening sky outside. Poppy ran her hands through her wet hair. Around her, men and women in different-coloured scrubs power walked past, holding clipboards and takeaway coffees. The cafe cart had a queue twenty people deep.

Poppy walked to the elevator and punched the up button. As the door pinged open, she felt a twinge in her lower back and grimaced. That would teach her not to jog in the rain while thirty-nine weeks pregnant.

Wenda met her in the reception area with a smile. 'Poppy, pet! How are you? We're getting to the pointy end now.'

Poppy smiled back. 'Good, Wenda. Same as before. Big, heavy, not as sweaty as usual, though. This is from the rain.' She pointed to her sodden dress.

Wenda chuckled. 'Wouldn't judge you either way, pet.'

They walked down to Wenda's office, chatting amiably. Wenda was worried about her cats getting stuck outside in the storm. Her husband was driving home from Mudgee but she was less worried about him.

In the office, Poppy hoisted herself up onto the raised bed and began unbuttoning her pinafore, ready for Wenda to put the heart rate monitor on her stomach. Her back twinged again and she winced. How embarrassing she couldn't even manage a light jog anymore without her body failing.

Wenda hummed to herself as she unlooped the cords of the heart rate monitor and strapped it around Poppy's belly.

'Do you feel that?' she asked, gesturing to Poppy's stomach, which had become hard and tense.

'Feel what?' asked Poppy, confused.

'The contraction.'

'The *what*?!' Poppy's head swivelled from her stomach to Wenda and back again. 'I'm having a contraction?!'

'It's either a Braxton Hicks or you're on your way, pet,' said Wenda gently. 'You're thirty-nine weeks and four days—I think this could be it.'

Poppy's mind whirled. She wasn't due for another three days. *Shit!* She hadn't bought a breast pump yet. Or a cabbage! There was still so much to do. This baby could not come now. She wasn't ready!

Wenda checked the monitor. 'Have you been having pains in the lower back area, anything like that?'

Poppy groaned. She was a dense, fucking idiot.

'Yes,' she admitted. 'But I didn't put two and two together.' She groaned again. This was a disaster.

'Now, pet, there's nothing to worry about. You're in the best place possible to be having contractions. Normally I'd send you home to wait until they were coming more frequently, but I think it's best to keep you out of that weather.' She nodded to the window. 'Why don't we organise a bed so you can settle in and relax before the big dance?'

Poppy nodded mutely.

'Alright then, let's get you organised.'

Like a zombie, Poppy followed Wenda through the ward. A blur of people in white coats and scrubs rushed past her, monitors beeped, lights flashed. Poppy had never been good with surprises but she'd had a few big ones recently. Surely she should be handling this better?

The labour room was wide and windowless, with a starchy white bed in its centre. A CTG machine and an IV drip stood ready in the corner and a shelving unit was stacked with towels and boxes of plastic gloves and surgical masks. Wenda began reorganising the shelves with the ease of a practised expert.

'Uh, Wenda?' A young brunette whom Poppy recognised as the ward receptionist popped her head through the door. 'We have a call for you.'

'Sorry, pet, I'm busy at the moment.'

'It's your husband,' the receptionist said apologetically.

Wenda narrowed her eyes and turned to Poppy. 'Make yourself comfortable, pet. I'll be back in a jiffy.'

Poppy sat on the bed. The sheets were a blinding white, tucked under the mattress with pinpoint precision. She flicked open her phone and stared at it. There were people she could call, people she probably should call, but this moment felt private. She turned the screen facedown and looked around at the grey walls. *So this is it*, she thought bleakly. *The big dance.*

Above the door, the cheap plastic clock ticked loudly. Poppy wondered how long she'd be here. Would anyone notice she was missing? Certainly no-one would know if she didn't make it home tonight. She was a wolf pack of one. The realisation sunk her deeper into the starchy mattress. She suddenly craved a double espresso and a shot of whisky. She wished she'd never met Patrick and his stupid sperm-filled penis.

Wenda burst back through the door, looking livid. 'That silly man has flooded the engine and now I have to go and get him! I told him he should have left earlier—or later—and did he listen?' She groaned, exasperated. 'I'm so sorry, pet, but I have to go.'

'Wh-what?' stammered Poppy.

'My husband! Stuck in the storm. Tried to drive through a flooded causeway and now the engine's cut out. He's stuck out there, forty k from Bathurst, and roadside assistance can't get there for four hours because they're dealing with real problems, not idiot men who've decided to take stupid risks. He could have got himself killed!' She spun around the room, dragging the CTG machine to the power point and piling towels on the end of the bed. 'One of my colleagues will take over. They're all lovely, I promise, and they will take good care of you, Poppy. This stuff actually happens all the time.' She gave a dry laugh. 'You can never tell when a life disaster and a labouring mother will appear at the same time. I wish I could stay here, pet, but I promise you're in safe hands.' She wrapped Poppy in a quick hug and then she was gone.

The door swung shut behind her, muffling the beeps and chatter from outside, cocooning Poppy in silence. What now? The windowless room felt smaller than it had moments before. The white bed was a lonely island on the linoleum and Poppy was stranded. Patrick had walked out without a second glance too. There was a discomfiting pattern emerging here.

'Incoming,' called a man in scrubs, pushing the door open with his butt as he reversed into the room. He was wheeling a trolley laden with medical paraphernalia. As he straightened up, back still towards her, Poppy got an eyeful of his thick, dark blond hair.

'You?' she cried, pointing at him with an accusing finger. 'What are *you* doing here?'

'I work here,' said the Ken doll, gesturing to his scrubs. 'I'm here to take over from Wenda. I'm the midwife.'

'The what?' cried Poppy. 'But you're a *man*! A fully grown man!' She waved her hands at his torso. 'You cannot be my midwife.'

He raised an eyebrow. 'I *am* your midwife. My name is James.'

'No, no, no.' Poppy shook her head. 'That's not possible. You go away and I'll have the baby when Wenda gets back.'

'You'll hold it in?' he asked, his eyes showing the faintest glimmer of amusement.

Poppy seethed. How dare he almost-laugh at her? 'I have been practising my Kegels religiously, so you bet I'll hold it in.' She glared at him. 'You can go now.'

'I can't actually.' James started moving around the room, pulling things off his trolley and plugging monitors into power points. 'I need to put that on.' He pointed at the CTG machine that he'd moved up next to her bed. 'It'll be difficult if you're not cooperating.'

Poppy glanced down at her dress. He clearly needed to get under there to put the monitor on. *Fuuuuuck! This day!*

'You could change first,' he said, reading her mind. 'Where's your hospital bag?'

'My what?' Poppy asked. She had the distinct impression this guy thought she was thick.

'Your hospital bag. You know, with pyjamas, toothbrush, clothes for the baby.'

A sweet arrow of relief shot through Poppy. Mercifully, thankfully, *gloriously*, she'd packed her hospital bag last week and it had been sitting in the boot of the LandCruiser ever since.

'It's in my car. I'll go get it!'

'I'm not sure about that, ma'am. The weather is pretty crazy out there. I'll organise someone to get it for you.'

Poppy bristled. 'First'—she jabbed a finger at his face—'do *not* call me ma'am. I am not a hundred years old. My name is Poppy. And second, I will do what I want.'

Poppy heaved herself off the bed and marched out of the room.

By the time she reached the main entrance of the hospital, she was sincerely regretting her stubbornness. It was bucketing down. The trees in the distance swayed like drunken clubbers, their leaves being dashed to the ground. Tentatively, she stepped out under the portico and felt the rush of cold air fall damp on her skin. Another twinge of pain spasmed up her back. Of course he would trap her into doing this with his evil reverse psychology. What an absolute dick! Flexing her toes in her Birkenstocks for better grip, Poppy braced for the inevitable.

The rain was hammering down and she could hardly jog for the tension in her lower back. By the time she reached the LandCruiser, she was soaked to the bone. Her hair was plastered to her neck and her skin was covered in goosebumps. She quickly opened the boot, grabbed her bag and turned to head back, when one of her shoes came loose and ricocheted under the car. Poppy's head roared. *DAMN IT!* As torrents of rain attacked her, she crouched next to the wheel and tried in vain to reach her shoe.

'WHAT ARE YOU DOING?!' roared a voice behind her. 'Quick! Take this!' It was evil-Ken-doll-James, shoving an umbrella into her hand. He flattened himself onto the tarmac and slid under the chassis to retrieve her shoe. 'Now, move!' he commanded, standing up. 'Let's go!'

He was still fuming as they re-entered the hospital. 'What were you thinking?! You could have slipped and hurt yourself. Not to mention the baby!'

'I was being careful,' Poppy snapped angrily.

'Is that how your shoe ended up under the car?' He was as wet as her. His scrubs were clinging to his shoulders and thighs, and his hair was slick with moisture.

'That was an accident.'

'Yeah, well, you're lucky,' he grumbled, looking away.

'I'm hardly lucky!' Poppy retorted. 'Look at me—I'm drenched! Actually, don't look at me; I look like shit. So do you,' she added spitefully, clocking his wet shirt stuck flat against his stomach.

Ignoring her, James began striding to the ward. 'Hurry up,' he ordered.

Scowling, Poppy reluctantly obeyed.

★

Back in her hospital room, Poppy prised a pair of dry tracksuit pants and a clean t-shirt out of her bag. The contractions were still manageable, so James had left her with blunt instructions to keep walking around to 'hurry things up'.

She was going to do the exact opposite, because: screw him. She was going to buy chocolate and a trashy magazine and lie on this starchy bed and pretend she was somewhere far away where she didn't need a brain or a body or a yellow card that said 'not present' where it should define a life partner.

She picked up her phone and swiped the cool glass. There were so many people to call but her brain couldn't compute what she'd say. *Hey there, sitting here ready to pop a baby out my vag! Just about to cross that threshold into single motherhood, don't mind me!*

She stood up and began the walk to the hospital cafe. She'd known logically that this day would come, but she hadn't *really* known. In her bones, she still didn't feel ready to be a mother. On an intellectual level, she knew exactly what she had to do: feed the baby, clean the baby, give it shelter and love. But how did you actually *do* all that?

She'd watched Dani pick it up, slowly learning to recognise what Nella needed. At first it had been a giant convoluted puzzle. They'd cried with laughter together at how stupid they felt, trying to calm the crying baby with their singing and dancing. They laughed and laughed because otherwise Dani would cry.

'Contractions, love?' asked an elderly volunteer behind the cafe counter. She had blue eyebrows pencilled on her forehead and Poppy wondered if it was a fashion statement or an eyesight failure. She looked like a very kind circus clown.

'Yep.' Poppy grimaced, picking up a magazine with Princess Kate and Meghan on the cover.

'Would you like a curry pie on the house? The curry might speed things up for you?'

SPECIAL DELIVERY

'Thank you, that's very generous, but I'll stick to sugar.' She dropped the magazine and three chocolate bars on the counter.

The woman took Poppy's money with a smile. 'This is a very exciting time for you and your husband, so make sure you enjoy every moment.'

'Oh . . . er, yes, thanks,' Poppy faltered. She tucked the magazine under her armpit and tried to smile but her face felt frozen. It wasn't the first time it had happened—not even close—but the blow it caused in her chest never dulled. She wasn't normal anymore. She was a statistic now, a minority, a cautionary tale to be traded over cocktails and coffee—and she still couldn't work out how it had happened. Patrick was the kind of guy who, on a good day, could have thrown himself into parenthood. She could imagine his reaction to the birth if they'd still been together. He would have posted a family shot on Instagram within the hour. *Welcome to the world little one!* he'd write. *Mum was incredible! Dad was a blubbering mess!*

But with the benefit of seven months of cold, hard hindsight, Poppy knew now that Patrick was deeply unoriginal. He did what other people thought was funny and interesting, and then he did it ten per cent more so he seemed funnier and more interesting than everyone else. If people were posting on Instagram, Patrick would too—but with more exclamation marks.

The pains were definitely coming harder and faster now. Poppy paused and leaned against a wall, gritting her teeth as she breathed through the latest back spasm. Around her, people scurried past on their own missions, oblivious to the labouring woman in their midst. *These are the easy ones*, Poppy reminded herself miserably. It was going to get a lot worse before it got better.

When she reached her room, she found James there. His hair was still shining wet but he'd found a new pair of scrubs. Shame. The sight of his wet uniform could have really lifted her spirits.

'They're getting worse,' Poppy announced, pointing to her belly.

James continued pressing buttons on the CTG machine. 'That happens.'

This man was horrible. Empathy level: zero. Annoyance factor: through the roof.

'I need to put the monitor on now,' he said, unlooping a canvas belt attached to the CTG machine. 'This will go around your stomach so we can track your contractions.' He pointed to the bed. 'Lie down and lift up your top.'

'Gosh, what a bedside manner,' Poppy muttered, heaving herself up. Uninvited, an image popped into her mind: James curved above her in bed, his shoulders bare and his dark eyes glittering. *Argh!* These were not helpful visuals at all.

Poppy lifted her t-shirt and James leaned over to fasten the CTG belt around her. Poppy shifted her body towards him and tried to breathe normally. He smelled of soap and fresh cotton and the slightest trace of aftershave. Unbidden, the vision of shirtless James reappeared in her mind and she scrunched her eyes closed in disgust. God, she hadn't been near a guy for so long; she was pathetic.

'Done,' he announced, straightening up and returning to the monitor.

'Great,' she grunted, tilting her head so he wouldn't notice the heat creeping up her neck. This was routine work for him and she was having erotic daydreams like a sex-starved hermit.

'Have you thought about drugs?' asked James.

'Recreationally?'

'Pain relief,' he clarified dryly.

Poppy rolled her eyes. *It was a joke.* 'I am open to anything so long as no-one's forcing me into it.' Another contraction gripped her torso like a vice. She flinched as it rippled up her spine like broken glass. As the pain receded, she gasped, 'And I am open to starting now.'

James studied her. His eyelashes were abnormally thick. 'This is the start of a long journey. We shouldn't go too hard too early on the pain relief.'

Poppy scowled. There was no 'we' about it. She was doing this by herself. 'Whatever,' she mumbled.

'Normally I'd do an internal examination to check how far you're dilated.' He glanced at her pelvis. 'But in this case, I think I'll call for backup.'

Poppy unclenched the thighs she didn't know she'd tensed. Thank the lord for backup. That would have been way too much. Way, way too much.

CHAPTER 5

The wheels under the white bed squeaked pathetically as Poppy lunged wild-eyed at the guardrail. The bed frame rattled three centimetres to the left, even though the brakes were on. A wave of pain was shuddering up her spine and she folded at the hips and moaned in agony.

Where was that fucking button to call someone?! Where was that fucking midwife?!

The pain was clouding her vision, blending colours and merging shapes. Blindly she grabbed at the cords connected to the bed. She knew that magic button was connected to one of those damn cords.

Finally, she found it and punched the green button. *Where the fuck was he?* Punch, punch, punch. *She would kill him!* Punch, punch, punch.

James had left forty minutes ago, announcing he had to do 'various things'. His condescending aura of calm had tricked her, and now she was all alone with a seismic fucking tornado ripping through her and no-one to help. *ARGHHHHHH!*

She heard a knock and saw the silhouette of James's shoulders in the doorway.

'Where the hell have you been?!' she cried.

James approached her carefully, glancing at the CTG machine. 'You seem to be progressing well.'

'Well?!' Poppy screamed. 'I am not *well*! I need drugs! Shit has fucking escalated!'

'Want to try the gas?' James asked, unwinding a tube from a grey machine next to the bed.

Poppy snatched it. Another contraction was starting, coiling like steel around her organs and smothering her to death. She shoved the mouthpiece in and inhaled deeply. Through her haze of pain, she could sense James was amused. The fucker.

'The trick is to inhale the gas before the contraction arrives so you're already relaxed when the pain comes.'

Poppy grunted. Words. Too hard. She inhaled again, feeling the cool gas slide down her throat. Slowly the contraction receded.

'Is it helping?' He searched her eyes for an answer.

Poppy winced. She could feel another contraction stirring in her abdomen, about to engulf her.

As if reading her mind, James grabbed her hand and guided the mouthpiece back to her lips.

'Quick, inhale now,' he urged. 'Before it really hits.'

Poppy did as she was told, breathing deeply again and again. The contractions came—still torturous and powerful, the pain only slightly blunted by the gas. She whimpered helplessly. The contractions were sucking the air from her lungs, they were strangling her arteries, they had filled every capillary with thorns. She couldn't survive this. 'Please,' she begged, reaching for his arm. 'Please make it stop.'

James checked his watch. 'I'll see if we can organise an epidural,' he said. 'I'll go find an anaesthetist.'

'No!' Poppy yelped, gripping him harder, her fingernails digging into his forearm. She moaned as the contraction peaked, sending waves of pain reverberating up her spine. 'Please don't leave!'

James gently prised her fingers off his arm. 'I'll yell from the door.'

Poppy closed her eyes and dug her fists into her thighs as James strode to the door and stuck his head out. 'Can we get the anaesthetist up here? Quickly, please?'

'Oh my god,' Poppy wailed.

James was by her side in an instant. 'Gas?'

'No—I need to go to the toilet.'

Through the blur of the pain she saw James almost smile again. HE WAS FUCKING INFURIATING!

'What kind of trip to the toilet?' he asked.

'What the hell do you mean?!' shrieked Poppy.

James's lips curved into a wide smile. It was the first time she'd seen him do that. It cracked his whole face open so it shone like the sun. It was golden and warm and fuzzy and, oh god, she was too exhausted to be thinking like this! She cried out as another contraction coursed up her body and out to her extremities, warping her fingers and toes into claws. She needed sleep. She needed a tranquilliser. Even death would be

SPECIAL DELIVERY

okay right now. She wanted the bed to swallow her whole so she'd never wake again.

James put a hand on her shoulder. 'If you're thinking it's more than a wee, then it might not be what you think. We might have a baby on the way.'

A nuclear warhead exploded in Poppy's brain. A baby? A poo? A smile?! *It was all too muuuuuuuch.*

'You do it,' she begged. 'Just pull it out of me. I don't care if it's a poo. Just pull it out.' She paused and drew breath. 'Sorry,' she sobbed, her voice cracking. 'I don't mean that, I didn't mean to say that. Sorry, that's disgusting. Just pull the baby out. I just can't do anything anymore.' She heaved another sob. 'I can't do it, James. I can't.'

'Poppy, look at me,' James commanded, putting both hands on her shoulders. His liquid eyes bored into hers. 'You *can* do this. I promise you.'

Another contraction surged through her body, and Poppy threw herself into his arms, her fingernails digging through his scrubs. 'ARGHHHHHH!' she screamed. 'HELP ME!'

'Poppy, you need to trust me,' James said slowly. 'You need to lie on the bed and I'll help you take off your pants. I've got a hospital gown we can put on straight over your t-shirt.'

Her vision was blurred. She couldn't see. The pain was an anaconda and it was choking her to death. She let herself be lowered back onto the mattress and feebly tried to push down her tracksuit pants. Somehow there was another body in the room, a woman, and she deftly grabbed a handful of Poppy's clothing—tracksuit and undies—and yanked them down.

A hospital gown materialised over her and Poppy felt her legs being eased into steel stirrups.

'We're getting you ready to push,' James explained. Through the fog in her eyes, Poppy could see the silhouette of his arm pointing at the woman. 'This is Becky, one of my colleagues, and she'll be here to help us through the next bit.'

Poppy's brain was mush. Words floated in, untethered, and made no sense. *Use the contractions. Breathe through the pain. Push when we tell you.* She threw her head into her pillow and sobbed. It wasn't supposed to be like this. She wasn't supposed to be a single mother. She was a good girl, a loveable girl, someone who deserved a husband, someone to parent with. She didn't want to be doing this alone. She was scared.

A warm hand landed on hers and squeezed. 'I'm here, Poppy,' James whispered, his head beside hers. 'We're doing this together. I promise everything will be okay.'

CHAPTER 6

'YOU *WHAT*?!' screamed her mother.

Chrissie McKellar was a woman whose outdoor voice could pierce holes in glass, thanks to a combination of a well-used diaphragm and a sonorous nasal cavity not dissimilar to Barbra Streisand's.

'WHY DIDN'T YOU CALL ME?'

Poppy pulled the phone away from her ear to avoid permanent hearing loss. A baby girl lay tightly swaddled in a perspex crib in the corner.

'Darling, I would have been there in a jiffy! Oh my goodness, I can't believe I missed this—my first grandchild! I can't wait to tell the girls at golf!'

'PAUL!' she roared in the background. 'Turn that bloody football off. We're going to the hospital!'

'It all happened very quickly, Mum; even the midwife didn't expect it to go so fast. He said it was one of the quickest he's had in a while.'

'*He?*' her mother repeated, aghast.

'He,' Poppy confirmed. 'Wenda had to leave so another midwife stepped in.'

'PAUL, HURRY UP!' her mother yelled. Returning her attention to Poppy she said, 'Darling, we're coming as fast as we can, or at least I am. Paul! Your boots aren't there; they're in the laundry where you left them. Darling, you just hold tight. We'll be there before you know it. It sounds like it was an absolute debacle. Oh gosh, the girls at golf will not believe their ears.'

Her mother hung up and Poppy dropped the phone on the bed. She rose gingerly, unsure whether her limbs could still function. She'd escaped with just three sutures which stung as she moved but felt like tiny prickles of rain compared to what she'd been through. More disconcertingly, she had the feeling of having been completely disembowelled, her insides scooped out, leaving her a hollow deflated shell with no connective tissue linking her limbs to her torso. It was disorientating. Every time she moved, she wasn't sure how it happened.

She padded quietly across the linoleum and pulled the crib next to her bed. 'Hi, little one,' she whispered.

Her daughter's chest rose and fell infinitesimally and her eyes were squeezed shut, blocking out the noisy, beeping world around her. Under the halogen lighting, her skin was pale and slightly downy, her ears tiny miraculous coils of skin and cartilage. *You are so small*, thought Poppy reverentially. *You are so precious.*

'Hello?' called a deep voice from the doorway. 'Can I come in?'

'Yes, I'm decent,' Poppy replied, immediately regretting her choice of words and the allusion to her prior non-decent behaviour and state of undress. God, she'd talked about poo with this guy. There was no coming back from that.

'You okay?' asked James, examining her with those dark eyes.

He moved to the side of the bed next to the crib. The baby was sleeping deeply, oblivious to everything around her. James smiled. Without the haze of contractions, Poppy could see the fatigue in his face.

'Yes, I'm good . . . good,' she repeated, nodding her head. Was she good? She couldn't tell. She felt okay at this precise moment, with a sleeping baby and the relief of no pain and an expert at her side in case things went wrong, but would she be okay if any one of those variables changed?

It didn't help that an inconvenient undercurrent of guilt was swelling, starting to course through her veins like a virus. She should tell Patrick about this. It was a pretty big deal, if not the biggest deal he'd ever encounter. He would know the news was imminent. He might be selfish, but he wasn't an idiot.

She'd been planning this conversation for seven months. How she'd coolly inform him that he had a child, and that no, even if he did want to get back together, she wasn't so sure. He deserved to sweat a little. She fully expected him to argue back. As a benevolent compromise, she'd decided she would allow joint holidays and visits every weekend. They could build up from there.

The problem was, in among all this scheming for imaginary confrontations, Poppy had a growing fear that it might amount to zilch. Despite all her expectations that he'd try and win her back, Patrick had hardly contacted her since the breakup. There had been one cursory text to point out her due date clashed with the Sydney Test and that had been it. It was both embarrassing and unsettling. Had they grown apart or had she never really known him? At uni, she knew he'd been the party guy. By the time they'd met, he was the career guy who worked hard and partied harder. Travelling, he was the guy who'd befriend the locals and next minute you were sitting in some old nonna's house eating fresh pappardelle and doing shots of homemade grappa. But was that Patrick or a high-energy facade?

James coughed and Poppy realised she must have been staring. He checked his watch. 'I'm going home now.'

'Oh, right,' said Poppy, remembering they weren't actually friends. Why would he stick around and keep her company? That whole truce during labour had been a purely functional midwife–patient relationship thing.

'Right then, bye.' He raised his hand in an awkward wave. 'Becky will be here if you need anything.'

As he closed the door, Poppy lay down on the bed and rolled onto her stomach. The weight of her exhaustion washed over her, pushing her deeper into the foam mattress. Never again would she take sleeping on her stomach for granted. Her eyelids fluttered and closed as though weighted down by every muscle she'd used in the last twenty-four hours. She took a deep breath and a sigh seeped from her lips. For a moment, everything was still. There was no energy left in her body. A leaden, dreamless sleep was beckoning.

On the trolley table, something buzzed. Poppy cracked an eyelid. If it was her mother, she would kill her. She grabbed her phone and saw a photo of a grinning brunette with the bone structure of a Filipina princess.

'PARPEEEEE! My beautiful, beautiful girl,' Dani cried, half-sobbing, her serious mode fully activated. 'I just got your text. Tell me everything!'

Poppy smiled. She may suffer from acute verbal diarrhoea more than was healthy, but with Dani as her audience, she was a master storyteller. Everyday chores could become comical inside jokes and disasters became hilarious sitcoms to be pored over in side-splitting detail—and the last six hours had the makings of an *SNL* Christmas special.

'Dani, old girl,' she began auspiciously, 'you are going to wet your frickin pants.'

CHAPTER 7

The memory of the recent storm had been erased by seventy-two hours of incessant January sun which had pummelled any moisture back out of the earth, leaving it flaky and dry again. From the doorway of her rented house, Poppy could feel the heat reflecting off the Betadine pavers. In the crook of her elbow, she held a capsule with a sticky label on the top with big black letters spelling *MAEVE*.

'Darling!' exclaimed her mother, rushing from the kitchen. 'My darlings!' she corrected herself, joyfully extending the 's'. 'I love you both so much, to the squiddly-umpy-dumps and back!' She shoved a cup in the dishwasher and spun to her daughter, embracing her like a rose-scented cyclone. Through the thick of her mother's hair, Poppy could see her kitchen bench had been scrubbed sparkling clean. A bunch of fresh hydrangeas sat next to the sink.

Her dad appeared from the hallway, his arms spread wide. 'My precious Poppy! A mum! Can you believe it?' He looped

SPECIAL DELIVERY

his arms around his daughter and wife, bringing them into a group hug.

'We'll put little Maeve over here,' said Chrissie, breaking away and confidently taking the capsule from Poppy. She placed it in a corner of the open-plan kitchen-living area.

Maeve kept her eyes tightly shut, her tiny hands balled in fists on her chest. The stripes on her onesie rose up and down as she breathed.

'She's so beautiful, Poppy,' said her dad. 'You should be so proud of yourself.'

Poppy knew she wasn't expected to respond but nodded anyway.

Her mum grabbed the kettle, filled it up and pulled a box of teabags from a Harris Farm bag on the bench. It was the expensive brand of tea that her mother would never normally buy for herself.

'We've got treats in there too,' said her dad, nodding towards the fridge. 'Not every day our girl comes home from the hospital with our granddaughter. We need to celebrate.'

From a brown paper bag, three shiny neenish tarts were produced. Poppy closed her eyes and smiled. They had been her favourite growing up.

Her mum laid out three plates and teaspoons on the kitchen bench, and Poppy sat down with a sigh, picked up her spoon and broke the glossy surface of the tart, watching the cream and jam ooze out.

'I've stocked Maeve's room with nappies and left a bag of hand-me-downs in your bedroom,' her mother announced.

'For Maeve?'

'No, for you, darling. I had lots of trendy tops that are a bit raggy now but would be great for nursing around the house. And some old leggings too—nice and elasticated.'

'Oh, er, thanks, Mum,' Poppy said. 'Great idea.' She would wear each item once, she decided, take tactical selfies as evidence, then orchestrate a small, accidental fire to get rid of them—possibly via hair straightener.

'What time did Maeve last feed?' asked her mother. 'Should we wake her now?'

Poppy blinked. 'I thought you shouldn't wake a sleeping baby?'

'No, no. Babies need to feed constantly in these early days. I'll wake her now, shall I?'

'Oh, um . . .' Maeve had only been asleep for an hour. That didn't seem excessive.

'Best wake her now,' her mum said, beelining for the capsule.

'Ah . . .' Poppy didn't know what to say. She'd only been a mum for seventy-two hours; it wasn't like she was an expert. 'Okay.'

Her daughter's cry was a wavering bleat. As her mother brought her over, Poppy unclipped her maternity bra with clumsy fingers.

'She's latching wrong,' Chrissie observed, hovering over them. 'Don't do it like that or her nose will be covered and she'll suffocate.'

'The midwives didn't mention that.'

'Oh, they're too distracted. Understaffed. Move your arm like this . . .' She pulled Poppy's elbow to an awkward angle. 'There, that's better.'

SPECIAL DELIVERY

It wasn't better. It felt completely unnatural. Her upper arm immediately began to ache.

'So,' said her mother briskly, 'what do you want to do after the feed? I've already changed her bed linen in the nursery. I thought cotton would be better on her skin. Do you want a sleep, or do you want to watch that Diane Keaton movie I was telling you about? Or I could whip something up for dinner? You'll be needing some iron. How about some chops?'

Poppy's forehead creased wearily. Could someone else decide?

Her dad patted her arm kindly. 'You need to take advantage of this, Poppy. Soon her grandparent hormones will fade and she'll be back at golf.'

'Paul! I've already told Poppy I'll always be available to help with the baby . . . just not between nine and one on Mondays and Wednesdays.'

Poppy and her dad glanced at each other and smiled.

'What?' demanded Chrissie. 'A woman needs a hobby. Don't pretend you want me home twenty-four seven, Paul!'

'Of course not!' said her dad quickly, winking at Poppy. 'Golf all you want, darling.'

'Well, Mum, if you're wanting to do something . . .' Poppy paused, chewing her lip. 'Do you think you could help me, um . . .?'

Her mother looked confused.

'I know it's stupid, and if you don't want to go out in this heat I completely understand, it's just . . . I don't really know how I'd take Maeve outside and, well, I've only breathed hospital air for the last few days. So . . . will you help me . . . go for a walk?'

Chrissie laughed, clapping her hands. 'Of course, darling! Gosh, I thought you might need help going to the toilet, or need me to check your bits or something. A walk I can certainly do. Although,' her mother's smile abruptly faded, 'don't go poking around your bits without me. We don't want a hand-held mirror getting stuck up there.'

On his stool at the kitchen bench, her dad covered his ears.

★

The neenish tarts disappeared even faster than anticipated, and fifty minutes later—after a breastfeed, a nappy change and some tense moments connecting the bassinet to the pram frame—they were ready to go. Poppy's dad settled himself onto her second-hand couch and flicked on the cricket while her mum opened the door and Poppy eased the pram outside, a muslin cloth protecting Maeve from the sun. Her mum followed them, carrying the fully stocked nappy bag 'just in case'.

'I think she needs a singlet,' Chrissie said for the fortieth time.

'It's over thirty degrees, Mum.'

'Yes, but newborns get so cold. I'll wait here while you go change her. Make sure you get a hat for yourself too.'

It was stiflingly hot but Poppy's sluggish brain was not prepared for resistance. She lifted Maeve from the pram and walked back inside like a robot.

As they re-emerged through the front door, her mum smiled, vindicated. 'Much better.'

The air was warm and heavy with the scent of mown grass as they rolled onto the footpath. The stark afternoon sunlight

SPECIAL DELIVERY

sharpened every vignette. Maeve's eyes drifted closed and Poppy yielded to the therapy of the motion. Left foot, right foot, left foot, right foot. There was so much to think about but she was doing her best to avoid thinking at all. Some people strived for mindfulness; Poppy strived for mindlessness. If she reduced everything to its smallest component parts—ignoring the terrifying synergy of it all—she felt less overwhelmed. It was all her brain could cope with right now: left foot, right foot, left foot, right foot.

'Have you spoken to—'

'Dani, yes,' interrupted Poppy, knowing that was definitely not where her mother was heading with that question. 'I've spoken to her a few times.'

They continued on in silence. She'd tried to call Patrick on her first night in hospital but he hadn't answered. She'd stared at the phone for a full fifteen minutes afterwards waiting for it to ring. She'd seen Patrick walk out of funerals to take a business call, but after fifteen agonising minutes she realised with a white-hot pain that he wasn't calling back. At a loss for what to do, she'd texted him a photo of Maeve wrapped in a pink blanket in her perspex bassinet. A message came back almost instantly: *She's beautiful Pops! Just like her mother.*

That was it. No promise to call back, no questions about how she was feeling, no questions about the weight or height or labour. He didn't even ask her name, for god's sake. It was a message you'd send to anyone who'd had a baby. Poppy had buried her head into her pillow and cried herself to sleep.

Now, as she traipsed gingerly around the parched suburb with her mum beside her, Poppy tried to settle her thoughts.

Left foot, right foot, left foot, right foot. She needed a goal.

Obviously she had to get a job. She didn't have to worry about money yet—her maternity leave payments would run out eventually but her savings would see her through for another twelve months, and she could always move back in with her parents if she got really stuck—but finding a job would help ward off any anxiety about impending doom (aka moving back in with her parents).

She also needed to meet people. She could not survive in this town with only her mum and dad for company. All the conversations about Rockmans would test her mental fortitude more than a surprise pregnancy.

So, okay, she needed a job and friends. Jesus, they were not small things. Maybe she needed a different goal, something with more straightforward, actionable steps. French lessons, maybe? A coding course, perhaps?

The pram bumped over a tree root and Poppy flinched. Maeve was unperturbed, which was strange because the pram had really jolted. Poppy peered at the wheels. Maybe the suspension on the pram was faulty. She made a mental note to double-check the promo video on YouTube and compare it with how her pram was functioning. If she had been ripped off, she should probably write a letter to the CEO. With whole days stretching out before her with nothing to do, she'd have to keep herself busy somehow.

The pram rolled along in front of her and the realisation hit her like a semitrailer. That should be her goal: *being a good mother*. How embarrassing she hadn't thought of that

SPECIAL DELIVERY

before. Thank god no-one could read her thoughts. What kind of mother forgot to prioritise mothering?! She'd assumed it would be automatic (i.e. birth baby > undergo maternal transformation), but her brain was still in young-and-dumb mode—though she was way more dumb than young.

Poppy cleared her throat. 'Mum, will I ever feel confident about this?'

Her mother smiled cheerfully. 'Never, darling. This is a life sentence.'

CHAPTER 8

Maeve was dressed in a floral onesie that covered her feet and hands. Yes, she was tiny and divine and smelled like heaven in human form, but good god, this child was *hers*. After twenty-four hours at home, twenty of which she'd spent alone (apart from Maeve), the reality of her circumstances were beginning to sink in. Unlike her two nights in hospital, where she'd slept under the leaden weight of exhaustion, last night she'd barely rested at all, springing up at Maeve's every sound, nervously checking the swaddling wasn't tangled and waiting for her eyes to adjust in the darkness so she could watch for the minuscule rise and fall of Maeve's chest. It wasn't just tiredness. She felt like she'd ridden three rollercoasters back to back and was still waiting for her insides to settle.

Poppy considered the installation of half-drunk tea mugs littering her hard surfaces; an affecting portrait of modern motherhood. The bassinet was parked in a shaded corner

SPECIAL DELIVERY

of the kitchen with Maeve happily sleeping inside, but even this was cause for anxiety: she was supposed to sleep while the baby slept! But it was only 10 am. Her circadian rhythm hadn't adjusted yet. When would that happen? Day five?

A knock rattled the door and Poppy jumped. Any unanticipated sound—no matter the volume—now prompted a visceral reaction. She glanced anxiously at Maeve but her daughter didn't stir.

'Coming!' she whispered, checking her maternity bra was clipped up as she hurried to the door. The unpacking of the dishwasher would have to wait. Again.

A pair of broad shoulders was visible through the opaque glass. *Oh crap.* She'd expected Wenda would do her home visits, not James.

Annoyed, she opened the door.

'What?' asked James, and Poppy realised her nose was crinkled as she looked him up and down. He was carrying a backpack and wearing jeans and a white polo; an outfit that was uncannily reminiscent of a standard-issue Ken doll.

'I was expecting Wenda.'

James gave an almost imperceptible shrug. 'I already had a personal engagement in this street so I figured I should swing by. May I?' He gestured inside.

Poppy turned and led him to the kitchen. 'Would you, er, like a cup of tea?' she asked, vaguely wondering if she should have baked something. Also—what kind of 'personal engagement' could he have had in this cul-de-sac? Did he moonlight as a fax machine salesman?

'No,' James said curtly. 'This isn't a social call; I'm working.'

Poppy glowered. Did he not understand common courtesy? She wished she *had* baked something, so she could have sneezed on it.

James glanced around the kitchen, seemed dissatisfied, then walked to the living area, talking over his shoulder. 'I need to ask you a few questions, check your stomach, then I'll weigh Maeve. Understand?'

Poppy nodded, feeling her mouth curl in disgust. He didn't need to speak to her like she was thick. It was unfortunate that the kitchen looked like a bombsite and she'd gone batshit crazy during labour, but they were hardly reasons to doubt her mental capacity. There had been extenuating circumstances.

James pulled a clipboard from his backpack and sat on the sofa. 'How was last night?' he asked.

'Fine,' replied Poppy irritably. She sat at the opposite end of the couch.

'I'll need more information than that.'

'She woke quite a few times and I hardly slept at all, but I don't think anything went *wrong* wrong. Like, she fed okay and she seemed to fall asleep pretty well after I breastfed.'

'Good,' said James and made a note.

Poppy nodded, relieved her breasts had (literally) risen to the occasion. The thought of discussing her nipples with James was supremely discomforting.

'And you're getting wet nappies?'

'Yes.'

'Any poos?'

'Yes, two.' (Should she clarify they were Maeve's?!)

SPECIAL DELIVERY

'Next question,' continued James, making a show of reading from the clipboard. 'Have you considered what you'll be using as contraception going forward?'

Poppy's breathing stopped halfway between an inhale and exhale and came out as a hacking cough. The What-to-Expect articles had not mentioned this. She felt her neck redden and prayed the blush wouldn't reach her face. How on earth should she answer that? She'd been on the pill on and off during her years with Patrick, but she'd hated how it affected her mood and her skin. (God, that made her sound so vain.) Before she fell pregnant, they'd been using the pull-out method, but she was definitely *not* mentioning that. 'I haven't really thought about it . . .' She trailed off, looking at the floor. 'But it's not a huge priority for me as I'm kind of, um, closed for business.'

James cleared his throat. 'It's important to remember that breastfeeding is not the foolproof contraceptive method some people would have you believe. Contraception may be the last thing on your mind after having a baby, but the reality is that you could become fertile again much earlier than you expect, so you need to be prepared.'

James began to run through the various options for contraception—the pill (hard to remember to take it when you're distracted by a baby), condoms (may be uncomfortable because of lower oestrogen levels), IUDs, the morning-after pill, and everything else—in excruciating detail.

'Right,' he said finally. 'That's all you need to know about that. Okay, last question: are you experiencing any anxiety?'

Poppy rolled her eyes. 'No.'

'I need a serious answer.'

'That was serious.'

'You're telling me you're completely fine?'

Ugh, he was a dick. Of course she wasn't fine.

'I'll ask you again: are you okay?'

Avoiding his eyes, Poppy picked a loose thread from her t-shirt. It was a big question. The obvious answer was yes. Yes. Or was it no? Poppy couldn't remember what new mothers were supposed to say. A level of uncertainty was surely normal, but you were supposed to say something along the lines of 'tired but happy', right? And your eyes were supposed to say it with you. They should have bags and lines around them but be filled with an incandescent maternal sparkle. But in the same way Poppy's skin hadn't acquired that indefinable glow, she suspected her eyes were lagging too.

'I . . . tired?'

'Just tired?' asked James, his eyes probing.

'Fatigued.'

'I know what tired means, Poppy. I was asking whether you feel tired above all else. Or are you feeling anything else?'

What could she say? That she was tired, yes, but more than that she was scared. She was unsure. She was alone. Every time Maeve squeaked at night it was her ears that heard it, her eyelids that sprung open. She couldn't poke someone across the mattress. She couldn't have a day off; she couldn't have a minute off. She couldn't rely on herself to remember to buy cereal but she had to rely on herself to feed and clothe and raise this child. And yes, she had her parents in town, and yes, she had some great friends on speed dial, but was she really going to call them at 2 am? And 3 am? And 4 am? Every night?

SPECIAL DELIVERY

'I'm a bit ... numb,' she confessed quietly. It wasn't the whole truth but it wasn't a lie. She was running on tea and adrenaline, surviving by not overthinking, or hardly thinking at all. Feed, sleep, walk, repeat. Left foot, right foot.

'That's not unusual,' said James. 'It's a big change, after all.'

That was the problem, though. It was a big change but it wasn't the only one. It was like she was working her way through the encyclopaedia of life-changing moments. Fall pregnant: tick. Break up with partner of nine years: tick. Leave job: tick. Move towns: tick. Have baby: tick. Poppy's world had turned on its axis so many times in the past twelve months she was practically spinning into another dimension.

'If you want to lie down on the couch, I'll check your uterus now.'

'Do we have to?' Having the nurses check her stomach in hospital had been fine, but having an annoyingly attractive man feel up her misshapen belly after an in-depth conversation about contraception was a completely different proposition.

'Yes, we have to.'

'Why?'

'Because this is a routine check-up and checking your stomach is part of the routine.'

Poppy glared at him. He glared back. If this were a staring contest, then Poppy sure as hell was going to beat this douchebag. She didn't care if she was so tired her eyes felt like sandpaper and ... ah, damn it. She'd blinked.

She lay down on the couch. 'Why are you a midwife anyway?' she grumbled. 'Unconventional career choice for a man.'

James raised an eyebrow. 'I'll ignore the inherent sexism in that statement.'

'Whatever,' Poppy said. 'I did a whole semester of gender studies and am fully aware of how that sounded. I meant *statistically speaking*, midwifery is an unconventional career choice for a male. I was merely inquiring about your job, the same way you'd ask the person sitting next to you on the bus.'

'I don't do small talk, especially on public transport.'

'I can't imagine why not,' snapped Poppy. 'You're a gifted conversationalist.'

'Fine,' said James. 'I became a midwife to pick up chicks. That, and I have a messiah complex and felt summoned to bring new life into the world.'

'If you're not willing to engage in a civil conversation then I won't waste my breath on you.'

'Finally we agree on something.'

He pointed to her stomach and Poppy grudgingly lifted her top, making sure her milk-stained maternity bra remained securely out of view.

James kneeled next to the couch and that cotton and aftershave scent washed over her. She briefly thought of closing her eyes to avoid the awkwardness but just as quickly decided that might imply some kind of erotic pleasure on her part. Instead she stared resolutely at the ceiling, willing herself not to blink. His broad palms gently wrapped around her torso.

'Your hands are cold,' she muttered.

James ignored her and moved his fingers carefully along her abdomen, testing pressure points with a subtle massaging motion. Her stomach muscles tightened under his fingertips.

SPECIAL DELIVERY

'Done,' he said, standing up. 'Everything feels fine.'

'Good,' said Poppy, quickly pulling her top down and hastening to her feet—anything to correct the power imbalance.

'It's time to wake up Maeve now,' said James, walking over to the bassinet where she slept. 'Will you wake her, or shall I?'

'I will.' Poppy strode over and placed her hand self-consciously on the wooden frame. She hoped this body language displayed the correct amount of instinctual maternal devotion. Too much and he'd know she was a fraud; too little and he'd call family services.

She knew Dani had struggled to bond with Nella at first, mystified by her crying and smallness, but Sam's love for Nella had been instant. Poppy couldn't deny that her daughter's skinny alien arms and legs freaked her out, but in her bones she could already feel a fervent connection to Maeve, even though they'd only known each other for four days. They were a duo; each other's only other. She wasn't sure if it was love yet, but there was an indivisible bond.

Poppy slid one hand under Maeve's back and another under her velvety head. Her daughter scowled at being moved and began to cry in her tiny rattling voice. 'Come on, Maeve,' Poppy cooed as James moved a collection of mugs to the sink so he could set up the portable scales on the kitchen bench. 'This is something we've gotta do.'

She undid the buttons on Maeve's onesie as James averted his eyes. She was going as fast as she could but this process was unbearable with an uncooperative baby. Had her fingers always been this fat and useless? She immediately resolved to throw out every onesie unless it had zippers. James seemed to be fixated on her fruit bowl—probably judging its barrenness. With a final exhausting effort, she pulled the last tiny button out of its tiny hole and laid her daughter gently on the scales.

'Three point five,' James said, scribbling on his clipboard. 'That's more than her birth weight.'

'Is that bad?'

'No,' said James. 'It's unusual . . . it's good.'

Poppy felt a heady rush of pleasure, as though she had received a glowing compliment. It was such a small thing in a week full of big things and, inexplicably, she felt tears forming in the corner of her eyes. She lifted her daughter to her chest and kissed her soft head. A lump in her throat had emerged from nowhere. These hormones were having a great time running the show.

James seemed to notice the change in energy and looked away, frowning at her messy sink as he gathered up his things. He was probably one of those guys who couldn't cope with untidiness—or female emotion. Poppy glanced at him, his nervous discomfort a welcome distraction from her own.

'What's wrong?' asked Poppy, pointing to his face. She felt compelled to provoke him, she couldn't help it.

'Nothing,' replied James.

'You're frowning.'

'No, I'm not,' he said, his expression dissolving into blankness.

Poppy studied his face for a flicker of emotion. Nada. This was the guy who'd held her hand when she'd pushed a human out of her vagina and he couldn't even break a smile in her company and offer a pat on the back.

SPECIAL DELIVERY

'Do you even remember the birth?' she asked. 'Or do all the labouring mothers blend into one? Like a giant conveyor belt of screaming women?'

James looked at her, confused. 'Of course I remember.'

'Then why can't you be nice?'

James zipped up his backpack and started towards the door. 'I'm not here to be nice,' he said over his shoulder. 'I'm here to do my job.'

CHAPTER 9

There was no time for coding courses. Hell, there was hardly time for hair washing. At this point, Poppy couldn't decipher whether Maeve's gas was burp-related or fart-related, let alone decipher HTML. Twelve weeks into parenthood and Poppy was surviving on a strict diet of coffee, tea and fork food. She hadn't used a knife in three months. She might never ever use one again.

Poppy eased the pram through her front gate, her eye catching on her elderly neighbour who sat on the verandah next door in a wicker armchair.

'Morning, Mary.' Poppy lifted her hand in a wave.

'Morning, love,' replied Mary cheerfully.

Poppy had met Mary during her first week in town. She'd been exploring the street and her eighty-nine-year-old neighbour had beckoned her over. Mary had proudly informed her that she sat on her verandah every day so knew everything about the street, including that its newest resident was a

SPECIAL DELIVERY

soon-to-be single mother. 'I knew from how often your mother visited,' she told Poppy, tapping her nose. 'If there'd been a man, he'd have been out of there like a shot.' Mary seemed delighted about this situation, declaring conspiratorially that as single girls they should stick together.

Mary had invited Poppy to join her on the verandah for some of her famous jam drop biscuits and proceeded to regale her with a detailed recount of her life, which revolved around her dynasty of grandchildren and great-grandchildren, who all had nineties sitcom names like Bobby, Jimmy, Davy, Mikey and Katie. Her other passion was buying useful (read: useless) trinkets via mail-order catalogue. Her latest purchase—a rainbow-hued silicone tea cosy—was proving far more practical than the word-of-the-day toilet paper which, as Mary put it, was 'more arse than class'.

Any remaining spare time of Mary's was consumed by her zealous commitment to neighbourhood snooping. Thanks to Mary, Poppy knew that number seven had a pool, number three played jazz too loudly and someone in number eleven was possibly having an affair. Everyone was aged over sixty-five apart from the woman in number five, who dressed entirely in yellow and regularly washed her (yellow) car in a (yellow) bikini. It wasn't necessarily useful information, but the gentle meandering of Mary's conversations amused Poppy, whose grandparents had long since passed away. She'd found herself looking forward to her regular chats with her neighbour.

As Poppy came to a halt in front of Mary's front gate, her neighbour hoisted herself up in her armchair to peer at the pram. 'How did our girl sleep last night?' she asked.

'Woke three times,' replied Poppy. 'Or maybe four?'

'Good girl,' clucked Mary. 'She's learned her day from night already.'

Poppy was continually bemused with how people were overly keen to praise her daughter for all manner of things—her blinking, her burping, her sneezing. Lauding her for waking up four times during the night, however, felt supremely disingenuous when a full night's sleep was clearly the actual goal.

'You're doing a wonderful job,' added Mary kindly.

Poppy wanted to smile, for Mary's sake, to make the old lady feel as though she'd done a good job of allaying her fears, but she couldn't. Her neighbour had no clue if she was doing a good job of mothering. No-one knew. No-one was watching her stumble in the darkness trying to find the bassinet. No-one was making sure Maeve latched on properly. For all they knew, Poppy could have been feeding her daughter Fanta from a bottle, setting her up for a lifetime of sugar addiction and expensive dentistry.

The hardest thing was that even Poppy didn't know if she was doing a good job. She wouldn't know for years, and—horrible thought though it was—she might never know. She might be on this hamster wheel of guilt and fear and self-doubt for the rest of her life, always second-guessing whether she'd made the right choice for her daughter, wondering whether bringing her into the world without a father was ruining her life from the start.

She wanted her old boss to walk into her house with a spreadsheet and a PowerPoint presentation and say, 'These are your KPIs, Poppy. Achieve these targets and you will raise

SPECIAL DELIVERY

a healthy, well-adjusted child.' Poppy could work with KPIs. She could work longer hours, she could read more reports, she could pore over the data sets until her eyes watered. It was what she was used to. But her metrics and optics and vision statements wouldn't work here. For all the love and energy she'd thrown at it, her big shiny career was worthless now. The only thing she could rely on now was her breastmilk—and that, to be perfectly frank, had the pong of old yoghurt.

She finally forced a weak smile as she pushed the pram down the road. 'Thanks, Mary. You're always lifting my spirits.'

The first autumn leaves littered the ground beneath her feet and an icy breeze tickled her bare hands. Maeve was wailing irritably in the pram, a lopsided beanie on her head. Poppy had no idea why she was crying. Her daughter was fed, changed, wearing mittens and three layers of clothing—all organic cotton and wool, like an Eastern Suburbs ski bunny ready for schnappy hour. *Maeve*, she wanted to say, *smarten up*. Actually, she didn't want to say that at all. In fact, the only thing worse would be saying, *Let it all out like Mariah*, while wearing a hot-pink golf skirt with leggings underneath. And yep—she looked down at her hideous, saggy leggings—she was halfway there. Why did no-one warn you that when you became a parent you became *your* parents? What kind of messed-up Freudian crap was that?

Poppy hitched up her leggings and turned onto the walking track that skirted the golf course. The air was thick with mist and pine. Mercifully, the track was deserted, free of judgemental ears. Thank goodness capitalism had burrowed through the Blue Mountains to the Central West, forcing people off walking tracks and into offices by 9 am sharp. Poppy checked her watch. Minus the crying, the day was running to schedule: breastfeed, walk, breastfeed, coffee, breastfeed, breastfeed, more breastfeeding. It didn't calm her anxiety.

Suddenly a kelpie bounded out of nowhere. 'Argh!' she yelled as it jumped up on her, leaving streaks of mud down her leggings. 'Get off!'

'Ga-ga!' cried Maeve, suddenly delighted. Her curious eyes were fixed on the dog and its thumping tail.

'Sorry!' a man yelled, running up to them. 'Ran away before I could get the lead on.'

'You!' Poppy scowled at the too-tall silhouette jogging towards her. 'Your dog jumped on me!'

Her former midwife came to a stop in front of her. His hair was dishevelled from the breeze and his long-sleeved t-shirt was a stark white under his puffer vest. 'Oh,' James said, without enthusiasm. 'Hi.' He'd clearly forgotten her name. His eyes whisked from left to right as if computing the fastest getaway route. He didn't even have the decency to look embarrassed. 'Eileen's only twelve weeks old,' he said, by way of unsatisfactory apology. 'I'm trying to train her.' He held up the leash as proof.

'Good,' Poppy said. She spun around and marched off, but within three paces Maeve was wailing again. As if it were a siren song, the kelpie trotted up and Maeve quietened.

James jogged over and grabbed his dog by the collar. 'Come on, Eileen, we're going the other way.'

'Waaaaaaah!' screamed Maeve.

'Come. On. Eileen.' James tried to pull the puppy in the opposite direction but it was refusing to budge.

SPECIAL DELIVERY

Poppy began walking away and the dog strained against its collar, barking at full volume. Maeve started thrashing her head against the pram, which took her wailing to an eardrum-piercing new level.

'I think Eileen is trying to get back to your daughter,' called James. 'I've seen this happen before. It's a protective instinct thing.'

'I don't care,' snapped Poppy. If he thought she was interested in the psychology of canines, he had a sorely misguided idea of what she found interesting (i.e. Mecca sales and pelvic floor war stories). As she strode off, the puppy barked like a maniac and Maeve's screams rattled the windowpanes of nearby houses.

'If we walk next to each other'—he was jogging back to her—'your daughter will stop crying, and Eileen will slow down so she can get used to the leash.' As if to demonstrate his point, the kelpie parked itself beside the pram and Maeve instantly stopped wailing.

Poppy glared at his perfectly windswept hair. The fabric of his t-shirt was fluttering in the breeze but his features were set in stone, as detached and inscrutable as ever.

Poppy tightened her fingers around the pram. 'No way,' she said. Her walks around the golf course gave her time to think and listen to cheesy podcasts and call Dani and her mum and do whatever she pleased while feeling the wind on her face and enjoying the sense of control and purpose that came with steering a pram. Most of her days felt like treading water—waiting for Maeve to go to sleep, waiting for Maeve to wake up—but when she was pushing a pram, she was in charge.

She did not need an intruder, especially such a douchey one, ruining this sacred ritual. 'I walk in silence,' she added over her shoulder as she stalked away.

'Waaaaah!' screamed Maeve.

RUFF-RUFF-RUFF-RUFF, barked the psycho dog.

'How's that silence going?' called James.

Poppy spun on her heels, her blood turning to molten lava. She could *feel* his smirk. 'I don't want to walk with you,' she hissed. Somewhere inside her consciousness, her mother tutted. Poppy had never been so openly rude in her life. If he hadn't realised he wasn't welcome, then he was either outrageously stupid or, as she was beginning to suspect, a bona fide robot.

He shrugged. 'The feeling's mutual, but I need to train my dog and my shift starts soon so my time is limited.' He looked bored now. 'So we going?'

Poppy's knuckles whitened on the pram handle. What was worse? His company or a screaming baby? Her brain was not cut out for this mental arithmetic. With a dull clunk in her frontal lobe, she realised the worst would be a combination of the two: her walking ahead with a screaming baby while he walked behind, judging her every parenting move with a full view of her saggy-bum leggings.

'Fine.' She pushed off, leaving him to catch up. The nerve of him! Trapping her in this predicament, especially when she'd made it clear how much she didn't want his company.

They strode in silence, Poppy's muscles so tense with irritation she was almost spasming. She needed to work out a way to get rid of him. Could she do something to the dog?

Suddenly, Poppy's phone dinged in the cup holder. She

pulled it out and blinked at the name on the screen. Patrick. *Of all times!*

Her eyes darted to James, whose gaze was locked on the path as if trying to manifest her non-existence. Poppy angled the screen away from him and opened the message.

What was name of shipping heir from Mykonos? Need asap for meeting

The three dots under the message indicated he wasn't finished. And just as well. After ten months of almost zero contact, this couldn't be it. You couldn't spend nine years with someone, have their child and tell them about the birth, only to be met with virtual silence until he needed a business lead.

The next message appeared.

Urgent!

Poppy stared at the phone. Seriously?! This was how he was playing it? No *hi*, no *how are you*, no *how's my firstborn child?*—just a demand for help remembering the name of a hairy dude from an underground bar. Poppy's hand dropped to her side and she lifted her face to the sky. Hot tears were suddenly welling behind her eyes and she needed gravity to tip them back down.

This was classic Patrick. He'd hardly acknowledged Maeve's birth. Why would he suddenly reconnect out of the blue? She should have known better than to expect anything meaningful from him. But then, why did her stomach suddenly feel like a cement mixer on acid?

She snuck a glance at James. For a fraction of a millisecond their eyes met, but just as quickly his gaze darted away. Well, good. She did not want his pity.

Suddenly: another beep.

URGENT!!!

Jesus! Poppy swore under her breath and began tapping furiously. A litany of responses swam through her mind, all of them heavy on the f-word. He'd ignored her for ten months but still expected an instantaneous response?! She tapped and deleted and tapped and deleted. Finally, she pressed send.

Theo Caryannis.

Ah, fuck it. *Next time*, she would tell him that his behaviour was completely unacceptable. She would *definitely* do that.

The pram bumped over a crack in the pavement. The phone had absorbed the chill in the air and was cold in her fingertips. Poppy stared at the screen long enough for James's eyes to flit in her direction again, but it was useless. No matter how hard she stared, she could not make those three dots reappear. Waiting for thanks from Patrick was like her mum's Zumba era: utterly pointless. She shoved the phone back in the cup holder.

The path beneath them was now carpeted with reddened pine needles, slippery under foot. Poppy tightened her grip on the pram and steered it around the pine cones that cluttered the pavement. They were just what she didn't need right now: more speed bumps.

She'd always thought of herself as a strong woman—*a feminist!*—but regardless of how long she spent daydreaming about reducing Patrick to a stuttering mess with her biting put-downs and dazzling intellect, it always seemed that when she was in his orbit, she became a spineless wallflower.

Maeve extended her chubby hand towards Eileen, and James flashed her a tiny smile. When he saw Poppy looking,

SPECIAL DELIVERY

he quickly turned away, his features morphing back into a square-jawed mask. *Men!*

Poppy was so intent on staring straight ahead and *not* looking at James that she hardly flinched when Maeve let out a giant fart. It wasn't until both James and the dog looked over, and her nostrils registered the acrid smell, that Poppy leaned over the pram hood to assess the damage. She saw it immediately. A mustard-brown splodge was emerging from her daughter's left buttock with alarming speed.

For god's sake! Poppy quickly pulled off the path for an emergency nappy change. She looked frantically from left to right, but there was nowhere to lay a change mat. It was a sea of pine cones. She tried to kick one away but the pine needles were slippery and she toppled clumsily, landing with an ungainly crack on a spiky conifer. 'Ow!' she cried.

James had pulled Eileen to a halt.

More hot tears were building behind her eyes. Embarrassment tears. 'Keep walking,' Poppy hissed. This was precisely why she liked to walk alone. Poonami crisis management was hard enough without an audience.

She clambered up to unbuckle her daughter. The poo was halfway up Maeve's back and down to her knees, and the kid hadn't even started solids! What the hell would happen when they introduced fibre?!

'Ah . . .' James shifted on the balls of his feet.

'Go!'

He began walking away, tugging at Eileen, who began barking emphatically.

Poppy tore off all Maeve's ski bunny layers, opened the nappy and began scraping as fast as she could. At the sight of the puppy leaving, Maeve screamed louder, flung her body to the left and rolled with a slow thud onto her belly. Poppy quickly grabbed more wipes and began scraping away at Maeve's bottom, but the rolling motion had displaced even more poo.

Maeve's cries were met with a booming bark, followed by a roar from James. 'EILEEN!'

Poppy looked up to see the kelpie running full pelt towards them. Without thinking, Poppy grabbed Maeve and hugged her to her chest, just as the kelpie came to a skidding stop on the change mat.

'This fucking dog!' yelled Poppy, as James ran up to them. She gripped her daughter tighter, feeling her sweater transform into an ombre-brown monstrosity. 'She almost killed my daughter!'

'She wanted to *see* her, not kill her!'

Poppy glared at him. Her sweater and singlet were both soaked through. She could hardly breathe from the smell. She'd packed spare clothes for Maeve, but not herself. What the hell was she going to do? Walk home topless?

James was already tugging Eileen away. Poppy scowled at his back. First Patrick, now James—scarpering when they could be helping! She closed her eyes helplessly and a fat tear plopped onto Maeve's head.

'Give her to me,' James said gruffly, suddenly beside her again. Eileen was tied to a nearby lamppost.

Without waiting for permission, he took Maeve from Poppy's arms. She wiped her eyes roughly as James fished a spare blanket from the pram's undercarriage, laid it flat on the ground and

SPECIAL DELIVERY

lowered Maeve onto it. Pulling more wipes from the nappy bag, he began rubbing her clean. Maeve blinked up at him, dazzled. Before Poppy could unclench her molars, her daughter was somehow wearing a new nappy and a clean onesie, babbling contentedly to a pine cone. It had all happened so fast.

James turned to Poppy. 'You got hand sanitiser?'

'I'm not a total heathen,' she retorted, throwing him a bottle. She knew she looked like a murder victim, but brown. She was determinedly not inhaling through her nostrils.

James cleaned his hands, wiped down the pram and lifted Maeve back into it. Poppy glowered at him. He was acting like a better parent than her, the show-off.

When he turned back to her, his eyes were so stormy that Poppy unexpectedly felt a surge of triumph through her veins. His mask of irritating calm had been smashed!

'Poppy, I swear . . .'

'What?' she demanded, dimly registering that he'd remembered her name.

He threw his hands in the air. 'I've never had so many *issues* with one patient.' His eyes flashed over her like lightning in a thunderstorm. Angrily, he unzipped his vest, threw it on the ground then pulled his t-shirt off over his head.

Poppy glared at him. Even shirtless, he was so obviously lacking a normal human level of self-consciousness. He had the smooth, honed ridges of a swimmer and his chest was firm and taut. He looked like he could perform tumble turns under the pressure of Olympic glory and then sell you a box of Nutri-Grain. Poppy's skin tingled with a sensation that was foreign to her, as though someone had double-bounced her on a trampoline and statically charged her with electricity—*angry* electricity. Her eyes flared as she spoke. 'I've never met someone whose *issue* was being so unfriendly.'

'I'm not your friend,' he snapped. 'I'm your midwife.'

Poppy bristled, feeling the static electricity transmute into something more flammable. 'Newsflash, *James*, I stopped being your patient three months ago, so you can stop being a condescending prick.'

'I'm maintaining *professional boundaries*.'

He was half-naked.

'You're maintaining a pole up your arse.'

He thrust his t-shirt at her. 'Take this.'

Poppy snatched it. 'Turn around.'

They turned their backs to each other and Poppy tore off her soiled layers and grabbed more baby wipes to clean her stomach. She pulled his t-shirt on and—*oh, sweet Jesus*—she could breathe normally again. The cool autumn air flooded her nostrils, spiked with that same aftershave scent she remembered from the hospital. The cotton was still warm from his body.

When she turned back, James had zipped his puffer vest over his bare torso. His arms were rippled with goosebumps. 'You're lucky I had this vest.'

'Yeah, I'm so *lucky*,' Poppy replied sarcastically. 'You and your dog have ruined my only decent sweater and because I forgot to buy laundry powder *again*, tomorrow I'll have to start wearing hand-me-downs from my mum from *Rivers*! Do you realise how embarrassed I feel on a daily basis, without having to wear my sixty-three-year-old mother's hand-me-downs? As if I wasn't deep enough in battler mode, this is really going to tip me into ultimate loser territory, so yes, James, I feel so incredibly fortunate!'

Fluttering at their feet were mountains of used wipes which would have to be bagged up and binned. (Oh, the landfill! Oh, the guilt!) Poppy leaned down and began scrambling to scoop the wipes into plastic bags, which she heaped into the base of the pram. There was no way she could finish this walk now.

She spun the pram to face the opposite direction, at which point, Maeve began screaming and Eileen responded with her own wolverine howling. Over the cacophony, it briefly occurred to her to say sorry, but then she remembered she hated this guy and he knew it and, oh, what a relief not to care about hurting someone's feelings.

'Later!' she called over her shoulder, in what she hoped he would recognise as the verbal equivalent of the rude finger.

She stormed away, her blood boiling at everything: his smirk, his nappy-changing skills, the perfect tessellation of his chest muscles. She could feel a bruise forming on her butt cheek, and as Maeve continued to scream Poppy bit her cheek to keep from joining in.

Rounding the corner back into her cul-de-sac, the woman from number five was carrying a sud-filled bucket to her car wearing nothing but a yellow string bikini and pair of rubber gloves (also yellow). The sight was a welcome distraction from the thundering rage still battering her rib cage.

'Hi!' called the woman, her pert breasts shaking as she waved. Her legs were impossibly long and cellulite-free and her long, glossy hair swirled in the breeze. She was almost as tall as . . . oh, of course, James. Poppy smirked wryly, remembering how he'd arrived for her home visit after a mysterious 'personal engagement'. He must have been visiting this Bella Hadid clone.

Poppy waved back and smiled, a smug understanding blossoming in her chest. Just as she suspected—James was as unoriginal as an Ikea flat pack, shipped straight from the factory floor. Good-looking men made such obvious choices.

CHAPTER 10

The Bustle had quickly become one of Poppy's favourite places in town. A converted Masonic hall, its cathedral-like walls housed a café, a homewares shop and a fashion boutique, all nestled together in an energetic jumble. Floral installations hung from the ceiling and the white-painted brick walls were decorated with a rainbow of artworks. Shelves were heavy with jewel-toned crockery, cushions and other trinkets, while reams of vibrant outfits weighed down the clothing racks. Light streamed in from skylights and the floor-to-ceiling windows, bathing the place in a phosphorescent glow. It was so different from anything else in the wind-bleached town and so unapologetically colourful compared to anything in Sydney that it felt like an escapist dreamland.

Parking the pram next to a duck-egg blue table, Poppy settled herself into a chair and pulled her laptop out of the nappy bag. After a quick shower at home, she'd changed out of her saggy-bummed leggings and was now wearing her denim shorts in steadfast denial of it already being jeans season in Orange.

'The usual, Poppy?' asked a twenty-something waitress in a Breton-striped t-shirt.

Poppy loved that the friendly waitress (whose name she had awkwardly forgotten) already knew her order by heart. It made her feel like a cast member of *Home & Away*.

'Yep, soy cap for me,' she replied, smiling brightly to compensate for the forgotten name.

'Coming right up.'

The waitress left and Poppy opened her laptop, sliding her fingers across the touchpad to bring up Seek. In her weekly budget, she could justify the daily coffee by using her time at The Bustle to search for jobs.

Engrossed in her browsers, she didn't register the footsteps shuffling closer until a shadow fell over her shoulder. 'Poppy?'

She turned, and her heart fell through her stomach with a painful jolt.

'Henry?'

It had been almost a decade and Henry Marshall looked exactly the same. His hair still curled over his ears, his cheeks were still dimpled, his nose was still smattered with freckles. He still had all the requisite features of a typically cute country boy.

'Here you go, Poppy,' said her waitress, reappearing from nowhere. She placed the coffee on the table with a flourish and looked at Poppy expectantly.

'Oh, er, yes,' Poppy stammered, trying to get her brain into gear. 'Um . . . thanks . . . so much.'

SPECIAL DELIVERY

Henry's hands were shoved deep into his pockets, so that he appeared to be one long line of checked shirt and moleskins. No limbs, just a monolith of man.

The waitress looked between them, realisation dawning on her clear young face. 'Oh, you two are friends?'

Poppy was mute. She couldn't answer. Were they friends? They had been the very best of friends, but that was a lifetime ago. Poppy waited for Henry to respond, but he looked as tortured as she felt.

'Old friends,' said Henry eventually, nodding at the waitress as if that were her cue to leave.

'That's awesome,' said the waitress, cheerfully immune to his hint. 'I love how everyone here knows each other. It means you can't get away with anything though. That was never an issue in Perth.' She flashed them a smile and bounced back to the counter.

Tracey from Perth! That was her name!

'Thanks, Tracey,' called Poppy meekly. The waitress's perkiness—and obliviousness—was overwhelming right now. Warily, she turned back to Henry.

'Poppy McKellar,' he said slowly, the syllables heavy in his mouth. 'It must have been, what, nine years?'

'Almost ten,' Poppy confirmed too quickly. Not a word of contact since that night.

'And wow, I see . . .' He nodded towards the pram. His voice was friendly but his face was tight.

'Yes.' Poppy nodded. 'This is Maeve.' Her daughter had fallen asleep and was sucking the fabric cuff of her onesie. She hoped Henry wouldn't think that was disgusting but he wasn't looking at Maeve. His eyes were fixed on her.

'I guess . . . Patrick?'

Poppy winced. She had never wanted to have this conversation. Those worlds had collided once and it had not been pretty. 'Yes . . . Patrick. He's the father. But we've . . . separated.' The word felt sandy on her tongue. 'Separated' sounded closer to 'divorce', which sounded simultaneously more grown up and more hideous. But she didn't want Henry to think she and Patrick had merely broken up, as if their relationship had been just a summery, drunken whim. Of all people, she didn't want Henry to think that.

'And you're . . .' She pointed towards his hand, which was still bare. 'Oh—I mean you're about to, um, marry?'

About to marry?! She sounded like an Edwardian princess.

'Yes,' said Henry, his expression unchanged. 'Engaged a few months ago actually. Very . . . exciting.' If it had been ten years ago, Poppy would have burst out laughing at how unexcited he sounded. Now, his emotionless voice was excruciating.

'I hear you're taking over the family business?' Poppy continued, attempting some semblance of a normal conversation.

'Yes.' Henry brightened slightly. 'Dad's over it. Reckons financial planning's a dying craft in the age of crypto, so he's busting to hand it over. Basically mailed me the keys when I was still in Brissie.'

Poppy smiled gently into her coffee. Henry's dad had a thick handlebar moustache which, in high school, they had decided was the source of all his powers, like a middle-aged dad version of Thor's hammer. His dad had a similar Thor energy: he was gruffly passionate about everything from rugby to business to a good pub lunch.

SPECIAL DELIVERY

'I can't imagine him ever getting sick of it,' she said to her cup.

'I know,' said Henry, reading her mind. 'Who's he going to rant to now? Mum? She'll go insane.'

Poppy looked up to meet Henry's eyes and understanding buzzed between them. It didn't matter how much time had passed, they were still like this. They thought the same, they *knew* each other. A chain between them, which had laid loose and dusty in the dirt for ten years, was suddenly pulled taut.

Henry must have felt it too. He changed the subject. 'What are you up to these days? Apart from the obvious.' He gestured towards the pram.

'Well, the *obvious* is actually taking up a fair bit of my time.'

Henry chuckled, and Poppy's heart lifted slightly, glad he could still recognise her jokes. 'You're living in Orange?' he asked. 'Long term?'

Truthfully, she had no idea. Sydney rent was out of the question at the moment, but once Maeve was older she'd be stupid not to consider it.

'I'm finding my feet,' she said vaguely. 'I'm looking for jobs but not looking too hard at the moment. I've got a few things I need to sort out before I can start working again: child care, sleep, stopping breastfeeding, that kind of thing.'

Henry's cheeks reddened slightly. Poppy registered that she probably shouldn't have mentioned her breasts, but she talked about them so much these days she'd forgotten it wasn't part of normal conversation. It was all she talked about now: boobs, and poo.

'Gosh, kids,' said Henry. 'We haven't properly started thinking about . . .'

He trailed off and Poppy felt a body blow to her solar plexus, suddenly aware of a bridge they were very close to crossing. *Of course* Henry and his fiancée were thinking about kids. It made sense. It would be weird if they weren't, and Poppy had no right to feel this slight queasiness in her stomach.

She'd already stalked his fiancée as much as she could. Her name was Willa and her social media accounts were expertly set to private. Her Instagram profile pic showed long limbs silhouetted against a European sunrise. You couldn't see her face, but Poppy could tell she was beautiful. Girls that tall and slim always looked effortless.

Poppy felt properly sick now. 'Babies certainly keep you busy!' she persevered. She hoped the comment was generic enough to make it seem as though she hadn't spiralled down that Henry-Willa-offspring rabbit hole. The *certainly* might have been too much, though. She wasn't *actually* Edwardian.

'I can imagine,' Henry replied, his eyes vacant again. He shifted towards the coffee counter and glanced at it. 'I won't keep you,' he said.

'Okay,' said Poppy, blindly searching his face for that connection they'd shared only moments ago. It was like trying to find a safety rope in a dark cave. 'I'll see you around.' She tried to smile but couldn't. That was happening too often these days.

CHAPTER 11

Her AirPods secured in place, Poppy spoke to the voice inside them as she pushed the pram through her front gate. 'He started talking about having kids with his fiancée and I almost died. I mean, what was I supposed to say?'

'Shit, Pops,' replied Dani. 'That's full-on. I can't believe he was there. Like, after all these years, he just appears.'

'It was only a matter of time, I guess. This town is so small.'

'How did he look?' asked her friend.

'Good,' Poppy admitted regretfully. He'd looked really good.

'Hmmm. This is inconvenient.'

'Tell me about it.'

Through Poppy, Dani and Henry had become firm friends during their university years, sharing a similar enthusiasm for a meat pie after 2 am. When Poppy had lost Henry as a friend, Dani had too. Another thing to feel guilty about.

'What were you wearing?' asked Dani.

'Nothing terrible. A pair of denim shorts and a gingham shirt.'

'Ha! Look at you, Daisy Duke, getting all country on me! Since when do you wear gingham?'

'Since now, you loser. Gingham is actually very fashionable at the moment. Have you not looked at any shops lately?'

'Um, no. As if I browse shops anymore. My sleepy newborn days are long gone, my dear. I can't even browse the nappy aisle. I need to be in and out. First thing I see, that's what I get. I see nappies for boys, Nella is getting nappies for boys. I see a non-hideous shirt that will fit, that's the shirt I'm getting. Honestly, Pops, you have all this to look forward to.'

Poppy rounded the corner onto the golf course track and suddenly felt a ballistic missile explode between her temples. 'Dan, while I'd love to continue this chat about my descent into momcore, I have to go.'

'What's with the angry voice?'

'I'll explain later.'

James was waiting by the oak tree with Eileen barking and straining against her leash. 'I do this walk most mornings,' he said stonily. He brandished a sleek cardboard bag with thick ribbon handles towards her. 'Here.'

Poppy grudgingly slowed the pram and snatched the bag. She peered inside. 'Is this like hush money?'

Inside was a pristine white sweatshirt. Poppy glanced at the designer label. He'd guessed her size correctly.

'Take it back.'

'No.'

SPECIAL DELIVERY

'Take it,' she repeated. She would never spend that much money on a top, especially in this phase of life, where every morning was a high-stakes game of cup-size bingo. She also didn't need to be any more indebted to this guy—he'd already delivered her baby.

James shook his head once. 'No.'

He was like a hostile battleship: all steel and muscle and latent missiles beneath the surface.

'Fine.' Poppy shoved the bag into the base of the pram. Maeve stuck her hands out to catch the dog's thumping tail. 'But don't think we're doing this again. You have to walk ahead of us. Maeve should be looking at the trees and nature and stuff. She needs to learn there is more to life than dogs.'

A muscle ticked in his jaw. 'So we walk separately and put up with the screaming and the barking, despite having an obvious solution?'

'Yes.'

James's lips pressed into a thin line but he began pulling Eileen away.

Maeve—who was clearly too astute for her own good—noticed the ploy first. 'Waaaah!' she cried as the kelpie drifted ahead.

'Keep going!' Poppy commanded. 'They'll get over it.'

James strode ahead as the barking continued and Maeve's screams reached fever pitch. Poppy glanced at her daughter who was now screaming so hard she was turning a shade of beetroot. *Character building.* There were only three and a half kilometres to go, after which Maeve would be hopefully cured of her canine fixation. They would get through this.

Suddenly there was a choking sound from the pram. Poppy slammed on the brakes, instantly prepared to administer the Heimlich manoeuvre.

Hic! Maeve giggled, and suddenly James and Eileen were beside them again.

'I thought I heard her choking,' he said.

Poppy narrowed her eyes at her Machiavellian daughter. 'I think she screamed so hard she gave herself the hiccups.'

'Right,' said James. 'And you want us to leave again?'

The tiny smile in his eyes was like napalm to her bones. Her chaos was a joke to him, and now she was being forced to choose between walking with him or having her daughter choke and die. With a furious huff, she moved the pram fractionally to the right. Eileen skipped straight into the space and wagged her tail. Maeve made a gesture that looked suspiciously like an air punch.

Poppy marched ahead, her eyes fixed on anything but the figure beside her. The undulating path was lined with poplars and evergreens. Birds tweeted, butterflies flew, a lone rabbit gambolled across the green, and with every metre they strode the silence intensified like steam whistling in a kettle. Were they really going to pretend James hadn't just bought her a one-hundred-and-fifty-dollar top? Were they really going to pretend it was normal to walk around a golf course with someone you despised? The pine trees creaked in the breeze until Poppy couldn't take it any longer.

'What is wrong with you?' she exploded. 'Why can't you be a normal person and *speak*? You're making this horrible!'

James raised an eyebrow. 'No I'm not.'

'Yes you are!'

'You're being dramatic.'

'I'm allowed to be dramatic!' She was almost yelling but the douchebag hath brought the fury and the lady doth give no fucks. 'I'm a single mum with no clue what I'm doing. My life is already at diabolical levels of crap without your attitude getting in my grill!'

James looked at her sideways. To her satisfaction, he looked vaguely startled. 'I'm just walking,' he muttered.

'Yeah, well . . .' Poppy's eyes blazed at the pavement. She couldn't look at him. It was the tension in the jaw and the confidence of his stride. It was how arrogant his shoulders looked under that vest. It was *him*. He was too much. They walked a few more paces in a deafening thunderstorm of silence.

'Okay,' James conceded gruffly.

'Okay what?'

'Okay, I get this is not ideal for you.'

Poppy's eyes jerked to his. Something unreadable flashed across his face and his grip tightened on the leash.

'Good,' she said abruptly, equal parts confused and mollified.

They continued on. After a few minutes of awkward silence, he cleared his throat. 'Read any good books lately?'

Poppy glared at him. 'Are you quoting Mark Darcy?'

'Um . . . not intentionally?'

'Then why the hell are you asking about books?'

'I'm trying to make conversation.'

Poppy huffed. 'Then be a normal person and comment on the shit weather.' She added in an undertone, 'You really are a robot.'

'What was that?'

'Nothing!'

The corner of James's mouth twitched. 'I actually heard you. I wanted to see if you had the guts to say it to my face.'

'Fine!' She swivelled to look him dead in the eyes. His irises were dark as coal and she could tell he was laughing at her. This was all a game to him. 'You. Are. A robot. An annoying one.'

'What makes you say that?' he asked.

'For starters,' Poppy said, gripping the pram with an unnecessary force, 'you have zero social skills, which indicates a distinct lack of emotional intelligence. Second, you are unable to deal with any display of human emotion, which indicates a clear lack of empathy. And finally, your taste levels are clearly subhuman, as evidenced by the fact you named your dog Eileen.'

James shrugged. 'I thought it would be funny. Like the song. "Come On Eil—"'

'I got it,' Poppy bristled.

The soles of her sneakers were going to wear thin with all this stomping. Trust him to like *bad music*. Bad music which was actually *excellent music* but most people were too embarrassed to admit it. He probably only liked it in an ironic way; he'd probably never had a genuine emotion in his life. And now he was asking about books when he should know new mums never had time to read, apart from that one book she'd read in those early weeks which had turned out to be surprisingly addictive and she'd had no-one to discuss it with since her mum only read *Country Style* and Dani hadn't read a book since first-year uni.

SPECIAL DELIVERY

Poppy gritted her teeth. 'If you must know, I just read the one about the girl with the dragons and it was brilliant and—*don't* look at me like that, it was really good—and now I'm not talking anymore.'

She marched down the footpath, resolutely ignoring the flicker of a smile she could see growing in her periphery.

By the time they'd finished the walk, Poppy estimated she'd spent thirty per cent of the time devising ways to publicly embarrass him, thirty per cent praying Maeve's nappy held up, and the other forty per cent trying not to breathe too loudly in case he used it against her in some way.

'Bye,' James grunted when their paths diverged.

'Nrrrhmph,' Poppy replied to the footpath. She still hadn't worked out how to engineer a public shaming, so communicating via gorilla sound effects would have to suffice. It was all he deserved.

CHAPTER 12

'Come On Eileen' was still stuck in Poppy's head when Henry appeared to pick up a takeaway coffee later that morning at The Bustle. At least she'd been prepared for this. He looked more prepared too. She wondered whether he'd considered avoiding the cafe like she had. Or had he come hoping to run into her?

'Hi again,' he said, smiling. 'I like your dress.'

'Oh, er, thanks.' Poppy flicked a muffin crumb off her lap. He'd always liked polka dots. 'Is this your regular place?'

'Pretty much,' Henry said. 'Our office is—'

'Around the corner, I know. I mean, I remember.' She'd been to his dad's office countless times as a teenager to drop off schoolbags so they could roam the streets of Orange unencumbered. The receptionist used to wink at them as they'd leave, tugging each other by their school shirts.

Henry nodded. 'I'm here a fair bit. I like the country mum vibe of the place.'

Poppy smiled. 'I'm sure you do.'

His eyes still twinkled like a joke was on the tip of his tongue. Knowing how his brain worked, it probably was. He'd never been the class clown, or the biggest star on the sports field, but everyone knew Henry Marshall had *good chat*—and for a boy who was polite and past the acne phase, there could be no higher praise.

'How's your week been?'

'Busy,' he replied. 'Dad had all these ways of filing that are so archaic, I'm trying to get up to speed. I want to start trying some new things to increase our activity levels, get more money coming through the door. With the current state of the stock market, there are so many opportunities to make better investments for our clients.' He paused and laughed. 'Sorry for the finance babble; I get a bit excited. It's so good to finally be here and actually be able to put my ideas into action.'

A hollow feeling swelled in Poppy's chest, but she smiled over it. 'Sounds like all your dreams are coming true.'

'Oh.' Henry looked to his coffee, his ears turning pink. 'Something like that, I guess.'

'So how do you plan to get your ideas out to the market?' Poppy asked.

Henry chuckled. 'I haven't thought about the marketing yet. Always a one-track mind with you, though, isn't it?' He paused and winced. 'Sorry, that's not how I meant it.'

Now Poppy blushed. 'It's fine,' she said, waving the comment away. 'But I'd be happy to help. You know, if you need it.'

'Thanks.' Henry shifted his feet. 'How have you been?'

'Since yesterday?'

'Well, yes. But also, like, generally. I think I forgot to ask that yesterday, sorry.'

Poppy smiled. 'Good, I guess.' She pointed to Maeve lying in the pram sucking on her fingers. 'We're settling into a bit of a rhythm. I've got the house set up now. We're getting a bit of sleep. It's not too bad.'

Henry peered at Maeve, whose eyes darted around the contours of his face. 'She's very alert, isn't she?' he said, staring at her.

Poppy nodded. Maeve's eyes had also been described as wakeful, beady and restless, but alert was her preferred term. It implied intelligence.

'And jeez, her nose is really—'

'Yes.' Poppy cut him off, knowing exactly where he was going with that. She happened to love Maeve's tiny ski-jump nose. It was perfect on her.

Henry's ears turned pink again and he glanced at the floor.

'How's your mum enjoying having you back in Orange?' Poppy asked, retreating to safe territory.

'Over the moon, as you'd expect. We're already locked in for dinners almost every night of the week. And she keeps popping around to the office to drop off things she thinks I need. RB Sellars polos, handwash, that kind of thing. She's forgotten I have managed to dress and wash myself for more than a decade without her.'

'What about those undies she used to send you? Don't tell me you started buying them yourself?' At uni, Henry had firmly refused to buy his own underwear, complaining the price per square centimetre of fabric was absurd. This wasn't an issue because his mum sent him care packages every six months, always containing three new pairs of Bonds briefs. Both Henry and his mother considered this a logical arrangement.

Henry laughed. 'She started giving them to me in bulk as Christmas presents, so I think that's fair enough?' Poppy giggled and he grinned appreciatively. 'I knew you'd find that funny. As soon as I opened that Christmas present, I knew you'd tease me.' His smile faltered. 'Well, anyway, that was a while back.'

He was right. Poppy would have crowed with laughter if he'd told her. *Henry Mummy's Boy Marshall*: it was one of her favourite jokes. It made her hurt to realise he hadn't been able to tell her, to pick up the phone slightly tipsy after Christmas lunch and gleefully recount his reaction and his mother's satisfied smile. She could imagine it so clearly. Had it been a couple of years ago? Or was it long before that? She wished she knew.

'I'm glad to see my good friend Henry Marshall is growing up.'

'Aren't we all?' he replied, motioning to the scene before him: Poppy, Maeve, the colours and sounds of Orange through the window. It was all so different now; gentrified, glossier, busier. The sleepy town of their youth was long gone—just like their stupid teenage dreams.

CHAPTER 13

The next few days passed at a pace that was either dizzily fast or agonisingly slow. What was she doing apart from walking, breastfeeding and sneaking in a coffee with Henry? Nothing, it seemed.

On Monday, James was waiting by the oak tree again. It was sunny and his hair was scattered with threads of gold. He was optimistically wearing rugby shorts. It somehow made him look more muscular, which made Poppy even angrier. She strode past without greeting him and James fell into step with her. It was infuriating how he was basically strolling, his strides long and languid while she was puffing away as she tried to walk faster.

'Is this the part where I ask about the weather?' he asked.

Poppy shot him a withering look. Just thinking about him waiting at the oak tree so presumptuously made her feel physically violent. In the pram, Maeve's hands were clasped as though in prayer. Poppy's mind scrolled through futile

SPECIAL DELIVERY

escape plans. He looked too sturdy to be waylaid by an 'accidental' karate kick. She couldn't use speed to her advantage either. She had no chance against those damn legs. Deciding to try the opposite approach, she slowed subtly, hoping James might overtake them. When she got to bridal procession pace and registered she was still shoulder to shoulder with James, she snuck a glance leftwards. The corners of his mouth were struggling to stay neutral. Huffing furiously, she resumed normal pace.

When they passed the golf course entrance James inquired about what music she liked.

'Death metal,' she retorted sarcastically.

'I like everything,' said James. 'But not death metal.'

'Then someone needs to explain the definition of *everything* to you.'

James shrugged. 'Maybe I need to give death metal more of a chance,' he mused, as if he hadn't heard her.

Poppy sniggered.

'What?' asked James.

'You wouldn't like it. You're too . . .' Too what? Too clean maybe. Too polo-shirty. 'You don't fit the mould,' she muttered.

'What mould *do* I fit?'

Ralph Lauren model sprang to mind but she sure as hell wasn't verbalising that.

'Country music fan,' she said flatly. It was the first thing that popped into her head and she instantly regretted it. She loved country music and she didn't want this sacred subject tarnished with his douchey opinions. Still, she hoped he was offended. Patrick would have been offended.

James spun towards her, bright-eyed. 'I deadset love country music!'

Poppy side-eyed him, her neck muscles tensing as Maeve squealed spontaneously. *Seriously?* He was choosing this moment to reveal he had a mode other than bored-to-smirky? Country music was *her* thing. She shouldn't have opened her stupid mouth. It was infuriating how his AI brain could read her mind just to piss her off.

James scanned their surroundings. 'What's your favourite type of, um . . . tree?'

Poppy levelled him with a scowl. What did he expect her to say? *Oh, I'm partial to a paperbark but a river red gum really floats my boat.* Good lord.

'This'—she waved her hands between them to indicate the gaping absence of passable conversation—'is terrible. This is possibly worse than the silence.'

'I thought the silence was fine,' muttered James, shaking his head.

'Nope. That was terrible, this is terrible. You need to try harder.'

James rolled his eyes. 'Or what?'

'Or else,' Poppy retorted. *Damn it.* Her sass was always so excellent in her daydreams but here she was sounding like an evil dictator about to *mwahaha* as she pressed the World Detonate button with a menacing pinky finger.

James raised an eyebrow. 'I think you can do better than that.'

'You think too highly of me,' she snapped.

He gave a low chuckle. 'I doubt that.'

SPECIAL DELIVERY

Poppy glared at him. What the hell was that supposed to mean?

Maeve's hand brushed the tail of the dog and her daughter giggled in delight.

'We're reverting to silence,' Poppy ordered.

James flexed his wrist to tighten his hold on the leash. 'Whatever you say.' The smile in his voice was as clear as a bell.

★

That afternoon, as she sat in her parents' garden and watched her mum pull weeds out of the garden bed, James's voice kept interrupting her thoughts like a skipping CD player. *I deadset love country music!* Maybe everyone here liked country music. In Sydney, she'd been the only one who annoyed DJs by requesting Luke Bryan and took over the aux cord to play old-school Taylor Swift. It was her schtick and now he'd stolen it. God, he was infuriating.

In her hot-pink shirt and tailored floral shorts, her mum looked like a Bible Belt frat boy on spring break. Poppy sat on a chequered rug next to the Chinese elm with Maeve lying next to her, her frog-like arms and legs curled into her torso, one cheek pressed into the rug.

'I don't know why you do that,' said her mum, nodding her head towards Maeve. 'When you were born, we never had to do that and you turned out fine.'

Her mum was full of wisdom like this: care less, do less, and your child will turn out better.

'It's called tummy time, Mum. It's to build up her core strength. Maybe you should have tried it. Maybe that's why I'm terrible at sport.'

'Nonsense,' said her mother. 'Besides, Maeve is half Patrick, which means she has fifty per cent more sporting genes than you were blessed with. Have you spoken to Patrick yet?'

Poppy grunted noncommittally. No, she had not spoken to him, and she resented the implication that *she* should be reaching out to *him*. She had a lot on. 'Garden's looking great, Mum,' she said, desperate to change the subject.

Her mother gave a laboured sigh. 'Oh, it's a disaster.'

'What do you mean? It looks fantastic.'

Her mother pulled a giant weed from the soil. 'Have I told you Martha and Peter are re-landscaping? They got an arborist in to cut down that tree like I told them to, and next thing you know, they're talking to a landscape designer and all hell has broken loose.'

Poppy was confused. Was this a big deal? Her mother's tone warned her it was.

'Martha mentioned they're thinking of getting rid of the magnolia. The magnolia!'

'Mum, it's their garden, who cares what they do?'

'I do, Poppy! If they rip out all their crabapples, where do you think the rosellas will go for food? Here, that's where! The apricot tree will be ripped to shreds! And I may as well say goodbye to the camellias now.'

'What? Why? Do rosellas eat camellias?' (Poppy had no idea why she was attempting to find logic in this conversation.)

'Ideally not, Poppy,' huffed her mother, as though explaining an adult concept to a small and fundamentally unintelligent child, 'but for lack of better options they probably will, once Martha pulls everything out.'

SPECIAL DELIVERY

Her mother eased back onto her haunches, wiping her brow. 'Let's not talk about that or I'll give myself a panic attack. Have you caught up with any of your old schoolfriends yet?' She looked at Poppy with pursed lips. This topic came up every time they talked, no matter how often Poppy explained none of her schoolfriends still lived in town.

'Did I tell you I saw Maddie Harrow at the nursery the other day?' continued her mother. 'She was always such a bright spark. Four kids now, too! Lots of the girls from that year are still in town. Maybe you could catch up with them?'

Maddie Harrow had been the ultimate cool girl in high school. A few years older than Poppy, she had married her high-school sweetheart and ended up back in Orange where she could continue to rule her cool girl empire. Poppy had seen her gaggle around the place, all wearing the latest fashions from The Bustle, never seen without a pair of expensive hooped pearl earrings. On average, it seemed they had a million kids each, and when they weren't coordinating adorable family photo shoots they were holidaying in Noosa.

'Mum, I hardly knew her at school.'

'Yes, but you might—'

'I don't think we'd have much in common.'

Poppy's mum looked at her sharply. 'What does that mean?'

Poppy shrugged.

Chrissie pointed her finger dramatically. 'You're not better than those women just because you had a high-flying Sydney career, Poppy. I'm worried about you. You need some friends here.'

Poppy flicked a clod of soil off the picnic rug. She didn't need to be reminded of her acute friendlessness by her own mother. 'I have some friends,' she mumbled.

'Who, Poppy?'

'Mary.'

'Your eighty-seven-year-old next-door neighbour?'

'She's eighty-nine, but yes, Mary and I are great mates.'

'Anyone else who was born after World War Two?'

'Henry.'

'Henry Marshall?' Her mother's eyes narrowed. 'I didn't know you'd been seeing him. Do you know he has a fiancée?'

'God, Mum—yes!' Poppy cried, turning away as she felt a mortifying heat creep across her cheeks. 'Can't two old friends catch up and people not read anything into it?'

Her mother gave an irritating *hmmm* and turned back to her weeds. 'I suppose we should organise a dinner then. I could invite his parents and fiancée. I've heard she's a paediatrician with the most lovely skin, and it *would* be good to meet her. A dinner together would be nice, wouldn't it?'

Poppy waved a fly off Maeve's back. She knew what her mum was doing. She was laying a trap. Either commit to a dinner that already made her feel queasy or decline and be forced to admit why she didn't want to go. Well, her mum didn't have a newborn; she forgot that Maeve provided an excuse for flaking on everything.

She wasn't concerned about seeing Henry. Their conversations at The Bustle were the highlights of her day. The awkwardness of the first meeting had eased into a warm familiarity. She had no problem with him; it was Willa who was the wild card. Poppy didn't want to hang out with them as a couple. The current arrangement suited her fine.

'Dinner sounds great, Mum,' she said with feigned brightness. If the past few months had taught Poppy anything, it was that she was excellent at lying.

CHAPTER 14

The next Wednesday, Poppy almost didn't go for her daily walk. There was a biting wind and, frankly, she was concerned for the state of her molars, which were the innocent victims of anger-induced grinding whenever James appeared. But it had been raining for two days and this was *her* neighbourhood and *her* baby's schedule. She was going to walk whenever and wherever she goddamn pleased.

When she reached the oak tree, James was waiting for them. There was a devilish gleam in his eyes.

'What?' she challenged him as he matched her stride.

He put his hand into his puffer vest and pulled out a neon yellow deck of cards, patterned with tiny stars. 'A solution to our problem,' he announced, holding out the packet. The cursive font was embossed in gold foil: *HOW TO WIN FRIENDS AND IMPRESS ACQUAINTANCES; 100 NAUGHTY AND NICE CONVERSATION STARTERS.*

Poppy's eyes snapped to his. If he thought he could hide his

SPECIAL DELIVERY

smile just by tightening his jaw, someone needed to tell him his glinting eyes were a dead giveaway. 'No way,' she said.

'Yes way,' James replied, looping Eileen's leash around his wrist. He pulled the cards from the cardboard case. 'Choose one.'

Poppy ignored his outstretched hand. 'Where did you buy those?'

'I didn't buy them. I borrowed them.'

Oh, right. They were yellow. He'd probably swiped them post-coitus from Miss Yellow Bikini's bedside table.

'So are we doing this?' He held the pack out. 'Or are we resuming the death metal chat?'

Poppy sighed and plucked a card from the deck. '*Tell me about your most embarrassing sexual experience,*' she read aloud. *Thanks, universe.*

James laughed and yanked the card away. 'No way, José. Choose again.'

Blushing, Poppy snatched another card; the last thing she wanted was another sex-themed conversation with this man. '*Tell me about your favourite person in the world.*'

'Good one,' he said. 'I would say it's a tie between my mum and my sister. Mum is a crazy high-school teacher who wears those long maxi-dress thingies. My sister, Kate, is a crazy high-school teacher who gets around in sports gear. Other than that, they're pretty much exactly the same.' He nodded as if pleased with this summation. 'Do you want a go now?'

Poppy sighed. 'Do I have to?'

'In order to have a *conversation*, Poppy, there have to be two people involved.'

'Fine,' she said, reaching for the cards. 'Give me one.'

'Nope,' said James, pulling them away. 'First you tell me your favourite person.'

'Who came up with these rules?'

'Me.' He flashed her a sarcastic smile. 'So? Who is it?'

Poppy glowered at him. 'Dead or alive?'

'Alive, obviously.'

Poppy's mind drifted to Dani. Sparkling, bubbly Dani, who could read her like a book and make her laugh like a hyena. Jeez, she missed her. Then she thought of her parents. Her mum would probably be offended if she didn't choose her. *Oh shit*, she thought as the realisation hit her. Maeve! She'd forgotten about her own daughter. God, she was a terrible mum. She definitely had to choose Maeve as her favourite person. Then again, maybe babies didn't count.

'Can I choose a baby?'

'Nope,' replied James, as though these rules were actually real.

'Okay then, I choose my best friend, Dani.'

'Why?'

'Because she's a legend.'

'How so?'

'Because . . .' Poppy's mind struggled for words. She was hilarious, empathetic, pragmatic, a great dancer, an amazing mum, she had helped Poppy study for her final exams and then taken her out for five-dollar schooners when she failed statistics. She had a great dress sense but never worried about how she looked because she always looked banging. There were no words to convey how utterly great her best friend was. 'She's my everything,' she said simply.

SPECIAL DELIVERY

A moment passed, the silence feeling a little less combative than usual. 'She sounds . . . important,' said James quietly.

'She is,' Poppy agreed, tears suddenly welling behind her eyes. She blinked them away, embarrassed. She was so lucky to have Dani on speed dial, but it couldn't replace a cuppa in her kitchen or a walk through Centennial Park. It had been four long months and her best friends in this town were an eighty-nine-year-old widow and a fourteen-week-old baby who routinely shat herself.

'Shall we do another one?' she asked, hoping he didn't hear the wobble in her voice.

James's eyes met hers briefly. 'I'm happy with silence.'

To their left, a ride-on lawnmower buzzed over the fairways and a lone golf ball sailed through the cloudless sky. Poppy swallowed her tears and a huge wave of relief.

★

The next day, James and Eileen were back by the oak tree, which was a blaze of red and gold. The grass around them was still wet from the morning dew.

'What are you wearing?' asked Poppy.

'Hello to you too,' replied James.

'You know I don't waste time on pleasantries with you.'

'I do know that,' admitted James, shifting to the left so the pram could have the bulk of the footpath.

'So enlighten me,' Poppy said. 'Do you not own pants?'

James was wearing a pair of rugby shorts over compression tights.

'This is a look,' he argued. He pronounced it like *leeeewk*.

'Says who?'

'The Sydney Swans, the Parramatta Eels, the Wallabies, the Western Sydney Wanderers. It's a high-performance look. Would you prefer I wore tights without the shorts?'

'No way,' Poppy said firmly. She had witnessed too many misguided old men in Centennial Park who favoured the tights-only look for their weekend walks. The memory of their jiggly ball sacks was burned into her retinas.

James shrugged. 'That's a bit sexist, if you ask me. You wear tights every day.'

'Yeah, but when guys wear tights it's too revealing.'

James's eyes skimmed across her backside. 'I hate to break it to you, Poppy, but tights are revealing on anyone.'

Poppy felt an unwelcome heat creep up her neck. She ignored it. 'Where are your cards?'

James pulled them from his pocket. 'You sure you don't want to keep talking about my fashion choices?'

'I'm picking.' Poppy reached over and plucked a card from the deck.

'*Tell me about your greatest fear*,' she read.

'Heavy stuff,' said James. 'Wanna pick again?'

'You're not game to tell me?' What was this sadistic part of her that liked seeing him squirm?

'Okay,' said James slowly. 'My greatest fear is . . . spiders.'

Poppy raised her nose. 'Cop out.'

'Okay, okay. I'll be serious. I just need to think.' He furrowed his brow and gazed into the distance. 'Alright, I've got it. You ready?'

'I can barely stand the suspense.'

'Okay, I don't really know if this is a good one, but I think it's kind of—'

'Hurry up, you're annoying me.'

'That's unusual.'

'Just being honest.'

'It's one of your best traits.'

'Actually it's not. I'm normally an overly nice people pleaser and avoid confrontation at any cost, even with my best friends and parents. I'm not this honest with anyone else.'

'Lucky me.'

'It wasn't a compliment,' said Poppy. 'Stop stalling and spill.'

'Okay.' James looked straight ahead and spoke. 'My greatest fear is . . . settling.'

'Like settling down?'

'Well, kind of. It depends, I guess. I don't want to wake up one day and realise I've wasted years of my life by blindly settling down. I want to *choose* my life.'

They walked in silence for a few moments.

James turned to her. 'Was that answer acceptable?'

Poppy considered this. 'It's passable, I suppose, but it does make you sound like a douchey bachelor.'

'What do you mean?'

'Your greatest fear is commitment? That's some A-grade douchebag shit.'

James shook his head. 'That's not what I meant. I meant I don't want to settle for just anything. I don't want to drift along and find myself somehow living a life that's not what

I want. If I do settle down, it's going to be my choice, and with someone who is really, properly amazing.'

'So essentially your greatest fear is not marrying a Victoria's Secret model?'

'I think you're deliberately misunderstanding me.'

'Whatever,' shrugged Poppy.

'What about you then?' asked James. 'What's your greatest fear?'

Poppy gave a bitter laugh. 'Easy. I'm afraid of being a bad mum.'

'Poppy—'

'I'm not fishing for compliments,' she interrupted. 'I know I won't be a bad mum in terms of brushing her teeth with Coca-Cola or anything. I'm just . . .' She paused, registering she should probably stop before she revealed her greatest insecurities to the most unempathetic human in the world. But really, if there was anyone whose opinion she couldn't care less about, it was the man next to her. 'I'm worried I won't be enough,' she sighed. 'I mean, Maeve only has me. I worry enough about whether I can be a good mum, let alone whether I can be a good dad too. I mean, seriously, I'm shit at sport.'

'Maeve's dad isn't around much?' James's voice was quiet.

'No,' she said flatly, a vision of the labour ward flashing behind her eyes: James holding her hand, Patrick hundreds of kilometres away in Sydney. 'You already know he didn't even come to Orange for the birth. He had tickets to the Test.'

'He missed the birth of his child for a *cricket match*?'

'And he hates cricket,' Poppy said. 'It was just a convenient excuse. He didn't want to be at the birth. It would have made it real to him and he's more of a fantasy-land kind of guy.'

'Jesus,' muttered James. 'He sounds like an arsehole.' He looked at her quickly. 'Sorry, he was obviously great if you were with him . . .'

Poppy laughed darkly. 'Don't worry. He *is* an arsehole. I just assumed he'd grow out of it. Like, when we were younger, he'd come back from the pub with all these crazy stories and I just thought it was funny. Now, I'd be like, "Dude, you're thirty-five—go home."'

James shook his head.

'I don't want your pity,' Poppy muttered.

'But who hates cricket? I can understand indifference, but *hate*?'

Poppy repressed a sardonic smile. Her dad used to say the same thing.

The distant purr of traffic hummed around them as the pale sun filtered through the clouds. They walked the rest of the loop in silence to the metronome swish of Eileen's tail. For some reason, it felt less suffocating today.

Before they parted, James paused for a moment. 'If it makes you feel better, my dad wasn't around growing up and I turned out fine.'

Poppy stilled the pram and glanced at him. His eyes looked almost earnest but it was hard to tell when she'd become so used to his smirk. Maybe after prolonged exposure to him, she'd just recalibrated her sense of social propriety. She narrowed her gaze sceptically. 'By whose definition of fine?'

James smiled. 'Well, my siblings turned out fine. See you tomorrow.'

He raised his hand in a wave as Poppy pivoted back towards her cul-de-sac, a confusing mist suddenly clouding her brain. Thoughts were trying to form but were fading like holograms before she could grasp them. A faint uneasiness settled in her gut. She didn't like talking about Patrick—that must be it. And then James had started saying things like 'catch you Monday' and 'see you soon'. She couldn't decide whether it gave her the ick.

The breeze whipped against her neck as she rounded the corner into their street. Her daughter's arms were thick with woollen layers, giving her the appearance of a knitted teddy. Poppy wondered whether it would be overkill to buy a point-and-shoot thermometer to check whether Maeve was cold on these walks. Would that be helicopter parenting or good parenting? The line was so blurry.

'Poppy, love!' called a voice up ahead. 'Want to pop in for a cuppa?'

Poppy could see Mary's hand waving over the hedge.

'Love to!' she called back.

Even though the wind was getting icier, her neighbour still spent her days sitting on her verandah. According to Mary, there was no such thing as bad weather, only bad clothing choices. Today, she wore thick stockings under her arrow-print shift dress, with a quilted flannelette jacket over the top.

'Morning, Mary,' Poppy said, pushing the pram through her neighbour's gate and levering it up the verandah steps. 'Thanks so much for the cardigan. Maeve is better dressed for this weather than me now.'

SPECIAL DELIVERY

'My pleasure, love.' Mary glowed. 'As I told you, my great-grandchildren are too old now for anything I knit. They're addicted to rugby league–branded polyester.'

From her vantage point on the verandah, Mary had quickly worked out Poppy and Maeve's daily routine and had taken to exploiting it for her own social enjoyment. She was constantly inviting them over for a cup of tea and a jam drop.

'See anything interesting on your walk today?' asked Mary. She always began with the same question, eager to fill any gaps in her neighbourhood knowledge.

'Not today,' replied Poppy. 'Just the regulars out and about.'

'No dog poo, then?' asked her neighbour. Dog walkers who didn't pick up after their pets were a particular bugbear for Mary, even though she rarely walked the footpath herself. It was the principle of the matter. She had written to council about it.

'None today,' said Poppy. James was always militant about picking up after Eileen.

'That's good, I suppose,' Mary said, disappointed. 'Well, I'd best put the kettle on.'

Poppy sat down on the wicker chair on the other side of the table as her neighbour heaved herself up and pushed through the squeaky door to her hallway. Despite Poppy's offers to help prepare the tea, Mary always refused. Even now, with the weather cooling, Poppy was never invited inside.

Mary returned to the verandah a few minutes later carrying a tray laden with cups and saucers, a teapot, milk jug, sugar bowl and a plate of jam drops. The tray rattled onto the table and Mary eased herself back into her chair. 'I've got a blanket down there if you need it,' she said, pointing underneath the table.

Poppy pulled out a thick crochet blanket and spread it over her lap. 'Thanks, Mary.' She poured the tea then put two jam drops on her plate.

'Have you had one of those mummy meetings yet?' asked Mary.

'I had the first mothers' group yesterday actually,' replied Poppy. 'It was'—she swallowed a mouthful of biscuit—'okay.'

Mary noticed her hesitation. 'What was the problem?'

Poppy wasn't sure how to answer this. There was no specific problem; she just didn't see the point. After agonising over whether she should arrive slightly early or slightly late, she had arrived at the community health centre right on time—a feat in itself, considering the punctuality handbrake she'd given birth to.

It had been stupid, really, to care so much. It was just a bunch of women sitting in a circle on plastic chairs, like they were at Alcoholics Anonymous, but the only addiction they suffered was clicking 'add to cart' at 3 am. They were all just tired and tender and probably a bit hungry.

It was fine. So, so, so fine. But . . . it wasn't. These women weren't like her. If she was still with Patrick, she would have been exactly like them, but she definitely wasn't now. They reeked of normality with their husbands and mortgages and Mazda CX-5s. They had shiny hair and wore fashionable activewear. Poppy picked up the milk jug and poured a generous slosh into her tea. 'I think the other mums are a bit different from me, that's all.'

The crow's feet around Mary's eyes deepened. 'How so?'

Poppy sighed. 'They just seem . . .'

SPECIAL DELIVERY

How could she explain it? They wore different clothes? They had nice hair?

'They looked like girls who just happened to have babies. Like, their babies were just accessories or something.' She was aware of how stupid she sounded, but the words kept coming. 'They looked as though they had their babies and kept on being the same people.' Expensive-athleisure-wearing people.

Mary raised an eyebrow. 'What gave you that impression, love?'

Poppy looked at her daughter. She was so little and innocent. She had no idea she had such an insecure, ridiculous mother. 'Their clothes?'

Mary's other eyebrow rose.

Poppy changed tack. 'I guess it felt a bit like high school.'

It had been eerily similar. The hard plastic chairs, the halogen strip lighting, the animal kingdom group dynamics. A community nurse led a conversation and, just like in school, some people spoke up confidently while others—like Poppy—were essentially mute, eyes flicking constantly to the clock near the door. When any of them made a joke about their partner's inadequacies when it came to nappy-changing or night-feeding, the others laughed knowingly while Poppy stared at her shoes.

Poppy sighed into her teacup. 'I know I sound like an idiot, but it felt like everyone knew how they fitted in apart from hot-mess Poppy over here.'

Mary chuckled. 'You're not a mess, love. You're doing better than you think.' She pointed to the pram. 'Look at little

Maeve. She's as happy as any baby I've seen and you're doing it all on your own, too. You should be proud.'

Poppy took a sip of tea. She was getting used to biting her tongue when people said things like this. 'Doing it on her own' was what she was most ashamed of.

'Anyway,' continued Mary, 'I think these mummy catch-ups sound fantastic. When my four were born, no-one could care less about what I was up to. I just had to get back into it—cooking, cleaning, helping on the farm, squeezing in the baby stuff when I could. I would much rather have been sitting with my girlfriends chatting about nappies.'

'They're not my friends, though,' Poppy pointed out.

'They will be,' said Mary. 'Parenting gives you something to laugh about together, and if you're not laughing together, you'll be crying together. That's what friendships are founded on.'

Poppy chewed her jam drop. She didn't have the heart to argue. Mary meant well but she had no idea about how female friendships were forged in the twenty-first century. She didn't know you needed to get inordinately drunk and harass DJs, and then wet your pants laughing together the next morning remembering the photoshoot with the bouncer, the decision to buy ten Snickers bars and almost tearing a hammy trying to do the worm on the dancefloor. That was how true adult friendships were formed.

'Humans are social creatures,' Mary went on. 'And if I've learned anything from my eighty-nine years and my inspiration-of-the-day desk calendar, it's that you need to have an open heart.'

SPECIAL DELIVERY

Poppy swallowed the last of her biscuit and reached for another. Easy for the old lady to say. She'd never known the cesspit of Tinder or the feeling of seeing your friends tagged at a party you weren't invited to. It wasn't easy to have an open heart these days—especially when you were so out of practice. Poppy had been in a relationship for nine years and had hardly made a new friend since uni. Sure, she'd met some awesome people through work, but those relationships were sustained by water-cooler gossip—which suited her fine, because her books were already full. She had enough people to love and be loved by. She'd never needed more, which meant she didn't need to be vulnerable. Pre-tween childhood, the start of high school, the start of uni: those were the occasions when it was acceptable to ask for friendship. If you missed those windows, you'd better be next-level charismatic, because it sure as hell wasn't easy otherwise.

Poppy spent the rest of their tea date avoiding more inspiration-of-the-day advice by asking Mary's opinion on the jazz playlist booming from number three ('pretentious and tone deaf' was her neighbour's assessment). But while they debated the cultural influence of Elvis Presley and Austin Butler's fake accent, Poppy couldn't shake the words gnawing at the back of her consciousness: *you need to have an open heart.*

They were still there as she pushed the pram back around the hedge. *You need to have an open heart.* When they reached the front door, Poppy scooped her daughter from the pram and bumped the door open with her hip as her daughter's head fell lazily against her chest. Maeve's body was tired and sleepy against her own, her breathing deep and content, like she couldn't be more certain of her place in the world, which was right here: her body moulded like latex against her mother's frazzled heart. Poppy felt a familiar stirring in her chest. She loved this kid so much it made her want to cry sometimes. It made her want to give her anything, do anything for her.

As she shifted Maeve onto her hip and walked into the kitchen, Poppy whipped out her phone before she could second-guess herself. She needed to have an open heart.

FaceTime tomorrow? she wrote. *Maeve would love to meet her dad.*

CHAPTER 15

By any objective measure, it had not been a good start to the day. The spontaneous text to Patrick had proven to have properties similar to all-you-can-drink espresso martinis, in that she'd woken every hour after midnight, anxious and sweaty, drawn to her phone like an addict, desperate for notifications. Maeve had then woken at 4.45 am with a series of screams which loosely translated as: *I WILL NOT BE CALMED*. Thus, Poppy's day also began at 4.45 am—though everyone knew that this only counted as morning if you were an Olympic rower and with their abnormally powerful quadriceps they were hardly human anyway. Poppy was so tired she suspected she was dribbling but lacking the brain capacity to realise.

As she perched on the couch to try to feed her daughter, Maeve writhed in her arms, knocking Poppy's toast—which had (foolishly, in hindsight) been balanced on the arm of the sofa—onto the carpet, Vegemite-side down.

While she was cleaning the mess, she heard the garbage truck rumble past her driveway. *Classic.* She'd forgotten to put the bins out. Again. The carpet cleaner was starting to foam, which was a good sign apparently. According to the bottle, she needed to leave it for five minutes then wipe it off. Poppy checked her watch. She was not rushing. Why would she be rushing? She had all the time in the world. She had no deadlines, nowhere to be. She lived her life to Maeve's schedule, no-one else's.

But a thought nagged at her. *Oak tree at nine thirty.* May as well try to be on time, she reasoned with herself, otherwise James would be a hundred metres ahead and it would be weird to follow him around the golf course, especially if Maeve was still in this grizzly mood. It might also give off stalker vibes, and that was an impression she did not want to convey—especially to him. But she was aware of the irritating irony: somehow, James had weaselled his way into her routine to the point that walking around the golf course *without him* would be more awkward than walking *with him.*

Poppy scraped the foam off the carpet, sponged it down, then lay a towel over the top. By the time they arrived at the oak tree it was 9.42 am. Poppy looked up and down the path but it was empty save for her and Maeve. On cue, her daughter wailed louder.

★

The crying didn't stop until Maeve fell asleep in Poppy's armpit as she carried her daughter to the car. It was an impressively brief catnap. Maeve woke up the moment Poppy clipped her into the capsule. Now, as she headed from the car to the supermarket, Poppy was navigating a new-found commitment to attachment parenting. Maeve had fallen into a restless sleep in the baby carrier on her chest.

'Do *not* think about the text,' commanded Dani through the AirPods as Poppy entered the store. 'Get a coffee with someone to distract yourself. Is Henry around?'

'No, he has an off-site meeting,' said Poppy. 'And he only ever gets coffee around eleven-ish because he schedules client meetings beforehand.' *Hmmm.* She probably shouldn't know his schedule by heart. 'Besides,' Poppy added, 'you told me I had to call you urgently. What's up?'

A pause.

'Dan?'

'Well . . .'

'Wah!' Maeve yelped.

'Shit! She's awake again. Oh, wait . . . okay, she's gone back to sleep. Start again, Dan.'

'Okay, so . . .'

Poppy's phone beeped. *Eek!* 'Hold on, Dan! Oh, sorry, it's not Patrick. Just the mothers' group WhatsApp thread going off. Oh, actually . . .'

One of the perky girls in a P.E Nation top had collected everyone's numbers at the last meeting and connected them in a WhatsApp group optimistically titled Mumz Gone Wild. They were meeting at The Bustle in fifteen minutes, which was just across the car park—about a two-minute walk away. The conversation would no doubt be inane, but there was a chance it would distract her from her emotional turmoil about

Patrick's non-responsiveness. 'Maybe I could go and meet them for coffee . . .'

Dani was quiet on the end of the line.

'Sorry, Dan, what were you saying?'

Dani sighed. 'Nothing, it's all good.'

'You sure?'

'Yep, you're having a busy day. We'll chat later. You go to mothers' group, and if Darth Vader texts, make sure you call me.' She paused before adding solemnly, 'May the force be with you.'

Poppy adopted a Jedi voice too: 'And also with you.'

They both convulsed into cackles.

'Love you, Dan.'

'Love you too, Pops.'

Still smiling, Poppy hung up and placed her AirPods back in her pocket then beelined for the checkout. As they waited in the self-service queue, Maeve opened her eyes and blinked miserably. No wonder. By this time of the day, she'd normally had a two-hour nap already. Today, by Poppy's calculations, Maeve had only had fifteen minutes of unbroken sleep since quarter to five. Poppy began some surreptitious squats to lull her back to sleep. In front of her, baby boomers made terrible decisions: not weighing grapes correctly, not putting their reusable bags in the bagging area, choosing cash when the signs clearly said CARD ONLY.

'Wah!' Maeve admonished.

Poppy checked her watch nervously and began squatting deeper, aiming for a full glute burn. Her daughter would be unhinged if she didn't get some quality sleep. 'Time for bed,

SPECIAL DELIVERY

Maevey,' she whispered. These ignorant sexagenarians had no idea that the bomb on her chest was about to explode.

'Waaaaaaaah!' repeated Maeve more vociferously.

A couple of baby boomers glanced in their direction.

Hurry up! Poppy willed them. Why were they moving so slowly?!

Maeve's body was becoming rigid on her chest. 'WAAAAAAH!'

More grey heads swivelled towards them. Poppy flinched and checked her watch again. This was the scream of a hungry baby dragon, but Maeve wasn't due for a feed for ages—she'd been cluster feeding all morning. Though, come to think of it, precisely nothing had gone to schedule today. Why would it start now? She was still a two-minute walk away from The Bustle, and judging from the pace of these boomers, a Jurassic period away from getting through the checkout.

'WAAAAAH!'

Poppy cursed herself inwardly. She should have predicted this! It was the rule of three—and four and five and six and one hundred fucking million; if one bad thing happened, at least a hundred million other bad things had to happen before you had a clean slate to start again.

An empty checkout appeared behind a man in a tartan vest who was shuffling away at the speed of a comatose snail. Poppy raced over and shoved the nappies under the barcode reader and—*oh no.*

UNWANTED ITEM IN THE BAGGING AREA.

No! How had she stuffed that up?!

'WAAAAAH!'

This had escalated so quickly! Her daughter was screaming under her chin like a car alarm. She shouldn't have called Dani! She should have been more efficient in the nappy aisle! She shouldn't have wasted so much time thinking about bloody Patrick! And why did she continually let her grocery supplies get so low?! She needed to get better at weekly shops—that was how real adults did it!—but if she didn't need to go to the shops every day, would she ever have a reason to leave the house?! She'd trapped herself in this vicious cycle of consumerism. Poppy did some more squats and added some useless patting. Random passers-by were staring openly.

'WAAAAAH!' Maeve reminded her, for lack of any other vocabulary.

A checkout assistant had still not materialised. Were they on strike? Wildly, Poppy weighed up her options: steal a (small) pack of nappies or risk being thrown out of the shop for noise pollution (was that a similarly indictable offence?!). Poppy suddenly wished James and his distractingly thumpy-tailed dog were here.

Her phone buzzed in her pocket and she seized it as if it were some kind of lifeline.

K.

'WAAAAAH!'

K? K?! Poppy's eyes bulged in disbelief as she stared at the screen. Patrick finally deigned to respond to her FaceTime invitation, and this was what he said? *K?!* He couldn't even spare the time for a fucking vowel?!

'WAAAAAAAH!' Two lines of snot were now streaming down Maeve's face and onto Poppy's chest. It was very possible she was going to commit her first non-alcohol-induced felony.

SPECIAL DELIVERY

'Voila,' announced a portly gentleman, appearing at her side and tapping the screen with a magic swipe card. 'Someone's grumpy,' he said with a chuckle.

You bet I'm grumpy! Poppy fumed, before realising he was referring to her screaming child.

'Thanks.' She smiled weakly, paid with superhuman efficiency, and hightailed it out of there, quickly hammering out a text to confirm she'd call Patrick later. She didn't make eye contact with a single soul until she emerged into The Bustle and spotted the phalanx of prams.

Hearing Maeve, two mums sprang into action, clearing a path for Poppy to cannonball onto a chair, where she whipped off the BabyBjörn and shoved Maeve onto her boob.

Oh, the relief. She was still panting from the adrenaline. Her lungs were at post-cardio levels of deoxygenation, like she'd just won the Tour de France and celebrated with a jumping-jack floor solo. On her left, a ginger-haired mum beckoned to a waitress. 'Caffeine needed here asap, please.' Poppy glanced up in thanks. The ginger-haired mum smiled back.

As Poppy wiped the beads of sweat from her hairline, the conversation washed over her. Away from the confines of the white-walled community health centre and without the hard-backed plastic chairs forcing them into frigid schoolgirl postures, the group seemed livelier than she remembered. Projectile vomits, night feeds, backing the car into a telegraph pole while the baby was screaming. To Poppy's surprise, the chat wasn't completely terrible.

When the coffees arrived, there was a flurry of movement as everyone cleared rattles and bottles off the table to make space. It was refreshing being around people who had the same amount of *stuff*.

'Seriously, call me a Sherpa and send me up Everest,' groaned one mum. 'I'd be a real asset to any trek, I'm so highly proficient in lugging around crap.'

'You try formula feeding,' quipped another. 'If anyone needs a few tins, I'm your girl. My nappy bag weighs, like, twenty kilos.'

Poppy snuck in a few glorious sips of her hot soy cappuccino before Maeve, now sated with milk but apparently existentially unsated with life, began to cry again.

'She looks so much like you,' said the ginger-haired mum, who—subversively—was not wearing activewear.

'Like the kid from *The Exorcist*?'

The mum laughed. 'I meant she has your eyes.'

Poppy set down her coffee and repositioned Maeve on her lap so she could balance her in the crook of her arm. She could not get past Maeve's little nose, which was unequivocally perfect on her but also an exact replica of her father's. At least it didn't overwhelm anyone else.

'I'm April,' the mum said. 'You're Poppy, right?'

'Good memory,' Poppy replied. 'I can't remember anyone's name. My brain isn't fully functional yet.'

'You're telling me. I left my sunnies on the top of the car today and drove straight off without them. Sayonara, Ray-Bans. I was so sad I cried.'

'Ha!' piped up another mum. 'Today I filled out my Medicare forms and used my maiden name. I've been married six years! Poor hubby, it's like all his help getting up in the middle of the night counts for nothing!'

SPECIAL DELIVERY

'That's nothing,' said another. 'I clean forgot my husband's birthday last week. No presents at all!'

'Better than Hello Kitty lingerie, which is what my husband bought for *my* birthday,' said a brunette mum.

'Ooh'. The group winced in sympathy.

'Sell it on Marketplace?' suggested one mum.

'Sell *him*,' suggested another.

The table laughed and at that moment, Maeve let out the scream that Poppy felt. She had to find a way to be more chill about husband jokes but she hadn't worked out how. She shook her keys in front of her daughter, trying to shake off her suffocating awkwardness. Could they tell she was a single mum? For some reason, she felt she should keep that detail quiet.

As the conversation continued, Poppy cycled through a combination of breastfeeding, knee-jiggling, back-patting and key-shaking. Nothing worked. Maeve continued to oscillate between disgruntled whingeing and outright shrieking. Shoppers and coffee-drinkers jerked their eyes towards her, probably thinking, *Shut that kid up.*

I'm trying, Poppy wanted to cry.

Maeve was normally a straightforward baby but nothing was making sense today. People often said marketing was an imprecise science but Poppy knew that world like a chemist knows a periodic table. She could drill down into those market segments and find the missing links, the answers to the CEO's questions, the untapped opportunities. There was no problem that didn't have a definitive solution.

As Maeve continued to wail inconsolably on her lap, Poppy made ineffectual shushing noises. She couldn't hear herself think, let alone follow a conversation. Her eyes lost focus, the colourful art on the walls merging into a hazy kaleidoscope. If she blinked for too long, she might fall asleep. She suddenly wished that for a moment—just one moment—someone else could hold Maeve; that someone would see her confusion and fatigue and know how to help. That was all she wanted. Just a moment to herself. She didn't even need to go to the toilet. She just wanted to stand up and stretch her legs, arch her back and flex her fingers without the weight of another human barnacled to her body.

Poppy stared at her now-cold coffee. The women sitting around her wouldn't think to offer. They had their own babies to hold. With husbands and partners at home, a cafe jaunt with bub was probably a treat: more one-on-one time! The guilt lanced Poppy's heart like a poison dart. She loved the one-on-one time. Really, she did. But god, she was tired. She was so, so tired.

The pressure of the last few weeks had been building. Every day she'd been doing it by herself—feeding Maeve, swaddling and re-swaddling, changing nappies, making sure they both got fresh air, searching for jobs, making dinners, vacuuming, hanging out the washing, sweeping the verandah—and this was what no-one seemed to fully grasp: she was doing it *by herself.* Her mum and Dani and Mary would say things like, *You're doing so well, Maeve is so lucky, You should be so proud,* but what she needed was someone who *really* got it, who really understood the mind-warping hamster wheel, who could feel in their bones how terrifying and exhausting it was, and she wanted them to say, *What you are doing is so hard and you deserve a fucking medal.*

That's why, when the fellow mums collectively decided to dismantle the pram blockade and head home, Poppy felt the hormones threatening to engulf her yet again. She was going home—alone, like always—to clean her house for a FaceTime date with a man who still didn't know he shared a nose with his daughter.

When April gave her a firm hug goodbye and quietly whispered, 'You've got this,' it took all Poppy's remaining courage to lie and blame unseasonal hay fever for her watery eyes. She thought her laughter had masked her helplessness, but of course they could spot it: she stuck out like a sore thumb. She wasn't like these mums at all.

CHAPTER 16

Poppy turned a slow three hundred and sixty degrees and exhaled. Who knew you could clean an entire three-bedroom house while wearing a three-month-old? She could be hired as a back-up dancer and tour the world; she had the core strength of a stripper!

The floors were mopped and vacuumed, the toothpaste spit had been scrubbed off the bathroom mirror and she'd degreased the shit out of the stovetop. It was a scene from *The Stepford Wives*, minus the dystopian robots. She wasn't sure whether the clean grout would be visible to the naked FaceTime eye, but hopefully the cumulative shininess would create an aura of domestic bliss. At the very least, the cleaning had been a distraction from her anxiety.

By the time Poppy settled onto the couch in a shirt she'd spontaneously ironed, Maeve—who sat on her lap—had even deigned to stop crying. She tapped her phone and the FaceTime dial tone jingled through the living room before a giant smile filled the screen.

SPECIAL DELIVERY

'Hey, Mum.' At least, she assumed it was her mum. She couldn't tell under the blowfly sunnies and face-scaldingly-pink visor.

'Darling, how are you? Have you washed your hair? You look lovely.'

'Yep.' Poppy swelled with pride. 'And Maeve is wearing the new outfit you bought her.'

'Oh, good girl. It's pure wool so make sure it doesn't go into the hot wash pile.' (Poppy made a mental note to commence the adult practice of separating her laundry. Maybe after she finished the ironing. Ha!) 'What's the occasion?'

'No reason,' lied Poppy. 'Just wanted to show you Maeve in her outfit.'

'Oh, thank you, darling. I'm just about to tee off for Twilights but should I pop over afterwards?'

'No thanks, Mum.' (Who knew how long they'd be on the phone to Patrick? There was a lot to catch up on.) 'Good luck with the bunkers. I'll chat to you later.'

Her mum rang off, and Poppy re-hoisted Maeve on her lap and relaxed her jaw into a breezy smile. She'd left nothing to chance. This was it.

The FaceTime dial tone filled the room again, and Poppy and Maeve stared at their faces on the screen, Poppy noting with satisfaction that her experimental contouring had dulled the black circles under her eyes. She couldn't wait for Maeve's eyes to blink in surprise when Patrick's face popped up. Finally, her daughter was going to have a father—on screen, if nothing else. This was a momentous day.

Regardless of how the conversation went, Poppy had resolved to be positive. Today wasn't the day to confront

Patrick about his hurtful behaviour. She'd ease into that conversation after a few more FaceTime chats. Confrontation had never been her strong point and she didn't want to lash out during Maeve's first meeting with her dad. Kids ended up in therapy for much less.

The dial tone rang out.

Poppy checked her watch. She had purposefully waited until 4.30 pm to call. Patrick ritually moved to the pub by 4.30 pm on Fridays. She decided to try again. Maybe he was still in the elevator.

It rang out again.

Frowning, Poppy opened up her text thread. His message had definitely said *K*—she hadn't imagined that. And surely that was short for 'OK'? Poppy checked her watch again. She'd try in ten minutes. Maybe he had a new boss and had been held up in a meeting.

At 4.40 pm, he didn't pick up.

She tried again at 5 pm, but he still didn't pick up.

At 5.15 pm, he didn't pick up.

At 5.30 pm, he didn't pick up.

Poppy pinched the bridge of her nose, determined to stay optimistic. She'd give him until 6 pm. It was time for Maeve's bath anyway.

As she ran her hands under the water to test the temperature, Poppy forced herself to attempt some yogic breathing. *Inhale for four, hold for four, exhale for four.* There was no reason to get upset. It wasn't even that late. It wasn't Patrick's fault that she'd been up since 4.45 am with a clingy baby. Lots of people's days—Patrick's included—only started once the sun went down. Poppy lowered her daughter into the bath, cradling Maeve's head on her forearm as she filled a cup with bathwater and poured it over her daughter's belly. It wasn't Patrick's fault she was already thinking about bedtime routines. He had no idea their days began winding down now.

At 6 pm, with Maeve in fresh pyjamas, she tried again. The ringtone pitter-pattered up and down and up and down, like her rollercoaster of a day, then abruptly cut out. *FaceTime Unavailable* it said.

Breathe. Poppy punched out a text.

Hi ☺ *I thought we were going to FaceTime? Maeve is about to go to bed.*

Instantly, three dots appeared. Proof of life! Poppy waited, but the three dots disappeared.

Swallowing hard, she punched the green button and called him. It rang out.

Breathe, breathe, breathe. It was proving hard to exhale through her rigid jaw. She *knew* he had his phone with him. Why couldn't he just pick up? Why was he forcing her into this obsessive version of herself? She couldn't give two shits if he wanted to ghost her, but this was about her daughter— *their* daughter. Maeve's future self-worth depended on it.

Her phone beeped with an incoming text: *FT not gonna work today. At Ryan's.*

Poppy's neck muscles went stiff. *We don't mind. Just call us from the beer garden* ☺

Nah—will call later

When?

The air outside was now liquid black. Poppy waited and waited. No three dots appeared.

Screw it. She called him again. This time it didn't even ring. She tried him again and again and again. She carried Maeve to her bedroom and lay her gently in her cot, kissed her goodnight, closed the door, and she called him again.

A text arrived. *FFS Poppy! I'm meeting with clients.*

Poppy barked a bitter laugh. Of course—so-called 'clients' appearing on the very day he'd agreed by singular consonant to meet his daughter. How convenient.

She stormed to the kitchen. She needed to do something with her hands—squeeze the life from a broom, scrub the bench till her elbows ached, scrape a cloth against the oven racks until her fingertips bled—but her house was already spotless. For him.

A fat tear slid down the curve of her cheek. She'd wasted a whole day worrying about this FaceTime call, wilfully ignoring the fact that Patrick had never—not once in the last three months—shown any interest in contacting his daughter. She'd buried that truth bomb in the unused part of her brain (the maths part) and pretended she was being optimistic when, really, she was being a naive imbecile.

Poppy wiped her cheeks roughly. There was no-one she could call about this. Dani would declare that Patrick was an arsehole who deserved to have his balls chopped off in a speedboat accident. Her mum would insist Patrick had the potential to be a great dad. The problem was, depending on the speaker and audience and time of day and astrological moon patterns of Venus and Saturn and the NASDAQ, Poppy could agree with both of them, which confirmed her theory that when she was in Patrick's orbit, she became a spineless idiot, incapable of autonomous or rational thought.

A familiar pressure was building in her rib cage, squeezing her organs and tightening her throat. The gleaming benchtop jeered at her. The stovetop sparkled in pity. Everything was too clean and too shiny, her gullible face reflected off every surface and she couldn't stand it a second longer. Poppy grabbed her phone and ran for the door.

★

The air outside was white-hot ice. It scalded her bare feet, the freezing chill warping her toes, but she would run until she couldn't feel them. She would run until her sweat soaked into the fabric of this stupid ironed shirt. She would run until the voices in her head dissolved like steam in this chill-ridden air.

A bat flew overhead, its wings spread wide. Poppy stopped abruptly and a sob heaved from her chest as she sank onto the kerb of her driveway. The concrete beneath her was an arctic tundra, but that seemed inconsequential at this point. Sports bra or no sports bra, she couldn't run further. This was the outermost edge of her bubble and she already felt guilty for being so far from Maeve. If the police found her now—crying like a madwoman in her gutter, neglecting her daughter who slept peacefully inside but could wake at any moment due to any number of life-threatening issues—they could whisk Maeve away and hand her to Patrick. He knew how to play the game. He'd definitely pick up calls from the police.

'Poppy, is that you?' The voice came from across the hedge.

'Mary? What are you doing outside?'

'I could ask the same of you, love.'

'I was . . .' Poppy looked at her bare toes, already blueish in the cold. *I was losing my mind.* 'I was just going back inside.' She stood up and pulled her sleeves over her hands. Her toes were a lost cause.

'You okay, love?'

Not really. Not at all. But totally fine, if anyone's asking. Fine enough to raise a daughter. 'Yes,' she called back.

'You sure?'

Poppy had lost all feeling up to her ankles. 'Never better, Mary. See you later.' Poppy hurried to her front door. She stepped into the warmth of her hallway, where the light from the tulip-style fixtures cast a peachy glow. Quietly, she turned and padded towards her daughter's bedroom. Opening the door, she could hear the tiny whisper of Maeve's rhythmic breathing, as soft as an eyelash fluttering in the wind.

Poppy curled her still-unthawed toes against the tiles. A painful lump had thickened in her throat, making each breath razor-sharp. She may have already lost Patrick and her right to a safe, predictable future, she might soon lose whole limbs to hypothermia and properly lose her mind, but that didn't mean that her precious, unprejudiced daughter had to lose her father. Poppy closed the bedroom door and prised her phone from her pocket.

A fervent need throbbed in her chest. She wasn't sure if she was doing this for herself or her daughter, but her fingers tapped the keypad on the screen.

Hope the client meeting goes well. We're always free to talk, whenever you are ☺

CHAPTER 17

It appeared Maeve was in a 'leap'—a period of cognitive development impacting sleep, behaviour and mood. Poppy had downloaded the app but it wasn't doing jack shit. Suffice to say, the morning had been a disaster. She'd texted Patrick again—just a quick *FT today?* Only two words, abbreviated, totally his style, hopefully completely safe from accusations of nagging, but she'd heard nothing back—and then Henry had bounced into The Bustle this morning looking like a curly-haired Hemsworth cousin. His cheeks were pink from the wind and tiny diamonds of rain were scattered across his curls. 'Dad's getting a labrador,' he announced, sinking into the seat beside her with his takeaway coffee. 'That's his retirement plan.'

Poppy readjusted Maeve on her lap. 'What about your mum's allergies?'

'He's getting a doodle one.'

Poppy couldn't repress a grin. 'A male one?'

Henry grinned back. 'No, a doodle one, you dumb-arse.'

'A *labradoodle*?'

'I *knew* you knew what I meant.'

She always knew what he meant. 'Why a labradoodle?'

'Penis size.'

Poppy snorted into her coffee and Henry's eyes twinkled, thrilled with himself. A mental image of Henry's dad with his blond handlebar moustache popped into her head, and Poppy felt the bubble of something hilarious in her throat. 'I always thought . . .' she began, but nope, the giggles were already fizzing through every vein. 'I always . . .' she tried again, but the laughter was sucking the air from her lungs.

Henry's grin expanded and he began to chuckle. Their eyes locked and they laughed harder, and Henry had no idea why they were laughing, which made it even funnier.

'I . . .' Poppy gasped, holding Maeve tighter before she lost full control of her body.

'Tell me,' pleaded Henry. They were both shaking now, vibrating like caffeinated tambourines. Every time their eyes connected, that link between them was pulled tighter and they laughed harder. Random customers glanced at them, smiles tugging at their lips too, as if whatever was happening between them was contagious. They were making a scene for no good reason other than this was how they were together. Still.

'WHAT, POPPY?'

The blond moustache. *She couldn't*. It was too stupid.

'GOLDENDOODLE!' she gasped, clutching her daughter as a tear rolled down her cheek. 'Always had you for a golden-doodle family.'

Henry's head fell into his hands. 'Poppy!'

'I know!'

'Not! Funny!' More laughter rumbled from his core and his eyes sparkled. Everything about this man thrummed with life. The gloss of rain in his hair, the twinkle in his eye, the creases of his laugh lines. He looked like a man who slept for eight hours a night.

'I'd forgotten this,' Henry wheezed, settling back into his chair.

'How hilarious I am?'

'No, how you crack yourself up two hours before the punchline.'

'It's because I'm hilarious.'

'It's because you're a deadshit.'

If there were a warmer compliment, Poppy didn't know it.

'I've missed this, Pops.' His hand landed on the table as he tried to steady his breathing.

Poppy wiped her palm across her cheek. 'Same, Hen. No-one gets my crap jokes like you do.'

'You mean no-one gives you sympathy laughs like I do.'

'And that's why I love you.'

Oh god. Poppy blanched. It had just slipped out. Like another giggle, but a giant wrecking ball of verbal diarrhoea. *Loved.* She had *loved* him. Past tense. He knew that! They could be grown-ups about this. It had been an innocent slip of the tongue. It was the giggles; she'd deprived herself of oxygen. She'd basically taken a nang! She could not be trusted to speak coherently after such oxygen deprivation. And anyway, people were allowed to love their friends. She loved Dani. She could love Henry in the same way—even if he was her first true love, whom she definitely still found attractive even though he was engaged to a megababe. And besides, maybe he hadn't heard anyway.

Poppy glanced at him. Oh shit. He'd definitely heard. His ears were tinged with a tell-tale pink.

'I'd better be going,' he said, standing abruptly.

'Definitely,' agreed Poppy, hugging Maeve closer.

'Bye.'

This was excruciating. 'Cheerio.' And *that* would help.

Henry fumbled with his wallet, trying to slide it into his chinos, and Poppy watched in slow motion before she realised what was in her sightline and she hastily snapped her eyes away. Maybe she should say cheerio again, just to make it clear this was one hundred per cent platonic?

'I didn't mean to say I love you!' she blurted.

Henry flinched.

'I didn't mean to make it weird, it's just . . .' She paused, trying to find the words, but she wasn't used to thinking before she spoke. (It was unnatural!) She shrugged wearily. 'Most people don't laugh at my jokes.'

Henry picked up his coffee and eventually, to her overwhelming relief, he laughed. It was a soft tinkle, not a booming full-body laugh like before, but it was better than nothing. A cool rush of relief flooded her nervous system. If she could have loved him any more (in that extremely platonic long-time-friend kind of way), his smile made it possible.

'Don't stress, Pops.' He placed a hand on her shoulder as he walked past on his way out. 'I know what you mean.'

SPECIAL DELIVERY

Now, as Poppy stood in her garden, leaning on a useless rake that was providing zero assistance in overcoming this leaf-sludge travesty on her front lawn, it dawned on her that she had not thought about her unanswered text to Patrick for over two hours. Instead, she'd been ghoulishly rewinding back and forth through her conversation with Henry. Maybe this was how she'd survive in life: by obliterating the memory of recent disasters with the memories of new ones. Genius!

From her bouncer on the verandah, Maeve was watching her like a sniper. The reproachful look on her daughter's face made it clear Maeve was extremely displeased with their geographic separation and the resultant lack of skin-on-skin contact. Poppy began raking again and smiled encouragingly at her daughter. Maeve responded with an unimpressed blink.

The wooden handle of the rake was splintery under her hands—a comes-with-the-house accessory she'd found in the corner of the garage—which required her raking motion to be perversely gentle and therefore perversely inefficient. At this rate, she'd be done by next autumn.

Out on the street, a HiLux ute was parked next to her driveway. She'd seen it there before. The sun bounced off the ute's windows obscuring the view inside. There was a sticker on the rear windscreen that looked like a cartoon duck. Then again, it could be a rego sticker. Poppy still had clear memories of the social currency that bumper stickers earned in high school. A boy who had a Cowra Races sticker on his ute was cool, but a boy who had a Louth Races sticker was the ultimate. She sighed at the memory. Everything had been so simple back then.

Poppy glanced at Maeve. Her daughter was now fascinated by a fly on the wall so Poppy decided to edge towards the fence to check out the car. Mary's neighbourhood snooping was rubbing off on her.

This HiLux wasn't giving much away. It didn't have enough gear to be a tradie's ute. It didn't have enough branding to belong to a real estate agent. It was too small to be a family car. The dust could have come from anywhere, but maybe it was from somewhere exotic. Somewhere like Louth?

Mary would want to know. After checking that Maeve was still distracted, Poppy quietly unlatched her gate and tiptoed closer to the car. It was slightly exhilarating to be on a mission. This was how you amused yourself as a suburban mum—you became a Desperate Housewife.

She reached the driver's window and squinted through the dust. Hmmm. Not much, not even an empty Macca's bag or a chocolate wrapper. There was loose change in the centre console. That wasn't much of a hint. But, aha! There was a green canvas bag sitting in the footwell of the passenger seat. It looked full of . . . cash? Drugs? She couldn't wait to brainstorm with Mary.

'Poppy?'

She swivelled. Oh bugger.

'Hi James,' she said, forcing herself to make eye contact.

'What were you doing?' he asked.

'I was . . .' Poppy looked around desperately for inspiration. 'Raking!'

Damn it. There was nothing more unbelievable than the truth. 'I didn't know it was your car.' (Damn it again. The truth thing was not helping.) She hoped he wouldn't notice the redness creeping across her cheeks.

'Okay,' he said slowly, his eyes narrowing. Poppy held his gaze determinedly. *Play it cool. Do not let him see you blush.*

'What are *you* doing here?' she asked. (The oldest trick in the book: turning defence into attack!)

'Visiting someone,' he said. 'Before I start my shift.'

'Oh.' Poppy suddenly remembered her yellow-string-bikini neighbour. The thought of their combined tallness made her feel mildly sick. They amount of eye contact they could make. Imagine what their other body parts could do together.

'Rightio,' she said. (That sounded more middle-aged soccer dad than she'd intended.) 'I hope you enjoyed your visit, though next time you should dress to match.' She smirked as she gestured to his non-yellow attire of jeans and a grey jumper.

James raised an eyebrow.

'I won't hold you up,' Poppy continued, bravely filling the silence. 'You must need to rush off. Babies to deliver and all that.'

James's eyebrow was still raised. Poppy wished she could smack it down. It had a real air of condescension, that bloody eyebrow.

'Okay then, McKellar. I'll see you round.' His lips twitched slightly, and Poppy had the distinct impression that as soon as he turned away, his face would break into a big private grin. Douchebag.

He got in his car and started it as Poppy stood rooted to the footpath, watching him. Driving off, he raised his hand in farewell and Poppy found herself raising hers in return. A wisp of a thought formed in her head, but it vanished like smoke. She sensed, like a dream fading, that it had been significant.

'Poppy, love. Is that you?'

'Mary, yes,' answered Poppy, startling from her thoughts.

'Cuppa?'

'I'll grab Maeve!'

Five minutes later as they settled into the verandah chairs with Maeve next to them in the pram, Mary got straight down to business. How was Maeve sleeping? (Okay.) More jam drops? (Emphatic *yes*.) Any neighbourhood gossip? (Hot dude still sleeping with hot chick in number five, but we don't like to talk about him so pretend I said nothing and let's move on as though he doesn't exist—except Poppy didn't say that. She went with a polite: 'Mmmm . . . no.')

Mary's fourth question was new: 'Any men in your life?'

'Er . . .' Poppy swallowed a mouthful of jam drop. 'Nope.'

'What about Maeve's dad?'

'Uh, er . . .' Poppy waved a non-existent bug from Maeve's head. How could Poppy explain this to a lovely old lady who probably didn't want her verandah sullied with such liberal use of swearwords?

'And what about that old high-school boyfriend you told me about?'

'Um . . .' Poppy couldn't even remember mentioning Henry to Mary. 'Ah . . .'

Mary smiled at her expectantly. 'I've got all the time in the world, love.'

'Okay, well . . .' Poppy cleared her throat and ran through a condensed timeline of both relationships, laying the detail on thick when it came to the last forty-eight hours, and by golly, there had been some details.

'Goodness me,' exclaimed Mary somewhat gratifyingly after she'd finished. 'You know what you need?'

'Please don't say you have a lovely grandson.'

'Oh, I have hordes of lovely grandsons, love, but that's a discussion for another day. In the meantime, I think you need a holiday.'

'A holiday?' Poppy's mind immediately drifted to tropical island getaways with all-you-can-drink swim-up bars. They were obviously out of the question in terms of both price and alcohol content.

'Yes, for the Easter long weekend. I have a cabin at Burrendong Dam, but I won't be able to go with my dodgy hip. I could give you my keys and you can take Maeve up. You'd both love it.'

'Burrendong?' Poppy wrinkled her nose. 'I'm not really into fishing.'

'Oh, love, that doesn't matter at all. Go for the bushwalking and stay for the skies. It's really magical. I think you should go. You deserve it.'

'I don't know,' she said. The idea of a holiday—even in a dusty country caravan park—felt too indulgent when she should be focusing on getting her life sorted for Maeve. Yes, this had been a crazy week, but she was making progress. For example, the house was clean. (*Victory!*) And soon her lawn would be denuded of those frost-muddled leaves. (Possibly.) There was real and significant progress happening on the other side of the hedge. You just had to look hard—and at very specific times. It would be risky to stall the momentum now.

No, she would stick to her current plan and have lunch with her parents and the neighbours, then watch TV while they played a round of digestive golf after pudding. Great. Yes. Fifth-wheeling on her parents' double date and enduring endless questions about single parenting in the age of social media.

'It's so quiet up there,' mused Mary.

Poppy thought of her mum's screechy storytelling. *And then it was a MALE midwife!*

'How quiet?' Poppy asked.

'Quiet enough to hear the magpies swoop, love. Pure serenity.'

Poppy lifted her daughter into her lap. *Serenity*. No questions about Patrick, or assertions that leaps were a figment of the modern imagination. Big skies and no-one in the world to judge her. That's what she needed right now.

Poppy grabbed another jam drop from the plate and a smile spread across her face. 'Okay, Mary—I'll do it.'

CHAPTER 18

The cabin's corrugated-iron walls were painted pale yellow and the tin roof was a weathered green. A stack of cobwebbed plastic chairs sat on the verandah with a crusty welcome mat at the door. There was not a breath of wind and the water shimmered at the base of the valley like a mirror of the sky. Poppy heaved her luggage up the stairs, grimacing in the unseasonal heat.

Mary had given her the keys to the cabin along with two Tupperware containers of lemon slice and jam drops. The jam drops were for Poppy and the lemon slice was for Mary's family, who would be staying in the cabins nearby. Her instructions to Poppy were simple: watch out for snakes and *relaxez-vous*.

Inside the cabin, a scratchy canvas couch faced a small television with a mustard-coloured kitchen in the rear. In the bedroom, the sateen mustard bedspread threw sepia-toned light like an Instagram filter. If you shimmied the bedside table into the corner and pushed the bed frame against the opposite wall, a portacot could fit in the gap. Maeve was already making good use of it, exhausted from her first long drive. The cabin was kind of beautiful in a nostalgic, seventies kind of way. Poppy opened the kitchen windows and breathed deeply. It smelled of eucalypt and dust and . . . yoghurt?

She opened the esky and groaned. Her half-litre tub of Chobani had split at the base and a goopy white paste covered everything inside: the figs, the strawberries, the tomatoes, the cheese, the bread rolls. Everything was ruined. The lone champagne bottle was so covered in yoghurt it looked like milk, but at least it could be rinsed off. She turned on the kitchen tap, which made a guttural choking sound. Brownish water spurted out, ricocheting off the sink and sending brown splotches all over her white linen shirt. Poppy swore and tucked her shirt under her bra so the water now spattered her bare stomach. She waited until the water ran clear then began washing the fruit under the tap. The cheese and bread which had been wrapped in paper bags were already starting to sour. At this rate, she'd be on a fruitarian diet for Easter.

'Hello-ooo?'

Poppy jumped at the sound and spun around.

What the hell?!

James's tall frame filled the doorway. 'Hi,' he said, the corners of his mouth twitching as he glanced at her stomach.

'Oh shit.' Poppy pulled down her top. 'I was just . . .' She gestured to the sink and the fruit. He would have no idea what she meant. 'What are you doing here?'

'I'm here to get the slice.' He pointed at the Tupperware on the bench. 'Mary said you'd bring it.'

SPECIAL DELIVERY

'Mary? What?' *Ohhhhhhh.* 'Mary is your *grandma*?'

'Yep.'

'But why do you call her Mary?'

James shrugged. 'She hates being called Grandma. Makes her feel too old.'

Poppy's mind drifted back to James's ute in her street. 'That . . . explains a lot.'

'I thought she would have told you.'

Poppy shook her head, her sluggish brain struggling to keep up. 'I guess that means you and the bikini model . . .?'

James creased his forehead. 'Who?'

'Oh, er, I thought you and our neighbour were . . . um, you know.' She pulled at her shirt to make doubly sure it wasn't still tucked into her bra.

'Oh!' James sounded shocked. 'No, no, not at all. Happily single, I am.' He coughed and glanced at her quickly. 'Sorry, weird thing to say.'

Poppy's brow tensed slightly. Was that embarrassment she'd witnessed? From the robot? She turned to the lemon slice. 'You're lucky your grandma is such a great baker,' she said, handing over the container.

'I know.' James nodded. 'We don't need it at all—we've got mountains of food—but it wouldn't be Easter without Mary's slice.'

Poppy glanced at her own measly pile of soggy food on the bench. 'I bet.'

James tilted his head towards the wet baguette poking out of the esky. 'What happened there?'

'Yoghurt explosion.'

'Right.'

'I may be on a liquid diet this Easter.'

James glanced between her and the food. 'I guess, er, you could join us? For Easter lunch tomorrow?' He hesitated. 'Only if you want to, of course.' He held up the Tupperware container. 'We'll have slice.'

'Oh.' Poppy felt her cheeks redden. 'I wasn't angling for an invite.' Her conversations with this man always seemed to veer off course. It was his damn eyes. They were so distracting.

'Not at all. It would be my—I mean, *our* pleasure.'

Poppy grimaced. There was no way out from all this politeness. She was trapped. 'Oh, um, okay then,' she stammered. 'Thank you, um . . . James.' His name sounded so formal on her tongue.

'Right.' He nodded as if concluding a business meeting. 'I'll pop by tomorrow morning and let you know the plans. You would think lunch would be at lunchtime, but you can never be sure when my family is concerned, so it pays to check. I guess, I'll . . . I'll see you soon.'

He turned and walked down the stairs. Poppy squinted into the sunlight, watching him go. In the distance, a kookaburra laughed until its cackle was absorbed into the hot, dry air. She turned back to the kitchen and leaned her elbows on the bench then dropped her head into her hands. The Tupperware of jam drops sat next to her, as duplicitous as a poisoned chalice. Poppy straightened up and rubbed her eyes. Mary had a *lot* of explaining to do.

CHAPTER 19

Poppy's fingers hovered over her phone. Would it be positive parenting or soul-sucking suicide to send an Easter message to Patrick?

'Happy Easter!' called a familiar silhouette from the doorway.

Argh! Poppy's phone clattered onto the table and Maeve looked up from her play mat.

'I thought you might need sustenance,' said James, opening the door and waving a box of Cornflakes and a three-litre bottle of milk. 'I can't leave these with you—you have no idea how much my nephews eat—but if you're hungry you could make a bowl now and I'll take the rest back.'

'Oh, er, thanks,' said Poppy, wishing she wasn't still in her pyjamas. 'I'll just change. Can you watch Maeve?' She didn't wait for an answer, just raced into the bedroom, grabbing a t-shirt from the floor and pulling a hairbrush from her suitcase to smooth her bed hair. It was only eight thirty, for god's sake.

Being in your pyjamas at this hour was completely acceptable on a public holiday, especially when you had a newborn. It wasn't her fault James always looked so fresh.

When she came out, James was cradling Maeve in the crook of his arm as he rummaged in the cupboards. 'She started grumbling so I picked her up,' he explained, as if this were the most natural thing in the world. His forearm was so big that Maeve lay on it like a bed.

'Do you mind if I join you?' he asked, pulling two bowls from the cabinet. 'It's chaos back at our cabin.'

'Um, okay,' said Poppy. 'Can't refuse a man who brings me food.'

'Good to know.' James grinned and, inexplicably, she felt her stomach drop. Hunger pangs, obviously.

James filled the bowls with Cornflakes and poured the milk all with Maeve on his forearm. It was so *dexterous*.

'I haven't had Cornflakes in years,' remarked Poppy to distract herself as she took Maeve back. 'Not since I was back-packing. Cornflakes always remind me of hostels.'

James pulled out two spoons from a drawer under the sink—Poppy would have never found them there—and put them in the bowls.

'They remind me of camping,' he said, making his way towards the verandah with the bowls. Poppy followed. 'When I ate them overseas, they always tasted different from the ones back home.'

'I seem to remember they were saltier in Europe,' said Poppy grabbing the play mat with her spare hand.

'And sweeter in America,' said James.

Poppy nodded. 'Yeah.' She'd been about to say that.

She lay the play mat on the verandah and placed Maeve on top.

'When was the last time you had Cornflakes?' asked James.

'No idea,' Poppy said with a sigh. 'Probably about ten years ago, when I went backpacking with my best friend. We were so skint we always had to choose the cheapest hostels. Rickety beds, crap showers, the constant stench of booze and BO. It was the best.'

James smiled and Poppy accidentally smiled back.

'I went travelling with my brother for a few months after uni,' he said. 'We were those Aussie guys you meet at every hostel—wearing footy shorts and thongs even when it was freezing, surviving on beer and baguettes. Unhealthiest I've ever been in my life, but jeez it was fun.' He looked down towards the dam and then back at her. 'Couldn't do it now, though.'

'No,' Poppy agreed, her gaze settling on Maeve, who was tugging the fringing on the play mat. 'Somehow we all grow up.'

'Or we try not to,' said James. 'I'm going back to uni next year. Hopefully studying medicine. It'll be strange being the oldest guy in the lecture hall, but I don't care. I made the decision for me, no-one else.' He lifted a giant spoonful of Cornflakes to his mouth and gulped them down. 'FYI, you don't need to fill up on cereal today. There's so much food up there.' He gestured towards the cabins up the hill. 'My mum starts planning Easter lunch before we've even digested Christmas pudding. It's an affliction.'

Poppy smiled at the spoon in her hand. 'Thanks for inviting me to join you,' she said.

'Not at all. You're doing me a favour.' James scraped the last of his Cornflakes from the bowl. 'She always tries to force-feed me the leftovers so it's always useful to have someone else to share the eating load.'

'I wonder why she thinks you'd be hungry.' Poppy smiled, inclining her head towards his empty bowl. 'You inhaled that.'

James shrugged. 'Cornflakes are fucking delicious.'

Poppy looked down at her bowl to hide her chuckle. The sun felt warm on her face as it slid long shadows across the verandah. It was so quiet she could hear the patter of a magpie's feet as it landed on the corrugated-iron roof. She scooped up a spoonful of Cornflakes. She'd forgotten: they *were* delicious.

As they stood up to clear the bowls, James said, 'Hey, I'm sorry I showed up with no warning. I forgot to consider you might not be up and at 'em yet.'

Poppy turned to him, puzzled. Maeve was still happily turtle-backing on the play mat.

'What?' he asked.

Poppy picked up her daughter and playmat. 'I don't know.' She shook her head. 'You seem so different from when we first met.'

James grimaced as he opened the screen door for them. 'Yeah, I feel bad about that, sorry. It had been a weird day. Although'—a wicked smile crept across his face—'I'd like to remind the jury that you *didn't* have a pram.'

Poppy tried to elbow him as she passed. 'You try carrying a baby in the peak of summer. My parking choices were completely justifiable.'

SPECIAL DELIVERY

'It's okay.' James patted her on the shoulder. 'I forgave you instantly.'

It was like his hand left an imprint on her. Something ballooned in Poppy's chest and she tried to quash it. The conversation, the casual touching; this was veering into something she couldn't put her finger on and it was making her nervous. When had this truce sneakily emerged? She was supposed to hate him. Poppy racked her brain for one of those conversation starters to change the subject. Should she ask his views on organised religion?

James got in first. 'Do you have plans this morning?' he asked, pulling a scrubbing brush from the cupboard under the sink. The sunlight through the window had transformed his hair from dark blond to honeyed gold.

Poppy nodded. 'I'll put on the baby carrier and go for a hike. Maeve loves a walk. As in, she loves to sleep while I walk. It suits both of us.'

'Do you reckon . . .' He trailed off. 'Nah, don't worry.'

'What?'

'Nothing.'

Poppy narrowed her eyes. His blank-faced man-of-mystery routine was so annoying. 'Tell me,' she said.

James turned on the tap and began scrubbing the bowls. 'I was going to ask if I could join you with Eileen. But it's okay. I know you wouldn't want that.'

Poppy bristled. 'Don't presume to know what I want.'

'So you want me to come?'

Poppy felt a familiar twinge of frustration in her rib cage. Did he *practise* this reverse psychology?

'I can grab Eileen and be back here in half an hour,' said James, his inflection halfway between statement and question.

Poppy dropped the play mat in front of the couch and lowered Maeve onto her back. 'Okay,' she said. 'Sure.' This wasn't entrapment; she had implied he could come, and now he'd offered to come. She just wasn't sure she wanted him to—or if she'd purposefully made him think that she did. Had she? She stared at the garish colours underneath her daughter. She had to remember not to be so ambiguous around this guy. Somehow, he had the power to make her second-guess her every word.

CHAPTER 20

Thirty-five minutes later Maeve was dressed and strapped in the BabyBjörn wearing a tiny hat and they were ready to go.

She could see James walking down the road from his cabin. His broad chest stretched out his t-shirt and his calves were still tanned from summer. He looked like a guy who should run up these hills, not walk them.

He arrived at the foot of her verandah stairs with Eileen. 'You okay if I take her off the leash once we get going?' he asked.

'Sure,' replied Poppy. 'She seems much less skittish now.'

'Only around you and Maeve. My last dog was a good judge of character too, and I should have paid more attention to that.'

Poppy raised her eyebrow but it seemed James was done with that conversation.

'You ready?' he asked.

'Ready,' she confirmed.

They set off up the bitumen road, following it past the cabins further up the hill before turning onto a gravel track that veered back to the dam. Poppy had spent the last half-hour worrying about how they'd cope without his conversation starters but somehow the chat flowed easily. With all those walks around the golf course, they'd developed a companionable rhythm and she hadn't even realised. Something inside her flared with irritation—he'd forced her into that; she'd never wanted to hang out with him!—but then she remembered eating Cornflakes on the verandah with the sun casting its glow over the dusty furniture and she felt her frustration dissolve like motes of dust in the autumn air. She'd needed help post-yoghurt explosion and he'd offered. That didn't seem sinister. It seemed kind of decent.

As they crested the hill, James said, 'So I have to warn you, my whole family will be at lunch. Aunties, uncles, cousins, everyone.'

'But not Mary,' said Poppy.

'Yes,' conceded James. 'And . . . not my dad.'

Poppy nodded. 'I remember you mentioned something about that.'

'Yeah.' James tugged the collar of his t-shirt. 'We never see him.'

Down at the dam, a trailer reversed a boat to the water's edge and gleeful cheers from wetsuited kids rang up the valley.

'What happened?' asked Poppy. 'You don't have to tell me if you don't want to. I'm just interested.'

James glanced at her quickly then back at the gravel path. 'He and Mum broke up when I was in high school,' he said.

SPECIAL DELIVERY

'He didn't treat her very well. He wasn't a good guy, to be honest. We were living in Forbes, but as soon as we'd all graduated from high school Mum moved to Orange. My siblings and I followed fairly soon after. We're pretty close like that. None of us speak to Dad.'

He said it matter-of-factly, as though reading from the dictionary: succinct, without caveats and unnecessary detail. In the distance, the boat puttered to the centre of the dam, its wake rippling wider until it was absorbed into the stillness. She'd never noticed before but he seemed so sure of himself. The way he spoke about his father. Even the way he announced he was going back to uni, like it wasn't a big deal to reverse your life into quasi-adolescence. Poppy couldn't imagine doing either so confidently or so freely, but as James loped along beside her, she doubted he'd spare the brain power worrying about what other people thought. Maybe that was why he came across as such a douchebag.

'What about Maeve's dad?' asked James. 'He's still in Sydney?'

Poppy felt a reflexive pinch in the pit of her stomach but she tried to ignore it. There was no point lying. James had been in the delivery room. He already knew too much.

'Yep, he's in Sydney,' she replied. She kicked at a pebble in their path. 'He's still stuck in his inner-city, work-hard-party-hard lifestyle. We'd been together nine years, but when I fell pregnant I realised I'd grown up and I didn't want that life anymore. I mean, Maeve was very much a surprise, but when I saw those two lines on the stick, I felt a sense of "Yes, okay, this is what I'm doing now." I was ready, you know? When Patrick couldn't get on board, I finally understood how unsuited we were. He hardly cared when I said we should break up, so it was very mutual, which is worse than it sounds.'

On her chest, Maeve dozed peacefully in the carrier, her fingers curled into the fabric of her onesie. Poppy hadn't talked about the break-up like this with anyone. Dani and her parents had witnessed it happening in real time, so hadn't received the condensed version stripped of the adrenaline and hormones and swearing and tears. Telling the story like this made it sound kind of simple. A guy and girl who'd fail any Instagram quiz on compatibility. They'd been a big Jenga tower with blocks sliding out all over the place, and they hadn't realised until it all came tumbling down.

Poppy sighed. 'I never wanted to be a single parent. Like, I would love someone to help me with Maeve so I could rest sometimes, but I don't regret the decision to have Maeve for a second, and I have to keep telling myself it won't always be like this. And Patrick wouldn't have helped anyway. He would have worked too late or been too hungover to do anything. It's probably easier this way, knowing I only have myself to rely on rather than being constantly disappointed. That would drive me insane.'

James was silent, his eyes on the path. It was easy to talk when no eye contact was required. 'Will he be involved in Maeve's life?' he asked.

'I'm open to it,' said Poppy. 'It would be easier if I could cut him out properly and move on, but you know, a kid needs a dad.'

She thought of her own dad. Quiet, comforting, pretty hopeless at lots of things but always a steady shoulder to lean on. She felt tears spring up just thinking about him that way. She blinked them away, embarrassed.

'Do you have any support in town?' James asked. 'Your parents live in Orange, don't they?'

Poppy nodded. 'Yep, they do, which is great. I see Mum at least every week. She's a very passionate grandmother. Lots of love, lots of opinions.'

James smiled. 'Sounds normal.'

'I know. I'm lucky, really. I just wish I had some other opinions to balance out Mum's. I don't really know anyone else in town.'

James looked across to Maeve, sleeping contentedly on her chest. 'I'd offer you a place on my cricket team, but I'm guessing that's out of the question?'

Poppy groaned. 'That would be out of the question whether I had a baby or not. I'm used to getting kicked off sports teams for lack of ability, so I avoid the humiliation by never signing up.'

'You wouldn't get kicked off a *social* team.'

Poppy gave a wry chuckle. 'I have seen *social* teams where grown men have punched umpires over a mistimed bounce pass.' She shook her head. 'Nope, sports are not for me. I'm going to grow old gracefully and non-actively.'

'That's a lie, you walk every day.'

'That doesn't count as sport.'

'I suppose not, but I'm glad you do it.'

Poppy glanced at him.

'It's been great for Eileen; she's come a long way in her puppy training. And I benefit too, obviously.' He smiled at her and, if Poppy wasn't mistaken, his eyes did a quick slide up and down her body. Was he checking her out?! *On purpose?* How mortifying! She was literally wearing a baby.

They walked a few paces before James spoke again. 'Have you tried to make friends?'

Poppy was so glad he'd broken the silence she wasn't even offended by the implication she was a friendless loser.

'Of course,' she muttered. 'I'm friends with Mary.' (Okay, maybe that sounded a bit loser-ish.) 'I've also met a few people through mothers' group. So, you know, I have prospects. I won't be a loner forever.'

'Hmmm.'

'You're saying "hmmm" like you don't believe me.'

'No, I'm not.'

'Then why are you hmmm-ing like that?'

'You're reading too much into it.'

'It obviously means something if you said it with that expression on your face.'

The corners of James's lips curved upwards. 'What expression was that?'

Poppy stepped over a tree root and Maeve bumped against her chest. His almost-smile could be so infuriating. A nerve-crackling mix of smugness, condescension and complete obliviousness to its power.

'Hmmm,' said James again, then laughed. 'Sorry I didn't mean to do that. I was actually thinking about how hard it would be to make friends without sport or work. You could borrow the conversation starters if you need to?'

Poppy rolled her eyes. 'I'll be fine, thanks.'

'Well, I may have grown up in Forbes but if you want my advice on what brings people together in Orange these days, I'll tell you: real estate chat. Buying, selling or renovating, it doesn't matter which one—they're all acceptable.'

Poppy readjusted Maeve's hat in the carrier. 'Maybe I'll have to start watching *The Block*. As a single, jobless mum, that will be the extent of my involvement in the property market.'

'Not a bad outcome,' James said approvingly.

'You're a fan?' asked Poppy, glad to be veering away from the heavy topics.

'Yep, it's a tradition. Work, gym, dinner, *The Block*. I get sad whenever a season ends. I'm like: what do I watch now? *A Current Affair*? Kill me.'

'That's funny,' said Poppy. 'I would not have picked you as a reality TV fan.'

'I'm not. *The Block* doesn't count. It's very manly and practical. You pick up lots of useful tips—manage your budget, waterproof on Wednesdays—and the auction finales are epic.'

Poppy smirked. 'I'll take your word for it.'

'You don't watch *The Block*?'

'Nope, never. I'm too busy. And a bit too cool.'

'No-one is too cool for *The Block*, Poppy. *The Block is* cool. Scott Cam is cool. When the next finale is on, you can come over and watch it at mine, if you want? I'll commentate for you. You'll be on the edge of your seat, I promise.'

Poppy glanced at him. He'd issued this invitation so casually, so confidently, like having a single mum over to his place to watch TV was normal. Was he being friendly or was he a serial killer? In this present moment, with his eyelashes looking so dark and soft, even the latter sounded acceptable. Which was weird.

By the time they'd looped back to the cabins, Maeve had finished her sleep cycle and was awake again, as wide-eyed as a baby lemur. They hadn't reached her verandah before Poppy started pulling off the BabyBjörn. As she fiddled with the straps and clips, James held out his hands to take Maeve as though they'd done this a million times before. It made her feel strangely shy.

'I'll swing back at one to pick you up,' said James.

'Sure,' said Poppy as she took Maeve from him. 'It's a date.'

Ugh, why?! The words had slipped out before she realised how they'd sound. It wasn't actually a date. She hoped he didn't think *she* thought it was a date.

James was smiling, apparently unflustered. Poppy quickly shifted Maeve over her shoulder for a spontaneous burping session to avoid unnecessary eye contact.

'See you then,' he said, turning up the hill.

'Yeah, bye,' Poppy mumbled. If a sky-writing aeroplane were to spontaneously appear overhead, she suspected it would waste no time in spelling out: TYPICAL, MCKELLAR.

CHAPTER 21

As Poppy emerged onto her verandah wearing a red wrap dress printed with tiny white daisies, James looked up from where he sat on the front step. 'You look nice.'

'Oh . . .' Poppy wasn't sure how to respond. 'Nice' was the blandest compliment you could get; she tried not to feel so happy about receiving it.

James was freshly showered, his still-wet hair glistening. The collar of his navy polo stuck up as though he'd dressed in a hurry.

'Let me get that,' he said, standing up to grab the pram and carry it down the three stairs. As he flicked on the pram brakes, he remarked in surprise, 'It's heavy, isn't it? You should be careful carrying it around.'

Poppy came to a halt at the top of the stairs. 'Sure, I'll get my monkey butler to carry it for me.'

James moved to the foot of the steps. 'You *know* that's not how I meant it. I just don't want you to hurt yourself.'

Poppy crossed her arms. 'Regardless, you still sound exceptionally patronising.'

James's mouth quirked upwards. 'I heard exceptional?'

Poppy rolled her eyes.

'Kidding!' He smiled, stepping onto the lowest stair, his eyes now level with hers. 'I promise my intentions were honourable.'

'And yet again, you sound like a tool.' She shrugged. 'You're really bad at reading the room.'

He came a step closer, his mouth tilting. 'I'm only bad at reading you.'

His hands reached up to rest on the handrails that framed either side of her hips and as his smile inched higher without breaking her gaze, Poppy was abruptly aware of the sun's warmth on her bare arms. It felt like the heat was swirling across her skin like smoke across water. In fact, it was too hot. She needed more SPF. She needed to cover up. She needed to move but she couldn't because *his eyes*. From this angle she could see they were scattered with tiny flecks of hazel, like hidden seams of gold. There was an ominous fight-or-flight sensation tingling up her spine. She needed to look away. Now.

'I'll grab the nappy bag,' she said, too loudly.

The screen door squeaked behind her as she pulled the bag from the couch, grabbed the champagne from the fridge and, after a moment's pause, twisted the tap at the sink. She put her fingers underneath the clear, cool water then dabbed at her temples, feeling her pulse slowly subside. She was being ridiculous. They were just two people. Who had eyes. Having lunch. With his whole family. No big deal.

SPECIAL DELIVERY

When she stepped outside, James was peering into the pram making faces at Maeve. 'I'm trying to make her laugh,' he explained. 'But she's a stone-cold ice maiden.'

'Like her mum?' said Poppy.

On cue, Maeve giggled.

'Oh, that's how it is, is it?' said James to Maeve. 'Only laughing at Mum's jokes?'

Poppy smiled at her daughter, glad for the comic relief. 'As my daughter, she's genetically predisposed to some serious ice maiden energy.'

'Whatever you reckon,' said James, taking the nappy bag from her and looping it over his shoulder. 'You're sweet as pie.'

Poppy's eyes jerked sideways. *This guy.* He said things that were So. Hard. To. Read. 'Let's go,' she said and began pushing the pram up the hill, steadfastly ignoring the prickle of heat across her clavicles. That would be the beginning of the sunburn. And what was 'sweet as pie' supposed to mean anyway? Was it some kind of weird backhanded compliment? Was he patronising her? Again? That would be so like him.

Unless—a thought snagged like driftwood in the babbling current of her brain—maybe he was being friendly and she was overthinking it. Maybe he'd been making a passing comment fuelled by that no-filter honesty and self-assurance that seemed to emanate from his broad shoulders. He thought she was 'sweet'—however he defined that—ergo he'd said so. Case closed. Nothing more to see here, people. She needed to get a grip. It was unhealthy to analyse human behaviour to this extent; she'd give herself an aneurysm.

They arrived at a cabin surrounded by utes and SUVs. Somewhere in the background a Bluetooth speaker was pumping Cat Stevens. Kids were running up and down the verandah stairs and there was the unmistakable sound of beer bottles clinking.

'James!' cried a woman in a Camilla-esque caftan. She was holding a tray of smoked salmon blinis. 'I've been looking for you everywhere.'

'Mum, I was gone for two seconds. How did you even notice? I already moved the eskies around the front and plaited Maisie's hair, like you asked. I even sorted out Uncle Pete for beers. I went to get Poppy, like I told you. I couldn't have her turn up at the lion's den alone.' He looked at Poppy. 'Oh yeah—Poppy, this is my mum, Donna. Mum, this is Poppy.'

Poppy held out the chilled bottle of champagne that was sweating in her hands. 'This is for you.'

'You shouldn't have!' said James's mother, happily lying. 'We'll have a special glass of that later. James, put it in there.' She nodded towards the nearest esky, which was covered in Bundaberg Rum stickers. 'Don't let me forget that's where I put it. I'm not having those pesky teenagers sneaking our special drinks. It's so nice to meet you, Poppy,' she said, turning to look at Poppy with the same dark eyes as her son. 'You're the one living next to Mum, aren't you? She raves about you, so it's lovely you can join us here. Feels like you're part of the family already!' She smiled warmly and squeezed Poppy's arm; Poppy felt a rush of gratitude. 'I'd love to stay and chat but I promised Norma I'd take these blinis straight to her. She gets so antsy about the canapés. Then I've got to sort the potatoes and, oh gosh. . .' She walked off, the caftan billowing behind her.

'She's not normally so flustered,' James remarked.

'She's lovely,' said Poppy. She meant it too.

Within seconds they were surrounded by people clapping James on the shoulder, hugging him and wishing him a Merry Easter. (Was that a thing?) Drinks were offered by friendly uncles and aunts, and Poppy laughed shyly at the chaos, clutching the pram in one hand and a half-glass of champagne in the other. Compared to her own family, this was an army.

'Jimmy!' cried a woman, emerging from behind a swarm of children. She had long, dark blonde hair and legs up to the sky. 'We just arrived! Where have you been?' She punched his arm playfully.

'Ow!' cried James, rubbing his arm. 'Poppy, this is my sister, Kate. Kate, this is Poppy, Mary's next-door neighbour.'

'I've heard so much about you,' said Kate as she drew Poppy in for a hug. She pulled away and looked Poppy up and down. A sly grin crept onto her face. 'I can see why—'

'Kate!' yelled a voice in the distance. 'I need your help with this cheese plate *now*!'

Kate grinned. 'I'd better go. Don't hog Poppy to yourself, Jimmy boy. I can tell she's out of your league.' She winked and disappeared around the back of the cabin.

James ran a hand through his hair. 'She's so weird. Sorry about that.'

Poppy chuckled. 'I'm just loving the "Jimmy" revelation. Can't wait to bust that one out.'

'You wouldn't dare. Now let's go check out the set-up.' James put his hand on the small of her back, steering her towards the backyard, and Poppy's abdomen tightened at his touch. Her lower back suddenly felt glazed with sweat. She prayed he couldn't tell.

'Always so over the top,' groaned James, as they rounded the corner. The grass behind the cabin was still crisp from summer. A towering scribbly gum cast a welcome shade and lines of trestle tables covered in white tablecloths were decorated with garlands of gum leaves, foil-covered chocolate eggs nestled among them. James plucked an egg from the garland and began peeling off the foil.

'Hey, don't eat the decorations!' Poppy tried to shove him but James effortlessly dodged her swipe and poked her in return.

'I cannot be blamed for eating Easter eggs on Easter Sunday,' he said. 'They shouldn't have made edible decorations if they didn't want them eaten.' He popped the entire chocolate egg in his mouth and grinned.

As more family members arrived, James was swept away in more hugs and to-do lists. Poppy tugged the rug from the nappy bag and unfolded it under the gum tree. Bodies moved in all directions. Children were running across the grass and adults were marching through the cabin like ants. Some kids threw her curious glances. To most of them, she was invisible.

A bevy of teenage girls—cousins, she presumed—drifted over, delighted to find a baby in their midst. 'Can we babysit?' asked one, a curly-haired girl who couldn't have been more than fifteen.

'Oh, that's very generous . . .' Poppy began. She'd only ever left Maeve for an hour or two with her mum, and even on those rare occasions it had been heart-wrenching.

'I babysit all the time,' said the girl, waving at the crowd as if to indicate she'd raised this lot.

'Harper *is* great with babies,' said Kate as she walked past with a cheese platter. 'She basically parented the twins by herself, but don't hold that against her.'

'Oh, um . . .' Poppy glanced around uncertainly.

Kate called over her shoulder, 'You can trust her.'

The girls were already sitting on the blanket and pulling toys from the nappy bag. 'Um, er, okay,' Poppy heard herself say. She stood up and took a tentative step to the left. The teenage girls had already forgotten she was there. So had Maeve apparently; she was transfixed by the gum leaves overhead. Poppy swallowed and assessed the situation. There were adults everywhere and it was a relatively small place. If Maeve screamed she would hear it immediately. She was going to be cool about this. She would not make a scene.

'Dying of hunger!' Kate laughed.

Poppy's head spun around. 'Who? Maeve?!'

'No, the boys,' said Kate, gliding back with a massacred cheese plate. 'Cooper tried to take the whole wheel of cheese for himself. Reckons he's bulking and needs the protein. He's *twelve*!'

Poppy giggled. Under the tree, her daughter's eyes were closing, as though hypnotised by the dappled light.

'I think I'll put her to sleep in the pram,' announced Harper.

'Oh.' Poppy had been about to suggest the same thing. 'Sounds good, thanks.'

'The kid's maternal instincts are strong,' said Kate approvingly, turning back to the cabin.

Poppy smiled cautiously. 'Let me help you,' she said, falling into step with her. 'I need a job.'

As they entered the kitchen, Kate raised her voice. 'Everyone, this is Poppy. She's the one staying in Mary's cabin.'

The room was heaving with people, and they all turned around, curious. Some of them waved, most of them smiled, and a few aunts bundled her up in a flurry of bosom-y hugs. Plates and glasses covered every surface and the air was humid from the roasting oven and the mass of bodies. Poppy surreptitiously lifted her arms to minimise underarm sweat.

'Are you sure we're ready to put the salads out?' cried one of the aunts, as Kate picked up a giant bowl. 'We've barely finished the appetisers.'

'Norma, unless we start filling those boys up with something vaguely healthy, they're going to gorge themselves on chocolate and be more hyperactive than usual. I'll let you deal with that, if you want?' Kate didn't wait for a response; she just strode out with the couscous salad, as poised as ever.

Poppy was handed a wide bowl of cauliflower and pomegranate salad which was surprisingly heavy and awkward to hold. She turned and began walking to the verandah, dodging the kids who were racing around her feet. She tried to shift the weight of the bowl more evenly across her arms. The bowl was bigger than her torso and seemed to be made from a surprisingly dense form of ceramic. She could feel her sweaty hands slipping slightly. *Oh god*, she thought, *please don't let me drop this. Please, please, please.*

SPECIAL DELIVERY

It was too late. The bowl was definitely slipping. Irrationally, she rushed towards the screen door, hoping to sandwich the bowl between her body and the flyscreen to keep it from falling. *Fuck*, the salad looked delicious too. This was going to be a travesty.

'Hey,' said James, suddenly appearing in the doorframe, easily steadying the bowl with one hand. (*Arrogant.*) 'What's going on here?'

'I'm taking the salad outside,' Poppy huffed. 'Obviously.'

'Were you trying to hammer throw it out there?'

'No, I just . . . my hands . . . it was quite sweaty.' She suddenly remembered the threat of armpit sweat and raised her arms away from her body. She was now holding the bowl like someone would hold motorbike handles—totally cool.

'What are you doing?' asked James, his gaze locked on hers.

'Nothing.'

'You're being a bit weird.'

'No, I'm not.'

'True—you're often like this.'

Poppy narrowed her eyes. 'Can you give me a hand or what?'

James smiled, taking the bowl from her. 'It would be my pleasure.'

Poppy followed him to the tables, where he set the salad down and surveyed the chairs that were slowly filling up.

'Let's sit over here,' he said, walking towards Kate. 'The key is not to get stuck on the kids' table or they'll make you tell jokes all day and try to pull down your pants.' He glanced at her dress. 'Well, maybe not you, but you get my drift. You don't want the drunken aunts and uncles, either; they'll try to bait you about all this woke Gen Y stuff. And you don't want to be sitting with the teenagers, because the boys use too much Rexona and it can put you off your food. And then . . .'

Poppy let his commentary wash over her, enjoying how he connected the dots in a busy, colourful mosaic. Within ten minutes, she had a plate heaped with turkey, ham, green beans with slivered almonds and lemony baby potatoes, there were plump slices of tomato with shreds of basil and silken burrata. There wasn't even room for the cauliflower and pomegranate salad. The cotton of the white tablecloths brushed her legs as she sat down next to James and another half-glass of champagne materialised from a friendly uncle. Maeve was still snoozing in the shade. Poppy suddenly wished everyone would pick up their forks. She was starving.

'Ahem.' The friendly uncle cleared his throat. He had James's jawline and shoulders, giving him the appearance of a retired tennis player. The man tried again and clinked a fork against his beer. 'Hey, shut up, you lot!'

The table fell silent. He cleared his throat again. 'I want to say thank you to everyone who helped prepare this feast for us.'

'You could have helped!' piped up James's mum, and the others roared with laughter.

The man grinned sheepishly. 'Thanks, Donna-tron, but no-one wants food poisoning at Easter, especially with the septic tank situation out here. I'll shut up soon, I just wanted to say how special it is to have you all here this weekend—even you, Cooper.' His laser eyes homed in on Kate's son, who immediately stopped flicking peas at his twin brother. 'I know Mary is so sad to be missing this, but nothing makes her happier than knowing how much we all enjoy each other's company.'

'Speak for yourself!' yelled an uncle from the back, and another wave of laughter erupted.

'Alright, alright, that's enough from you, Barry! I can see you're not enjoying this at all.' He pointed to Barry's overflowing plate. 'Well, let's all dig in and be thankful for having such a motley crew of a family. Cheers!'

The table raised their glasses and a hearty 'cheers' rang out across the valley.

James's siblings and their partners were all warm and friendly, with the athletic frames that Poppy was starting to associate with this tribe. It was like a Noah's ark of Olympians: Kate and Dereck, Michael and Maggie, Dave and Trudy. Poppy ate slowly, squeezing in mouthfuls between answering questions. They wanted to know about Maeve, her job, where she lived, why she'd left Sydney. Poppy hadn't spoken about herself in so long, it amused her to think how neatly she could summarise her life for strangers: Maeve was sleeping okay, she'd worked in marketing, she lived in Orange now, she'd left Sydney to raise her daughter.

When James's youngest brother, Michael, asked how she'd become friends with James, Poppy realised she had no idea. Forty-eight hours ago she wouldn't even have said they were friends, but they'd just spent a whole day together, their conversation floating from funny to sad to serious to stupid.

James bumped her knee under the table and caught her eye. Poppy bumped his back with a playful smirk. She hadn't realised their legs were so close, and now, wow, yep, his thigh was touching hers. Did he realise? Poppy tried to surreptitiously inch her leg away, ignoring the fact that all the heat in her body now seemed to be redirecting to her left knee.

'I helped deliver Maeve,' James said.

'No way!' cried Kate. Her expression twisted from wonder to shock to alarm. 'How . . . was that?'

Poppy tried not to wince and wrenched her knee cleanly to the right. 'No comment,' she replied, grimacing.

'Wait, wait, wait!' interrupted Michael, turning to James. 'You mean you pulled the baby out? You were at the *business end*?!' His eyes were wide with horror.

'Not quite,' said James. 'But I will say . . .'

Kate threw a scrunched-up serviette at him. 'Patient confidentiality, Jimmy boy!'

James threw up his hands in surrender. 'Poppy was a star, that's all I'll say. But yes, it is quite funny that we're friends now.'

Poppy's ears were burning suddenly. The casual compliments from James were starting to accumulate like weights in her chest. She didn't know what to do with them. Ignore them? Assume he was like this with everyone? Was she so emotionally stunted after nine years with Patrick that she'd forgotten guys could be friendly, no strings attached?

'Even if you had been swearing like a truck driver there would have been no judgement from me,' said Kate, and her sisters-in-law nodded vigorously. 'These men have no idea what we go through.'

Michael piped up, 'I dunno, sis. Maggie almost tore my hand off she was gripping me so hard and her fingernails were *sharp*. It was pretty intense for me too.'

SPECIAL DELIVERY

Kate and Maggie looked at each other meaningfully before walloping him over the head in unison. The rest of the table laughed.

'Well, Poppy, since you had to go through childbirth with James, I think it's only fair we share some of his embarrassing stories,' declared Kate.

'Where do we start?' quipped Mike.

'He was *obsessed* with Adam Gilchrist,' supplied Dave.

'Ah yes!' cried Kate. 'The cricket phase!'

'And remember his side fringe?!'

'The emo phase!'

'And when he'd play Blink 182 at the cricket nets!?'

'The emo cricket phase!'

The barbs volleyed across the table as James looked on in mock horror. When Michael began telling a story about an ex-girlfriend, James finally interrupted. 'That's enough,' he said, laughing. 'A man needs to maintain an air of mystery.'

It was like Poppy had snuck into a secret society of coded in-jokes and they were delighted to have a new audience. Among themselves they argued about who ate the most, who whinged the most, who was funniest, who was smartest, who was their mum's favourite, who was Mary's favourite. Everything was a competition with stakes that were tiny but hilarious and they laughed till they cried as they fervently tried to one-up each other.

It wasn't long before trays of cakes and slices appeared on the table and Kate declared the kids were allowed to eat the rest of the decorations. Lunch had flown. There had been so many jokes to keep up with and stories to file away for later,

Poppy had barely had time to chew. She'd just finished her second piece of Mars Bar slice and was packing her stuff to walk back to her cabin when Kate appeared beside her.

'You coming later?' she asked, as Poppy shoved the picnic rug into the pram undercarriage.

Poppy stood up and brushed her hair back. 'Later?'

'All us young ones—and I use that term very generously—head down to the dam at sunset. It's a tradition. Didn't James tell you?'

Poppy glanced over Kate's shoulder to where James stood chatting to some of the aunts. She felt a stab of . . . something. Why hadn't he mentioned it? Two days ago she wouldn't have expected anything from him. After today . . . well, he'd had plenty of chances to bring it up.

'Maybe he doesn't want me there.' She tried to say it jokingly but it came out stilted. 'I couldn't come anyway,' she said. 'I can't leave Maeve.'

'Of course he wants you to come!'

'What's this?' asked James, strolling over.

'I was telling Poppy she has to come to the dam for sunset. Harper can babysit Maeve.'

'Yeah, sure,' said James, waving the flies off his sister's shoulder. Was Poppy imagining it, or did he look uncomfortable?

'No, really, I don't want to intrude. I've imposed enough already.'

'No way, you should come!' cried Kate. 'It's very chill. Just drinks and music. The chat gets very funny once the rum comes out.'

James sniggered. 'I don't know if you're selling it that well, sis. Poppy might not want to see that side of us.'

SPECIAL DELIVERY

'Honestly, I'm fine. It's your special family time.'

'You're coming,' said Kate firmly. 'Jimmy, you can walk Harper over later and pick up Poppy. Bring a jumper,' she said to Poppy. 'It gets cold.'

James shrugged as if to say 'decision made'. His expression was as unreadable as ever.

Poppy pushed the pram back down the road. A flock of galahs swooped across the valley like rose-tinted gossamer in the breeze. If James didn't want her there, she didn't want to go. But then, Kate had invited her, and she liked Kate.

She didn't know what to do. She didn't want to seem clingy, but if they were friends (were they?) he wouldn't think that, would he?

The dam was now dotted with boats. The distant whirring of motors purred on the breeze and gum leaves rustled above her. Did everyone find the real world this tricky? She wondered. Before she'd had Maeve, she'd been insulated by corporate life, where there were clear standards of behaviour and you could trace your course of action on a neat decision tree. If yes, do this; if no, do that. Even at school, everyone had been institutionalised enough to decipher wrong from right and weird from cool, but out here, in the real world, every line was so fuzzy. People could be vague and chatty and bump your knee, and it was up to you whether you read into that or not.

Poppy asked herself again, more sternly this time: *Should I go to the dam?* Despite using her most intimidating internal voice, she still had no idea.

CHAPTER 22

'Ding-dong!' James's silhouette filled the doorframe again. 'We're here.'

'Hi,' said Poppy, standing up from the floor, where she'd been lying next to Maeve scrolling through her #FoodBaby-filled Instagram feed. For lack of making a decision, it seemed she had—by default—decided to go to the dam. She'd also, for lack of active decision-making, not texted Patrick. All things considered though, this was progress.

'You guys match!' exclaimed Harper. Poppy had changed into a pair of leggings and a baggy old Canterbury rugby jumper. James was wearing an old rugby jumper too, similarly faded and ratty around the cuffs.

'Lucky I didn't wear my leggings,' said James with a smile, and Poppy felt a rush of fondness, as though she'd known he was going to say that. She hurriedly pushed the thought away.

Poppy showed Harper around the cabin—somewhat pointlessly, given they all had the same floorplan. 'Here are the bottles and the dummies. I've sterilised everything, so you don't have to worry about that, and her toys are here if she gets a bit grumbly, and her nappies are here, and I've written a list of what calms her down. And here's my phone number. You won't need to bath her, but all her moisturisers and things are in the cabinet in the bathroom. I don't think you'll need them, but it's probably good to know . . .'

Harper smiled. 'I'm sure we'll be fine.'

'Okay . . .' said Poppy. She had nothing else to say. She picked up Maeve, held her tightly and kissed the crown of her head. 'Bye, my precious girl. I'll miss you.'

'I'll take good care of her,' said Harper, prising her gently from Poppy's arms. 'You just relax.'

Poppy's insides were a tightly coiled spring. She was leaving her only child with a teenager in a cabin with paper-thin walls. It would probably blow over in a strong wind! It could burn down! There could be a snake in here somewhere (the oven?!). There could be murderers in this campground. Come to think of it, this was the perfect setting for a true-crime documentary.

'Ready to go?' asked James, placing a light hand on her shoulder.

His touch startled her, yanking her back to the present. Harper was cooing at Maeve, whose eyes were flickering delightedly over the teenager's dangling earrings.

Poppy picked up her phone from the bench and nodded. 'I'm only a phone call away,' she reminded Harper, who bobbed her head, smiling.

Outside, the cool sunset air tickled the skin between her ankle socks and leggings. The gum trees were black etchings on a neon sky. They trudged down the gravel path in silence and Poppy pulled the cuffs of her jumper over her fingers. She hoped Maeve wouldn't do a poo—she hadn't reminded Harper that the nappies had to be put on with the picture of the monkey on the front, not the back. That could be confusing. She looked behind them to check how far they'd walked. Should she quickly run back and tell her? She checked her phone. No reception to text her. Damn.

'Just over there,' James said, pointing to a cluster of chairs and utes around a campfire by the water's edge. Legs dangled from the open ute trays and the tune of Keith Urban's 'Somebody Like You' floated across the breeze. The surface of the dam reflected the pink and gold of the sky.

Poppy looked back at the cabin. She could say hi to everyone and then jog back and tell Harper. That would be the polite thing to do, right? She couldn't make James wait here-but-not-quite-there while she faffed about.

'Hey guys!' called Kate, swinging down from the tray of a Ford Ranger. 'Drinks?' She opened an esky and pulled out a Carlton for James and something pink and bottled for Poppy.

'Guava Cruisers?' exclaimed Poppy, taking the bottle and turning it over in her hands. 'Is this the 2000s?'

'They still sell them!' quipped Kate gleefully. 'You have to admit, they *are* delicious—and super convenient in removing the burden of drinking wine from plastic cups.'

James snorted. 'Because that is such a burden, sis.'

'Shut up, Jimmy boy, I know you love a guava Cruiser. You'd be drinking them too if you weren't trying to impress.'

SPECIAL DELIVERY

'I'm fine for anyone to see me drinking Cruisers. I just don't want to deal with the pink teeth and bad dancing that seem to follow.'

'Dancing?' asked Poppy. She had the distinct impression that Kate and James were having a whole conversation beyond their actual words.

'I can confirm dancing is inevitable,' said Kate. 'You should see these young kids once the sun goes down. Everyone's an Usher. Or a Bieber. Or whoever's dancing for the kids these days. Don't ask me, I still have the 2009 *So Fresh* album in the car. Let's sit down and chat before we get interrupted. I want the uncensored labour story.'

Kate steered Poppy to a tartan blanket covering the back of a ute and they sat down. Poppy glanced back towards the cabin. When would be a good time to jog back? Maybe in the dark, so her neurotic mothering wouldn't be so obvious? She probably had forty minutes until Maeve's bowels kicked in. She checked her watch.

'Cheers,' sang Kate. 'To sunsets and teenage babysitters.'

'. . . Cheers,' Poppy agreed after a pause, willing herself not to look back at the cabin.

'You don't need to worry about Maeve,' Kate assured her. 'Harper is a pro. Nothing phases her.'

'I was thinking I might pop back . . .'

'Noooo! That would be a waste of energy and important socialising time. What are you worried about? Harper not knowing Maeve needs to sleep on her back? Or which way the nappy goes on? Or how long the bottle needs in the microwave? I promise you, she knows it all.'

Far out, thought Poppy. *I didn't tell Harper half that stuff. I already failed and I didn't even realise!*

'Don't worry,' Kate repeated. 'Being a new mum is the best experience you'll ever have—but also kind of the crappest, so when you have access to a free babysitter and deliciously fizzy bottled cocktails, you need to seize those opportunities.'

The music was slowly cranked louder, and as dusk settled into night the ute's headlights were turned on, casting a hazy glow across the campfire. Poppy curled her toes in her sneakers and angled her face towards the warmth of the flames.

The dust, the fire, the flannelette, the hands scrunched into rugby jumpers warding off the cold, everyone drinking cans of beer and pre-mixed rum—Poppy hadn't seen this world in forever. It made her feel young again and, simultaneously, ridiculously old.

'What's this boom-boom-tap-tap crap we're dancing to?' asked James, appearing at the ute. In the light of the fire he was all jawline and cheekbones and glittering eyes. Poppy wished half-heartedly he was a tad less attractive; it kept causing embarrassing sensations under her skin. Then again, under the cover of almost-darkness and with a pleasantly tipsy buzz, it was prime time for a perve.

'Who kidnapped you from the retirement village?!' shrieked Kate. 'You sound senile, Jimmy!'

'I can't keep dancing, sis. This music is making my ears bleed. It doesn't have any lyrics, for god's sake. You can't just replace words with synthesisers and think that'll make a song.'

'I think the youth of today would beg to differ,' said Kate, pointing at her cousins breakdancing in TikTok-style shuffles on the other side of the campfire.

'Give me some Lynyrd Skynyrd or Garth Brooks over this crap any day,' muttered James.

Poppy smiled. When she was in year ten she'd paid thirty dollars for the latest Garth Brooks CD and had studiously learned all the lyrics by heart.

'Oi!' yelled Kate to the dancing teenagers. 'Can we get some music for the oldies over here?' She turned back to James. 'As thanks for taking control, I will expect a full dancefloor contribution from you.' She strode over to the teenage aux cord controllers, and within seconds a familiar twang of guitar chords sounded across the melee.

'Ah, good choice, kids.' James eased himself up onto the ute tray next to Poppy. '"Sweet Home Alabama" was my theme song in high school.'

'God, you are a loser,' Kate teased as she rejoined them. 'You've never even been to Alabama. How could it have been your theme song?'

'It was in my cowboy phase.'

Kate cackled. 'That's right! The John Deere and belt buckle phase. How did you ever pick up?'

'She has no idea what she's talking about,' James said to Poppy. 'I was a stud.'

'*Was* being the operative word,' Kate retorted.

James shrugged good-naturedly. 'I peaked too early.'

Poppy chuckled, trying to ignore the flare of intrigue in her chest. Was that a confession that he'd been a massive player—and was he still? Was that what 'happily single' meant? He definitely had player potential, in that he was over thirty and still had a full set of teeth. The fact he was here, though, with his family, was somehow comforting.

Poppy tipped more guava deliciousness down her throat as the stamping boots stirred clouds of dust around the campfire. The last notes of 'Sweet Home Alabama' rang out and James cheered and clapped his hand against his beer. Poppy grinned. Who cared if he was a player? *Definitely* not her—especially when she was drinking stuff that tasted like sherbet and listening to embarrassingly sentimental music with people who loved it as much as she did. This was so *fun*. She hadn't done anything like this in . . . well, years.

With Patrick, she had bounced around the same suburbs and workplaces and bougie travel destinations as their friends. Anyone new they met was already a friend of a friend—a PLU, as Patrick called them: People Like Us. They were people who drank craft beer and twenty-five-dollar cocktails, who holidayed in Aspen and Santorini, and drove Teslas to offset their air travel. Ugh, and Patrick drove the biggest Tesla of all. If there was a more ostentatious way of virtue-signalling, Poppy didn't know it. But she'd stayed with him for *nine years*. She was the mother of his baby. It all seemed a blur now. He'd convinced her so easily that every day was an excuse for more fun, but that more fun required more money, and more money required more work, and more work required more opportunities to let off steam, and so the cycle continued. There wasn't time to breathe or think because there was always another flashy event to attend, another gift to be opened. It was a dizzying whirlwind which she'd let herself be caught up in—for *nine years*.

'What's your dancefloor song of choice, Poppy?' asked Kate, breaking her train of thought. 'What am I requesting next from the teenyboppers?'

'Well,' said Poppy slowly, dimly aware through the Cruiser buzz that no matter the crowd, her taste in music was generally considered embarrassing. But what the hell. 'I do love "Wagon Wheel".'

'Yes!' exclaimed Kate. 'That is exactly what we need right now.' She hoisted herself off the tray again.

'"Wagon Wheel", hey?' asked James, looking at her sideways. His eyes danced with amusement.

Poppy shrugged. 'I may be recently relocated from Sydney, but I am born and raised Central West—Central *Best*,' she clarified with a salute of her bottle.

'You forget I'm born and raised Central West too,' said James, a mischievous glint flashing across his eyes.

'So?'

'"Wagon Wheel" is my jam. And'—he paused dramatically—'I've got some moves.' He plonked his beer on the edge of the ute tray and grabbed her hand. 'Come on, McKellar. Let's show these young ones a thing or two.'

Poppy felt herself being dragged off the ute and pulled towards the makeshift dancefloor. Her body had no choice but to follow her hand. Her foot tripped over the uneven ground and her cheek bumped against the cotton of his jumper. She could smell his aftershave through the smoke.

'Follow my lead,' yelled James over the music as he tugged her wrist, propelling her towards him. She landed against his chest with an ungraceful head knock and he grabbed her other hand to spin her around.

With every beat of the music, James pulled her close then pushed her away, twirling her outwards then yanking her back. His hands guided her as their bodies moved in a chaotic rhythm, both of them shaking with laughter. Around them, boots swirled in the dust and everyone—Poppy included—roared the lyrics from the bottom of their lungs.

They twirled and dipped and swung and spun and it was exhilarating and exhausting and frankly surreal. It was like a time machine had pulled up and offered free rides to the noughties—pimples and alcohol poisoning not included. Poppy could hardly breathe she was laughing so hard.

At the final chorus, James spun Poppy to his chest, one hand on her back, the other clasping her hand and Poppy was suddenly aware of their closeness. She could see the fibres of his shirt, the creases around his eyes. Her singing dropped in volume as she realised their eyes were locked. James had gone quiet too. They were still dancing, swaying awkwardly together in the campfire glow, but singing seemed too frivolous now. She wanted to blink but she couldn't. The song was going to end in less than thirty seconds. This would all be over in an instant. She felt James's fingers tighten on hers. His eyes were glittering more than she'd ever seen. She looked at his lips. *Fuck!* She hadn't meant to do that, but it had already happened! And the intensity in his eyes hadn't wavered. Was his hand slipping towards her lower back?

Shit! This nanosecond had become too intense. What was happening?!

James suddenly jerked his head back as though he had whiplash and dropped her hand like it had burned him. The song faded to the finish and a Taylor Swift crowd-pleaser began to blare through the ute speakers. 'Er, right . . . thanks,' James stuttered. He tipped his head and gave an awkward bow, stepping backwards.

Poppy's head was spinning. The Cruisers and the twirling and that . . . *moment*—what the hell had happened? 'No problem,' she said, putting her hand to her temple. 'I think I'm getting too old for that kind of cardio. Or Cruisers. Or both.'

James didn't laugh—or even smile—as she'd expected him to. He just turned abruptly and stalked back to the ute as if he couldn't stand to be in her company for a moment longer.

The campfire smoke suddenly tasted bitter in Poppy's throat. Around her, teenagers stamped their feet in the dust, bellowing an unapologetically tuneless rendition of 'Shake It Off.'

CHAPTER 23

'So in summary, you're not fucked.' Dani's voice rang out in Poppy's AirPods as the paddocks whizzed past outside. 'You had a fun weekend, did your ten thousand steps, ate some good food, there was a tiny moment of . . . let's call it *intrigue*, in which you did nothing—and I repeat *nothing*—embarrassing other than a teensy-weensy tongue perve, and then everything after that was fine. So, I repeat: not fucked.'

Poppy groaned into her speedometer. 'Um, first, can you never say *tongue perve* again as though that's an actual thing? And second, it was not a tongue perve. I just happened to glance in his lower face region. And third, all of this is easy for you to say from your sunshine-y harbourside city, but you have no idea what my weekend was like. Everything at that bloody dam was so full of subtext.'

'You're making it sound very dramatic.'

'It was!'

SPECIAL DELIVERY

'Hon, have you considered that maybe you're reading into things too much?'

Dani did have a point. It was a point that Poppy had rolled around in her head constantly since she'd left the campfire. She'd been thinking about it when Kate and James cheerfully popped in the next morning, when James offered to check the radiator before she drove home, when he said, 'See ya later,' when he could have said, 'Bye.' Had she forgotten what friendliness was? Or was this something more?

'You've got a four-month-old, Pops. You have enough excitement in your life already; you don't need to add another layer of complication.'

'I know. In between the poo explosions and leaky boobs, it's one big excitement-fest with me.'

Dani laughed. 'I'm serious, dude. You've got enough on your plate. If this bloke wants to be friendly, let him. If he doesn't want to be friendly, let him do that too. You don't need him, so it's no skin off your back whatever he does.'

'I hate you being so bloody wise.'

'I know, my dear, but I hate you for moving away from me, so we're square. Seriously, though, I have to tell you something important.'

'Is Nella finally accepting porridge?'

'Ha, no—' There was a muffled scratchy sound.

'What was that, Dan? The reception here is so crap.'

'It's Sam's'—*rrrr-rar-rar-rrrr*—'Can you hear me? It's Sam's . . .' *Rrrrr-rar.*

'His rum?'

Rar-rrrr.

'Oh no, I've lost you again, Dan.'

Rar-rrrr-rar-rar-rrrr.

'Sorry, Dan, I think the reception's dropped out, so I'll go now, but if you can hear me, I love you. Bye!'

Poppy ended the call and glanced in the rear-vision mirror at her sleeping daughter. Maeve had passed her first teenage babysitting experience with flying colours. (Well, perhaps it was Harper who had passed the test, but there was no harm in taking credit for her daughter's good behaviour.) Maeve had accepted the bottle, there had been no nappy leakage and she'd obligingly drifted off to sleep with barely a whimper.

When Kate had heard this, she declared it was proof that Poppy deserved the night out. 'A sign from the universe,' had been her exact words. Poppy wasn't keen to burst Kate's bubble, but she suspected it was more a case of dumb luck. She'd lost confidence in the power of the universe.

It hadn't always been this way. Once upon a time, when her greatest concern was her daily commute, a deep, unacknowledged part of Poppy had believed in the intrinsic power of balance. Without ever having verbalised it, at a cellular level she believed things would work out. Sometimes, for example, you missed the bus or had to spend the whole journey standing up with an armpit in your face. Other times, you could score a whole seat to yourself and watch a soothing episode of open-heart surgery on *Grey's Anatomy*. If you expected life to be pretty good, but also a tiny bit shit (for the sake of equilibrium, and yin and yang, and possibly feng shui), you could lead a fairly comfortable existence.

But then she'd discovered she was pregnant.

SPECIAL DELIVERY

In the first few hours after those two lines appeared, everything had absorbed a new level of significance. Cellophane-wrapped flowers for sale at the train station: a sign of new life. Random kids making eye contact on the escalators: attuned to her inherent motherliness. Pigeons stealing hot chips for their babies: the circle of life. Every moment and person around her suddenly felt *meaningful*. Until Patrick came home.

She'd waited up for him, nervously placing and re-placing the pregnancy test at different angles on the dining table that sat near the entry of their one-bedroom rental. She hadn't texted to see where he was because she didn't want him to think she was in a 'naggy mood'. She wanted him to arrive home fresh and unencumbered and full of love for her and their future(!).

As it happened, he arrived home in a sulk because someone had parked in his favourite car space. He was wearing his gym gear, but she could tell he must have had a few schooners afterwards as his arrival was tinged with a faint whiff of Coopers. It was just past 9 pm.

'Good day?' she'd asked, looping her arms around his waist in an effort to distract him from his mood.

'Fine,' he'd replied, disentangling himself. 'Need to shower.' He'd completely missed the pregnancy test lying on the table next to where he'd chucked his keys.

As the noise from the hot-water system filled the apartment, Poppy had the unsettling feeling that, already, this wasn't going to plan. She'd imagined him arriving home with a big smile, a kiss for her, maybe a sneaky bum grab and a heartfelt inquiry about her day. She'd imagined she'd be coy, but he'd see through her beaming happiness and notice the test with its two pink lines. He'd sweep her into his arms and spin her around like a princess—the kind of move he pulled when he had an audience.

'What?' he asked, noticing her pacing when he emerged from the shower.

Poppy's eyes were wide and she couldn't speak for nerves. She jerked her head towards the dining table, the pregnancy test perched atop it like a ticking timebomb.

Patrick swivelled his head from Poppy to the table and back. 'What's this? Is this a joke?'

Poppy shook her head.

'What the hell? Really?' Patrick snatched up the test and peered at the plastic window with the two pink lines staring back at him.

'I did a test at work this afternoon. I wanted to tell you in person.'

Patrick suddenly dropped the test. 'Yuck, I forgot you peed on this—gross,' he said, wiping his hands on the back of his pyjama pants.

Poppy giggled nervously. 'I didn't pee on the whole thing, only the bit that's covered by the plastic cap, which . . . oh it doesn't matter . . .' He'd already stopped listening to her babble.

'How?' asked Patrick, glaring at her. 'You're careful, right?'

Poppy scoffed. Their pull-out method of contraception was definitely *not* careful, and definitely *not* her sole responsibility. The very name of it indicated the onus was on the guy: he literally had to *pull out*.

'What do we do?' asked Patrick.

'I think it's obvious, isn't it? We're having a baby.'

'What?' A muscle tensed in Patrick's neck.

With a sickening thud in her stomach, Poppy realised that this scenario was rapidly veering off course.

'Babe, we're not ready for this.'

'We've been together for nine years, Patrick. I'm thirty. We are textbook ready. I mean, yes, it would be nice to have planned it better, but we would have reached this point at some stage.'

'Whoa, babe! These are some huge assumptions you're making.'

'You're telling me you don't want this?' spluttered Poppy.

'No! But yes. I dunno. Jesus, Poppy! You drop this shit on me out of the blue and expect me to go along with your crazy plans!'

'Patrick, I didn't get pregnant by myself! I wasn't turkey-basting myself with your stolen jizz, for Christ's sake. You know what sex does. You're a grown man. You knew the risk.'

'And that's what it was! A risk, Poppy!' He sighed. 'Fuck me, do you really think we're ready for this?'

A switch flicked in Poppy's brain and it dawned on her that this was it. This was how they'd reached the end. With a pregnancy. It could have been the happiest day of her life. In a fog of confusion and swelling anxiety, she realised it was about to turn into the worst.

'I mean, seriously, babe, we're too young for this stuff.' Patrick was assuming her silence indicated agreement. 'We've got too much living to do, too much fun to have.'

He moved towards her, his arms open. 'You can't seriously have thought—'

'Don't touch me,' Poppy snapped. She rarely spoke like that to Patrick—she couldn't bear the conflict—but this had triggered something visceral. She stepped around him and stalked to the bedroom, slamming the door behind her.

Poppy never asked for anything from Patrick. She never expected anything from him. Most of the time, she was happy to go along with his plans, laugh at his recycled jokes and play the role of the awestruck girlfriend, but this felt different. This was a moment they could seize, this was a moment they could recount at sweet sixteens and weddings: the moment they discovered they were pregnant. Of all his stories, this could be the craziest. But not even that was enough.

Poppy stood at the foot of their bed and flopped face first onto the mattress. She wanted to scream into the pillow. Less than ten seconds later, she heard the television flick on. Patrick didn't speak to her for the rest of the night.

Now, as the paddocks whipped by in a haze of greenish brown, Poppy realised it didn't matter if she had 5G service or not. Patrick was never going to call.

CHAPTER 24

With her quilted jacket and muumuu-style dress with the cartoon-sized buttons, the elderly woman before her looked so innocent. Her face bore wrinkles of long-past stories. Her eyes twinkled with the joy of a life lived in digital detox. She was a vision of ageing gracefully. She was also a sneaky rat.

'Good morning, *Mary*.' Poppy lowered herself onto the wicker chair next to Maeve, who sat in the pram trying to ingest her whole fist.

'Morning, love,' replied Mary, clamping her lips shut in poorly concealed glee. How had Poppy not realised that smile was genetic? Her neighbour turned to the teapot and began pouring. The teacups tinkled on their saucers: *tee-hee-hee!* Maeve gurgled happily. The amusement in Mary's eyes was contagious. Poppy clenched her cheeks to suppress a reluctant smile. She'd been aiming to convey Extreme Indignance, but Mary was cracking her like an egg.

'How was Burrendong?' Mary asked.

'Why don't you ask *James*?'

'Already have.'

'Mary!'

Mary smiled kindly. 'I know, love, but I really did think you deserved a holiday, and I knew you wouldn't go if you knew James was going to be there. He told me as much.'

In the pram, Maeve bobbed her head between them, intrigued. Her ears always pricked at the mention of James— probably because she thought he was the dog.

Poppy raised an eyebrow. 'How did that even come up?'

'Oh, you know, we got talking after I lent him my pack of conversation starters.'

'They're yours?!'

'Of course. Did you like them? They're from the Innovations catalogue, last November. Anyhow, when James mentioned you might need a break, I suggested inviting you to the cabin and he agreed . . .'

He agreed?!

'. . . but he said you wouldn't go if he was there because of some dilly-dally about tomato paste, so then we just resolved to, er, I think his words were "play a straight bat, Granny".'

'Is that cricket speak for deflecting the truth?'

'I have no idea. I was too distracted by the granny jibe. I'm much too young for that nonsense.'

Poppy snorted, a bubble of laughter swelling in her chest. The idea of James scheming with his grandmother was outright ridiculous. She leaned over and grabbed a jam drop. 'I thought you said us single girls need to stick together.'

'Oh, we do, but families have to stick together too. So really, this was a convenient merging of the Venn diagram.'

Poppy bit her lip, torn between laughter and exasperation. There was a shrewd mastermind underneath that old-lady facade.

'Lucky for you I'm very forgiving,' said Poppy, popping the biscuit in her mouth as Maeve made a clapping motion at nothing in particular.

'And lucky for you,' said Mary, smiling, 'I've been asked to get your phone number.'

Crumbs shot out from Poppy's mouth. 'Wh-what?!' she choked, thumping her chest.

'Kate wants your number so she can organise a girls' dinner.'

'Oh.' *Ohhhh!* Thank god no-one else saw that awkwardly presumptuous reaction. She definitely wasn't handing out her number to anyone unless they could offer medical advice, handyman services and/or extremely platonic friendship. Poppy cleared her throat of the jam drop blockage. 'Oh, okay, yes, definitely. I can give you my number. It would be great to catch up with Kate.'

'Lovely,' said Mary, producing a pen and paper from the breast pocket of her jacket with a flourish. 'And I'll keep your number on the fridge in case there's an emergency and my family need to contact you.' She flashed Poppy a smile. 'I'm getting so old, you see.'

Poppy narrowed her eyes and took the pen. As she scrawled her number across the pale pink notepad, Mary's eyes shining with a barely suppressed smirk, Poppy had the distinct impression she was walking straight into a trap.

CHAPTER 25

The Bustle was heaving. The food festival always brought a few thousand interlopers into town who worked their way through a checklist of Orange's most Instagrammable hangouts. Winery with Shetland ponies: check. Pub with open fire and Chesterfields: check. Coffee-shop-slash-art-mecca: check. There was a distinctly Sydney vibe in the air. The leather caps and Balenciaga sneakers were a dead giveaway.

'Reckon it's worth trying Coffee Bucks?' Henry was standing by her shoulder in an olive green wool jumper.

'Depends. Are you comfortable with arsenic in your coffee?'

'Fair comment. I rue the day I was introduced to good coffee. I never used to mind a Coffee Bucks flat white. Amazing how they could press a button and that frothy goodness would magically appear.'

'I hear they have a vegan menu now. You could try that out?'

'Nah, if I went back, I'd have to go a vanilla slice, for old time's sake. Sometimes I actually miss that taste of rubber.'

Henry sighed. 'I guess I'll have to wait in line like the rest of these Eastern Suburbs plebs.'

'Did you have a good Easter?' asked Poppy as they waited.

'Nice enough,' replied Henry. 'Mum made too much food. Dad fell asleep watching television, snored like a foghorn, got grumpy when we tried to wake him up. Pretty standard Marshall behaviour really.'

'Did Willa enjoy it?'

'Oh.' Henry paused. 'She had Easter with her family. Not married yet, so we decided to divide and conquer before the "one-off-one-on" starts for good, you know?'

'Of course,' Poppy agreed, her brain replaying that look of unease which had flitted almost imperceptibly across Henry's face. *What was going on there?*

'What about you?' asked Henry. 'Did you do the obligatory photo shoot of Maeve wearing bunny ears? My feed was clogged with stacks of that content so I might have missed your post.'

'Shame,' deadpanned Poppy. 'We went the whole hog. Got Maeve in a bunny suit, in an Easter basket, surrounded by live ducklings, doves flying overhead.'

'Gutted I missed it.'

They grinned at each other; another one of those 'I know you get it and I love that you get it' moments that always gave her a slightly teenage rush.

As was their rhythm, they neutralised the moment by moving on to generic topics: Henry's nieces and nephews becoming extremely hyperactive and then sugar-crashingly depressed after gobbling all their chocolate; modern kids getting fruit from the Easter Bunny; the guesstimated annual turnover of Coffee Bucks. After they'd finally ordered coffees, they went to find a table.

'You'd think we were at a yacht club,' said Henry, looking around at the crowd as he sat down and Poppy parked the pram. 'I've never seen so many pairs of white jeans in a confined space.' It was true; there was an excessive amount of slim-legged white denim surrounding them. 'Are they the people who actually buy this stuff?' he asked, tipping his head towards the artwork-laden walls. 'Most of it looks like a four-year-old painted it.' He pointed at a canvas on the wall behind them, a jungle of pink lines on a lime green backdrop. 'I could do that in ten minutes. It looks like fingerpainting.'

'As if, Henry,' said Poppy. 'That composition is genius. And besides—who cares if it looks like a four-year-old painted it? Maybe that's the point.'

The art was one of the main reasons Poppy kept coming back to The Bustle. It was like having coffee in a gallery without all the self-conscious white space and echoey austerity. Looking at the canvases was meditative and restorative somehow, like therapy by osmosis.

Henry looked confused. 'I don't get it. Why would you buy something that looks like a kindergarten project?'

'Because it speaks to you. Art doesn't need to fit a definition, Henry. It's about how it makes you *feel*.'

She glanced at one on her left which she was desperately hoping no-one would buy. It was a swirl of pink, orange and yellow on a crimson background. The colours were startling but beautiful and the lines were hypnotic. Sometimes she thought it looked like a giant flower in the breeze; at other times it looked like a cyclonic whirlpool. Blossoming, drowning, it was all so similar.

'My *feeling* is that someone is making a lot of money ripping off kindy kids,' said Henry. 'I will save my money for a framed Wallabies jersey, thanks.'

Poppy rolled her eyes. 'Then I sincerely hope Willa is in charge of your home decorating.'

Henry smiled but it didn't reach his eyes. 'Definitely.'

Poppy's phone pinged with a new message and it vibrated across the table.

'Unknown number,' Henry said, pushing her phone back towards her.

Poppy picked it up.

Hi Poppy. James here. Been on night shifts so haven't been doing the golf course loop but realised the Block finale is this Sunday. Let me know if you're keen to watch. J

Another message buzzed: *PS Got your number from Mary.*

Poppy bit her cheek to stifle a reluctant smile. *Mary!*

'Spam?' asked Henry, as she put the phone facedown on the table.

'No, a friend,' said Poppy. 'Need to save his number.'

'His?' asked Henry.

'Yeah, this guy I know is obsessed with *The Block* and wants me to watch it with him.'

'*The Block*, like the TV show?'

Poppy nodded. Was Henry prying?

'Sounds like a very lame attempt at getting you to hang out with him, if you ask me.'

'Oh, it's not like that at all,' Poppy said in a rush. 'We're hardly even friends; he's just random like that. We spent Easter together and somehow we got talking about *The Block* and he said I should watch it. As I said, he's a bit random.'

Henry's brow creased. 'So you're not really friends, but you spent Easter together and now you're pretty much making plans to Netflix and chill?'

'Yes . . . and no,' said Poppy, feeling her neck redden. 'It's just a dumb show. And he's clearly not interested in me, so it's nothing like that . . . if that's what you're thinking.' *Jesus, how did this conversation end up here?!*

'Is he gay?'

'No—well, I'm not sure, but I don't think so. But then again, maybe. Why?'

'Then how do you know he's not interested?'

'Well, he clearly isn't,' said Poppy. 'I'm too, you know . . .' She gestured at Maeve, who was watching the whole exchange, fascinated. 'He wouldn't be interested in me . . . in this. That would be ridiculous.'

Henry levelled his gaze at her with disconcerting force. 'Poppy, you're single and attractive, and believe me, men aren't always good blokes—no matter how much crap reality TV they watch. Just be careful, okay?'

'I'm not . . . you're being . . .' Poppy trailed off as the waitress arrived with their coffees.

Henry stood up and grabbed his takeaway cup. 'I'm being a friend,' he said. 'You need to watch out for yourself, Pops.'

Poppy watched him weave his way to the door through the throng of white-jeaned women. Henry was being ridiculous.

SPECIAL DELIVERY

James *was* a good guy. Like, sure, he could be dickishly robotic sometimes, and on first impression he'd appeared devoid of basic social skills, but she knew him better now. He wasn't an arrogant, unfeeling prick. Underneath that coolly self-confident exterior, he was a guy who twirled his cousins around a campfire dancefloor just to make them laugh. And *besides*, even if he was an infuriating robot man at times, what did it matter? He had no interest in her beyond sharing his love of Scott Cam.

And *also*, thought Poppy frowning angrily into her mug, Henry had no right to be so *annoying* about who she hung out with. He was still in his engagement love bubble with Willa. Why should he care about who she was spending time with? He hadn't shown much interest in the last ten years.

That's because you didn't let him, squeaked a voice in her head.

What did 'be careful' mean, anyway? Be careful of what? Men in general? Bad reality TV? Getting carried away, getting hurt? She wasn't likely to fall in love, for god's sake. There were certain babies who would get in the way of that, and it wasn't as though anyone would be seeking her out for some torrid one-night-only-style bedroom action. Lord knows, the nursing bras would turn off even the keenest bloke. James was a single guy with great shoulders and great hair in a town of single women. If he wanted a steamy night in Orange, there were much younger, hotter prospects on the Royal Hotel dancefloor every Saturday night who came with much less baggage and much better grooming.

Everyone could settle down. James had no interest in her— he had made that clear enough at the dam when he'd pretty much cricked his neck trying to get away from her after their dance. Henry had nothing to worry about and therefore she had no need to *be careful*. Her nights were free to spend as she pleased (minus the breastfeeding, obviously).

She texted back: *Sounds good. But can we do it at mine so I don't have to organise a babysitter?*

See? She had just invited a handsome guy over to her house with no pretext other than watching crappy TV. She would not overanalyse this invitation; it could be read as intended, and if it wasn't, then, whatever. She was Zen; she was not overthinking this.

A text buzzed back instantly.

Sounds great. J x

Poppy shoved her phone in the nappy bag and stood up to go. It was great she wasn't overthinking things or that 'x' could have really messed her up.

CHAPTER 26

'I'm redecorating!' called her mother from behind a tangled mess of eucalyptus branches and what appeared to be Paterson's curse.

'Mum, are they weeds?'

'I foraged them, darling! It's the new thing! The girls and I went down to the wetlands and we found all these glorious branches. Desmona said you'd pay a fortune for them in Sydney. I'm going to hang them from the light fixtures in the kitchen. It will be very French provincial. Like giant bushels of lavender, only—'

'Only Paterson's curse.'

'No need to be so snippy, darling, I hear this is all the rage in the city. Now, where is my beautiful girl?' She heaved the bunch of branches onto the kitchen bench and dusted herself down, looking around Poppy for the pram.

'I left her with Dad. They're in the front room watching the Panthers game.'

'We can't have that,' said Chrissie, brushing past her daughter to walk down the hall. 'Paul! I'm coming to get Maeve. I will not have you indoctrinating her with all this rugger-bugger palaver. It is her right as a child of a single mother to never have to endure a sports match unnecessarily.'

They entered the front room to find Maeve bouncing happily on her grandfather's knee and sucking a Jatz cracker.

'Dad!' cried Poppy. 'Maeve hasn't started solids yet.'

'What?' asked her father, oblivious.

'Ugh,' groaned Poppy, pulling the cracker from her daughter's mouth. 'I was hoping her first food would be slightly less trans-fatty.'

'She's enjoying it,' her father insisted.

Poppy picked up a teething ring from the carpet, wiped it on her shirt and gave it back to her daughter. 'Here, Maevey. This is a more age-appropriate chew toy.'

'I gave you *one job*, Paul—make yourself scarce—and you still manage to stuff it up,' groaned Chrissie theatrically.

'If you want my help in the kitchen, I'm ready,' he replied.

'No!' cried Poppy and her mum in unison. Paul had a habit of burning everything, including the utensils, which infused everything with a poisonous plasticky smell.

Paul laughed and squeezed his granddaughter. 'Your first life lesson, Maevey: incompetence brings rewards.'

Chrissie rolled her eyes and took Maeve from her husband. 'My granddaughter is not being raised on this drivel. Modern men are not hapless fools, like the men of our generation. She will marry a man who can mow the lawn *and* cook her dinner.'

'Or a *woman* who can mow the lawn and cook her dinner,' countered Poppy's dad.

SPECIAL DELIVERY

'Or she'll be single and do it all herself,' added Poppy.

'Of course she will,' agreed Chrissie. 'My point is, Paul, you need to start helping around here so Maeve has some positive male role models in her life. She can't grow up seeing you glued to the television screen all the time. You need to contribute . . .'

Poppy and her dad shared a glance, barely stifling their amusement. They knew this rant back to front. It was long and superlative-laden, with just a touch of truth to it. (Poppy's dad may have been prone to burning things but he was also Chief Washer-Upper and Chief Calmer of the Head Chef—both critical duties in the kitchen.)

'Oh bugger!' cried Chrissie suddenly, thrusting Maeve at Poppy. 'I forgot to turn the oven off!' She raced into the kitchen, swearing at herself.

Poppy's dad smiled. 'Don't worry—I put the timer on. I knew she'd forget.'

Poppy laughed. Her dad was always quietly fixing things in the background.

A voice rang down the hall. 'I must have put the timer on! Clever me! Don't worry, lunch is saved!'

Poppy and her dad chuckled. Chrissie McKellar would never change.

Half an hour later, they sat down to a steaming homemade moussaka, the Panthers game still playing in the background and a bushel of Paterson's curse festooning the ceiling above them.

'This is going to be a lovely family tradition now you're back in Orange,' declared Chrissie. 'We should have family lunch at least once a month.'

'Why not weekly?' asked Paul.

'I have golf every third Sunday,' his wife reminded him. 'You should tell Dani to come one weekend,' she continued. 'And we could invite Henry and Willa.'

Poppy choked on her side salad. 'What? Why?'

'We talked about this, darling, remember? We said it would be good to all get together.'

'Oh, right,' muttered Poppy. So many plans flitted in and out of her mother's brain and yet this one had stuck? She noticed her mum and dad exchange a look and felt her hackles rise. They could be so *parental* sometimes. She swallowed her mouthful of lettuce. 'That sounds great,' she said brightly. 'I would love that.'

'Excellent,' said Chrissie. 'Now, next thing, I think I should take Maeve for one day a week.'

'Why? I'm doing okay, aren't I?' Poppy looked to her dad for support. 'Maeve is happy; we're making things work.'

'No-one's questioning your parenting, Pops,' said her dad.

'Just imagine a day for yourself,' continued her mum. 'You could do all those errands you're always telling me about. You could get a haircut. You could go to the gym. You could do whatever you want—and the upside is, I get more quality time with beautiful Maeve.'

Poppy's dad raised his napkin and spoke to Poppy behind it. 'Your mother wants an accessory for coffee with the other grandmas.'

Chrissie ignored him. 'I think Thursdays would be best, because Martha and Susie also have their grandkids on those days.'

SPECIAL DELIVERY

Poppy squeezed her daughter, who was sitting on her lap. The idea of letting her mother take the caregiving reins was slightly nerve-racking, but the prospect of a whole day of freedom was shamefully tempting. She would love a few hours to herself, though she felt guilty for even thinking that. 'Maybe we could start with the afternoons,' she suggested cautiously.

'Perfect,' her mother said. 'Thursday afternoons with Grandma. No sports viewing allowed.'

'No problem,' agreed her dad. 'We'll watch *Judge Judy* instead.'

Poppy laughed, a bubble of excitement swelling inside her. She was going to have *time*. She was going to have *space*. She could go places *without the pram*. Maybe she could even organise some job interviews, get her career back on track. She would be able to achieve so much!

'That reminds me,' said her mother cheerfully. 'A lady at golf mentioned I could sue Martha and Peter for removing the magnolia because there's legislation that covers tree disputes with neighbours. I could go to the Supreme Court!'

'What?!' spluttered Poppy. Her mind had drifted to visions of Thursday afternoon Reformer Pilates classes wearing cream leggings or something equally baby-unfriendly. 'You literally just said you were going to have grandma babycino dates with Martha. Why would you sue her?'

'It would be nothing personal, darling. I'm just upset that as a *good neighbour* and friend of more than twenty-five years, they haven't even consulted me about their landscaping.'

'Not true,' interjected Paul. 'They invited us over weeks ago to look at the plans.'

'That was all for show, Paul,' Chrissie retorted. 'They'd already had them drawn up by that stage.'

'They weren't likely to take you to the meetings with the landscaper now, were they?' he replied.

'You're missing the point. I mean, did Martha even consider my hellebores when she was making these decisions?!'

As Chrissie nattered on about the inadequacies of over-priced landscape architects, Maeve fell asleep in the crook of Poppy's arm. Hopefully those cream leggings from Nimble would be on sale soon. They'd be perfect for her vision of baby-free Pilates chic. And she could organise a coffee with some prospective employers. Network a bit, get her CV out there. This would be so achievable when she didn't have to leave the house with twenty kilos of baby paraphernalia.

On the table, Poppy's phone buzzed with a message.

Still on for Block epicness tonight?

Ah yes, James. In all the excitement she'd forgotten their not-date was tonight. Maybe they could have coffees on Thursday afternoons too, now that they were kind of friends? How civilised and delightful!

Using her left hand, so as not to disturb Maeve, Poppy tapped out a quick thumbs-up emoji.

?? was the response.

Poppy checked the thread and swore under her breath. She'd accidentally sent back an eggplant emoji. Oh bugger.

SORRY! she texted.

Fat fingers!

Meant to send thumbs up.

Penic texting now!

SPECIAL DELIVERY

*PANIC!
Sorry for all the texts!
Stopping now!

Poppy put her phone down and tried to slow her breathing to match her daughter's. Oh jeez, nothing was ever straightforward, was it?

'Who are you texting?' asked her mother, interrupting her own commentary on the merits of magnolia canopies.

'Ah . . .' Poppy didn't know how to introduce the concept of James to her parents. 'Dani,' she lied.

Her mother peered across the table to Poppy's phone, where an oversized eggplant emoji was still visible.

'Oh, of course,' said Chrissie. She turned to her husband. 'They're texting about my moussaka.'

'The lasagne?' he asked.

'It's moussaka, Paul. It's made with eggplant, you dill, not pasta.'

'What's the difference?'

'Less carbs,' explained Poppy.

'Yes, lots of women prefer eggplant,' added her mum.

Unbidden, a vision of James's chiselled body flooded Poppy's central cortex, his jeans stretched to the perfect tension across his butt. It was wildly inappropriate to think about friends that way, but she was dog-tired and clearly delirious. Her mind dipped to the denim below his belt buckle and she inexplicably felt like exploding with laughter.

She swallowed the final mouthful of moussaka and nodded enthusiastically. 'You're absolutely right, Mum,' she said. 'Now and then, we all love a bit of eggplant.'

CHAPTER 27

Poppy ran to the mirror for a quick check. Her hair was loose over a cashmere-blend jumper that she had paired with her 'good' leggings. She was aiming for casual, but not slobby, but still kind of attractive and, you know, clean. Cleanliness was a seriously hard vibe for new mums to nail.

'Pizza delivery,' called the voice behind the door.

'Shush,' Poppy said, opening it. 'You'll wake Maeve.'

'Shit, sorry,' said James, looking around as if Maeve might be asleep somewhere on the verandah. 'I'm just excited about super supreme with extra olives.'

'You won't regret it,' said Poppy, moving aside to let him in. 'The veggie to meat to olive ratio is perfect.'

James walked into the kitchen and put the pizza boxes on the counter. 'I got garlic bread too,' he said, fishing an aluminium-wrapped roll from a bag on his elbow. 'And this.' He handed her a bottle of red.

Poppy inspected the label. 'Nice. Your choice?'

SPECIAL DELIVERY

'I know you like your drinks guava-flavoured, but I wasn't sure how that would go with pizza. And the pepperoni is a red meat so I figured a shiraz would be a good match.' He spoke in that almost-smiling way she was getting used to. 'Maeve go down alright?'

'Oh, you know, with a complex combination of milk drunkenness, swaddling, patting, rocking and singing. Piece of cake. Actually, she slept through until four this morning. That was a record. By the time I'd finished feeding her it was five and I was so well rested I kind of thought of staying up. I didn't, obviously, that would be dumb, but I can tell you, four am wake-ups are actually amazing after months of broken sleep.'

'Wow, go Maeve!' said James. 'Who knows? Maybe tonight she'll sleep through till four thirty.'

'Don't jinx me!' hissed Poppy.

'Forget I said anything! This conversation never happened. Quick, change the subject!'

Poppy chuckled. 'It's fine. I should stop talking about our sleep patterns anyway. Sorry for boring you.'

'Not at all,' said James. 'It's my industry and Maeve happens to be one of my favourites, even though I am duty-bound to love all babies. But Maeve and I bonded, so we're tight.'

'Oh yeah?'

'Yeah. During her post-birth routine tests she was staring at me with those piercing eyes and I swear she looked deep into my soul.'

Poppy laughed. 'She *does* have piercing eyes! Sometimes she looks at me and I feel so intimidated, like she already knows her mum is a bumbling fool. Poor little Maeve. She's already past the ignorance-is-bliss stage.'

'Don't read into it too much. She's just a little girl with beautiful eyes.' James tipped his head towards her. 'They're exactly like yours.'

He held her gaze for a beat and Poppy felt her cheeks start to flush. She turned away and picked up the pizza. She was not going to overthink that accidental-but-maybe-not-accidental compliment. 'Shall we relocate to the TV?' she suggested.

'Definitely,' said James, checking his watch then grabbing the wine and garlic bread. 'The spectacle is about to unfold. We can't be late.'

James settled himself on the couch and began fiddling with the remote while Poppy fetched plates, cutlery and wineglasses. This was definitely the weirdest thing she'd done in a while. 'Channel Nine and chill,' Dani had dubbed it. She'd texted Poppy every day this week with obnoxious tips on how to make it a successful night (hence the eggplant lurking in her recent emojis). The advice ranged from Buzzfeed articles on '10 Hot Things Scott Cam Does With His Hands' to: *Put frankincense in ur essential oil diffuser for hypnotic properties. Handy in case u want light bulbs changed, beer refilled, sexy times with evil sexy man etc. etc. (NB making assumption this guy is sexy.) Please confirm/deny? Send pics if poss.*

'It's starting!' called James.

'Coming!'

Poppy settled herself on the armchair, tucking her feet underneath her as Scott Cam appeared on screen in a Bisley work shirt. James sat on the couch.

SPECIAL DELIVERY

The show itself was objectively terrible. So much contrived banter, so many toothy veneers, and way too many thick-framed glasses used to convey quirkiness. The contestants were so blandly typecast it felt satirical. James relished it all, nodding with satisfaction at the liberal use of power tools. His knee bounced reflexively to the determinedly upbeat soundtrack. It was a damning indictment of his cultural inferiority, she decided. A six-foot-four guy who was trained to care for vulnerable women and deliver babies was bound to have a chink in the armour somewhere.

When the final house sold for a cool $3.4 million and the camera zoomed in on the contestants popping a bottle of champagne, James grabbed the remote, dialled the volume down and turned to her.

'So?'

'So?'

'Can we agree that was epic?'

Poppy chortled, which made her choke on her wine. 'Sorry!' she gasped, trying to clear her airways and stifle the laughter that was fizzing up inside her. It was a losing battle. The giggles were shaking her whole body. 'Sorry!' she repeated. 'It's just . . . well, I think we can agree that was epic, but in a terrible way. Right?'

James stuck out his lower lip. 'I bare my soul to you through the medium of commercial TV, Poppy McKellar, and this is how you treat me?'

Poppy angled to face him properly and stretched her legs over the armrest of her chair. 'You give me wine and I will bare my soul in return. And my soul tells me that I never need to watch that ever again so long as we both shall live.'

'Luckily for you and unfortunately for me, we now have to wait a whole six months before the next season. Thanks for reminding me of that demoralising reality, Poppy. What will I do now at seven thirty every night? And don't you dare suggest *MasterChef*.' He picked up the empty bottle of wine. 'Damn, I need to drown my sorrows a bit more.'

Poppy sprang up. 'Hold on, I can help with that.'

She went to the kitchen and grabbed a bottle of red wine and a block of chocolate from the pantry and a punnet of strawberries from the fridge.

'Dessert,' she announced as she handed the bottle to James and put the chocolate and strawberries on the coffee table.

'Mmm, some nice aphrodisiac treats you've offered up here, McKellar,' said James, waggling his eyebrows suggestively.

Poppy waggled her eyebrows back. 'Ha! Glad you like Aldi chocolate. I aim to impress.'

'Clearly. I will assume this is your signature move. Ply a guy with red wine and then get him over the line with below-market-price chocolate.'

Poppy laughed. It was so far from the truth it was actually hilarious. She'd been with Patrick for so long, she had zero skills in the seduction game. She didn't have a Bumble profile, let alone a playbook for how to impress a guy. Come to think of it, maybe she should do more googling of that stuff. It would be a refreshing change from googling sleep regression articles. She may as well have it tattooed on her forehead: *Don't mind me, I have no moves.*

Although, it seemed she had said that last bit out loud.

'What do you mean you have no moves?' asked James. 'Everyone has moves. Even if they're crap moves, everyone has moves.'

'Not me. I've never needed moves so I never developed any. I am a woman without moves. No seductress potential here; everyone can keep calm and carry on.'

James was refilling their wineglasses. 'Didn't you have a boyfriend for almost a decade though? How did you nab him, if not with your seductive moves?' He looked at her and waggled his eyebrows again. For a good-looking guy, he looked embarrassingly stupid pretending to be sexy.

'We got together when I was twenty-two. We basically got drunk at a bar and went home together and then kept doing it until it became habit, so unless you count drinking my bodyweight in overpriced Jaegerbombs, I think I can say with confidence that I have no moves of the seductive variety.'

James peered at her over his wineglass. 'I don't believe you. You need moves even when you're in a relationship. How else do you get what you want?'

'Nope,' Poppy insisted, taking a large gulp of wine. 'I never needed to be sexy—just needed to know the routine. Tuesdays, Thursdays, weekends. Never after footy training, never after a three-course dinner. Super predictable, super easy—just a bit of him on top, me on top, maybe some doggie, then—'

'Stop!' cried James, covering his ears. 'Okay, you win, you have no moves. I don't need to hear about your past sex life!'

Poppy laughed, vindicated. How good was wine for eliminating oversharing anxiety? 'You asked for it. And that proves my point. I can't be sexy, so you are in no danger of being seduced while hanging out with me.'

James cocked his head. 'I don't think that's true.' He didn't waggle his eyebrows this time. He held her eyes for two long seconds and Poppy stopped laughing. A heat was creeping up her neck but also down to other body parts that hadn't felt like this in a long time.

James grabbed the remote. 'What are we watching now?'

Poppy exhaled and felt the adrenaline subside. After that moment, she would happily watch another twenty-four hours of soul-destroying reality TV if it kept things in neutral territory. 'Channel Nine and chill' was anything but chill.

★

As the credits began to roll after the re-run of *Happy Gilmore*, James stood. 'I'll clear up,' he announced.

With another bottle of wine under their belts, the conversation had flowed easily through the ad breaks. They'd magnanimously shared the last row of chocolate and thankfully there'd been no more talk of past sex lives. Poppy must have been imagining the earlier frisson. There was definitely none now that James had described cutting Mary's toenails.

'Honestly, don't worry,' said Poppy, jumping up, but James was already on his way to the kitchen with the pizza boxes and plates.

She found him with the dishwasher open, pulling out the clean plates.

'Here, let me,' said Poppy, trying to wedge herself in to help. The 1980s kitchen wasn't made for more than one user, especially if the second user was the size of James.

SPECIAL DELIVERY

'I've got it,' James insisted. 'You relax.' He looked around the kitchen. 'You can sit here and order me around.' He picked her up by the waist and lifted her onto the kitchen bench as casually and effortlessly as if she were a clean Tupperware container that he was unloading from the dishwasher. In the scheme of what usually went on in her kitchen, it was outrageously sexy. Poppy hoped her breathing wasn't as heavy and obvious as it sounded in her head.

She watched as he put the clean cutlery in the drawer and started opening cupboard doors to find her crockery shelves. The back of his t-shirt rose above his belt to reveal his toned back and Poppy's wine eyes enjoyed not looking away. When he began rinsing the dirty plates before putting them in the dishwasher, Poppy actually grinned. *This guy,* she thought. *This is the kind of guy who so many women would get off on. Handsome, house-trained, looks after his grandma.* She could imagine her mum foaming at the mouth with delight if she ever brought him home. She wondered if he liked watching sport as much as he liked playing it. She could picture him sitting in her parents' floral armchairs watching the cricket with her dad.

'Where do these go?' James asked, interrupting her daydreaming. He held up two breast pump attachments.

'Oh shit.'

James smiled. 'I am a midwife, Poppy, and a modern man. I know these bear no relation to your cup size.' He did the eyebrow waggling thing again and she rolled her eyes and laughed. She pointed to the bottom left drawer. She couldn't help grinning as she watched him put them away.

'What's that look for?' asked James.

'Nothing. You're just so . . .' She trailed off. Who knew what the wine would let her say tonight?

'I'm so . . .?' James wiped his hands on a tea towel and stood in front of her. His mouth was turned up slightly at the corners and his dark eyes were full of mischief, baiting her.

'You're so . . . tall.'

James bent his knees until he was eye level with her. With a jolt in her stomach, Poppy realised that their lips were also now level.

'This better?'

Poppy felt her hands rise to rest on his shoulders. 'Yes, this is a good perspective.'

James came closer, nudging her legs apart. His eyes were locked on hers and the mischievousness had vanished. As he stood to his full height, his hands tilted her head towards his and then landed on her waist. Poppy's eyes widened.

'And this? Is this a *better* perspective?'

The wind flew out of Poppy's chest. 'Yes,' she squeaked.

James's fingers spread out slowly to cup her butt and slide her across the bench towards him. This couldn't be happening. And yet it *was* happening. And whatever it was, she wanted it. She was sure of that. It wasn't just the wine speaking. She was a girl, he was a guy—a good guy who she'd once thought was a bad guy but now knew was fundamentally good—it made sense on so many levels, and yet . . . was this really going to happen with Maeve sleeping down the corridor?

Oh fuck it, said the wine. *You're a cool mom, not a regular mom.*

Poppy giggled and James moved his head closer.

SPECIAL DELIVERY

'I love your laugh,' he breathed, his lips millimetres away from hers. He moved his hand to her head and his finger slid down to stroke the skin behind her earlobe. Poppy inhaled sharply.

'Poppy.' He said it like a dusting of icing, it was so light and delicious. He leaned in and pressed his mouth against hers and both their eyes closed reflexively. Poppy felt herself sink, letting James absorb her, grateful for the bench propping her up. From the lightest touch, her whole body began to hum. Every part of her wanted him.

James pulled away slightly and Poppy opened her eyes. Their lips were still so close they would connect at the slightest tremble. His dark eyes were searching hers and she knew why. He was asking her, *Are you okay, is this okay?* Poppy's body responded on her behalf. She gripped his shoulders and slid her hands down his back, pulling him closer. She was basically straddling him now. Thank god for the wine; she didn't want to consider the inelegance of this because fuck it was hot.

Satisfied with her response, James leaned in again and this time his mouth parted. His tongue slid over hers and she felt like sugar caramelising under a flame. There was no going back from this. She was kissing James. James was kissing her. All she needed to remember was lips, pressure, release, again. Maybe forever. She could do this forever.

She brushed away the thoughts trying to distract her: *You're on a kitchen bench with a baby down the corridor; this guy delivered your baby; this guy knows you're an insecure psycho.*

His mouth moved to her neck and a warm ripple of pleasure rushed through her core.

Shut up, she told the voices in her head. This was nothing more than kissing, and oh god, after months in a barren wilderness, it felt *good*.

As if reading her mind, James moved his lips back to hers, soothing her with his mouth. He slid his hands up her legging-clad thighs and Poppy felt herself shift nearer to him. She could feel every part of his body pushing through his jeans to her. She tightened her thighs around him, her pulse spiking as he pulled their bodies flush. His hands roamed across her curves as their lips melted against each other. Suddenly she wanted this to be more than kissing. She wished she wasn't wearing her leggings and that his hands were sliding up her bare skin; she needed to be as close to James as possible.

Her mind performed some rapid calculations. Maeve wouldn't wake for at least another four hours, and their bedrooms were at opposite ends of the house. Conclusion: there was nothing to stop this moving to the bedroom and moving there fast.

She pulled away. 'Should we . . .?'

James blinked, his eyes searching her face. He exhaled. 'Yeah, I guess we should stop . . . right . . . okay, right, let's stop then.' He was babbling, breathless.

She stared at him, lost for words.

No! she wanted to say. *Keep going. Let's never stop this.* But her mouth wouldn't work. Her eyes were locked on James, willing him to understand, but he was looking away now, running his hands through his hair. *Speak!* she admonished herself, but it was too hard. Everything she said now would make it clear that she wanted something more when his automatic reaction had been to stop.

'I'll go then,' said James, straightening his t-shirt. 'I'll get a cab.' He put his hands on her shoulders briefly then let them drop. 'Bye,' he said with a weak smile. He grabbed his keys from the bench and the clang of the metal was like a steel gong in her ears.

What the hell had just happened? How had that gone so stupidly fucking pear-shaped so quickly? Why wouldn't her brain connect to her stupid voice box? For Christ's sake, normally she couldn't shut up and then at this once-in-a-lifetime kitchen-bench moment she becomes a dithering mute?!

As she heard the front door close, Poppy rubbed her arms where James had touched them. The crackling warmth from his grip had vanished and she suddenly felt a desperate, chilling cold.

CHAPTER 28

It was raining for the third day straight and, completely out of the blue, Patrick had texted.

Hey marketing pigeon. Is TV advertising still worth the money?

Poppy couldn't make sense of it. She felt like a Swiftie with an indecipherable Easter egg; like, if only she was better at code-breaking she could land backstage passes and solve world peace. Was 'marketing pigeon' an insult or a nickname, or an insult wrapped up in a nickname, or vice versa? Was it supposed to soften the blow that he'd reached out for work advice—again—like she was of no more value than her former career? The timing of the message was unsettling too. Sent at 3.34 am. That was a whole lot of context. It was a time for sleeping (or breastfeeding). It was not a time for making good decisions. It was booty-call hour.

Most likely, he'd been soaked in vodka trying to close a deal at the casino and wanted urgent advice from an obliging source, she told herself. Nothing more.

SPECIAL DELIVERY

She gazed out the window at the August rain pelting her garden. It was showing no signs of easing and Poppy was suffering from extreme cabin fever. Maeve was suffering from it too—she was lying on her play mat grizzling for no apparent reason. It could have been her teeth, but how would you know? Ever since Maeve had been two weeks old, every time she grizzled someone would say, 'Teething?' Poppy wanted to shake each one of them vigorously to convey how unhelpful she found that question. Yes, it could have been teething, but it could also have been the weather, the food, the lighting, the company. She'd never know until a) Maeve was old enough to tell her or b) a tooth popped up.

Against her better judgement, she'd committed to going to the mothers' group catch-up today. She'd missed the last few due to various reasons (appointments, family lunches, downright avoidance), but she needed a reason to get out of the house and stop spiralling over this Patrick text and the fact that James had gone completely off the radar after Kitchengate.

She'd waited for weeks to run into him on the golf course loop. She knew his shifts changed on a two-week cycle, so it was completely possible he wasn't avoiding her, but then she'd clocked a whole month with zero James sightings and had been forced to conclude that hospital rostering wasn't the reason. Maeve's sleep times had changed too, so now they were walking after lunch instead of the mornings, but it didn't matter anyway because somehow—in this town where everyone's paths tangled like the cords behind the TV—James had managed to neatly Ctrl+X himself out of her life.

So, mothers' group it was. Mary had been the one to suggest it. Poppy and Maeve had popped in yesterday to deliver some misdirected catalogues and then somehow stayed for two hours. As they gossiped with woollen blankets on their laps, Maeve's fingers poking through the crochet holes, Mary had asked about the next 'mummy catch-up'.

'There's one tomorrow, but I haven't been in ages,' confessed Poppy. 'I missed a few, and now I feel like *I'm out of the group*.' She used air quotes on the last bit, even though she wasn't sure Mary would understand what she was doing. As a woman in her thirties, it felt juvenile to talk about 'groups' despite it definitely still being a thing.

'How can you be *out of the group*'—Mary used air quotes too, which was both unexpected and yet completely predictable from her—'when the only entry requirement to the group is having a baby, which you do?'

On cue, Maeve laughed delightedly. The woman had a point.

★

Three mums were already there when she arrived and they eagerly made space for her and Maeve among the melee of prams. 'So good to see you!' they chorused as Poppy sat down and plonked Maeve on her lap. They sounded similarly starved of a social life.

As more mothers arrived, Poppy found herself breathless from chatting, surprised at how much she had to say. It was a relief to talk about the crazy things she regularly googled during night feeds (namely: *is a three-month regression a thing*; *is a four-month regression a thing*; *is a five-month regression a thing*).

SPECIAL DELIVERY

At one point, a couple of women started squealing with laughter about a husband gaffer-taping bottles to his chest to convince his son to drink formula. As the group laughed, Poppy hugged Maeve tighter, that familiar twinge of otherness clouding her vision. It wasn't shame, but it was a little bit of shame, and it wasn't anger, though it was a little bit of that, and it wasn't sadness, though there was a tiny bit of that rolled in too. It was a wistful alienation. She'd never be able to join in these conversations.

Suddenly one of the mums spoke above the group. 'Sorry, April. We should stop with our boring husband chat.'

'*De nada, de nada,*' replied April, who Poppy recognised from the first mother's group catch up. She had a ginger bob and the most dazzling emerald eyes. April waved her hands in a 'carry on' gesture. 'Being a single mum, I love hearing about how husbands add minimal value. Makes me feel so much better about my life choices.'

'Wait,' gasped Poppy. 'You're a single mum?'

April nodded. 'Correct.'

'But you're so . . .' Poppy was momentarily lost for words. 'Clean!' she said finally. She realised she sounded like a lunatic, but this woman had glossy hair and shining eyes and an adorable baby who looked chubby and healthy and content. She looked like a woman on top of things. She did not fit Poppy's mental picture of the single mum brigade.

April shrugged. 'I did shower yesterday . . . I think.'

The other women looked on blankly, apparently bamboozled by the exchange.

Poppy backtracked. 'I only say that because I'm a single mum too and I'm a hot mess. I'm a hot, steaming, sweaty mess, despite living in pretty much the coldest town in Australia. Look at me!' She lifted her arm to reveal the crusted-on Weet-Bix on her jumper that she'd only noticed when parking the car. 'I'm barely fit to be seen in public!'

The other women at the table laughed generously and Poppy felt a lightness she hadn't known in ages. No-one seemed scandalised, no-one seemed pruriently intrigued. Instead there was casual surprise and a rapid pivot to the next topic: when to start weaning on to cow's milk (answer: ages away).

Over the stories of exploding formula bottles and princeling babies refusing anything but freshly expressed breastmilk, April nudged Poppy. 'Should we start a single mums' club? Badass mums living in sin?'

Poppy glowed. 'Sign me up. I'll order the t-shirts.'

'Cool, I'll bring the beers,' said April. She hoisted her son onto her lap and pushed a teething ring into his mouth. 'So, you single by choice . . . or not?'

'Cutting straight to the chase!' Poppy said with a laugh.

'Would've got there eventually.' April shrugged. 'I already know you pushed a baby out your vag, so we're past the small-talk stage.'

'True,' Poppy conceded. She paused to consider April's question. It had been her choice to break it off with Patrick but he had forced her hand. 'A bit of both, I guess.'

'Same,' April said. 'I couldn't meet the right person and I was always going to have to do IVF to have a baby, so I decided why wait? IVF is fucking expensive, but I tell you what's more expensive: my ex-girlfriend. She was obsessed with home decorating. Now I get to eat my solo girl-dinners, I don't have random West Elm orders bleeding my bank account dry and I still get to have a baby. It's a win-win-win.'

'That's brave,' remarked Poppy.

'Woman, please. I'm not brave. I'm so scared of commitment, I decided to have a lab baby.'

Poppy laughed.

'Are you going okay?' asked April.

'We have our moments,' replied Poppy automatically, 'but we're fine.' It was what she told anyone who asked.

'I bet you say that to every random in the street,' said April. 'My line is: *The days go slowly, but the weeks just fly*. Like, ugh, am I a Hallmark card? Would I actually ever say that? Obviously not. But random old women in the supermarket want to know how I'm going, so that's the line I feed them. Hallmark quotes are like crack for the over-sixties.' She took a sip from her latte and looked Poppy directly in the eye. 'Single mother to single mother, how are you actually going?'

'I'm okay,' insisted Poppy. 'I mean, I am okay at this very specific point in time. Don't ask me about yesterday when the dryer blew up and I cried, and don't ask me what I'm going to do if I can't find a job before my maternity leave payments run out, but at this particular moment, sitting in an awesome art-filled cafe with a hot soy cappuccino in front of me, I can almost confidently say I am okay. Almost.'

'Good for you,' said April. 'If it makes you feel better, last week my bedroom light blew and I still haven't replaced it. I just use the light from my phone like a true Millennial.'

Poppy smiled. 'Are *you* going okay?'

April smiled back. 'I eat cheese and Sakatas for dinner and my iPhone fills any partner-shaped voids in my life. My son is alive and thriving, and I love him so much it makes my heart hurt. I am okay too.'

Poppy raised her cappuccino. 'To being okay.'

April picked up her son's bottle and clinked it against Poppy's coffee. 'To being okay,' she echoed.

★

It was 11.30 am by the time the mothers' group disbanded. There was a blizzard of sleet outside but The Bustle was toasty warm, so Poppy decided to hang around in case Henry popped in for a second coffee. She opened her phone to check her messages. Patrick hadn't sent a follow-up text but he might not have remembered sending the first one. On her lap, Maeve's body was slackening with sleep. Poppy lifted her carefully into the pram and covered her with a thick blanket. Then, on a cappuccino-fuelled high—before she could second-guess the impulse—Poppy deleted Patrick's text. If he couldn't be bothered asking about his daughter, who looked like a living angel sleeping so divinely under the pale pink blanket, then he didn't deserve a response.

She pulled her laptop from the nappy bag and opened it on the table. Her fingers tapped the keyboard, the spinning wheel of death took its sweet time, the blue-and-pink Seek logo appeared, and everything felt strangely normal. There was no plague of locusts, nor a biblical rain of fire. She'd just deleted a text from Patrick and the world didn't care.

SPECIAL DELIVERY

'I found a job,' Poppy announced when Henry walked in ten minutes later. 'Well, it's a job ad, but I reckon I'm qualified so I sent in my résumé. It's with Region Building Australia—the government agency. They've got a marketing and digital team.'

'That's great news,' replied Henry. 'The usual?'

Poppy gave him a thumbs up and he headed to the counter to order, poking his head under the pram hood to smile at Maeve as he passed. Poppy grinned at her laptop screen. Everything was turning out dandy.

'Poppy?' said a voice behind her. A queasy rush of adrenaline immediately saturated her nervous system. In this too-tiny town, it had only been a matter of time.

'James!' Her voice was an octave too high. He was standing there in his scrubs with a takeaway coffee. She hadn't seen him walk in; she must have been engrossed in her laptop. His hair was as lustrous as ever and his scrubs stretched taut across his shoulders. Why did he always have to look like this? Three months of no contact other than a texted gif of Scott Cam dancing. She'd responded with three laughing-face emojis and that had been it. The whole exchange had felt cheap and frankly sad after the highs of the kitchen bench encounter.

'It's been a while,' she said, glancing at Maeve, who was still serenely asleep.

James shifted uncomfortably. 'Yeah, I've been studying heaps. Haven't really seen anyone. I've been working, studying, working, studying. Bit of coffee in between. Not much else.'

Poppy's jaw tensed. What was she supposed to say?

'I've been coming here hoping to run into you,' James said quickly. 'I should have called or texted, but I left it too long and then I convinced myself that it would be better to have a conversation in person but . . .' He took a deep breath. 'It's proven trickier to run into you than I'd thought. Have you stopped walking the golf course loop?'

Poppy narrowed her eyes. Where was this going?

James spoke in a rush. 'I'm sorry,' he said. 'That whole thing in your kitchen—I got carried away and I don't want you to think I planned it or I was trying to take advantage of you.'

I wish you'd taken advantage of me, said Poppy's mind traitorously. She'd told herself again and again that breaking off the kiss had been the best outcome. She didn't need distractions; she needed to focus on her daughter. But then he turns up with his puppy dog eyes and his apology and her brain capitulates instantly. How embarrassingly un-feminist.

Since that night she'd tried to banish all images of broad-shouldered, dark-eyed men from her thoughts. Time had been helping to blur the memory of his breath on her neck—it was almost as though it had been a really hot dream, just a figment of her touch-starved imagination—but seeing him here brought back the crashing, desperate reality: that kiss had been the best of her life. Such a shame it would never happen again.

'Poppy, I'm really sorry and I really hope we can go back to being friends,' said James. His dark eyes were searching hers.

'Of course,' said Poppy automatically. She didn't need distractions, and his excellent kissing definitely qualified as that.

James breathed a sigh of relief and ran a hand through his hair. 'I'm so glad. You have no idea how often I've imagined this conversation.'

SPECIAL DELIVERY

I bet I imagined it more, thought Poppy dryly.

'I'm not lying when I say I've spent a small fortune buying coffee here hoping to run into you.' He leaned closer and lowered his voice. 'Controversially, I don't get the appeal. I think the coffee's better up the road.'

Poppy pursed her lips. 'I come for the ambiance.'

'I get that,' said James, glancing at the walls around them. 'The art is awesome. I wanted to buy some, but then I got targeted on Instagram and ended up buying these random prints from China instead. They took seven weeks to arrive and they won't hang straight but they make me feel more worldly. Also, they cost twenty-seven dollars for four and you can't put a price on that kind of bargain. Well, you can put a twenty-seven-dollar price on that, I guess—but you get what I mean.'

Poppy laughed despite herself. 'Buying art is a very'—she searched for the right word—'*mature* thing for a grown male to do.'

'I am mature,' he said, smiling. 'And tall.'

Poppy stared at him. Was that a reference to Kitchengate?!

'Ahem, hi there.' Henry was holding out Poppy's coffee.

'Thanks, Hen,' she said, taking it. 'James, this is Henry. Henry, this is James, my friend from—well, it's a long story.'

'I was her midwife,' explained James, reaching out to shake Henry's hand.

'Her midwife, right,' said Henry, brow furrowing as he worked through the implications of that. He returned the handshake. 'Thanks for bringing Maeve into the world. We can't imagine life without her.'

Poppy glanced at Henry quickly. *We?*

A slight crease of his forehead told her James had noticed too.

'Henry is an old schoolfriend who's moved back to Orange,' she explained. 'His office is around the corner so Maeve and I bump into him a lot when we're here.'

'Bit of a ritual for us,' Henry said in a deeper voice than usual.

God, he was being so *weird*.

'Henry's engaged to a paediatrician actually. Willa Prescott. Do you know her?'

'Oh yeah.' James brightened. 'I know of Willa. I haven't met her, but the other doctors rave about her. Her referrals are the best apparently; very detailed. She's been away for a while, though, right?'

A muscle tensed in Henry's neck. 'Yes, tying up some loose ends with her job in Brisbane. She'll be back soon.'

Poppy glanced at Henry in surprise. He hadn't mentioned that.

The two men looked at each other for a second too long.

'I'd better be going,' said James suddenly. He turned to Poppy. 'Are you going to the races this weekend?'

'Yep.' Poppy nodded, feeling Henry's eyes swivelling between them. 'Mum is booked in to babysit.' She turned to Henry. 'Dani is coming down too.'

'Great,' said Henry in that weird deep voice. 'It will be good to see her.' He turned to James. 'Another old friend,' he explained.

James nodded. 'I've heard lots about her.'

Henry's jaw tightened.

SPECIAL DELIVERY

'Nice to meet you, mate,' James said to Henry. 'Great to see you, Poppy. I'll call you.' He leaned over to kiss her cheek goodbye. 'Thanks for not rejecting me again,' he whispered.

'What?' Poppy spluttered. *He* had rejected *her*!

'So glad we're friends again.' James smiled then left them, striding into the blizzard outside with the sharp-shouldered confidence of a Marvel hero.

'What was he talking about?' asked Henry, his voice back to normal, if not a tad too high.

Poppy stared at James's disappearing silhouette. 'No idea,' she muttered truthfully.

CHAPTER 29

Dani was disproportionately excited about their impending trip to the races. 'Should I bring my Scanlan and Theodore or my Sass and Bide? Is Sass and Bide a bit, I dunno, *spangly* for Orange? I don't want to look like I'm trying too hard. Like, I have done country races before, I am not a novice. I need to give off a hot-but-not-novice vibe. Do you think there'll be heaps of cute country boys there? Bloody hell, my uterus feels like I'm twenty-two again!'

'Dan, literally no-one will care what you're wearing. The fanciest shop we have here is Sportscraft and it's designed for the sixty-plus market, so you'll look banging in anything. How does Sam feel about you having a weekend off to chase cute country boys?'

'He's pumped. After he takes his mum to some appointments, he's got lots of plans with Nella. They're going to the zoo, apparently. Good luck to them. He's most worried about me having a hall pass to sleep in—aka get a hangover. I don't think I've been drunk in eighteen months. He's made me promise not to drunk dial him. I tried to explain I'd be way too busy shimmying on the dancefloor with some hot belt-buckled twenty-somethings and he *laughed in my face*. Well, little does he know: Dani is back for one night only and it's going to be wild.'

Poppy laughed. Dani's enthusiasm for attractive members of the opposite sex was only surpassed by her obsession with her husband, who was a favourite topic when she was a few wines deep.

Meanwhile, Poppy's mum would be babysitting Maeve for a *whole twenty-four hours*. Not only would Poppy be able to go out with her best friend, she'd also be able to wake up and eat a cafe breakfast baby-free. The prospect of being able to eat with a fork *and knife* was making her giddy with anticipation.

The whole town seemed to be going to the races and Facebook was abuzz with people desperate to buy last-minute tickets. A few girls from the mothers' group were going (also sans babies) and had been eagerly texting all week with questions and advice on everything from dresses conducive to sneaky mid-races breast-pumping sessions to the best after-races venue (unanimously agreed to be the Royal Hotel dancefloor).

'Just remember to bring your coat, Dan. Honestly, this weather is the devil.' Poppy looked outside to see the rose branches being battered against the window.

'Already packed, girlfriend. I will see you in less than seventy-two hours. Put the champagne on ice!'

Poppy ended the call and put the phone on the kitchen bench. Seeing the bench every day had the discombobulating effect of amplifying the highs and lows of her love–hate attitude towards James. Every time she saw it she would think, *God, that was good*, while simultaneously thinking, *I wish that damn kiss had never happened*, but then she'd follow that thought up with, *But, oh god, that kiss was the best*, and the cycle of mind-fuckery would continue.

Maeve was settling into her dinner—literally—by joyously massaging her chest with pureed sweet potato. Such were the dilemmas facing Poppy these days: answer the phone and let Maeve control dinner, or reject the call and maintain a semblance of order.

'Ba-baa,' said Maeve, slapping the table of her highchair with sweet-potato hands. 'Baaaaaa! Ba!'

'Ba-baa!' agreed Poppy. 'Shall we try using a spoon again, Maevey?'

She picked up the silicone teaspoon that had been flung onto the tiles with half the puree and handed it back to her daughter.

'Ba-baaa!' said her daughter happily, flinging it back to the ground. 'Ba-ba! Da-da!'

Poppy froze. That last bit had sounded eerily like 'Dada'.

'Ba-ba!' she reminded her daughter, picking up the spoon again. 'Or Ma-ma! Let's try that. Mama! Mama!'

Maeve looked at her, confused. 'Ba-baaaaaa!' She threw the spoon away again and began massaging the puree through her hair.

Poppy's phone rang and she glanced at the caller ID.

SPECIAL DELIVERY

James.

She looked at her daughter, now sucking her puree-covered fingers. Oh well, at least some food was making its way into her mouth. She answered the phone. 'Hello?'

'Hey, Poppy, what's going on?'

'I'm feeding Maeve sweet potato and she is feeding it to the floor—and to her hair. You could say we are redecorating with sweet potato. If anyone is still saying orange is the new black, we are right on trend.'

'Sounds fun,' said James. 'I can also recommend dried Weet-Bix as an alternative to gyprock. That stuff is like concrete. I'm pretty sure the Egyptians used it to build the pyramids.'

Poppy smiled. 'To what do I owe the pleasure of this call?'

'Uh . . .' James faltered. 'I said I would call you, so, here I am calling you. You know, in an attempt to keep promises and not disappear for months. You're still coming to the races, right?'

'I am.'

'Great. What tent are you in?'

Poppy looked at the paper flyer stuck to her fridge. 'Twelve D. I think it's trackside. It's all you can eat and drink, which sounds potentially devastating, but apparently it's the place to be.' April and a few of the mothers' group girls had booked places in the same tent, so there'd be a few friendly faces.

'I'm Twelve H, just down from you. It's the cricket club tent, so there'll be too much testosterone flying around in there. I'll come find you.'

'Sounds like a plan,' replied Poppy. 'Unless I have an electric drill–induced trip to emergency, I'll see you there.'

'Wait, what?'

'Long story,' said Poppy, 'but a new dryer is being installed on Monday, which means I need to fix the laundry shelves I broke when I was trying to fix the dryer in the first place. Anyway, I'm going to attempt to fix them tomorrow so I don't have to do it hungover on Sunday. I've been watching a lot of DIY how-tos on YouTube so I'm at least thirty-five per cent confident I'll be okay.'

'Do you want some help?' asked James.

'No, of course not,' replied Poppy too quickly. She hadn't told him that to coerce him into offering to help. If she actually wanted help she would have asked her dad. 'It'll be fine. I promise I didn't tell you that to make you feel compelled to help.'

'You realise I enjoy that kind of stuff? I have the power tools to prove it.'

'Are you saying you want to help me?' asked Poppy.

'Are you trying to avoid asking me?'

Poppy exhaled. 'I wasn't going to ask for your help, James. We weren't speaking two days ago.'

'We weren't *not* speaking, Poppy. I just hadn't timed my coffee runs very well. I was definitely still speaking to you, I just hadn't *seen* you.'

'Okay, well, do you want to come help fix my laundry shelf?'

'Nope.'

Poppy groaned.

'Kidding!' James laughed. 'I'm on the early shift tomorrow so I could pop over in the afternoon?'

'That works.' Poppy made a mental note to clean the kitchen. Or actually—should she leave it dirty for maximum

SPECIAL DELIVERY

friends-without-benefits vibes? Oh far out, she had no idea what she wanted. 'See you tomorrow then,' she said.

'See you then,' agreed James. He clicked off and Poppy watched her phone go blank.

'Dada!' cried Maeve delightedly, pointing at the phone.

Poppy grimaced, sinking under a tsunami of too many feelings that made no sense. She picked up a wet cloth and wrapped it around her daughter's chubby fingers. 'Maeve,' she said sternly as she began wiping off the orange puree, 'please never say that in public.'

CHAPTER 30

James was wearing a tool belt. His hair was tousled from the breeze and the curves of his biceps were visible under his sweatshirt as he stood at her door.

'Is this a joke?' asked Poppy, eyeing the belt. 'The rest of the Village People couldn't make it?'

'There was an emergency at the YMCA.'

Poppy moved aside to let him in. 'I randomly always had a thing for the policeman.'

James locked eyes with her and raised an eyebrow. 'Noted.'

Poppy felt a familiar heat tingling up her spine. She wrenched her gaze away to break the current. 'Follow me.'

She led the way down the hall into the laundry, where the shelf hung at a forty-five-degree angle—completely useless for shelving things, but entirely useful for assessing the laws of gravity. For lack of any other shelf, she had piled her laundry detergents into the space where the slope of the shelf met the wall, creating a V-shaped stack of washing liquids.

SPECIAL DELIVERY

'I see how this could be a problem for you,' said James.

'Suboptimal,' Poppy agreed. 'I call it my Cleaning Tower of Pisa.'

'I would call it a clear lack of shelf-preservation,' said James.

Poppy smiled. 'I've been a bit shelf-destructive.'

His laugh was wonderful. The way his face broke into a broad grin, it was like dropping an Alka-Seltzer into water. Making him laugh made her fizz with pride. It was always better than she expected.

'It needs some shelf-care,' continued James, turning back to the wall.

Poppy smirked. 'Are we going to do this all afternoon?'

James shrugged. 'I have no shelf-control.' They grinned at each other like fools, before he added, 'Especially around you.'

Poppy felt her grin melt and she was suddenly hyper-aware that James wasn't blinking. She quickly looked away.

'Like I said, I'm getting the dryer installed on Monday so the shelf needs to be fixed before then. If you don't think you can do it, I'm sure my dad and I can manage.'

'Poppy, please don't underestimate my prowess with a drill.' James pulled a pencil from his belt, stuck it behind his ear, and Poppy watched as he pulled out a tape measure to calculate the height between the floor and the shelf. It was highly irrational, but she was feeling majorly turned on.

'You don't have to do this,' Poppy said for the hundredth time. (They'd been texting about it all last night.)

'I know,' said James. 'But I've been around enough kids to know that as soon as Maeve can try to use this as a ski jump, she will.'

'Maeve can't walk,' she reminded him.

'Ah, but can she ski?'

Poppy smiled. 'Unlikely.'

'I'm not willing to take that chance. Someone's got to think of the children, Poppy.'

He put his hands on her shoulders, moving her back towards the wall so he could slide past, his hands gliding down her arms ever so slightly as he did. His touch was electrifying, like a swarm of fireflies fluttering over her skin.

'I'll get this out of your way,' she offered, sliding back past him to pick up the laundry basket. She bent down to pick it up and felt his hands on her waist, playfully tugging her towards him.

'You're getting in my way, McKellar.'

Poppy straightened up, her back to his chest, his breath on her neck. She placed the basket on the top-loader and spun slowly. The humidity in the air seemed to build as her eyes met his. Her heart was suddenly whirring like an electric fan and her gaze travelled to where his jumper snagged at his waist. An inch of skin peeked out above his tool belt and she had an irresistible urge to slip her fingers under the waist of his jeans and pull him towards her.

All her synapses were suddenly firing, sending warmth to places in her body that hadn't felt this kind of heat in years. It was as though they were tightrope-walking on a single golden thread. If James made the slightest move, she would disintegrate on the spot, like a firework dissolving into air.

James's breathing was low and husky. How were they now so close? The room seemed even smaller than usual and she was acutely aware that her bedroom was less than ten metres away. It felt as though steam was floating off her body, condensation sliding down the windowpanes. The thought crossed her mind to move away, but another thought steamrolled in: *No frickin way.*

'Will I wake Maeve with the drill?' he asked quietly, his mouth perilously close to her skin.

Poppy heard herself whispering back, 'It's Thursday. She's at my mum's . . .'

The information settled between them, heavy with meaning, and Poppy felt the walls close in further, threatening to suffocate her.

'Poppy,' James said in a low voice. He moved his fingertips to her waist, light as mist, and she shivered with anticipation. His face tipped towards hers and she tilted upwards, their breath mingling as her eyelids fluttered closed.

Her brain wasn't cut out to perform these calculations. The risks of moving an inch forward were high, she knew that, but she also knew that sometimes you needed to succumb to temptation in order to refocus. Like a cheat day. Maybe she just needed to get this out of her system.

She pressed closer to James and his lips brushed her neck. Her skin burned hot underneath them as his grip on her waist tightened. She wound her arms around him, threading her thumbs through his belt loops, and his lips increased the pressure on her throat, sending a flame down her spine. 'Is this okay?' he murmured.

Before she could stop it, a tiny moan escaped from her lips. She felt his mouth smile against her skin and it made her want him more.

'I'll take that as a yes.'

'Clever man,' she whispered, kneading her fingernails into the fabric of his top.

Their stomachs met and a heavy longing gathered in Poppy's belly and everywhere else her skin touched his. James tipped her face upwards, his nose grazing hers until the heat of his mouth touched her lips. She gasped. It was exactly as she remembered, but softer, like the slightest strike of a match before it lit a pool of gasoline. His lips parted hers with the gentlest touch and her hands slid under his jumper and t-shirt, running over the coolness of his skin, the firmness of his muscles. She angled her neck to drink all of him in, like his mouth alone could quench her thirst. She could feel him smiling as his lips moved against hers, stronger now, and she felt she would melt in a puddle.

'James,' she whispered, because she needed to say something, anything, to have some sense of agency when she was clearly losing all control.

In response, James skimmed his hands down to her butt and around her thighs, and Poppy felt herself being lifted, wrapping her legs around him as he pulled her up. With one hand he struck the laundry basket to the floor and placed her on the top-loader. 'Sorry,' he breathed between kisses.

'Collateral damage,' she muttered.

His hips were firm against her and she could feel how much he wanted her. Her fingers ran through his hair as his tongue slipped into her mouth. She pushed her chest against him, her nipples hardening.

The steel lid of the washing machine was cold under her thighs compared to the fire between them. She pushed herself into him, demanding more contact, and he pushed back, filling the space, kissing her deeper. The washing machine squeaked underneath her and their hands slid over each other, hungry to learn every curve. It was as though they were on a timer, desperate to touch everything, feel everything, before someone yanked them back to reality. Poppy gripped his jumper, tugging him closer. She wanted him flush against her, and he obliged, grabbing her butt roughly as his lips traced her jawline. His teeth grazed a jagged path down her neck, the resistance sending a rush of pleasure to her core. Every touch was like fire—hot and fierce. He knew when to push and when to release, and Poppy could hardly stand it. Their lips met again and Poppy laughed into his breath as his hands slid under her top and she arched her back to give him better access. *This is not enough*, she thought blindly. Whatever this was, it was amazing, but she needed more. She wanted all of him, faster and harder and deeper, and she wanted it now, she needed it *now*.

Poppy pulled her lips away. 'Should we . . .?' Suddenly, a memory of them in her kitchen flashed up: her asking the same question, him misunderstanding, her crumbling, months passing. That couldn't happen again. 'I don't mean stop,' she blurted.

'Wasn't planning to,' growled James, moving his lips to the soft skin behind her ear as his fingers spread wide against her rib cage. He curved his hands under her butt and picked her up again, the tool belt wedged between them, and carried her down the hall.

'On the left,' she ordered.

Obediently, James pivoted and she felt her back against her bedroom door. He pushed it open, walked her to the bed and carefully placed her on the edge, pulling his mouth from hers to look her in the eyes. He kneeled on the floor in front of her. Gone was any trace of humour; his eyes were dark with focus. Poppy's breath hitched.

'Are you sure?' he asked.

'Yes,' she breathed, her eyes fixed on his, unafraid to ask for this. She tugged him towards her, pulling off his jumper. God, she was happy to see that chest. She wove her arms around him and pulled him on top of her. Her fingernails dug into his back and up towards his shoulder blades, the friction driving her wild.

His hands slid under her top, finding the curve of her breast, and she writhed in pleasure as his fingers seamlessly moved to unclip her bra. Her breasts fell free and she willed him to discover more of her. She wanted him to explore her body like a map, trace every part of her.

Her hands fumbled with his tool belt and she realised she was laughing. 'This stupid belt.'

'You're right,' muttered James. 'Police costume would've been better.'

He pulled the buckle undone and it fell to the floor with a thud.

'Next time,' she breathed.

'Don't tease me,' he moaned.

He reached both hands under her top and she raised her hands so he could peel it off, savouring every movement like he was unwrapping a present. Her skin sizzled under the heat of his gaze. She needed his skin against hers, now.

She began pulling at his underwear as he pulled against hers and they tangled themselves in desperation. 'You do you, I'll do me,' commanded Poppy as she began pulling down her own undies.

'No way,' replied James. 'I'm doing this.'

His eyes locked on hers and he slowly, purposefully slid her underwear down her legs, his warm hands sending electric sparks fizzing through her abdomen. Not breaking eye contact, he moved down to her chest and kissed her between the breasts, then quickly pulled off his own underwear and propped himself above her, his beautiful, naked body way too far away for her liking.

'Hold on.' He rolled across the bed to reach for his jeans pocket and pulled out his wallet. There was a crackle of foil, and he was back. She could barely stand the fact there was so much of his skin that she wasn't touching.

She glared at him. 'Don't make me wait for this.'

James leaned down and kissed her collarbone then moved up to her mouth, his lips parting hers greedily as he positioned himself above her. 'I've already waited for far too long,' he breathed.

The dappled light through the windows brightened, her soft cotton sheets cradled her body and her skin pulsed with an energy unlike anything she'd ever known. This was her home, she was safe and she knew what she wanted.

He moved inside her, gently at first, then deeper, and she bit into his shoulder to stifle the animal sounds she wanted to make. Her nerve endings crackled, filling her body with a rapacious heat.

'Poppy,' James moaned. 'I promise I don't normally do this.'

'You should,' panted Poppy, her mind swimming as she pushed against him, exerting all her focus to extract every inch of pleasure from his body.

'What am I saying? Of course I should,' James agreed, driving his hips against hers as she melted into him, arching in pleasure. 'I should do this, you should do this, *we* should do this.' He grabbed her hand and threaded his fingers through hers as he stretched her arm above her head. 'We should do this all the goddamn time.'

CHAPTER 31

They lay on her bed staring at the ceiling, their chests still heaving. Poppy's naked leg was draped over James's like it was the most natural thing in the world. It felt like an appropriate time in life to start saying crikey. As in: *That sex! Crikey!*

James began to laugh quietly to himself.

'What?' asked Poppy, smiling.

'I didn't come over here to seduce you. I actually charged the drill.'

Poppy grinned and glanced down at his naked body. 'Is that what you call it?'

'Very funny.' He slung a lazy arm across her waist.

'Well, now that you mention it . . .' Poppy twisted to look at her bedside clock. 'The shelf isn't going to fix itself and it's only two thirty, so . . .'

James propped himself up on his elbow to look at her. 'It's sitting pretty low on my priority list,' he said, skimming his hand across the dip of her waist, sending shivers down her spine.

'Oh yeah?'

'Yep. My current priority is checking you out.'

Poppy blushed and tugged a sheet around herself. No-one looked at her naked body anymore, not even her.

James smiled and wrapped his arms around her, pulling her close. 'Too late,' he whispered, his nose touching hers. 'I have committed every inch of you to memory.'

Poppy smiled into him. 'I actually have no idea what just happened.'

'Would you like me to explain it to you?' he teased.

'I mean, I don't know how we ended up here. Like, it's you.'

'And what? You hate me?'

Poppy shrugged. 'I definitely considered kicking you in the balls at least once.'

James grinned. 'Foreplay. This was always going to happen.'

'Um, as if,' retorted Poppy, feeling a familiar pang of irritation at his Smuggy McSmugface.

'Well, I wanted it to happen,' admitted James.

Whaaaaaaat?!

'Since when? *The Block*?' (This was unexpected and startlingly good news.)

'Nah, before that,' said James. 'Or maybe . . . I dunno.' He flipped onto his back to stare at the ceiling again. 'Even when we first met—even before you'd had Maeve—I just had this feeling you were . . .'

'What?'

'I dunno. You were . . . different . . . cool.'

Poppy crinkled her nose. 'Please tell me you're not some sicko who gets off on pregnant women or something weird.'

James laughed and wove his fingers through hers. 'I didn't mean I had the hots for you then, dumb-arse. You just made me feel . . .'

'Enraged, irritated, maniacally defensive of a crappy old car space?'

'All of the above, actually—and that wasn't necessarily a bad thing.'

Poppy chewed her lip. He *kind of* made sense. But really, he didn't.

'I think you must be a sicko.'

James chuckled, his fingers still intertwined with hers. 'Can I please make it clear that I am not a sicko? Work is work, pregnant women are pregnant women, and women who turn up at my family Easters looking stupidly hot in footy jumpers are in another category completely. I have lots of boxes in my brain where I keep things nice and separate, and Poppy-the-patient fits in the work box, while Poppy-in-front-of-me is in another box entirely. There is no overlap.'

Poppy's heart was fluttering way too embarrassingly at the *stupidly hot* comment. 'Are you breaking the Hippocratic Oath by being naked in my bed?'

'Nope.' James grinned and rolled over to face her.

'How can you be so sure?'

'I checked my textbook.'

Poppy raised an eyebrow.

'There's a bit on dating patients. Well, it's a case study about a consultant who starts dating this nineteen-year-old stripper, and long story short, it's fine because he only saw her in ED for half a day, and by the time they ran into each other at the strip club six months later, there was no longer a patient–specialist relationship and a very low chance she'd be an ED patient again—unless she had another pole-dancing injury.' His tone was pragmatic. 'So if they were fine, I figure we're fine too.'

Poppy snorted. 'I don't see many similarities between that situation and this.' She waved her hand around the clothes-strewn room to remind him of what *this* was.

'You're not a stripper?'

'That. And we're not dating.'

James cocked his head. 'True,' he said slowly. 'But that wasn't my point. It's more that you're unlikely to be my patient again.'

Poppy swallowed, the tiniest speck of something like disappointment settling in her chest. So he'd dodged the mention of dating. Totally fine. She didn't need any commitment. She already had a significant other: Maeve. If he didn't want to talk about dating, neither did she. She was a modern woman who used contraception and had consequence-free sex that did not lead to childbirth. Hurrah!

She smiled, trying to channel her inner bravado outwards. 'So if the old guy and the stripper can date, no-one will care we had sex on a random Thursday?'

James studied her, his eyes darkening. 'Something like that,' he said eventually.

Poppy willed herself not to overthink that almost unnoticeable shadow that had swept across his features.

'I also made sure I was extremely professional around you when you were in my care,' James continued. 'And for another six months after that, just to be safe.'

SPECIAL DELIVERY

'Professional?!' cried Poppy, remembering his refusal to smile in her presence. 'Is that code for soulless?'

A tiny crease appeared between his brows. 'I needed to keep my distance.'

'You could have been friendly.'

'But I couldn't,' he said intently. 'I was scared of . . . I dunno . . . it's like you got under my skin somehow. I'd spent my whole life thinking people are either good or bad, and then you accuse me of being a goody-two-shoes and suddenly nothing makes sense anymore.' James sighed and rolled back to stare at the ceiling. 'You'd think I'd be stoked to never see you again, but it didn't work like that and I was so confused. Like, was I accidentally riling you up for my own warped enjoyment? I couldn't understand it and I didn't want to do anything irrational, so I forced myself to stick to the guidelines by the letter. I guess I did it to protect myself.'

Poppy felt her face flush. 'I felt like you were always either ignoring me or laughing at me.' She hadn't meant that to sound so vulnerable but she realised she didn't care.

James twisted onto his side to face her. 'I'm sorry,' he said gently. 'I didn't mean to come across that way. I was *never* laughing at you. If anything, I was laughing at myself. Every thought in my brain felt so ridiculous around you. And the whole time—the car park, the supermarket, even with Mary's stupid conversation starters—I was trying to do the right thing. I *like* doing the right thing. It just came out all wrong.'

His expression was so earnest, Poppy felt her self-consciousness fizzle. She inched closer to smile against his skin. 'It's because you're a robot,' she whispered.

James's hands suddenly grasped her waist. With one deft movement, he flipped her onto her back and shifted on top of her. 'You wanna test that theory?' There was a wicked glint in his eye, and her body was suddenly aflame again. Before she could remind herself to breathe, and verbalise that *yes she was one hundred per cent open to testing that theory*—especially since they were already dressed for the occasion—James laughed and fell back beside her.

Poppy exhaled and laughed too, her mind racing. Their first impressions, their impulsiveness around each other, the whisper of something else darting around her consciousness: *he'd researched this in advance?*

'Why are you single?' she blurted.

James raised an eyebrow. 'It's complicated.'

Now it was Poppy's turn to look sceptical. One second ago she hadn't even meant to ask that question, but now, after that kind of response, she was ravenous for details. 'That sounds like a cop-out.'

He shrugged. 'Maybe I don't know how to talk about it.'

'So try,' Poppy urged, realising the fact he was single had been making her feel anxious for weeks. Surely he had to be hiding a problematic gaming addiction or some kind of perverted gambling habit? Maybe he was one of those deadbeats who watched cockfights on YouTube.

'I was engaged, we were together for four years, we broke up last October, she took my dog. End of story.'

'Oh gosh.' Poppy exhaled. She had not been expecting that. Four years—and an engagement. That was baggage. (And she could say that because *takes one to know one*.)

'I'm still not over it.'

'Oh . . . okay,' Poppy stammered. She hadn't been expecting that either. Was this a blatant declaration she was a rebound? God, how embarrassing. And also, could he be less of a dick about it?

'What?' asked James, seeing her expression. 'You asked.'

'You're so annoying.'

James shuffled closer to her. 'I can't help it around you, McKellar.'

Poppy rolled her eyes.

'It's something cerebral,' James continued. 'Or physical. Or both.'

'Ha!' said Poppy. 'I think you'll find the layman's term for that is lust.'

'There's definitely that,' he said, leaning in to kiss her neck. 'But I think it's something more chemical, something neuro-endocrinological.' He shifted his body to prop himself above her and Poppy felt herself slacken underneath him. His kisses moved down from her throat to her breasts, light as butterflies.

'If you're trying to impress me with some BS medical term'—she wanted to roll her eyes again, but they were locked behind her eyelids, letting her body fulfil the sensory obligations on their behalf—'you're seriously misunderstanding what impresses me.'

It was ridiculous that she was trying to string sentences together when she could hardly keep herself from shivering in pleasure. She didn't need words; she needed his hands, his lips, all over her, everywhere, now. Again.

James stopped kissing her and looked her square in the eyes. 'That's what I'm trying to say. I'm *not* trying to impress you. It's like you make my brain short-circuit. With you, I hear the words coming out, and think, *Why did I say that?* I just can't help myself. It's like the moment I see you, I shed this skin I didn't realise I'd been wearing and I'm just my real, idiotic self.' He smiled and moved his lips back to her stomach. 'So I say the dumbest things to you and you say the dumbest things to me and yet here we are,' he murmured, trailing his lips over the curve of her waist.

Poppy's ribs were vibrating now as his chin moved over her hip bones. 'I don't say dumb things,' she whispered.

'Yes you do.'

His kisses were circling her inner thighs now, the pressure and want in her building to an almost painful crescendo. 'You're going to pay for that,' she murmured.

'I intend to,' he replied.

CHAPTER 32

The laundry shelf was still no closer to being fixed, but who the hell cared?

James had just finished showering in the ensuite and was drying his hair, beads of water still shining on his muscled back as he searched the room for his clothes. She was tempted to take a photo for posterity's sake. The man was gorgeous.

'I don't want you to think I'm kicking you out,' Poppy began.

'But you are?'

'Reluctantly.'

James found his t-shirt at the back of her dresser.

'I need to pick up Maeve at four.'

He smiled. 'I get it,' he said.

There was a buzz in her solar plexus like a post-workout endorphin rush. She watched him pull his t-shirt over his head, the collar flattening his hair into a solid wet fringe. Reflexively, he shook his head and his hair fell back into place. It was the hottest thing she'd ever seen.

Okay, okay, okay, so he'd proved he wasn't completely perfect. She still couldn't believe he'd confessed his feelings for his ex so openly (wasn't it like some cardinal rule that if you were naked in someone's bed you should at least *pretend* to be properly into them?), but she was finding it easy to overlook that when she had a front-row view of his biceps.

There was no need to label anything yet. She may as well enjoy the dopamine rush while it lasted. She could deal with the adulting later. Or she'd workshop it with Dani. Oh yes, Dani.

'I can't hang out with you at the races,' Poppy announced. She wondered whether this was a completely redundant thing to say. Did he even want to hang out, or was he a wham-bam-thank-you-ma'am kind of guy? 'I mean, not presuming that you even wanted to hang out, but if you did, I can't, so . . .'

James's head was stuck behind her bedside table looking for more clothes. His muscly back looked excellent from this angle.

'My best friend, Dani, is coming from Sydney so I'll be hanging with her all day. And, obviously, if you weren't planning on hanging out with me on Saturday, just pretend this conversation never happened and I'll just, you know, die of embarrassment.'

James straightened, having retrieved his jumper. 'Can I say hello?'

Poppy felt a rush of happiness. He hadn't seemed like a ghoster but you could never be sure.

'A hello would be nice.'

James closed the space between them and kissed her on the lips. 'You're nice.'

SPECIAL DELIVERY

Poppy smiled. 'So are you.'

She wished there wasn't so much goodness in him. With the afternoon light streaming through her window and the memory of his hands on her skin, she couldn't remember how she'd managed to hate him so much. All the same, a pit of dread was deepening in her stomach. It was very unlikely this would end well.

CHAPTER 33

'I am feeling very mutton-dressed-as-lamb,' Poppy announced, tugging at her neckline. She was wearing a periwinkle-blue dress with a cowl neck and mid-length hem—borrowed from Dani, of course. (Her own wardrobe was almost exclusively milk-stained lycra.)

'Hon, you look smoking,' replied Dani, pulling her heel out of the mud as they wove through the car park to the racetrack entrance. 'You're just not used to getting your girls out.'

Poppy looked down at her chest. Breastfeeding had enlarged her boobs to basketball proportions and now they'd shrunk back to limp windsocks. She also had a sneaking suspicion they were now different sizes but she'd avoided measuring for fear of confirming the worst. So yes, it was fair to say the girls had been hidden for the last seven months—the Thursday afternoon interlude notwithstanding.

'I can't believe you convinced me not to bring a coat,' whined Poppy.

SPECIAL DELIVERY

'It'll be warm in the tent,' insisted Dani, who knew nothing about Orange's climate. 'Besides, that colour makes your eyes look like laser beams, Pops. I've always said you need to harness that laser power more. Your eyes were so wasted with Patrick and his one-dimensional ideas of hotness. I am still not over the fact he chose Gisele Bündchen as his hall pass. Like, could he be any more clichéd? He was definitely no Tom Brady.'

'Definitely not the GOAT,' Poppy confirmed.

'But in some ways, very similar to *a* goat,' mused Dani.

'For example, his voice,' said Poppy.

'And . . . penis size?' proffered Dani.

They cackled like two witches. Poppy's heart felt so nourished after having spent the whole morning with Dani, with no small children to interrupt their frenetically zigzagging conversations, which had so far involved lots of cathartic bitching about Patrick. According to Dani, he was still living in the same apartment and had the same job, just partying more than usual. The thought made Poppy's head hurt. He was always drinking and staying out late even when they were together. How was he finding the energy to do more?

The only topic they'd relished more than Patrick was James. How good was he in bed? (Amazing, obviously.) Was he messed up about his ex? (Well, apparently.) Was he likely to break Poppy's heart? (Of course not, because Poppy's heart had nothing to do with their recent bedroom shenanigans. That had been an animal instinct thing.)

Dear old reliable Dani—ever the assertive and confident decision-maker with the voice projection to prove it—had taken a black-and-white view of the whole situation. They should either never have sex again or Have The Chat.

★

'I can't demand we're official after one random hook-up!' Poppy had argued while sitting at her kitchen bench that morning. 'That would be so *cringe*!' There were *rules* about this stuff. Even she knew that.

'Pops, the guy sounds like a heartbreaker. He's already disappeared on you once—who's to say that won't happen again? Labelling things might protect you.'

Dani munched on her croissant and passed a jam-slathered crust to Maeve in the highchair. 'And you should probably have the chat before he touches your boob and milk squirts on him. How are you going to deal with those kinds of shitshows if you don't know where you stand? Although, no judgement from me if you've already told him your boobs are off limits. Mine were a no-man's-land for like ten months after Nella was born.'

'Really?' Poppy pulled the sticky crust away from Maeve and passed her a teething rusk. 'My nips are like leathery Tarzan's feet these days. Zero sensory capacity. He could touch my boobs all he liked and I'd hardly notice.' (She would *definitely* notice.)

Dani snorted. 'I'm just saying—'

'Okay, I get it,' Poppy relented. 'We need to cool off.'

Dani was probably right. What would have happened if they'd moved from the kitchen bench to the bedroom all those months ago? Would he have stayed the night? Would she have wanted him to? The thought of him waking to her unclipping her maternity bra at 3 am was so blergh. Maeve let out a yelp and Poppy grudgingly passed back the jammy croissant.

'I'm not trying to pressure you into making a decision, Pops. I just want you to be careful.'

'I know, Dan.' She sighed and moved the jam jar out of Maeve's eyeline. 'That's why I'll blame you if I'm celibate for the rest of my life.'

'Hon, I'll buy you a new vibrator. You'll thank me in the long run.'

An hour later as Dani sang a Miley Cyrus medley in the shower and Maeve slept off her raspberry jam high, Poppy heard a quiet knock at the front door. She opened it to find James standing there, looking offensively handsome in his chinos and navy blazer.

'I was trying not to wake Maeve,' he said, pointing at the doorbell he'd chosen not to ring.

Poppy smiled. He was a good egg.

'I thought you and Dani might want these for the races,' he said, pulling two paper wristbands from his blazer pocket. 'Gets you free entry everywhere. A friend had some spare so I grabbed them for you.'

'Thanks,' said Poppy, careful not to brush his fingertips as she took them from him. Just seeing him was numbing her brain to almost-paralysis. She needed to Not Think About His Naked Body. God, that was hard when he was looking so delicious in those slim-fit chinos, and his lips were so warm and firm . . . good god, she needed to simmer down. *Boundaries!*

She swallowed and ploughed ahead. 'We're friends, right?'

'Of course,' said James, his eyes narrowing as though trying to X-ray her. 'I don't drop off free wristbands to my enemies.'

'I mean, we're going to keep being friends, aren't we? Even though we've . . . well, you know. I'm just trying to say . . .' She paused, trying to find words that conveyed how reluctantly she was making this decision. 'I really want to keep being friends,' she said in a rush, 'but I can't escalate anything right now.'

The faintest trace of something flitted across his face and was gone just as quickly. 'Poppy, I love hanging out with you—'

'Oh, thank god,' she interrupted. 'I love hanging out too, and I didn't want anything to jeopardise that. Not that the other day wasn't great—it was amazing. I mean, you know that, you were there, you heard me. Oh sorry, that sounded inappropriate, but yeah, I needed to know that we're on the same page. The friends page. Obviously.'

James's brow was slightly creased and his always-about-to-smile lips were definitely not smiling. 'If you say so,' he said slowly, his eyes still X-raying hers. 'But I reserve the right to tease you about your horrible taste in TV.'

Poppy smiled. 'I'd expect nothing less,' she said, her anxiety fading. Phew. That had been okay. Thank god he was so nice.

★

Now, walking into the races, she couldn't wait to see him, which was completely normal for two friends who'd happened to have great sex one time, right? She was so excited for Dani to meet him and she desperately wanted them to hit it off.

SPECIAL DELIVERY

They arrived at the gate and flashed their wristbands to the friendly volunteers then meandered to their tent. Inside, Bunnings trestle tables groaned under the huge quantity of food. Underneath the tables were tubs full of ice and alcohol. There was enough for a small army. Dani let out a happy sigh. 'All you can eat and drink, hey? I think I'm going to like it here.'

'Poppy, hey!' called April, waving to them. She was dressed in a multicoloured jumpsuit. 'I'm so stoked you're here.' She gave Poppy a quick hug and a kiss on the cheek. 'And you must be Dani,' she said, bringing Dani in for a hug too.

'A fellow hugger!' exclaimed Dani, wrapping her arms around April. 'We're going to get on swimmingly! I love your jumpsuit.'

'Very breastfeeding-friendly,' April boasted. 'Not that anyone's getting near my boobs today unless it's for free drinks. Today it's MILFs Gone Wild, am I right?'

'Yes!' shrieked Dani. 'I'm so glad you've found some good influences here, Pops. I feel much more comfortable about your rural relocation now.'

The three women wandered deeper into the tent to find an open bottle of champagne. Everyone around them—lots of mothers' group connections—was dressed up, fascinators dusted off, heels sinking into the turf. It was just as cold in the tent as out of it, so Poppy committed to heating herself via champagne—a risky manoeuvre, admittedly, but Dani and April were doing the same.

Together they formed a stronghold around the canapé table and slipped from one hilarious story to the next. In April, Dani had found a soul sister. Poppy watched them, mesmerised. If you overlooked the fact Dani was a five-eleven Filipina and April was a tiny redhead, they were basically the same person.

'Fashions on the Field,' said Dani, yanking the cork from their next bottle of champagne. 'Discuss.'

'Horrible,' said April.

'Tasteless,' agreed Poppy.

'Gendered, archaic, possibly single-handedly propping up the fast-fashion industry, but *also*,' said April, 'if you think about it *deeply*, like as a casual observer casually observing dudes in hair gel and chicks with spray tans, Fashions on the Field is unequivocally *the best*.'

'My thoughts exactly,' said Dani.

'The white-tie-black-shirt-with-fedora look?' said April. 'Genius.'

Dani: 'And with white-framed sunnies? Chef's kiss.'

'Coincidentally,' said April, 'my grandma wears white Oakleys.'

Dani: 'Does she look rad?'

April: 'No, she looks like a speed dealer.'

Poppy choked on her mini quiche and they all convulsed into giggles. Listening to these women shit-talk was like Christmas. Poppy hadn't laughed so hard in forever.

The five horse races occurred between 2.20 pm and 4.47 pm apparently. Poppy spied one briefly from a distance, registering the thundering of hooves and a slice of colourful satin as the horses sped past a roaring crowd, and promptly turned back to her conversation. Everyone knew the races weren't actually for the races.

SPECIAL DELIVERY

As dusk fell after the final presentation and Dani and April went to source another bottle, Poppy swiped another mini quiche from the table (possibly her thirtieth of the day—they were buttery bombs of eggy-bacony deliciousness, and thank goodness, because she needed to soak up a lot of champagne). She was mid-chew when she felt a long arm loop around her shoulders.

'Hey, you,' said James thickly. His body was warm despite the chill and he smelled of aftershave and beer—not an unpleasant combination.

Wobbly on her heels, Poppy readjusted into his embrace. 'Hey, yourself.' She swallowed the last bite of quiche. 'How's your testosterone-fuelled afternoon been?'

'Superb. We got it catered by KFC and one bloke's dad is a horse whisperer so we've been making money on the punts all day. I'm fifty-seven dollars up.'

Poppy raised an eyebrow.

'I only bet in increments of two dollars,' he explained. 'Low risk, low reward. I'll never be Warren Buffett but I'll never be broke either. Some women would find that a turn-on.' He waggled his eyebrows suggestively.

Poppy tried to shove him but she was trapped under his heavy forearm. 'How many drinks have you had?'

'A few.' He grinned sheepishly and leaned in to whisper in her ear. 'I missed you.'

Poppy felt her insides vaporise to dust. *He missed her.* Her self-control around this man was laughable.

'Who is this?' demanded Dani, reappearing at Poppy's side. She pointed an accusatory finger. 'Are you James?'

James blinked. 'My reputation precedes me.' He moved his arm from Poppy's shoulders and held it out to shake Dani's hand.

Dani ignored it. 'Aha! You are just what I imagined.' She turned to Poppy. 'I can see what you mean.'

'What do you mean? What does she mean?' He looked at Poppy quizzically.

Please make Dani shut up, she prayed. *Please make her shut up.* She had described James in so many ways to her best friend, this was a real game of Russian roulette they were playing. Selfish douche with a pole up his arse? Yep, she'd called him that. Outrageously hot and possibly the best sex she'd ever had? Cringe, yep, she'd said that too.

Dani cleared her throat. 'She said you were'—*please pleasepleasepleaseplease*—'tall.'

Poppy almost fainted with relief. Thank god for beautiful, precious, clever, *clever* Dani.

'You must be Dani,' he said, smiling. 'Pleasure to meet you.'

Dani looked at him, her eyes blazing with something Poppy couldn't quite place. Her best friend could be terrifying when she wanted to. 'Pleasure's all mine,' she said curtly. 'I hear you're still obsessed with your ex.'

James choked on his beer and Poppy felt the wind rush out of her. There was the Dani sucker punch.

'Where did you hear that?' asked James, his eyes darting between the two women.

Dani looked pointedly at Poppy.

'You *did* say that you weren't over her,' Poppy said.

James turned his whole body towards Poppy. 'When?' He looked properly confused.

'You said you broke up, she took the dog and you were still not over it.'

Dani nodded and crossed her arms.

To Poppy's surprise, James began to laugh. It started small, a crinkle of his lips, but next thing she knew he was doubled over shaking and wiping tears from his eyes.

'What?' demanded Poppy. This was not just bewildering; this was embarrassing. Why was he laughing?!

James draped his arm around Poppy and rested his head against hers. 'I hate to disappoint you ladies,' he wheezed, 'but I am one hundred per cent over my ex. When I said I wasn't over it, I meant I wasn't over the dog.' His face suddenly became serious and he straightened up. 'She took my dog and I was devastated; I still am. We got him when he was a puppy but I felt so guilty about calling off the engagement that I let her have him. I miss him so much. That's why I got Eileen.' He turned to Dani, looking genuinely apologetic. 'Sorry—I know that story's not as juicy.'

Poppy could sense the same antennae pricking up in her best friend's brain. *He broke off the engagement? He wasn't on the rebound?* Oh, they would have so much to discuss tonight!

'April's gone to the ladies,' announced Dani. 'I'm gonna go too. You wanna come, Pops?'

Poppy looked between Dani and James and considered her bladder and the new information muddling through the quagmire of her brain. 'I'm okay, thanks, Dan,' she said.

Dani fixed her eyes on James and readjusted her clutch under her arm. 'Don't go anywhere, James,' she commanded. 'We can get to know each other later.'

As she stalked off, James let out a low whistle. 'What the hell have you told her about me?'

Poppy grimaced. 'In summary, everything. From the car park incident to now.'

'I see,' said James, rubbing the back of his neck. 'So she hates me?'

'She did at one point. In solidarity.'

'Did you try to change her mind? Did you at least tell her about my DIY skills?'

Poppy laughed. 'She was unimpressed you didn't finish the job.'

James's eyes glinted and a grin crept over his face. 'But I finished the most important job. Twice.' He watched her intently as her cheeks flushed at the memory; it seemed to embolden him. He slid his arm down to her waist and pulled her towards him. 'You look amazing,' he murmured into her neck.

Poppy was suddenly struggling to breathe. She could feel a hardness in his trousers. 'We decided we'd be friends, remember?'

'Circumstances have changed.' James's voice was low and gravelly.

'What circumstances?'

'That dress, for starters.' His thumb was tracing circles on her lower back and Poppy hoped he couldn't feel her shiver. What was she thinking, wearing silk?! Save for a few nano-particles of fabric, she was basically naked under his touch.

He was massaging her waist, edging her closer to him with every flex of his fingertips. She was forgetting to breathe, her nipples were hardening and he was smiling like he knew the power he had over her. She didn't know if she wanted to sink deeper into this dream or yank herself out of it.

Think, breathe, think, breathe, think, breathe. Oh god, that was too much to remember right now. She tried to focus her thoughts.

'Should we go for a walk?' he breathed.

Poppy felt a bolt of heat rocket up her spine. Was he suggesting what she thought he was suggesting?! She was not a horny teenager; she was almost middle-aged! They couldn't do something like that, not here, not in a public place. Could they? This was really teetering on the edge of that friend zone.

Think, think, think. 'No,' she whispered back, surprised she had the strength. She pulled away from him fractionally, steadying herself. 'Dani doesn't know anyone else. I should wait for her here.'

Poppy jerked her eyes away and took a gulp of champagne to wash out the impure thoughts flooding her central cortex. *Friends*, they had decided to be *friends*. It was proving very difficult to remember this.

'She knows April,' James reminded her.

He moved his mouth to her neck, his lips drifting towards her earlobe. They were basically already making out. Poppy remembered vaguely she should be embarrassed by the PDA but she couldn't make her brain work. At least if they went for a walk she could extricate herself from this blatant public-groping situation.

'Okay,' she heard herself say. She needed a bucket of cold water poured over her, stat. This was Orange, for Christ's sake.

Friends of her parents would be here. She needed to pull it together. She wrenched herself away from James and took a deep breath. 'Where are we going?'

James reached for her but she dodged him and picked up another mini quiche. She racked her brain for somewhere non-sexual they could go. 'Let's go to the stables,' she suggested.

'Aren't you sick of horses yet?' asked James. He picked up three mini quiches and wolfed one down.

'Ha!' laughed Poppy. 'I haven't even *seen* a horse today. I have *perceived* a horse in the distance. But could I tell you what colour said horse was? No. Could I confirm if it had four legs? No.'

'Then we're going to the stables,' James said. 'You can't go to the races without seeing a horse. It's unAustralian.'

He led her out of the tent, through the throngs of racegoers and around a brick pavilion. The sky was a swirl of lilac fading into blue as they stepped over crushed beer cans and plastic cups, and came to the quiet of the stables. The air smelled of wet hay and horses, and the din of the crowd was muffled. The horses were majestically quiet. They were tall and muscular, their manes gleaming in the fading evening light. A hilarious thought occurred to Poppy.

'What?' James asked, noticing her smile.

'Your spirit animal is definitely a horse.'

'Why is that?'

'They're tall. Great hair. Very . . .'

'Muscly?'

Poppy climbed up onto one of the fences to peer over. 'I was going to say hungry. You eat weirdly fast.'

SPECIAL DELIVERY

James came up behind her. 'I've had a lifetime of practice. How's the view up there?'

'Excellent.' She sat on the top railing and turned towards him. 'Quite the novelty being taller than you. Are you feeling emasculated?'

He came over and put his hands on the railing on either side of her, only inches from her butt. 'I'm feeling turned on, if you must know.'

Poppy felt a shiver reverberate down from her navel. She slid off the railing so she was standing centimetres from his chest. She steadied her breath and grinned. 'Lucky I'm so short then, since we're such good *friends*.' She ducked under his arm and walked into the stables pavilion, feeling his gaze on her back. He chuckled and followed.

'Where are you taking me, McKellar?'

'No idea,' said Poppy, wandering deeper into the building where the lighting was definitely not friend-zone-y. Most of the pens were empty, the chaff bags hanging untouched from the railings. She reached the end of the corridor and turned around to find James standing in front of her. The light was perilously dim, heightening her senses. There was a fizzing in her abdomen she was trying to ignore.

'Hi,' said Poppy, rooted to the ground.

'Hi,' he responded.

'Hi,' she said again. Goddamn that malfunctioning brain of hers.

'Hi,' he said, playing along. He was making her squirm on purpose, she could tell. His eyes were slightly crinkled and his lower lip had shifted to the left; he was clearly enjoying this.

'Should we go?' asked Poppy.

He smiled. 'No.'

'No?' Poppy squeaked. There was a war going on inside her. Her brain was screaming: *Remind him we're friends!* Her traitorous body was telling her mind to shut the eff up. This guy could melt her resolve like butter.

'I was thinking,' began James, closing the space between them, 'that the best thing about being friends with someone is that you can change your mind.'

'About what?' whispered Poppy, her adrenal glands on the verge of combusting.

'This dress, for example. I used to love it, but now I think I'd rather get rid of it.' He pressed himself against her and his hand found the slit in her dress.

A tiny moan escaped Poppy and she arched against him as his hand slid up her thigh. Body was triumphing over brain.

Their stomachs met and goosebumps rippled across her skin, a heavy want was gathering behind her ribs and belly button and all the places they were touching. James's other hand skimmed over the silk to hold her waist and he shifted her against the wall. Poppy levered against it to push back into him. This was probably not a good idea, but hell, she'd come this far.

Her breath hitched and she heard his do the same. Her heart was drumming in her chest as his hands manoeuvred the silk of her dress higher and higher until he could feel the lace of her underwear.

'Fuck being friends,' he whispered as he ran his hands over her thighs.

Poppy tried to argue but all that came out was a breathless whimper. She wound her hands into the fabric of his shirt, tugging it free from his waistband. James's lips parted hers with the lightest of touches and his tongue slid over hers. His hands skimmed up and down her torso, gliding from breast to thigh and back, and her body yielded under his touch, desperate for more. She pressed herself against him and his hands rose to her jaw, angling her mouth to his as he kissed her deeper. His fingertips were warm and strong, and they were somehow everywhere.

Poppy tugged the blazer off his shoulders letting it fall onto the dusty floor. She slid her hands up his back, feeling the resistance of his muscles. She caught the hem of his shirt and prised it up. He finished the job, pulling it over his head to reveal his broad shoulders. One hand gripped her waist and the other moved up to the lace of her underwear. His fingers lingered on her outer thigh, suggesting everything but forcing nothing.

James's inky gaze narrowed in on her, the muscles in his jaw tensing as he moved both hands to her zipper, and carefully undid it. The fabric bunched uselessly at her waist. They were half-naked in a dusty hay-strewn stable and nothing in the world had ever felt sexier.

Ravenously, Poppy lunged at his belt.

'Are you sure?' whispered James, his hands skimming her back, searching for her bra hook.

Poppy arched into him, guiding his hands there. 'You're asking that now?!' They were already at criminal levels of public indecency.

He laughed. 'I failed on the friends thing.' He pulled away slightly as he moved her bra strap down her arm, his dark eyes following with an almost giddy sheen.

In the distance, a bell sounded and a voice carried over a PA system. 'First bus leaves in ten minutes.'

Poppy's stomach dropped. 'Shit!' she cried, jerking away from him. 'Fuck, I'm supposed to be on that bus. With Dani. Fuck, I'd forgotten all about her. What time is it?'

James still had his hands around her back, her bra was half off. 'Do you really need to go?' he asked.

Poppy face-palmed herself. 'Yes,' she groaned. 'I'm such a shit friend. How long have we been here?'

James squinted at his watch through the dark. 'Not that long. I'm sorry—I shouldn't haven't dragged you here.'

'Not your fault,' muttered Poppy, suddenly furious with herself. She scrambled to put her dress back on properly. 'I'd better run.'

'Blame it on me,' said James, picking up his shirt and shaking off the dust.

'Thanks, but I might pretend I was knocked unconscious by a horse or something.'

'Hey,' said James, catching her hand before she could run off. He planted a strong kiss on her lips. 'I meant what I said. Fuck being friends.'

Poppy turned towards the door. 'We'll chat later,' she called. She hitched up her dress and began jogging away as quickly as her chunky heels would allow.

CHAPTER 34

The vibe on the bus was raucous and messy. Complete strangers were dancing with each other in the aisle, men were loosening their ties and women were shoving their heels in handbags and swapping to flats. One bloke was trying to crowd-surf.

Poppy's brain was trying to block the memory of James's hand sliding up her thigh. He was nowhere to be seen and yet he was all over her. The smell of his aftershave was on her neck. She could feel the lightning sizzle of his hands up her back. She was terrified Dani would ask a question and she'd blurt out something embarrassingly incomprehensible like *James! Thrusting! Horses!* Fortunately, Dani had hardly noticed Poppy was missing as it seemed the queue for the portaloos had wasted as much time as it took to get half-undressed in a stable. April, meanwhile, had been misplaced. She'd texted Poppy a burger emoji to confirm she was alive.

Poppy tried to focus her attention on hmm-ing in the right spots as Dani ranted about why Fashions on the Field was actually a joke (case in point: men in trilby hats always won but everyone knew guys who wore trilbies in real life were creeps and sociopaths). By the time the bus rolled into downtown Orange, Poppy felt only mildly less flustered. Dani, however, shrieked in alarm. 'Pops!' she cried, peering through the window of the Royal Hotel. 'Where is the dancefloor?!'

Dani looked so bereft that Poppy laughed. 'There, I think.' She pointed to a wooden floor currently covered with aluminium tables and some sexagenarian diners who'd not bargained on a busload of boozed racegoers interrupting their Saturday schnitzel.

'Oh man!' groaned Dani. 'My dancing feet are ready now!'

Poppy checked her watch. 'Relax, my dear. They pack away the tables at seven. We've got thirty minutes. We could order a quick pizza while we wait?'

'Yes!' Dani cheered, consoled. 'Hawaiian!'

The two women filed off the bus and snaked through the crowd to the bar, where they ordered a large Hawaiian pizza and two bottles of water. While they sat at one of the aluminium tables, a queue of racegoers began forming outside as the bouncers took a leisurely approach to ID-checking.

'How come they didn't check our IDs?' fumed Dani, watching a group of women pull their licences out of their purses. 'We don't look older than them, do we?'

The women at the door wore puff-sleeved midi dresses and minis with thigh-high boots. From this distance, Poppy couldn't tell if they too were scarred by motherhood's death-defying weariness. She had to admit, the thought of going home to sit on the couch and drink tea was crystallising in her mind as a very appealing option. Maybe after the pizza. No wonder the bouncers hadn't checked her ID; she probably gave off the aura of a seventy-year-old.

'Ooh, man alert, man alert!' announced Dani.

Poppy followed her gaze to see a head towering above the queue outside. 'The king of the jungle returns to find his prey,' she intoned in a David Attenborough voice. 'He scans the horizon, hoping to find her lurking on the crowded savannah.'

'I'm not his prey, Dan. I told you: we decided we're friends.' Technically true, if you discounted the events of the past hour.

'Please,' scoffed Dani. 'He couldn't take his eyes off you. And the way he kept finding ways to touch you, it was like he was marking his territory. I'm surprised he didn't pee on your leg.'

'Yuck, Dan.' Poppy shoved a giant piece of pizza in her mouth. 'How good is this Hawaiian?'

'Don't change the subject. I'm trying to do my best friend duty by reminding you to be careful—even if he does seem like your perfect man.'

Poppy spluttered on her pizza. 'What do you mean my perfect man?!'

'He has the looks of Patrick and the banter of Henry without the awkward history. I can see how it's an appealing combo.'

Poppy's windpipe suddenly felt airless and scratchy. 'No, no, no, Dan. I mean, yes, he's fun, and there's definitely some level of animal attraction there that I can't shake, but he is one hundred per cent *not* my perfect man. He legitimately drives me crazy sometimes. He brings out my inner velociraptor or something.'

Dani smiled. 'Well, my dear, after nine years of watching you in submissive girlfriend mode, it's refreshing to see this side of you.'

'But it's not real, Dan. The way I act around him, it's not me.'

Dani bit her lip thoughtfully. 'Maybe it is. Maybe he doesn't bring out your inner velociraptor, maybe it's just—you. Maybe you spent so long in Patrick's shadow, you've forgotten.'

Poppy stared at her friend wordlessly, the gears in her brain starting to turn. Was James really her perfect man? She'd been so blinded by lust she hadn't considered whether this could be anything serious. She gulped down some water, relishing the coldness sliding down her throat. She shook her head. This was a stupid hypothetical. It couldn't be anything serious, because she didn't have the time or capacity or brain space.

'I saw Henry before,' said Dani.

Poppy seized on the change of subject. 'Really?' She gulped more brain-defogging water. 'Henry didn't mention he was coming.'

'Yeah, saw him near the portaloos. He said his fiancée has been in Brisbane for a few months.'

Poppy frowned. 'There's something strange going on there. Henry has been acting a bit weird lately.'

Dani's eyes lit up. 'Ooh, I hope he turns up here. I'll find out what's going on.'

Poppy smiled wryly at her friend. 'You do that.' Poppy had no interest in the machinations of Henry-and-Willa. It had taken her and Henry so long to get back to a place of comfortable companionship, she didn't want anything messing with the precarious balance they'd established, which was largely based on pretending Willa was some sort of asexual roommate.

'Look who's made it into the inner sanctum,' said Dani in her David Attenborough voice again. 'The male of the species, following a mere sixty minutes of separation, has renewed his focus on his target. He scans his surrounds for a female companion, ready to lure her in with his mating dance.'

At that moment, James spotted them and waved. He began making his way over.

'Can we agree there'll be no more chat about mating?' Poppy pleaded. 'At least, not in front of James?'

Dani sighed. 'Okay. But I promise you, the sexual tension is on par with that silverback gorilla doco we watched the morning after my hens' party. Remember those humping noises? I still hear them in my dreams. I mean, only my sexual dreams, obviously—'

'Dani, stop!'

'Stop what?' asked James. His eyes were sparkling from the cold outside.

'Nothing.' Poppy glared at her friend.

A waiter in a black t-shirt arrived at their table. 'Hi, guys, sorry to interrupt, but we need to move this table now. We've got to get the dancefloor ready.'

'Finally!' yelled Dani, punching the air. 'This is what I've been waiting for. You guys coming?' She was already adjusting her dress straps ready for the exercise. Dani prided herself on her energetic moves, which both dazzled onlookers *and* counted as an aerobic workout.

'I'm not dance-ready yet,' admitted James.

'Fine, you two stay here. I'll go find April.' Dani strode off before Poppy could answer for herself.

'She definitely hates me,' muttered James.

'She's just protective and opinionated, and a dancefloor fiend. There was no way she was going to be impressed by you unless you challenged her to a dance-off to MC Hammer's "U Can't Touch This".'

James smiled. 'I'll save that for later.' He reached for Poppy's hand and pulled her towards him. 'Come on, McKellar, I'm buying you a drink.'

Poppy allowed herself to be led to the bar, enjoying the warmth of his hand on hers. Butterflies of . . . *something* pirouetted in her stomach.

Next to them, an older guy with a beard was yelling at the bartender while wobbling like an amateur rollerskater. James's arm slid around Poppy's waist and he steered her to the left, shielding her from the drunken man. Her skin crackled where he'd touched her and flashbacks from the stable suddenly flooded her. The pull of fabric, the tug of hair, the touch of his lips on her skin . . . *Pull it together!* she scolded herself.

Drinks in hand, they made their way back to the far corner of the room, where Poppy found a spare table and perched on a bar stool.

'Why *is* Dani so protective?' asked James as they sat down.

'Oh, you know,' replied Poppy vaguely.

'Tell me.'

Poppy picked up a cardboard coaster from the centre of the table and traced the edge with her fingertip, trying to find the right words. 'She's my best friend. She's been the one constant since we met in first-year uni. Other friends and boyfriends have come and gone, but she's always been there for me. She's my ride or die, and she doesn't want me to get hurt.'

'And she thinks you're in danger of getting hurt by me?'

'No—and yes,' Poppy admitted. She forced herself to settle the coaster on the table and placed her drink on top. 'She thinks I'm vulnerable right now, and she thinks you're interested in being more than friends, and she thinks I . . .' Poppy trailed off and tipped her head to look at the strip lighting on the ceiling. The way it blinded her felt kind of good.

'What else does she think?'

Poppy was suddenly exhausted. Exhausted from life, and today, and these heels . . . and most of all, she was exhausted from not knowing what to do. 'She thinks the friends-with-benefits thing is dangerous. She thinks I'll end up wanting more and getting my heart broken.'

James's charcoal eyes were still. The mischievous sparkle had gone and his knuckles tightened on his beer. 'And what do you want?' he asked quietly.

Poppy felt herself wilt under his gaze. He already knew what she wanted. Friendship. But that thing in the stables . . . she could see why he was confused. It didn't help that his knee was resting against hers and she hadn't pulled away.

'What do *you* want?' she asked. If she could just work out what was going on in his brain she could reverse-engineer her position.

'I asked you first,' he countered.

Poppy stirred the ice in her drink with her straw, her weariness surging like a king tide. If a troupe of shirtless men suddenly appeared with one of those portable Princess Jasmine–style beds, she would happily climb aboard for a nap. 'I don't know,' she sighed. 'That's the problem. The only thing I'm clear on at the moment is wanting to be a good mum. I mean, as a general concept, the idea of meeting a lovely guy who makes me laugh and drives me wild in the bedroom is amazing—but it's not a priority, especially not now. And besides, does that guy even exist?'

Her subconscious piped up: *Um, across the table?* She ignored it. This wasn't a conversation about James; it was bigger than that.

'And if this guy does exist, do I want him to be around my daughter? Is that drive-me-wild guy also father material, and if he isn't, is that okay? Does he have to be both? Do I have to decide for Maeve and me, or do I have to make the decision for myself and make Maeve go along with it? Or do I swear off all men to protect Maeve—or would that be worse, because then she has no chance of finding a father figure?' Poppy laughed slightly hysterically. 'Far out, I'm driving myself insane!'

James sipped his beer thoughtfully. 'I think it's only sensible that you have to think about Maeve. It would be weird if you didn't.' He set his beer down, studying her. 'Although, are we still speaking in hypotheticals?'

'We are,' said Poppy firmly. She was definitely not imagining him in bed next to her, his arm draped over her like a security blanket, flicking on the bedside light to help her find her way to the cot. He was only interested in getting hot and heavy when small babies were conveniently absent. She was aware of that. She was in control.

James's mouth curved into a smile. 'So hypothetically speaking, what would a guy have to do to drive you wild in the bedroom?'

Poppy's laugh was instant. 'You're not helping.'

'Sorry.' He laughed too and picked up his beer again. 'I get that you don't want any distractions to mess with your current set-up when it seems to be working so well.'

Poppy smiled at him gratefully. This was why he was so easy to talk to. He made her laugh *and* he listened.

James continued, 'But I don't think you should close yourself off from the world because of Maeve.' His eyes held hers for an extended beat, then he shrugged matter-of-factly and took a sip of his beer.

Poppy stared at him. Was he talking about closing herself off from the world or . . . from him? Were they still talking in hypotheticals? His gaze returned to her, his expression all sincerity and warmth, and despite herself Poppy felt her heart skip a beat.

'How are the uni applications going?' she asked, desperate for something platonic to discuss.

James gave her a knowing smile. He knew exactly what she was doing.

'What's the plan?' she pressed. Yes, she was changing the subject—but also, she was genuinely interested. She wanted to learn everything about him.

'I had the entrance exams a couple of weeks ago,' he said eventually. 'Our preferences are supposed to be decided this weekend. Actually, I might even have an email by now.' He picked up his phone and started scrolling. After a few seconds, he stopped. 'No way,' he breathed.

'What?' asked Poppy.

'I got it!'

'Got what?'

'Melbourne.'

'Melbourne, *Victoria*?' Poppy's head spun off her shoulders and fell to the floor. At least that is what it felt like. 'You're moving to Melbourne?!'

'Wow!' James grinned. 'I guess I am. I'll start next year. I'll have to find somewhere to live. Wow, this is insane. I can't believe I got in—this is massive.'

Poppy's mind was whirring like a centrifuge now, with everything pushed to the edges apart from one central piece of information. *He's moving to Melbourne.* It was like she'd been at the good part of a dream and woken up just before she got the ice cream or the puppy or the mind-blowing orgasm. She was completely disorientated. The logical part of her brain tried to tell her to congratulate him. The selfish part of her brain was screaming expletives.

'You okay?' asked James. His X-ray eyes were back on her.

'Yes, of course,' said Poppy, forcing a smile. 'Congratulations. I just . . .' She dropped her eyes. 'I didn't realise Melbourne was one of your preferences.'

James was looking at his phone again, re-reading the email. 'It was a wild card choice, but I figured there's nothing really keeping me here, and—'

SPECIAL DELIVERY

Poppy felt her stomach drop as James prattled on. *Nothing.* She was *nothing*. She furiously willed her tear ducts to keep themselves closed. She had no claim over this guy, he was free to move where he wanted and she shouldn't care—so why did her insides feel like they were being twisted inside-out? She stood up, realising she needed fresh air in her lungs. 'I think I should go,' she said.

James seemed startled. 'Poppy, I didn't mean to upset you.'

Poppy's veins hardened with resolution. 'What are we even doing?' She waved her hand between them. 'What is this?'

'We're . . .' James seemed lost for words. 'We're whatever you want to be. We're friends?'

'James,' she hissed. 'I almost had sex with you in a stable. I do *not* do that with my friends.'

'Stay.' He grabbed her hand, his long fingers wrapping around hers.

Her skin buzzed where he touched her but Poppy knew she couldn't do what he asked. There were some things you could gloss over and laugh off, but someone telling you that you were *nothing*? That was too much.

She wrenched her hand away. 'I can't do this, James. If calling me your friend with benefits means you get to enjoy commitment-free sex for a few months before you leave without a trace, then count me out. I'm not going to hook up with you to fill a void before you skip off to Melbourne and I never see you again. I'm not a space filler and I don't want to be that kind of friend.'

'Poppy, that's not how I think of you. I literally just found out about Melbourne thirty seconds ago. And I applied ages ago, long before anything happened between us. I have no idea what's going on; I still need to process everything. But I thought you'd be happy for me?'

'I am happy for you,' Poppy lied through gritted teeth. 'But I can't do this. I'm going home.'

James stood up. 'No, this is your night out. I'll go home.'

'No, you should celebrate, James. I'll go home.'

'This is stupid. We should both stay.' He put his hand on her shoulder and Poppy felt the weight of his gaze on her. His hand slid down to hold hers. 'Stay with me, Poppy.'

Poppy couldn't pull her eyes away and she knew that was where the danger lay. He could turn her brain to mush. She needed to be strong. She shook her head.

'Then I'm going home.' James put his near-full beer on the table. 'You stay and have fun with Dani. I hope you have a great night, Poppy. Cut a rug for me.'

Poppy jerked out of her trance like cold water had been poured over her. 'Fine,' she muttered. 'Perfect.'

James turned and weaved through the crowd towards the door, the strobe lights of the dancefloor flickering over his shoulders. Poppy waited for it, but he didn't look back.

Shell-shocked and on the verge of tears, she turned to the heaving dancefloor. Dani and April were in the centre, sweaty and breathless. Poppy downed her drink and marched towards them.

Dani squealed when she saw her. 'Hooray! You've come to your senses! Here, we saved you a space.' She pulled Poppy towards her. 'Where's James?' she yelled over the Black Eyed Peas.

'Gone home,' Poppy yelled back.
'Boring!' yelled Dani. 'You okay? Need a drink?'
'Drink!'
'Let's go then!'
The three women snaked their way to the bar.
'We're doing shots,' announced Dani, flagging down the barman.

Poppy grimaced but April laughed. 'When in Rome!' she said, clapping Poppy on the back. Poppy wondered briefly if it had been a mistake—from a liver-health perspective—to introduce these two.

With the acidic taste of tequila, salt and lemon curdling in her mouth, Poppy let herself be led back to the steaming dancefloor. Dani and April were women on a mission, unfazed by the lack of space and oxygen. They wedged themselves in the centre of the action, carving a gap with their arm-heavy dance moves. For the dancers surrounding them, it was a case of move or be decapitated.

With laser beams of pink and yellow slicing the air above them and a suffocating soundtrack of noughties pop, Poppy let herself be swept up in their maelstrom of sweat, energy, alcohol and temple-rattling dance moves. Feelings she hadn't felt in ages were coming back to her: physical sensations (high heels stepping on her toes, an extreme thirstiness for vodka sodas) and deep, fervent emotions (*I love my friends so much! What shit is this DJ playing?!*).

'When the fuck is he going to play Taylor Sssswift?' Poppy yelled at her friends, vaguely aware she was slurring. 'I gotta talk some sssense into this idiot.'

'I'm going home!' yelled Dani suddenly. 'I need to drunk dial my husband.'

'No!' cried Poppy helplessly as her friend ran towards the door. But there was no stopping Dani when she made a drunken decision. She made them hard and fast and delivered on them rapidly, hence the running.

Oh well, it had been fun while it lasted. Summoning the energy for the non-Dani phase of the night, Poppy turned to April and puffed out her chest. 'I'll sort out this music,' she yelled, and staggered across the dancefloor to the middle-aged man pressing keys on a laptop.

'Can you play some Taylor Swift?' she yelled.

'What?' he yelled back.

'Taylor Swift!' she hollered, squinting to read the playlist on his screen. She'd find the songs herself if only the words would stop moving.

'Heyyyyy!' shouted a voice behind her as two arms reached around to grab her wrists. 'Easy there, tiger. Are you requesting Taylor Swift again?'

'Yesssss,' she sighed, leaning into the familiar torso. 'I love her.'

'Knew it,' said Henry, spinning her around to face him. 'Please never change, Pops,' he said as he smoothed her hair back. 'I've missed you.'

'I see you nearly every day, Henry.'

'Not like this, though.'

'No,' Poppy admitted. 'Not like this.' She looked down at herself, her chest sheened with sweat, Dani's dress sticking to her body way too provocatively. She gave a pitiful whine and fell into Henry's chest. 'Oh, Henry, I'm druuuunk.'

'I can tell,' said Henry, wrapping his arms around her. His pores smelled of rum and his stubble was scratching her bare shoulder. 'Should we get out of here?'

Poppy looked over and saw April being lifted into the air by someone she recognised from the tent. Next thing she knew Henry was holding her hand and guiding her out of the pub. The deja vu from the early 2010s was uncanny.

'N-needed th-this,' stuttered Poppy, standing near the taxi rank, her body temperature falling rapidly. 'Air. Cold. Z'good.'

Henry stood next to her in his blue-and-white-striped shirt; his jacket was draped over Poppy's shoulders. She turned to him. His blue eyes were level with hers. 'I forgot about your eyes!' she cackled.

Henry put his arm around her and Poppy tried ineffectually to shake him off. 'Ya know the good thing about your eyes, Henry? Your eyes are at eye level.'

'Eye level?'

'Yesssss, Henry. Eye level! I don' have to tilt my head to look at 'em. Tall guys are sahhh annoying like that.'

'You calling me short, McKellar?'

'You *are* short, Henry.'

'I'm taller than you.'

'Ha! As if that counts. I'm basically a pea. Poppy the pea, thassss meee!'

Henry snickered. 'You're a real poet, Pops.'

Poppy elbowed him. 'And you suck, Henry.' She was suddenly starving. 'Can we get a kebab?'

Henry chuckled. 'Yes, Pops, and we can get extra hummus, just how you like it.'

Poppy leaned into his shoulder as thanks, enjoying the warmth of him. It was bloody cold out here. Willa would understand that.

They traipsed up to the neon-lit kebab shop. Poppy was wobbly on her heels and Henry seemed to be zigzagging as much as she was, which had a pleasantly neutralising effect.

Back at the taxi rank with two half-eaten kebabs, the air was saturated with freezing mist and the pungent smell of garlic.

'You're gross,' said Poppy, picking a shred of chicken out of her kebab. 'I can't believe you asked for extra garlic sauce.'

'Says the girl fingering her kebab.'

'See? You are gross, Henry.'

Henry harrumphed and rearranged his arm around Poppy's shoulders. It had been there for a while now and Poppy was ignoring it. Her need for his body warmth was purely functional.

Around her, people shivered and laughed, the steam from their breath clouding the air. There were too many people in this taxi line. She wanted to get home and out of these shoes and out of this bra and into her bed, now.

'You're both gross,' piped up a man in a flannelette jacket sitting in the gutter in front of them. 'Who wants a kebab at this hour of the night? Tomorrow you'll wake up and feel like a rat shat in your mouth. Rat turds, that's all you'll be able to taste.'

Henry and Poppy gaped at each other and Henry began to shake with silent laughter. Poppy felt herself wobble into him and gasped trying to stifle a giggle.

'I'm telling you,' the man continued. 'You need pure protein. Not some overpriced fifteen-dollar flat bread filled with possum

SPECIAL DELIVERY

meat and garlic sauce. Kebabs are just a marketing ploy. In my day, we'd go home and eat a block of cheese and drink a pint of milk and we'd be right as rain. Never had a hangover in the seventies, and I drank a fuck-load, I can tell you.'

A yelp escaped Poppy and Henry had his hands on his knees, trying to steady himself from laughing.

'You think it's funny, do you?' said the man, pulling a block of tasty cheese from the breast pocket of his flannelette. He peeled the plastic down and broke off a chunk. 'Have a chew on that and thank me later.'

Both of them were in fits of giggles now. 'Already full, mate,' gasped Henry, grabbing Poppy's hand and pulling her towards an approaching taxi. 'Maybe next time.'

They stumbled into the back of the taxi, heaving with laughter. Poppy's abs hurt. She tried to think of something to make her stop laughing, but the image of the block of yellow cheese emerging from the man's pocket was replaying in her mind like a gif.

'Two Penkivil Place,' called Poppy loudly, as Henry slumped in the seat beside her. 'What's your address, Marshall?'

'Nope, we're having kick-ons at yours, Pops. Two Penkivil Place for both of us, mate.'

The taxi driver flicked on his indicator and Poppy shoved Henry away from her. 'I'm not doing kick-ons, Hen. I'm too old. I'm *tired*.'

Henry grabbed her hand across the middle seat and threaded his fingers through hers. 'Come on, Pops. For old time's sake.'

Poppy snatched her hand away from him. 'Stop being weird, Henry.'

Henry smiled sleepily and patted her head.

The taxi glided through the dark streets, and by the time they pulled up to the house, Poppy could feel her eyelids closing. The night was a hazy black and everything felt so heavy and dizzy and cold. Apart from Henry. Henry seemed warm. But he was somehow already out of the taxi and opening her door and reaching in to help her out. His hands were so toasty, like warm bread. Mmm, bread. She could go some bread right now.

'This is the lair, hey?' Henry said, not letting go of Poppy's hand. He pulled her towards him into a one-armed side hug. He was so warm and solid, it seemed to help with her dizziness.

'Henry, I feel weird about you coming to my house.'

'Pops, don't make things weird.'

She wasn't trying to. It just felt important to say it. It *was* weird, right? He had a fiancée. They were ex-lovers. They'd seen each other naked. They had *liked* seeing each other naked. Even with such wobbly ankles and hazy eyes, it felt like a little person in her peripheral vision was stamping their feet saying, THIS IS WEIRD.

Henry suddenly turned to her and grabbed her face. She smelled the rum on his breath and before she knew what was happening, his wet lips were on hers. A part of her flickered with muscle memory—ha-ha, yes! A drunken kiss with Henry. How hilarious!

The other part of her reacted physically. 'Henry!' she yelled, pushing him off, causing herself to teeter on her heels. 'What the hell are you doing?!'

Henry stumbled back and blinked. The confusion on his face would have been comic if it wasn't for the coiling anguish in her stomach. A few years ago she would have dreamed of another kiss with Henry. But not now. Not like this.

The temperature seemed to plummet further and Poppy wrapped her arms around herself. 'Fuck, Henry!'

That little person in the periphery was getting bigger and stamping harder. *THIS IS FUCKING WEIRD.*

Oh no, wait. Shit. The little person really was getting bigger. It was turning into a really big person with really big shoulders.

'What's going on? Are you okay, Poppy?' James was on her verandah, walking towards her from her front door. Poppy's stomach plummeted. Oh fuckity-fuck, fuck, fuck.

'What the hell, James? What are you doing here?'

'I thought I'd . . . I was waiting . . . I wanted to say . . . I wanted to see if . . .' He looked from her to Henry and back. 'Why the fuck is *he* here?' he growled.

'Mate, fuck off!' yelled Henry.

James's eyes widened slowly. 'You brought *him* back here?'

How was this happening? The convergence of these worlds, at this moment, in this fucking freezing weather with these fucking uncomfortable shoes. What a *fucking* joke. A sudden pulsing in her temple told her the hangover tomorrow would be abnormally horrendous. She closed her eyes and whimpered.

'That's it,' James hissed. 'I'm going. I don't know why I came.' His words cut the freezing air like a knife. Disgust was etched across his face. She had never seen him look so terrifying.

'James, wait,' cried Poppy helplessly. A million words careened through her head. *It's not what it looks like! He kissed me!* But there was too much to explain and not enough time, so nothing came out.

'You think you know someone,' said James bitterly.

He stormed off down the dark street. Within seconds, he had been absorbed into the chilling blackness of the night.

She turned back to see Henry looking pissed. 'What's his problem?' Henry asked, putting his arm around her shoulder again.

'Henry!' cried Poppy, disentangling herself. 'Stop it. Just stop it!' Her drunkenness was morphing into a hazy hangover and the infinitesimal increase in clarity was making the searing pain in her gut even worse. 'What are you doing?! You're engaged! What about Willa? What about your model-slash-doctor fiancée? Are you coming back here to slum it with your ex before you marry the unicorn? Is this some kind of weird kink for you? You *know* me, Henry! I don't want to be that girl!'

'I . . . I . . . Pops, I thought we were having fun?'

'We *were* having fun, Henry, but then you tried to kiss me!'

Henry's eyes suddenly filled with tears and he turned away from her and kicked her garage door with an uncharacteristic ferocity.

'She's left me, Poppy. The love of my life has left me.' He was sobbing. 'I'm a mess. I'm a fucking mess. I thought coming back here might help me but now I only feel worse.'

'*You* feel worse?!' Poppy shouted. 'You come back here to my house, fuck with my head, piss off James and now have the audacity to play the pity card? You were going to sleep with me for your own selfish ego boost! Jesus, Henry!'

'Don't pretend you're innocent here, Poppy,' said Henry venomously. 'You've been playing with me for *months*. Coincidentally bumping into me for *months*, avoiding mentioning my fiancée for *months*. You've been pretending for *months* that I was single. Don't think I didn't notice.'

Poppy felt as if she'd had the wind kicked out of her.

'Fuck off, Henry.'

'Fuck off yourself, Poppy.'

They glared at each other and then, with a look of pure revulsion, the first boy she'd ever loved turned and stormed off down the street, following the same path James had taken moments before.

CHAPTER 35

'How did I not wake up for this?' muttered Dani, plucking the cashews out of a bowl of trail mix. Her hair was sticking out at strange angles, indicating a deep and motionless sleep.

Poppy grunted. The question had been rhetorical.

As she'd predicted, her hangover was immense. Her head was pounding, her skin was beaded with sweat, and, to make things worse, her glutes were abnormally sore, which suggested she was way too old for those dance moves.

She heaped a teaspoon of instant coffee into a mug and poured boiling water over it. *I'M A COOL MOM*, read the mug. The slogan seemed especially cringe-worthy this morning. Poppy reached for the milk and poured in a glug. Desperate times called for desperate measures and this coffee was the sign of a desperate woman.

'Can we *please* go out for breakfast?' asked Dani. This question was not rhetorical.

'No, we cannot. This town is too small. I cannot risk showing my face after last night.'

'What about Uber Eats?'

'This is Orange, Dani. There's only one Uber driver in town and it's a guy called Mal who plays the piano at church on Sundays, so he's not available. We can have Cornflakes and instant coffee and you will survive.'

'Who over the age of twelve eats Cornflakes?' The questions were back to being rhetorical.

Poppy grimaced inwardly. The Cornflakes had been a sentimental purchase, after the Easter getaway. Now they were a crunchily painful reminder of James and whatever had happened last night. She couldn't stop replaying—or trying to replay—the confrontation on her driveway. Why had he been there? What would have happened if Henry wasn't there?

And Henry—ugh, it made her shudder to think of his sloppy rum-soaked lips on hers. Every other kiss they'd shared had been so perfect, but last night had tainted the memory of them all. The thought of his presumptuousness made her blood boil. He'd just expected her to have sex with him, like she had no say in the matter. And he had a fiancée! Or ex-fiancée now, she supposed.

And that was the other thing. When Henry had called Willa the love of his life, a tiny part of her had died. A flame she hadn't even known was still flickering had been abruptly extinguished, and it left her feeling cold and clammy and so fucking stupid. She'd always assumed they were each other's Big Love. Soul mates who belonged together like two pieces of a jigsaw in which their families and friends and hopes and dreams all neatly aligned. She'd been swept away by the Patrick-ness of Patrick—he was loud and exuberant and a show-off and made her feel special—but he never understood her the way Henry did. She'd assumed it was a matter of timing that she hadn't ended up with Henry—they got together too early in life—but increasingly over the past few years she'd secretly believed it was a shame. They would have been perfect for each other. If Patrick had married her, he could have kept her in designer dresses and taken her on glamorous, champagne-filled holidays, and she would have made it work—hell, she would have really enjoyed parts of it. But there would never have been the deep, enduring peace of solid, boring, I-know-what-you're-thinking-so-don't-say-it love. The love that cushioned you when you sat on separate couches reading the paper, not even talking, but happier in each other's presence. The love you felt when having the other person nearby made you more complete, as if the light reflecting off them lit you up from within and made you the best and happiest version of yourself.

But no, that had all been in her head. Henry didn't feel the same deep-rooted connection. The love of his life was a paediatrician with luminescent skin. One who'd left him, no less. Well, life was a cruel joke, wasn't it?

Dani sloshed milk into her bowl of Cornflakes.

'Well, who knew?' she said (rhetorical again). 'Our girl is a man-eater.'

'No I'm not,' Poppy cried. The shame of the Henry kiss was throbbing painfully at her temples.

'It was a joke, Pops.'

'It wasn't funny,' snapped Poppy. 'This stuff always happens to me, Dan. My life is a fucking debacle.'

Dani lowered her spoon. 'Poppy, you're being way too melodramatic about this.'

'But my life is a disaster,' Poppy wailed. 'I screwed up the Henry thing ten years ago and now I've screwed it up with James before I could even work out what was going on.'

'Pops, that's literally two bad things in ten years. Most people would consider that a pretty solid track record.'

'Oh yeah? And would they consider it good form to waste nine years with an absolute prick who gets me knocked up and then leaves?'

'Poppy, listen to yourself. You didn't waste nine years; it wasn't perfect with Patrick, but you guys had fun, right? And look what you got out of it: a beautiful little girl. You can't say that relationship was for nothing.'

'Of course you'd say that.'

'What does that mean?' asked Dani, her voice becoming deathly quiet.

'You were the one who convinced me to hook up with Patrick, so obviously—'

'*I* convinced you to hook up with him?!'

'Yes! That night at the Sheaf. You literally pushed me into him!'

'Oh my god, Poppy, we were twenty-two years old! I was being a good wing woman!'

'Yeah but then Henry never called, and Mum thought Patrick was the bees' knees and then Dad never said anything, and no one told me I was living with a self-absorbed narcissist and look at how my life has turned out! I'm a single mother and—'

'Poppy, stop! You're a grown woman. No-one forced you to stay with Patrick for nine years. No-one forced you not to wear a condom! At some point you've got to take responsibility for your own life. I mean, I know my life is chaos, but at least I own that. Don't get me wrong, Pops, I love you to bits, but this constant victimhood is ridiculous. Some people have it so much worse. Maeve is a good baby, she's a *healthy* baby. I mean, she can link her sleep cycles! Some poor women never get more than forty minutes of unbroken sleep, or they have sick kids, or they can't even have kids. Everyone has shit going on, Poppy. It's not just you. Like, have you even bothered to ask how Sam is lately? Because he's shit. His mum's cancer is back and it's so fucking horrible and—'

'Why didn't you tell me?' Poppy interrupted, aghast.

'I tried, Pops,' said Dani sadly. 'I tried so many times, but you always had nappy-rash questions and breastfeeding crises, and there were so many other things going on for you it just wasn't a priority.'

'Of course it's a priority!' cried Poppy. 'Oh god, poor Sam. His poor mum. I'm so sorry, Dani. I had no idea.'

'Forget it,' said Dani, standing up to rinse her bowl and put it in the dishwasher. She checked her watch. 'I'd better get going anyway.'

'You're leaving *now*? I thought we were going to hang out?'

'It's a long drive back,' said Dani, pulling on her cardigan. 'And you said we're not going out for breakfast.'

Poppy stared at her friend. This was not what Poppy wanted. She wanted to curl up on the couch with mugs of tea and blankets and chat about nothing and everything with

SPECIAL DELIVERY

her dearest friend in the world, and she wanted it to be like old times, and she wanted to have done nothing wrong, and she wanted to apologise, and she wanted to be a better person, someone who didn't say dumb stuff. She wanted to be like Dani, she wanted to be in charge, and she wanted—more than anything—to take back everything she'd said and done last night and lock those memories up for good and throw away the key so she'd never have to feel those feelings again. But instead, she watched her best friend pack her things and walk out to her car. Poppy didn't have the words to describe how sorry she was.

CHAPTER 36

Poppy squinted into the mirror. It wasn't her imagination. Her skin was as grey and saggy as a baby elephant's. Maybe she was anaemic? Could that be the cause of all her woes? She made a mental note to defrost the mince just in case.

She hadn't heard from Dani since she'd reversed out of Poppy's driveway twenty-four hours ago and the silence between them was nuclear. It was a gloopy, radioactive, horrible mess and it was going to drown her. She'd sent four unanswered texts, including a gif of Ryan Gosling saying, *Sorry, I Love You*, which she immediately regretted. Apart from her lanky husband, Dani liked big beefy dreadlocked dudes with calf muscles the size of human skulls. Dani wasn't a Ryan Gosling girl; she was a Jason Momoa girl. What the hell had Poppy been thinking?! Now she had no idea what her next move should be. Did Dani want more space, or was she pissed off Poppy hadn't called already? Poppy was terrified of getting it wrong. She kept finding herself on the verge of calling Dani to ask her what she thought she should do before remembering she couldn't. She missed Dani so much already, she couldn't bear the thought of making it worse.

Making it worse in a financial sense was the handyman who'd arrived that morning to install the dryer. Since the shelf was still off-kilter, he'd cheerfully informed her he'd be charging an extra two hundred and fifty dollars to fix that too, and then had the gall to confess it was an easy job that she could have done herself.

Realising she was hovering around the handyman like a neurotic blowfly and suffering from a combination of irrational rage and self-induced claustrophobia, she'd invited her mum to coffee that afternoon. She couldn't show her face in The Bustle, obviously, so they'd agreed to meet at Coffee Bucks.

Looking around when she arrived, no-one seemed even vaguely familiar, which was perfect. The divide between the cafes of Orange was alarmingly wide. She pulled a plastic high-chair from the corner and placed Maeve inside. Next to her, two old ladies with blue rinses were poking at a factory-made carrot cake and trying to catch her eye. Poppy knew their type. They were hankering to say something highly unoriginal like, 'Wait till you have the next one! Har har har!' Poppy stared resolutely at her phone. She felt only marginally better than yesterday, which is to say she felt like shit. Her skin was grey, her hair was unwashed and her mind was playing a pitiless reel of James–Henry–James–Henry lowlights, sending her ever deeper into two-day-hangover oblivion. She'd only decided to meet up with her mum in the hope it would distract her from this spiral of despair. If anyone could be absurdly distracting, it was Chrissie McKellar.

'My darlings, hello!' bellowed her mother as she swooped towards the table, wearing a violet rollneck and matching scarf. She placed her giant magenta handbag on the spare seat and uncoiled her scarf in an expansive looping motion while updating Poppy on her brilliant reverse park. ('Just outside! Better than valet!') People at tables across the room all turned to look at them. Her mother had that effect.

'Tell me all about the races,' she said as she sat down. 'What did you wear? Did you see anyone fun? Anyone I know?'

Mercifully, Poppy's dad had dropped Maeve back home yesterday so she hadn't had to endure this interrogation at the peak of her hangover. Poppy's dad had only wanted to know which horses won. When Poppy confessed she had no idea, he nodded as though he'd expected as much and said nothing more.

'I haven't been to the races in ages, darling. Tell me all about it!'

Poppy coughed, a burning sensation building in her throat. 'It was . . . cold.'

'Yes, of course it was cold, darling. It *is* Orange. I hope you wore stockings.'

Poppy let her eyes lose focus as her mother launched into a monologue on the merits of wool versus man-made fibres and where to shop for the best-value thermals. (Her vote was the merino wool range at Best & Less, which Poppy already knew because her mother spouted these opinions at least once a quarter, even in summer.)

SPECIAL DELIVERY

Maeve began slapping the table in front of her and Poppy lurched back to reality.

'And you need some good winter boots,' her mother concluded.

'Mum, my shoes are fine.'

'Then shall we get you some thicker socks?'

'Mum, I'm an adult. I can dress myself.' She'd had this conversation so many times but it was grating even more than usual today. She fished in the nappy bag for a Tupperware container of parsnip and apple puree. When she saw it, Maeve's eyes lit up and she slapped the table harder.

'Better you than me, Maevey darling,' said Poppy's mum, crinkling her nose. As the waitress approached she said, 'I'm going to have the vanilla slice. What are you having, darling?'

Nothing in the sweaty glass cabinet appealed to Poppy. The slices had a waxy, synthetic sheen and the muffins looked like dry boulders.

'Just a peppermint tea, Mum.'

Her mother looked disappointed but she ploughed on as the waitress left. 'Who was at the races?' she asked again. 'Did you see Martha? Did I tell you we're not talking? Last week they ripped out the hedge, and do you know what they've planted along the fence? Jasmine! It's basically a weed, Poppy! Not to mention the ghastly scent. Thank goodness I'm not asthmatic or I'd have to do my gardening in a gasmask.'

Poppy couldn't decide which would be worse: validating her mum's garden drama or steering the conversation back to the races. Poppy took a deep breath. 'I went to the races with Dani and some of the mothers' group girls . . . Henry was there too.'

'How lovely!' exclaimed Chrissie, her garden rage instantly forgotten as a vanilla slice arrived at the table. 'Did you meet Willa?'

Poppy cursed inwardly. Why had she mentioned Henry? She'd gifted her mum this conversation starter on a platter.

Poppy shook her head. 'No, Willa wasn't there.'

'That's a shame,' said her mum, looking at her carefully.

Poppy used a serviette to wipe some stray puree from the table and passed Maeve a teaspoon to use as a drumstick.

'But speaking of Henry, I was talking to Peggy last week and we decided on Friday the eleventh for that dinner. We'll have it at the Marshalls. So it'll be you, Henry, Willa and both sets of parents. Does that suit?'

'Ah . . .' Poppy hesitated.

'I know you said you weren't going to the night markets so I assumed you must be free.'

'Mum, I can't.'

'Why not, darling? If this is to do with your hang-up about being a single mother, you need to get over that because no-one else cares. Honestly, darling, it's the twenty-first century and single girls get pregnant every day while their ex-boyfriends go on to marry doctors, and—'

'Henry kissed me!' blurted Poppy.

'WHAT?!'

'He, um . . . oh, I don't know, it was weird; let's not talk about it.'

'Unlikely, Poppy,' scoffed her mother. 'Tell me right now: what happened?'

'It was . . .' What was it? Weird? Upsetting? The universe playing a giant, soul-destroying prank? 'He, um . . . well, I think Willa left him, and I think he—'

'—wanted to make himself feel better by trying it on with you. Yes, I understand.'

For someone who seemed to exist in a permanent orbit of crazy, her mother could be remarkably astute sometimes.

'What did you do?' Chrissie asked.

'I pushed him off. Screamed at him.'

'Good girl.' Her mother chewed a piece of her slice thoughtfully. 'How did he react to that?'

Poppy winced at the memory. 'He got angry, accused me of—'

'—leading him on?'

There was that uncanny shrewdness again.

Poppy nodded and felt her eyes well up in shame. It had been a low blow from Henry—and the fact there was a tiny, mortifying kernel of truth there made her feel all the more wretched. Her hand shook, sending a glob of puree off the teaspoon and onto the vinyl floor. Maeve looked at it, dejected, then she slapped the table again to demand a replacement.

'Can't say I'm surprised,' sniffed Chrissie.

'What?!' cried Poppy.

'It was bound to happen.' Her mum dabbed the corners of her mouth with a serviette. 'You two were trying to pretend you were eighteen again, spending all that time together, living in each other's pockets.'

'We were not!'

'Coffee every day, darling? Two people with very limited spare time and you just happen to spend it together? You can't pretend you did that innocently. Why do you think his parents and I were so keen to organise this dinner? We needed to get you both in a room with Willa, so you would stop pretending.'

Poppy felt a firestorm of shame and rage engulf her.

'What the hell? I'm an adult, for god's sake. Henry and I are—were—friends. That's it, Mum! You have no idea! You have no idea what's going on in my life, and if you did, you'd know that never, not once, did I lead Henry on. What do you think I am, some scarlet vixen preying on the men of Orange? What a misogynistic view of the world, making Henry the victim and me the big, bad slut.'

Another spoonful of puree fell off the teaspoon and Maeve's lips began to tremble.

'Now look what you've made me do,' Poppy snapped as Maeve began to wail. She stood up and tried to pull her daughter out of the highchair, but her daughter's thighs were stuck in the plastic leg holes.

Her mum stood up too. 'I'll do it,' said Chrissie, trying to move Maeve's feet so her legs could slide out.

'I can do it myself!' cried Poppy, feeling the tears about to explode. 'Stop interfering! You're always telling me what to wear, who to hang out with, how to parent Maeve. Stop trying to run my life!'

Her mum reared back like she'd heard a gunshot. Poppy dimly registered the hurt in her eyes but she was so angry and humiliated and frustrated with this stupid fucking highchair that she didn't care. She finally managed to pull Maeve out and hugged her daughter to her chest, trying to absorb the goodness from her tiny innocent body.

SPECIAL DELIVERY

Her mum flitted at the edge of the table like a bird with a broken wing, her expression wounded and her breathing unsteady. Poppy couldn't summon the courage or grace to apologise. How dare her mother accuse her of leading Henry on?!

You accused yourself too, said a voice in her head, and Poppy scrunched her eyes shut. She wanted to hold her daughter against her beating heart, and every other sound and feeling and accusation could fuck right off.

Her mother spoke quietly as she picked up her magenta handbag. 'I think it's best if I go.'

To their left, the ladies with the blue rinses averted their eyes.

It was like Poppy was watching herself move through petroleum jelly. Everything was slow and blurry, everything was slipping from her grasp. 'Mum, wait,' she mumbled. 'You haven't drunk your coffee.'

Her mother spun around to face her, the lines around her eyes etched with sadness. 'Poppy, I didn't come for the coffee. I never come for the coffee.' She bent over and kissed Maeve on the head, hoisted her handbag onto her shoulder and quietly left the cafe.

As her larger-than-life mother returned to her brilliantly parked car, Poppy realised with a bone-shuddering certainty that she had reached a new level of rock bottom.

CHAPTER 37

A week had passed since the races and Poppy was an island. Not a tropical island with all-inclusive pina coladas; she was a solitary Nigel-no-friends island in a giant ocean of shame and anxiety. She was down to her last packet of pasta, and, in a town where every supermarket trip was a potential minefield, she was terrified to go shopping.

Poppy pushed the pram past an abandoned warehouse in Orange's industrial backstreets. The sharp smell of petrol filled her nostrils. Avoiding the leafy golf course loop felt like penance.

She'd tried her dad a couple of times, hoping he'd take a Switzerland-like approach to the whole thing, but even he was screening her calls. The only person she'd actually spoken to in the last five days was the comms manager from Region Building Australia, whom she'd cold-called in sheer desperation for human contact. It turned out they'd already filled the advertised role, but it didn't matter because Comms Manager was a human—and someone left on this planet who would still speak to her. They nerded out on marketing case studies, their discussion dipping and rising in all the right places with the light and shade of a Caravaggio masterpiece—but when Poppy concluded a hilarious story about doubling digital sales through a strategic *Betoota Advocate* partnership and Comms Manager had chortled, 'With that kind of ROI, I think Poppy McKellar will put Sarah Jones out of a job,' Poppy had realised Comms Manager wasn't called Comms Manager at all; she was called Sarah Jones. She was a real person with a real job. Poppy was leading this woman on too. She was pretending she was a competent adult who was ready for work but it was all lies. She didn't even have child care sorted.

As they passed a derelict building site, Maeve let out a mournful yelp from the pram. The blueness of the sky was doing nothing to soothe Poppy's soul. The loneliness was corrosive.

A week of introspection had confirmed, unsurprisingly, that she was a conflict-averse coward, and that all the crap in her life had one common denominator: her. Pretty much everyone important to her hated her right now, and she hated to be hated. She needed to start apologising. She just didn't know how to begin.

Henry was one of her oldest friends, and even though she was still furious with him, she knew he needed her right now if he wanted to win Willa back, because he was clearly bloody clueless when it came to understanding women.

James was ... well, whatever he was, he was special. The James compartment in her brain had a big red label that said *Handle With Care*.

The breeze whipped at the thin cotton covering her ankles. She dolefully recalled her mother's recommendation she buy thicker socks. Chrissie's silence had been deafening. She was either extremely angry or extremely disappointed, or both. Gardening tiffs aside, her mother was generally known for her obnoxiously glass-half-full approach to life. She was the kind of person who'd start telling you about her flat tyre and end in raptures about the helpfulness of the NRMA man. She even enjoyed going to the dentist. (When else did she get to read the *Reader's Digest*?) For Chrissie to dip below anything but mild annoyance for more than thirty seconds was rare, hence Poppy's current state of paralysis. How would she come back from this?

Without being conscious of where she was going, Poppy turned a corner and realised she was at the rugby field. Hundreds of cars were parked on the grass, most of which would stay there all weekend. Maeve's ears pricked up at the clack-clack-clack of football boots on bitumen. It was the sound of Poppy's childhood.

The old men at the gate waved her through cheerfully and Poppy pushed the pram towards the clubhouse. The stands were full of puffer-jacketed supporters, bracing themselves against the wind. On the field, players heaved themselves into each other and the mud. A whistle sounded and a sea of voices jeered at the ref. Poppy had no idea why. She'd been watching rugby her whole life and still couldn't understand the rules.

He was sitting in the grandstand. She spotted him immediately. If he wasn't going to take her calls, she'd have to ambush him.

SPECIAL DELIVERY

She parked the pram next to the canteen. The place smelled of damp earth and frying sausages. Hoisting Maeve onto her hip, she slowly climbed the concrete stairs. He didn't turn when she sat down, his eyes following the action on the field, a paper program folded in his hands.

'Dad.'

'Poppy,' he replied, eyes still on the game.

'I tried to call you.'

'I saw that.'

'You didn't want to call back?'

'I figured you didn't really want to chat to me.'

'No?'

'I thought you might be trying to get hold of your mother.'

'Ah.'

'Yes.' He turned and smiled at his granddaughter, who reached out to grab his finger. 'She's quite upset. I think she'd appreciate a call.'

Poppy felt her eyes well up. 'I didn't know if she'd want to talk to me.'

'Oh, Poppy.' Her dad smiled sadly. 'Don't be daft. She's been moping around like a cat without her cream. She's desperate to hear from you. She just didn't want to—what was the word she used?—ah yes, she didn't want to *interfere*.'

An ulcer of guilt burst in Poppy's stomach. 'I never meant to . . .' she began, her voice cracking.

'I know, Pops,' he said gently.

'I just . . .'

Her dad patted her knee. 'I know.'

They watched the rest of the rugby in silence. It was the way her dad liked it and she didn't have much to say anyway.

At the final whistle her dad turned to her, his face ruddy from the wind, and asked whether she wanted a lift home. Poppy gave him a hug goodbye instead. She hoped he felt that her grip was tighter than usual.

★

Two days later she pushed the pram through the doors of The Bustle. Bankers and real estate agents in country chic corporate wear were lined up for caffeine like it was sacramental wine. There was a possibility Henry had been avoiding The Bustle, but Poppy doubted it. With his office being almost next door, it was home turf for him. She glanced at her watch. He was due in any minute now.

The door squeaked behind her and a cold gust of air blasted in. She jerked her head around and there he was, as she'd expected. His curly hair was in need of a trim and there were bags under his eyes, but he was still as handsome as ever in his uncomplicated, happy-go-lucky way.

He glanced over and she held his gaze. A slight nod of the head invited him over. She wondered if they'd be able to communicate wordlessly like this forever.

'Hi,' she said.

'Hi,' he replied, looking nervous.

'I'm sorry!' they blurted in unison.

'Jinx,' said Poppy, a cautious smile emerging.

Behind them, a courier carried in a giant paint-spattered artwork. Henry probably thought there'd been an explosion at the Dulux factory. They watched the courier for a second before Henry grabbed at his curls. 'Pops, I'm so sorry,' he said.

'I was such a dick. I've been hating myself since it happened. I can't believe I was such a fuckwit. Of all people to piss off, you didn't deserve it. I'm so, so sorry.'

Poppy took a deep breath. 'Henry, I'm sorry too. I should have . . .' She trailed off. To admit what she'd done—even unconsciously—would make it real, and she didn't want it to be real. Was she really that woman who flirted with guys who were engaged? If so, she hated herself.

'Poppy, you didn't do anything wrong.'

'No, I did,' said Poppy, wincing in shame at the memory of the polka dot dress. 'I overstepped some boundaries and I shouldn't have. I feel terrible.'

Henry looked as anguished as she felt, which was gratifying in some ways, but she was about to make this so much worse.

'Henry, I also need to apologise for what happened ten years ago.'

'Poppy, you don't need to—'

'I do,' she interrupted.

Poppy had thought of that starless night more times than was healthy. The memory of Henry's face in the shadows, the hurt in his eyes. She'd never forgive herself for that moment.

Henry had been about to leave on a twelve-month secondment to his firm's London office. His employer had offered to put him up in a Sydney hotel before he flew out but Poppy had convinced him to crash with her. It had been one of those weekends when she'd offered her couch and he'd accepted, both knowing they'd end up in bed together after too many drinks at the Sheaf. Dani found it problematic, but that was because Dani didn't understand. What Poppy and Henry had was deeper than any normal friendship. It was basically no-strings-attached sex because it was *Henry* and he lived in *Brisbane* and he was moving to *London*, and they'd known each other for so long it was easier to be together than not be together. She was already excited to take him to the airport and be the last person he'd hug in Australia. She loved being that person for him.

But then Patrick appeared. They were at the Sheaf, and Patrick was wearing what she soon learned was his Double Bay drinking uniform: chinos and a Ralph Lauren shirt. This particular night he'd accessorised it with a pink baseball cap worn back to front. If there was ever an item of clothing more useless than a back-to-front cap, Poppy didn't know it, but at the time, the guy in the neon-pink cap had seemed so *cool*. It was a classic peacock move and she fell for it. For some reason, this confident guy with the loudest laugh had asked her to dance, which never happened. Guys like that went for flashy girls with Blake Lively hair and tiny bodycon dresses, not girls like her.

Dani was quick to nudge her in the ribs, urging her to accept, while Henry leaned in protectively. Their other friends looked from Patrick to Poppy, wondering whether this Eastern Suburbs playboy would pull it off. He looked like a brash idiot, the kind of guy who probably yelled at taxi drivers and flashed his parents' Amex, but Poppy heard herself agree and she took his outstretched hand. As Patrick led her away, Henry caught her eye. 'You sure?' he mouthed. Poppy nodded. Why not?

Within an hour, Patrick had spun her across the dancefloor, bought her friends two rounds of shots and regaled everyone with a story from Yacht Week involving an altercation with a Croatian nun and a leg of jamon. Poppy brimmed with pride at the way he'd captured everyone's attention. How on earth had *he* noticed *her*?

After more shots and too many vodka sodas, Patrick took her hand and insisted they get a cab. They were making out before they got to the taxi rank, and by the time they got to her apartment, Poppy was completely and utterly drunk and in lust.

She ignored the sound of her phone buzzing in her handbag as she slammed the door shut and kept kissing Patrick, layers of clothing sliding off with slippery efficiency. They crashed onto her bed, grabbing at each other, and when the apartment intercom buzzed she paused momentarily, her eyes uncrossing slowly. Who on earth . . .? *Shit! Henry!*

She jumped off the bed and ran to the intercom phone in the kitchen. 'Henry, you can't come up!'

'Poppy,' Henry pleaded through the tinny speaker, 'where will I sleep?'

'Work it out!' she hissed.

'Poppy, don't be stupid. Let me come up.'

'Don't call me stupid!' snapped Poppy. In her drunken haze, she was resentful. Henry couldn't just assume he was entitled to her couch—or her bed. In fact, he was probably the reason she'd never been hit on like this before. She was radiating taken vibes, even though they'd broken up years ago!

'Poppy,' Henry begged. 'Please, my bag is up there. At least buzz me up so I can grab it.'

'No!' She was irrational now. 'You're a big boy. You can sort it out.'

From her bedroom she could hear Patrick calling to her. She stuck her head out the window and saw Henry near her front door. In his boots and checked shirt, he looked so naively country. Normally she found it endearing, but tonight she found it embarrassing. She grabbed his R.M. Williams carryall from the couch and yelled to him, 'Henry, catch!' She tipped his bag unceremoniously through the window and watched it hurtle through the air, landing with a muffled thud on the hedge below. Henry looked up at her and in one split-second she saw the confusion, the disbelief and then the hurt. From her bedroom, Patrick was calling more loudly. Poppy slammed the window shut and pushed Henry from her mind. She would call him in the morning and smooth it over. He had plenty of other friends in Sydney; he would find somewhere to sleep. It would be fine.

But she didn't call him in the morning. Patrick stayed over and they went out for bloody marys and then gatecrashed a harbour cruise. She didn't get home—or sober up—for another twenty-four hours. By that time, Henry was already in a different hemisphere. Poppy decided she needed to call at the right time, probably when it wasn't morning for him. Then she decided she'd better call when it wasn't Monday. Or when it wasn't a weekday, or when it wasn't a Saturday, and she probably shouldn't call at night because he might be working late or recuperating after a busy day. And suddenly, weeks had gone by and she hadn't called him. And then weeks became months and Henry never called either. Her shame intensified whenever she remembered that night—and the flashbacks occurred with alarming regularity—but, she reasoned, how would she apologise to him and then explain that she and pink-hat guy had become a thing? Better to wait for him to reach out, when he was ready. But he never did. And suddenly, nine years had passed. She could still remember every line and freckle on Henry's face, how his eyes creased when he smiled, how his hugs smelled warm and comforting, like cinnamon. But they were just memories now—no more solid than the wind on her face.

Through those nine years, a thought often poked its way up and she'd clamp it back down and ignore it, but it was persistent, like a weed wriggling through the soil. *Had she lost a soul mate?* When she opened that window, did she not only throw out a bag, but throw out years of friendship and love? Did she throw out a future? She stayed with Patrick because the alternative was terrifying. To break up with Patrick would be to admit she'd made a horrible, unforgivable mistake and destroyed a relationship she valued more than any other. And she kept promising herself: *One day I'll apologise, one day I'll make this right.*

'Henry,' she said now. 'What I did that night was horrible, and that I never apologised is unforgivable. I've thought about apologising so many times and I've never been brave enough to do it, but now . . . well, I'm trying to be brave. I'm sorry, Henry—for everything, but I'm especially sorry for the last ten years. You've never stopped being one of my favourite people. I was just too selfish and scared to admit it.'

Henry tugged at his collar, his eyes downcast. 'I missed you like crazy for months, Pops. Maybe years. And I hated that fucking guy so fucking much. I thought I'd got over it, but then seeing you again this year, I thought maybe I hadn't . . .'

'Henry, please—'

'No, I need to say this too,' Henry interrupted. 'You broke my heart, Poppy. I know we weren't even together, but it killed me when you did that. I was as broken as that stupid bottle of cologne that smashed in my bag. But it was my fault too. We were young and we loved each other but we were too dumb and proud to commit to anything. I had so many chances to tell you how I felt but I never did. We were so obsessed with having fun, we ruined any chance of turning what we had into something real, something that would last.' Henry's voice sounded heavier than she'd ever heard it. She wanted to take his hand but she knew she couldn't. 'And then I met Willa and I realised I could find someone just as amazing—not the same kind of amazing but a different kind. Someone who is amazing for who I am now, not the person I was when I was sixteen. She makes me feel so happy and alive and . . .' His voice broke. 'Fuck, Pops. She said it wasn't working but I don't understand. My life only works when I'm with her. How have I stuffed this up again? Am I fucking cursed? Or just dumb as dog shit?'

Poppy bit her lip, a smile twitching at her mouth despite the tears clouding her eyes. 'Maybe both?'

Henry shook his head and smiled weakly. 'Friends?' he asked, proffering his hand. 'I don't want to waste another ten years.'

'Friends,' agreed Poppy, shaking it. 'I couldn't stand to lose you again, Hen. It was making me feel sick thinking we'd ruined everything.'

He smiled. 'Same.'

SPECIAL DELIVERY

They both looked at Maeve, her curious face a welcome distraction from all these complicated feelings.

'So,' Poppy said eventually, 'do you need some help winning back a certain paediatrician?'

Henry's ears reddened but his eyes lifted to meet hers. 'Thank goodness, Pops. I thought you'd never ask.'

For the next twenty minutes, as Maeve chewed her way through two teething rusks, Poppy asked all the questions about Willa she'd been dying to ask for months. How they met (through mutual friends), their first date (the zoo), when they moved in together (after thirteen months), what her family was like (quiet, smart, extremely competitive in the *Good Weekend* quiz).

By the time Poppy had weaselled a full recap of their first date out of Henry (the zoo being an unusually bold choice for him), Poppy felt herself becoming enchanted by Willa too. She was beautiful, she was intelligent, she donated money to the orangutans and her quiet equanimity was the perfect foil to Henry's gregariousness. For Henry, she was perfect. Which begged the question: 'Why did *she* fall in love with *you*?'

Henry groaned. 'I don't know. Because I'm funny?'

'Lots of people are funny.'

'I'm a good bloke?'

'My postman is a good bloke.'

Henry put his head in his hands. 'Maybe it's not something we can put into words. It's just a feeling. Like, we just clicked. She's clever and kind and witty, and I . . . I dunno, I balanced her. Like, when she got anxious, I could calm her down. When she was sad, I could cheer her up. When she was drowning in work, I was the one who'd make her come up for air, be spontaneous.'

And then it dawned on him.

'Oh.'

'Yep.'

'Do you think . . .?'

'Yep.'

'I've been too obsessed with the business? I didn't make enough time for her?' The last question lingered unsaid: *Do you think I spent too much time with you?*

'Yes to all of the above, Marshall. But the positive news is, it's not too late.'

'It's not?' Henry asked hopefully.

'No. You still have a conscience, which confirms my theory that you are not a terrible person. You stuffed up, got carried away—we both did—but you can fix it. You just need to apologise and then you need to be better. For a long time. Actually, for forever.'

'I can do that,' said Henry, eyes lighting up.

Poppy smiled. 'Then do that.'

CHAPTER 38

The escalators ascended into the fluoro-lit shopping centre, where the scents of doughnuts and deep fryers lingered on the air. Poppy had spoken to her mum on the phone four times since that unnervingly silent week and although she'd tried to apologise in every call, each time her mum had sounded shrill and distracted—which, admittedly, wasn't unusual. She hoped an in-person apology may prove more successful but that would depend on the amount of *40% OFF* sale signs within sight range.

As Poppy and Maeve reached solid ground, a turquoise haze descended on them from Suzanne Grae. 'Darlings!' it cried.

Maeve giggled and raised her chubby arms in delight.

Her mother dropped her bags and scooped up her granddaughter in a flurry of kisses. Around them, shoppers rerouted to bypass the blockage.

'It's been ages since I've seen you both,' cried Chrissie, pressing her granddaughter to her face. 'There is so much to catch up on. The magnolia got removed yesterday! There are branches everywhere! And you wouldn't believe who I saw at golf! That rugby league player . . . what's-his-face. The big one. You must know who I mean, darling. Giant of a man! Teeing off right next to us. What are the chances!'

Her mother was already strolling away with Maeve on her hip, nattering over her shoulder about the tuna baguette she had after golf yesterday. Delicious, apparently.

'Mum,' Poppy called.

'And the mayonnaise!' her mother replied. 'Light as air!'

'Mum!'

Her mother turned. 'Yes, darling?'

Poppy felt her eyes well up. She wished she wasn't standing in front of The Reject Shop. 'I just wanted to say . . . I'm sorry.'

'Darling,' said her mother. 'It's water under the bridge.'

'No, Mum, I was terrible. Especially when you've been so . . .' Here came the tears. 'You've been so . . . amazing . . . especially with Maeve . . . and me.' She choked on a sob.

'Oh, Poppy,' clucked her mother, closing the space between them. She wrapped her free arm around her daughter, her blow-dried hair sticking to Poppy's cheek. 'Don't worry about silly old me.'

'No, Mum,' said Poppy. 'That's the thing. I haven't been worrying about you. I've been horrible. I've only been worrying about myself and you've been so supportive. I've been a selfish idiot.' Her voice cracked.

'We can all be a ning-nong sometimes,' said her mother, patting her arm.

Poppy felt a laugh burst through her tears. 'You're so right, Mum. I was the biggest ning-nong ever. But honestly,

I couldn't have done the last nine months without you. You've been a lifesaver.'

'That's what mothers are for, darling. You'd do the same for Maeve.'

Poppy blinked, suddenly aware of a truth she'd never considered. Her mum was right. If her daughter came to her, single, pregnant, unmoored and scared, she knew she'd do anything to help her. The realisation made a lion roar inside her with a ferocity that surprised her. Maybe this was how she'd get through life: by summoning her inner lioness.

Poppy hugged her mother tightly. 'Thank you, Mum. I love you.'

On her hip, Maeve extended her chubby arms to lovingly pat her mother and grandmother. Poppy smiled. 'And thank you, Maevey-Maeve. I love you both so much more than you'll ever know.'

Chrissie exhaled theatrically and readjusted her glasses. 'I think what we all need is a nice cup of tea and a sweet treat.' She looked from left to right as if calculating the fastest route to a vanilla slice. 'I know you like the muffins at The Bustle. Should we go there?'

As far as olive branches went, this was a giant turquoise olive branch and Poppy realised with a pang of guilt how often her mum recalibrated her own needs to smooth the bumps for her. Maybe because her mother operated on a higher volume setting than most humans, Poppy had mistaken her extroversion for self-absorption. Poppy felt like a dim-witted brat. Chrissie had only ever loved her—bandaged her scraped knees when she fell, cuddled her when she cried, lifted her out of depressive funks with her relentless optimism—and Poppy had taken it all for granted. Her mum had shown Poppy how to find joy in the small things, how to laugh when everyone else was inclined to scream and how to pivot from disasters with her head held high. Poppy realised she wanted to grow up to be just like her.

'No, Mum,' she said. 'Let's go to Coffee Bucks.'

CHAPTER 39

The phone buzzed on the kitchen bench. An unknown number was calling.

'Hello?' Poppy said cautiously.

'Put your heels on, McKellar, we're going out.'

'What? Who is this?'

'It's Kate, James's sister! I've been meaning to get in touch for ages and I was speaking to April, who mentioned you were friends, so I decided you're crashing our dinner date. Mr Spice King at seven thirty.'

Poppy replayed the words in her head in case she'd missed something. Kate was calling? And she knew April? Since when? And why and how? And also: it was already five past seven.

'It's all sorted,' Kate continued. 'I called the restaurant and they've changed the booking and Harper's in the car ready to babysit.'

'Hi, Poppy,' called Harper from the background.

'We should be at your place in about twenty minutes. You're next door to Mary, right?'

'Uh, yes, that's right,' said Poppy, trying to catch up.

'Cool. We'll see you soon.'

'Wait!' Poppy said, trying to regain some level of control. 'Maeve is—'

'—sick, I know. I can't remember who told me. April? Or James? No, it was the lady at the pharmacy—she golfs with your mum. Anyway, her conjunctivitis will be no match for Harper. She's been around her fair share of pooing, spewing babies. A bit of eye gunk won't faze her.'

'But . . . but,' stammered Poppy. 'How do you even know April?'

'Played rep netball with her for ten years,' replied Kate. 'She's a monster on the centre court. A demon on the dance-floor too.'

Poppy chuckled. She could corroborate that last bit. 'Okay, I'll get ready. Is Mr Spice King the karaoke place?'

'Sure is,' replied Kate cheerfully. 'You're under no obligation to participate, but I must warn you that April gets very domineering with a mic. She calls herself a red-headed Beyoncé.'

Kate arrived twenty minutes later, flanked by a baggy-jeaned Harper. Poppy gave the teenager a tour of the house, detailed instructions for the baby monitor, a full rundown of bottles, nappies, formula tins and their precise locations, and finally, the password for the wi-fi. Harper looked most interested in that.

SPECIAL DELIVERY

As Poppy climbed into Kate's car, she checked her phone in case Harper had texted between her leaving the front door and reaching the driveway. Unsurprisingly, there were no notifications.

'Relax, mate,' said Kate. 'You've done this before, remember?'

★

The restaurant was packed, to the extent that Poppy had to suck in her stomach to squeeze between the tables. April was already seated, wearing an emerald lurex skivvy that made her eyes look even greener.

'Took the liberty of ordering a bottle,' she announced by way of greeting. 'What are you wearing, doll?' she asked Kate. 'It's, like, six degrees outside.'

'It's the first day of spring, hence . . .' Kate waved her hands at her leather miniskirt and legs that were preposterously tanned for this early in the season.

'Goal attacks,' said April, rolling her eyes. 'Such show-offs.'

'I knew it,' Poppy said, sliding into a chair.

'Knew what?' asked Kate.

'It's so obvious you'd play goal attack and April would play centre. You have very conspicuous GA and centre energy. Unco girls like me can pick it instantly. It must be evolutionary—my way of working out the leaders of the pack so I can convince them not to feed me to the wolves.'

'No wolf would want you,' scoffed April. 'You'd be too gristly now your boobs have deflated.'

'So true,' said Poppy with a groan. 'And you haven't even seen me naked.'

'Ha! You're not my type.' April winked. 'But I've been wanting to ask: did anyone get naked after the races? And I'm not actually asking you,' she said to Kate.

'Good,' said Kate. 'Because you know I don't have sex anymore. Three times for four kids was plenty enough for me. Happy to be celibate for the next few decades.'

'I'm sure Dereck is thrilled with that.'

'He loves me for my intellect,' Kate retorted.

April snickered. 'Back to my original question. Poppy, what happened after the Royal?'

A shaky movie montage flashed through Poppy's mind. Dancing, drinking, more drinking, Henry, James, him yelling, her yelling, her crying. Thinking about it still lanced her with pain.

'Nothing,' she lied.

'Nothing?' repeated April sceptically. 'From my vantage point on the dance floor, I absolutely thought you were on there. James was definitely keen.'

'He was?!' Kate exclaimed.

'He was totally keen,' said April.

'This is massive news!' cried Kate.

April grinned. 'Poppy, you need to tell us *everything* that happened between you and James.'

'Not everything!' yelped Kate. 'Remember I am his blood relation. Please keep it PG.'

'Nothing happened, I swear,' said Poppy. It wasn't entirely the truth but it was pretty darn close. If he hadn't told anyone, she sure as hell wouldn't.

'Damn it.' Kate banged her fist on the table. 'You would be so good for him. He should definitely have tapped that.'

Poppy coughed on her champagne. 'I thought we were keeping it PG.'

April laughed. 'Her definition of PG is—how should I put it?—loose.'

'Anyhow,' said Poppy, 'I'm a single mum. I have too much baggage. I'm sure he isn't interested.'

'Children, schmildren,' said Kate, waving her glass. 'He's obsessed with kids. He would not be turned off by you being a single mum and I definitely thought you'd be his type.'

April looked at Kate meaningfully. 'Especially given she's the opposite of . . .'

'Exactly,' nodded Kate.

Poppy was missing something.

'I'm the opposite of who?' she demanded.

'Adelaide,' said Kate, her voice dripping with revulsion.

'He's moving to Adelaide?' cried Poppy. 'But I thought he got into Melbourne Uni.' Adelaide was even worse than Melbourne. He might as well move to Moscow.

'He got into CSU Orange, too,' Kate said, 'but we're not talking about cities; Adelaide is his ex.' She scowled. 'They were engaged but they ended it last October. She had an affair with the drummer of the band that used to play at the Ex-Services' Club. No loss, really. We all hated her.'

'Oh my gosh,' whispered Poppy. This was critical new information. 'Did she break his heart?'

'Nah,' Kate said. 'That was what bummed him out the most. When it happened he realised he didn't even care that much. Like, he'd just got used to her being around and, being the good guy he is, he proposed because he thought he should, but when the shit hit the fan he realised he didn't actually love her. He'd wasted four years with a peroxide princess who thought Garth Brooks was a homewares shop.'

'Ouch.' Poppy winced.

'Precisely,' said April.

'So when you guys hit it off at the dam, our radars went completely haywire because we all knew Adelaide would never have come to the dam, let alone enjoyed it.'

'She was a grade-A bitch,' April agreed, gulping her champagne. 'He was always too good for her.'

'So why did they get together in the first place?' asked Poppy.

'Because it's James!' cried Kate, and April nodded as if that explained everything.

'I don't get it.'

'Because he's always the good guy,' said Kate. 'He never does the breaking up, he never pulls anyone into line, he just smiles and cops shit, and then deals with it stoically, because that's what he's always done. Ever since Dad left, he's just got on with it. He doesn't want anyone to think he's remotely like our father. He was so determined to never be the dickhead that he went to the other extreme and became this pushover who smiled and nodded when his girlfriend said she hated his hair and tried to tell us hippos were native to Australia.'

Poppy spluttered her drink. 'I know I should be concerned about the hippo thing, but you're actually serious that she didn't like his hair?!'

'The girl was a fool,' muttered Kate.

'Wow,' said Poppy slowly. For anyone to think James's hair was anything less than outstanding was criminal, but even more confusing was Kate and April's character profile of James. It was way out of sync with hers. 'I would never have picked James for a pushover. I mean, when we first met, I thought he was an arrogant douche.'

'What?' asked Kate and April in unison. They sounded confused now.

'Was that because you were in labour?' asked Kate. 'Because during all three of my labours I despised Dereck. During the twins' labour, I threw a custard cup at him.'

'She did,' said April. 'It split his lip. You can check the twins' baby photos.'

'I actually met James before I was in labour,' admitted Poppy.

'Huh?' said Kate. 'I could have sworn he said that's how you met.'

A distant alarm bell clanged in Poppy's mind. If James hadn't told his sister about their first encounter he must have a reason for that. (Was he trying to protect her reputation? Or his own? To be honest, they both deserved better than that first impression.) Poppy tried to keep her voice neutral. 'We did meet at the hospital,' she said.

Kate and April shared a look. 'There's more to this story,' said April. 'I can feel it in my waters.'

Poppy considered her options. Either tell the truth and unmask herself as a nutjob, or lie and have the truth catch up with her another day. It was a zero-sum game. She sighed. 'It was a really hot day . . .'

She told an edited version of the story—without mentioning Kate's brother looking like a sexily evil Ken doll—but touched on all the major points: stealing a car space she wasn't entitled to, the yelling, the sweating, the fact he probably saw her undies.

Kate exhaled deeply. 'No. Frickin. Way.'

Poppy looked at her plate, embarrassed. A common theme of recent weeks had been realising how selfish she'd been and it wasn't getting any easier to accept.

'No, no, no, you don't understand!' cried Kate. 'He told me about that car park drama! He literally called me after this happened! I had no idea it was you! This is a sign, this is a sign!'

'Hold up, girl,' said April, raising her palms. 'Explain yourself.'

'We'd been having some deep sibling therapy,' began Kate. 'Basically me ribbing him on FaceTime for being so clueless about life. So we'd just had this big D and M about how he needs to live his best life and stop putting up with the Adelaides of the world and blah, blah, blah, and I think nothing of it, like I've just done my sisterly good deed for the day, when he calls me twenty minutes later and I *swear* he is high. He's cackling like a maniac—well, James can't cackle, his voice is too deep—but he's laughing, because he reckons he followed my advice and this girl basically told him to stick it.'

Poppy cringed. 'Stick it' would have been so much better than the goody-two-shoes disaster.

'Then he mentioned this girl was pregnant and suddenly I'm all like, "Whoa, Jimmy, did you really need to lose it at a pregnant chick?" Because I understand that he needs to be his authentic self, but even though he's a midwife and a great brother, he's never been *pregnant*. And like, seriously, the world needs to go easy on pregnant ladies.'

'Hear, hear!' said April, nodding furiously.

Kate continued, 'But he was totally unapologetic. He basically said this chick could handle it, and when I asked how he knew he said, "Oh, she was a ball of fire."'

'Is that a good thing?' asked April.

'Yes, it's a good thing!' cried Kate. 'He's so black and white, he's basically a penguin. To him, everything is binary. People are good or bad, tall or short, pregnant or not pregnant. You're either allowed to park in the car space or you're not. The fact he could tell that your reaction came from a place of strength and not innate badness was huge.' She clapped her hands together. 'No offence, Poppy, I was stoked when you guys were hitting it off at the dam, but a part of me was like "he needs a fire girl" and now I find out you're the OG fire girl. Talk about next-level serendipity!'

Poppy gulped her champagne. This made no sense. She wasn't a fireball. She was a wet blanket. She'd been so afraid of confrontation it had taken her nine years to confront her own feelings about Patrick. That whole car park incident had been an aberration. And what were Kate and April talking about? James wasn't a pushover—she'd only ever known him to excel in confrontation. He was self-assured to the point of arrogance.

Unless ... James had definitely brought out her inner velociraptor—had she done the same to him? Her fingers trembled as she gripped her champagne flute. Were they so combustible together because they made each other burn brighter—in every way, good *and* bad? Then she remembered the disgust on his face that night after the races and her airways suddenly felt thick. She was being stupid. She was making crazy assumptions; they clearly didn't know each other at all. She was suddenly aware that Kate had no idea James hated her right now.

Up at the bar, Mr Spice King himself had appeared and was rolling out a portable karaoke machine.

'To signs!' declared Kate, raising her glass rapturously.

'To signs,' April repeated.

Poppy lifted her glass and attempted to smile. There was only one way to avoid feeling these feelings, so she tipped the rest of her champagne down her throat.

CHAPTER 40

Poppy shone her phone torch into her mouth and inspected the damage. Her left tonsil was the colour of red cordial. Of course she would get sick. Thirty-one-year-olds could not drink like twenty-two-year-olds without getting sick. It was a law of physics.

Turned out conversation starter cards were for suckers. If you really wanted to get to know someone—or a whole restaurant—all you needed to do was sing a few bars of 'Crazy in Love' and pass the mic around. With April and Kate by her side, she'd rolled through passionate renditions of Aretha Franklin, Macy Gray and Gwen Stefani before realising their superpowers (which were heavily reliant on their second and third bottles of champagne) could be harnessed perfectly for Carly Rae Jepsen and Miley Cyrus. The whole-restaurant singalong to 'Party in the U.S.A.' had been a life highlight, the kind Poppy would probably still remember in her nineties.

Too bad she'd be dead long before then. There was no way she could survive this hangover. She chucked her phone onto her bed and kicked off her shoes. Maybe a warm shower would cleanse her liver? At the very least, the steam might soothe her throat. She stepped into her ensuite, undressed and turned on the shower. She was about to step under when her ears pricked. Was that Maeve?

Poppy wrapped a towel around herself and stepped out of the bathroom. Maeve had only gone down ten minutes ago; she wasn't due to wake for at least another half an hour. Her temples pounded extra forcefully as she craned her ears. Bugger. Maeve was definitely crying. Poppy tiptoed down the hall, hoping Maeve might go back to sleep, but by the time she reached her room her daughter was screaming at full lung capacity.

Poppy eased the door open and saw her daughter lying next to a puddle of vomit. Oh god. She lifted Maeve from the cot and grabbed some wipes to scrub her face, which made Maeve cry harder. Her eyes were matted with a web of crusted mucus and two streams of green snot were running from her nostrils. *Fuuuuck!* This didn't look good.

Shifting her daughter to her hip—no easy feat while wearing a towel—she went to find her phone and began to type. Google, ever so helpfully, offered a range of options:

Is my baby teething?
Is my baby constipated?
Is my baby getting enough milk?
Is my baby sick or teething?
Is my baby lactose intolerant?

SPECIAL DELIVERY

Is my baby cross-eyed?
Is my baby too skinny?
Is my baby dehydrated?

Jesus Christ, she'd googled at least half of them. She rephrased: *Can a baby have conjunctivitis and gastro at the same time, and is that bad?*

The overwhelming response from Google was yes. Fuck. Again.

Maeve's cry had settled to a snivel but she still looked miserable. Her eyes were bloodshot and gooey and the snot was now smeared across her cheeks. Poppy put her hand to her daughter's forehead. It definitely felt warmer than usual.

Poppy's left tonsil throbbed and she let out a whimper. Of course this would happen.

She took her daughter to the lounge room and lay her under her mobile. As soon as Poppy put her down, Maeve began to wail. Poppy picked her up and patted her back to calm her and then lay her down on the play mat again, more gently this time. Maeve immediately started to cry. Sighing, Poppy scooped her up and then called her mother.

'She doesn't want to lie down,' she told her mother.

'Of course not, darling,' Chrissie replied. 'She's congested, so lying down will only make her more uncomfortable. She needs to be kept upright.'

Poppy wanted to wail. She'd heard tales at mothers' group of babies who got sick and had to be held constantly, with the parents taking it in turns. *But there isn't another parent!* Poppy fumed. *At some point I will need to shower! And pee!*

'Which doctor will you go to?' asked her mother.

Poppy grabbed a tissue to wipe Maeve's nose. She was embarrassed to admit she didn't have a regular GP yet. The hospital health clinic had sorted all her pre- and post-pregnancy needs and she hadn't needed medical help since. As her mum nattered on about how her bunion issues had been promptly fixed by her lovely young doctor (who was twenty years older than Poppy), her mind drifted to James. His knowledge of medicine, of Orange, his matter-of-factness, his innate decency; his recommendation would be rock-solid. Less bunion-reliant than her mother's, at least.

In one of those startling moments of maternal intuition, her mum asked, 'Why don't you call your midwife?'

Poppy's stomach lurched.

'You know,' her mum added, 'the old one with the ponytail.'

Wenda!

'Good idea, Mum,' said Poppy, glad her mother couldn't see the redness that had been creeping up her neck. 'I'll ring her now.'

She ended the call with her mother and looked up Wenda's number. She could feel a big wet patch forming on her shoulder. Poppy felt a mild sense of satisfaction that the snot was basting her bare skin rather than clothing. The last thing she needed was more laundry.

Her call was answered on the first ring.

'Hello, Orange Antenatal Unit,' said a deep voice.

Poppy froze. She had not anticipated this.

'Hello?' said the voice.

'James, hi,' said Poppy weakly. She'd walked right into this like a blind fool.

SPECIAL DELIVERY

She needed to say something. But what? The silence on the other end of the line was unbearable.

'I'm sorry to bother you; I was trying to get hold of Wenda. I was about to get in the shower and then I heard Maeve crying so I went and got her and then I called my mum and she suggested I call my midwife, so I thought of Wenda—not you, definitely not you. Not that I wouldn't trust your advice, it's just that Wenda popped into my head first—just like that!—and here we are. So . . . is Wenda there?'

Smooth, McKellar. Real smooth.

'I just—'

'Is Maeve okay?' interrupted James impatiently.

'Oh, ah, yes,' said Poppy, flustered. 'But no. She vomited. And she's got conjunctivitis. And I don't know if the two are related or if she's got a gastro bug *and* a conjunctivitis bug. I get that neither is life-threatening but I thought Wenda would be able to recommend a doctor, so could I talk to her? Her snot is going all over me. Maeve's snot obviously, not Wenda's.'

'Wenda is on long service leave.'

'Oh . . . right.' *Shit!* Wenda had told Poppy all about her plans to walk the Cinque Terre with her younger sister. And now that she thought about it, she was pretty sure she and James had talked about it too.

'Whoops. Mum brain. That's embarrassing. I just—'

'You can bring her in here.'

'Sorry, what?'

'You can bring her into the hospital to see the community health doctor. I can book you in.'

'Oh, that's nice of you, but honestly—'

'Just doing my job,' said James curtly. She could hear him tapping on a keyboard.

'Okay,' said Poppy meekly. She wondered whether she should try to explain that she really hadn't engineered the call to talk to him. It was purely accidental and Maeve was actually sick—a complete coincidence. Hilarious, really.

'There's been a cancellation. If you're free, you can come in now,' said James.

'Now?' replied Poppy. Her mind was whirling like a tornado.

'Now,' repeated James, as if she were thick.

'But I haven't got any clothes on,' she blurted. *Argh! Why?!* 'What I mean is, I'm not ready. I do have clothes on, I promise. Well, I mean, I don't have clothes on'—*stop!*—'but I have a towel on. No clothes under the towel, obviously, ha, because that would be weird. I was going to shower—did I say that?—but then I couldn't because Maeve was crying and now I haven't been able to put her down since. So, yes, I am still wearing the towel.'

Silence.

'So what I *really* mean to say is, thank you. For your help. I will get dressed and come straight in. Right now. Thank you. And good day.'

Poppy ended the call. *Ugh!* Could she be a bigger loser?! She sighed and carried her daughter into her bedroom, where she lay her on the carpet (Maeve immediately began to wail) and quickly changed into her cleanest jeans and jumper. Her brain might still not be fully functional post-birth, but she was going to remember to wear clothes to this appointment, thank you very much.

SPECIAL DELIVERY

As she started the car, Poppy spoke to the phone resting in the console. 'Siri, call Dar Nee.'

When life served her disasters in the form of accidental nude phone calls to infuriatingly handsome midwives, there was no other voice she'd rather hear.

'Hello?' Dani answered cautiously.

Poppy felt a bittersweet surge in her heart: the joy of hearing her best friend's voice; the self-inflicted pain of knowing it had been so long. 'Dan, I'm so glad you picked up,' Poppy said in a rush. 'I'm so sorry for everything. I'm sorry for being such a selfish brat, I'm sorry for not realising, I'm sorry for leaving it so long before I called, and most of all I'm so unbelievably sorry that I became someone who you thought wouldn't listen. You've been my lifeline this year, Dan, and since I met you really, and I honestly feel so, so stupid for taking that for granted. And now I'm prattling on like a tool and I haven't even asked about Sam's mum. How is she? I really hope she's okay. I understand if you don't want to talk about it, especially not with me, but I really want to know.'

Poppy slowed for the traffic lights, her mouth suddenly dry with fear. She really hoped Dani had understood that drivel.

'Sam's mum isn't great,' said Dani eventually. 'They're hopeful the radiation will work this time and she won't have to do chemo again, but she's scared and so is Sam. It's shit.'

'Oh, Dan,' said Poppy quietly. 'I'm so sorry. For all of you. That must be really hard.'

Outside, the streets blurred past. Poppy wished, not for the first time, that she could teleport to Sydney. 'If you need any help—someone to babysit Nella while you and Sam go to appointments, or someone to make dinners or clean the toilets or do the laundry—I can jump in the car and be there in four hours. You know I'd drop everything to help, right?'

Dani sighed. 'Of course, Pops. I know that.'

Poppy could feel herself choking up as she flicked on her indicator. 'I'd do anything for you and Sam and Nella, Dan. Like, I dunno, maybe I could do the laundry?'

'Yeah, you mentioned that.'

Poppy felt the tears erode her last vestiges of self-control and she sob-laughed. 'Dan, I've missed you so much.'

'Same, Pops. Life has been way too boring without you. Yesterday my Uber driver had a photo of Em Rata on his dash and tried to convince me they were cousins and oh my god, I almost peed myself it was so funny, but it also made me sad because I couldn't tell you.'

'What the hell?' cried Poppy. 'Of course you could have told me, you ninny; it breaks my heart that you thought you couldn't. But also, was this guy some kind of Polish–Israeli Adonis? Because if not, how on earth could he be related to Em Rata?'

'I know, right! As if a pasty old bald guy with a flavour saver could be related to Em Rata! That would contravene every theory of evolution.'

'Totally! And incidentally, I've never understood the appeal of flavour savers unless you're a Shannon Noll impersonator, and I'm not even sure that's a legitimate job.'

'Hundred per cent!' Dani laughed. 'Are you driving somewhere?'

'Yeah. Maeve's got an appointment at the community health centre.'

SPECIAL DELIVERY

'Is she okay?'

Poppy felt the panicky word vomit in her throat—Maeve's first sickness! She only had one bottle of baby Panadol in the house! There were so many things that could go wrong!—but she swallowed it down. This was nothing compared to what Sam and his mum were going through. 'She'll be fine,' Poppy said, keeping her voice steady. 'A few viral things, I think, but nothing to worry about hopefully.'

Dani was quiet, possibly considering whether to ask for more information. In the end she said, 'Okay, my dear, call me when you're done. I'm glad the band is back together.'

Poppy stifled another happy sob. 'Me too, Dan. I love you.'

'Love you too, Pops.'

Dani hung up and Poppy slowed as she drove through a school zone littered with clumps of teenagers in maroon uniforms. She was so lucky to have found Dani. A friend whose voice could calm you even when they were shrieking about baby goats on TikTok was a gift. And a friend who could lift you even when they were completely silent on the other end of the phone line was even rarer. Poppy had a best friend who could do both and she was never going to forget how lucky she was again.

Arriving at the community health clinic with four minutes to spare, Poppy parked the pram in the waiting room and held Maeve in her arms while her daughter snorted streams of elastic snot. Eventually Maeve's name was called by a grey-haired man with a receding hairline who introduced himself as Dr Gutherson.

The appointment was a wholly unsatisfying experience. Dr Gutherson told her genially not to worry about the gastro—'There'll be much more to come!'—and prescribed only a warm face washer for the conjunctivitis. As Maeve sat on her left knee grabbing at the stethoscope while Dr Gutherson leaned over to check her heartbeat, Poppy glanced up at the ceiling. On the other side of that gyprock barrier was the second floor of the hospital, and on the second floor of the hospital was the maternity ward. In that maternity ward were midwives: chatting, laughing, delivering babies. And one of those midwives would be going about his business fully aware that Poppy and Maeve were here. He could take the stairs, a right and a left, and come face to face with Poppy.

When the appointment ended, Poppy thanked Dr Gutherson and tried to slide Maeve into the pram. Her daughter glared at her accusingly and began to wail. Poppy tried singing quietly to shush her but Maeve continued thrashing her head against the pram liner.

'You'll find she'll be more clingy than usual,' said Dr Gutherson, handing Poppy a brochure appropriately titled *Gastro Passes*.

Poppy sighed and unbuckled her daughter. As she trudged to the car park through an icy wind, pushing the pram with one hand and carrying Maeve in the other arm, she asked herself again: *How do people have more than one child?*

At the LandCruiser, she flipped the pram brakes on and used her spare hand to prise her keys from her pocket. Her fingers found her phone instead. She fumbled and her phone dropped to the bitumen with a glassy clang. Poppy winced. She'd half-expected James to appear while she was at the

SPECIAL DELIVERY

community health centre, but that was stupid. He wasn't going to, and nor should he. He was on shift. He wasn't even really a friend at this point. Gingerly, she plucked her phone off the tarmac. Thankfully the screen was intact. It had landed right on the PARENTS WITH PRAMS ONLY sign.

I want to see him, she thought. It had been a vague, opaque feeling when she'd arrived, but now it was crystal clear. She missed him. She buckled Maeve into her car seat and walked around to the driver's side, poking the thought like a bruise: *I want to see him.* She was used to floating through life, saying, 'Yes, please,' and, 'No, thank you,' like a good girl, accepting whatever came next, and now it was possible she was going to float on the breeze away from James. She'd have to run into him around town for another few months, which would be horribly painful and sad, and then he'd move to Melbourne, which would be even more painful and sad.

Before she knew it, she'd arrived at the Woolworths car park. The wind was still howling outside and the clouds were darkening. She parked next to a HiLux that could have been James's, if not for the BO1TOY numberplate. A thunderclap cracked above her. The universe was tormenting her with terrible omens and terrible spelling.

Poppy strapped Maeve into the carrier on her chest and walked into the supermarket. It smelled like roast chicken and Maeve kicked her legs enthusiastically. *I want to see him.* She couldn't unthink it now, but was it merely lust? Was she just a sex-starved single mum? Was this a completely rational response to having slept with a guy whose arms were the perfect balance of muscle and flesh?

A tall man with dark blond hair walked out of the milk aisle and Poppy's heart skipped a beat before she realised he was her father's age. She exhaled slowly, and Maeve squawked and pointed down aisle four. Poppy turned, thinking for a moment Maeve may have spotted him down there. She shook her head in exasperation with herself. Of course it was another false alarm.

The shopping list app on her phone had neat ticks in all but one of the boxes. Poppy steeled herself and turned into the aisle with the pasta sauce. She knew logically that he wouldn't be there either but that didn't stop her heart beating like a jackhammer. She selected a jar of passata and placed it in the trolley. A thought nagged her. Did she like James? Like, *like* James? She pulled a second jar from the shelf. The linoleum where the sauce had exploded all those months ago had been scrubbed clean without so much as a pinkish stain left behind.

She steered the trolley to the checkout. She couldn't possibly *like* James. She was a smart girl and liking James would *not* be the smart choice. Notwithstanding his uncanny knack for unleashing her most embarrassing confrontational tendencies, he was moving eight hundred kilometres away. Liking James would be super dumb.

The cashier with an eighties fringe asked if she had her own bags. Poppy handed over the tangled ball of reusable sacks and began placing groceries on the conveyor belt. There were two separate things happening here: first, she was a hormonal (i.e. horny) mess, and second, James—despite his capacity to push all her buttons (including the horny ones)—was a first-class person. They were two completely unrelated facts: he was great at sex, and she liked hanging out with him. It would be ridiculous to confuse those two facts with having feelings for him. She was much smarter than that.

The passata jars clinked on the conveyor belt. There was something she was missing, the fuzzy outline of a thought she couldn't grasp. The cashier scanned her passata and suddenly she remembered. Kate had mentioned that James had been accepted into CSU Orange. Had he decided to stay here? Was that why he'd come to her place after the races? To tell her?

'Cash or card?' inquired Eighties Fringe.

Poppy pulled out her phone to tap the EFTPOS machine. If James was staying in Orange, what would that mean? Would they hang out? Would they booty call? Would they *date*? Her imagination scarpered ahead: visions of him on her couch, grinning as he pulled her to his lap and kissed her neck; the teasing bump of his hip against her waist; the touch of his lips against her bare shoulder; their pinky fingers linked on the couch; his ankle draped over hers in bed. A smile spread over her face and something warm and golden pulsed through her arteries. Her life was full of jobs and lists and duties and pressures, of bills and groceries and nappies and milk, of dreams and fears and laughter and tears, her brain was overwhelmed, her body was hardly hers—but there was a tiny keyhole within her that was empty. Maybe that's where James could fit.

At the checkout, the EFTPOS machine beeped. 'I think your phone is broken,' announced the cashier, pointing at Poppy's phone, where a giant black stripe now covered half the screen. 'Do you have your wallet?'

Poppy patted where her jean pockets were hiding under the hip strap of the BabyBjörn. Of course she wasn't carrying her wallet. She hadn't seen it in weeks. 'Can I leave an IOU?' she asked.

Eighties Fringe frowned. 'What do you think this is? The eighties?'

Poppy was too stressed to appreciate the tragicomic irony. She looked helplessly at the reusable bags already filled with sixty-seven dollars' worth of crap that was completely essential to surviving the next twenty-four hours. She did a frantic mental inventory of her pantry contents. She could eat Weet-Bix for dinner and forgo laundry until tomorrow, the no-toilet-paper situation would be an issue, but she could—

'I can help,' said a quiet voice. A willowy brunette brushed past her and pointed her credit card at the EFTPOS machine. 'There,' she said, her voice like a wind chime as the machine beeped authoritatively. 'Done.' She smiled at Poppy, her tiny diamond nose ring glinting under the strip lighting. Her skin was so youthful and bright it almost glowed.

Poppy looked around frantically. 'No, no, no, no, no,' she spluttered. A queue was forming behind them. 'Can you do a refund?' She patted her back pockets uselessly. 'That's so generous,' she said to the girl, 'but I can't accept.'

'Ahem,' grumbled Eighties Fringe.

The girl shrugged. 'It's done. And if you make her refund it, it'll be awkward for all of us, and it's a small town, so we'll never forget.'

'I, er . . .' stammered Poppy. *Was that a threat?*

SPECIAL DELIVERY

'I'm kidding!' the girl said, smiling. 'I have nieces. Things get busy, phones get broken and sometimes the smugly child-free need to step up and help out. This is my time to pay it forward. Honestly, don't give it a second thought.'

Poppy felt the prickle of tears at her eyelids. 'Thank you,' she said, wishing she wasn't wearing Maeve so she could hug this nose-ringed angel. 'Truly. This means more than you can imagine.'

CHAPTER 41

Poppy strode out into the sunlit cul-de-sac, the crisp spring air curling itself around her body while Maeve sat in the pram wearing a hat to shade her from the glare. After five months of bone-chilling purgatory, the mere act of switching from beanies to sun protection felt like a victory. Maeve nibbled a rusk and hiccupped contentedly. They'd survived their first Orange winter. It was something to celebrate.

Over the hedge, Mary's perm bobbed up. 'Off for a hot lap?' (Poppy had once used this term in front of Mary, who had neatly injected it into her everyday lexicon.) 'Fancy a cuppa when you get back?'

'We'd love that,' replied Poppy.

'You watch out for those magpies, pet.'

'I will,' Poppy assured her.

'You want some cable ties to poke through your hat? I've got some in the garage.'

SPECIAL DELIVERY

'No, thanks, Mary.' Poppy wondered whether she'd ever feel so anxious about magpies that she'd resort to wearing a hat with cable tie spears attached to it. Her initial feelings were: no.

She set off down the road, basking in the weightlessness of her long-sleeved t-shirt. Mentally, she was already boxing up the North Face to stow at the back of her wardrobe until next year. Everyone else walking around the golf course was obviously feeling the same. Middle-aged women had forgone the puffer vests and Gen Z-ers were wearing crop tops and bike shorts. The spring-fuelled exuberance was contagious.

The oak tree was covered in tiny green buds. In a few weeks it would cast a luscious shade. Poppy automatically glanced to her left but she was alone. She pushed her sleeves up to her elbows as her newly repaired phone began to ring in the cup holder. Pulling it out she saw it was an unknown number, but the dial code was local. Curious, she tapped the green button. 'Hello?'

'Hello, do I have Poppy McKellar?'

'Yes, speaking.'

'Great. Hi, Poppy. This is Sarah Jones from Region Building Australia. We had a chat last month.'

Comms Manager Sarah Jones?! What on earth did she want?

'Is now a good time to talk?' asked Sarah.

Poppy looked at Maeve, who was flexing her fingers in the sun. 'Sure,' she replied.

'I'm calling because we're starting a new brand-awareness project focused on cross-channel content and targeted outreach.'

'Okay . . .'

'I'll cut to the chase. I'm looking to recruit a digital platforms lead and I thought you might be a good fit. I've got to lock in my headcount asap for our end-of-year budgeting, so I need to fill roles fast with a view to sorting out specific working arrangements down the track. If you're interested, I can get this moving fairly quickly. Our conversation last month could be considered your first interview, and I've got your CV already, so with your permission we could go straight to reference checks. Of course, we could also negotiate a part-time arrangement or a job share—the main thing I need at this stage is confirmation you're interested so I can get the ball rolling on the rest. Does it sound like something you'd be interested in?'

'Uhhhh . . . uhhhh.' The words wouldn't form in her mouth; her brain was mush. 'Yes!' Poppy gasped, brain connecting to voice box finally. 'I am definitely interested.'

'Fantastic,' said Sarah. 'I'll send over the contract and job description now for you to review, but essentially the job is yours if you want it. If you could confirm your interest via email, I'll get you set up in our system. If you have any questions, you can call me on this number. Otherwise, I'll wait to receive your reply.'

In Poppy's imagination, cannons sent glitter and confetti rocketing into the sky, a chorus of dancing girls high-kicked from stage left, the guy from the Old Spice ad rode in on a horse. 'Thank you so much, Sarah,' she said, beaming. 'I'll look forward to the email.'

The call ended and Poppy stared at her phone in disbelief. *Yes!* She punched the air. This was living! Getting a job, making money, providing for her daughter—this was what life was all about. This was taking control!

She rounded the corner back into the cul-de-sac, energised. The blossoms were bursting! It was spring—and soon it would be summer! She was going back to work! She'd need to have her suit pants dry-cleaned and sort out day care and buy Maeve a lunch box and prune the hydrangeas and buy mozzie coils from Bunnings. She'd buy her mum a new Rockmans dress just because she could. There was so much life to get done!

She needed to call James. It was so obvious now. She needed to apologise and things could go back to the way they were. She could see it now: they matched. It wasn't the hormones or the heat or the fact his lips would curve slightly upwards in that almost-smile which could make her blaze with irritation because she was desperate to share every joke. It was just her, and him, and together they existed in some unfiltered, messy continuum where you could yell and cry and laugh and somehow none of it mattered, because what mattered was that they were real together.

With Patrick, she'd endured the boozy adventures, trying to convince herself it was fun. She'd posed at awkward, arm-flattering angles for his Instagram stories when all she wanted was a night on the couch. With Henry, she'd spent months pretending half his life—the Willa part—didn't exist. She'd warped her reality to make space for both of them, even if it meant ignoring parts of herself.

With James, she'd never hidden anything and gosh, it had been liberating. Imagine feeling like that forever. To feel like that even for a few more weeks would be a gift. There was no point worrying about Melbourne. She had so much to tell him. She was going to buy a leaf blower, Maeve was trying new food groups, her mum had plans to storm the council DA meeting. He'd listen to it all and know the perfect thing to say. He'd tell her she was stupid or amazing or that he didn't care about Maeve's foray into beetroot (but she knew he would). She missed his no-bullshit view of the world and she missed how his smile made warmth radiate through every cell of her body.

Her smile was irrepressible as she eased the pram up Mary's garden path and registered the table that was already laden with their morning tea. 'We're back, Mary,' she called. The plate of jam drops was there but the teapot was missing. Mary must be fetching it from inside. Poppy pulled Maeve out of the pram and sat down in her usual chair. When Mary didn't appear after a couple of minutes she rose again and knocked on the screen door. 'Mary, can I help you carry anything out?'

The sound of a buzzing dragonfly filled the silence.

'Mary?'

Poppy shifted Maeve to her other hip and eased the door open. 'Mary?'

She walked down the hall to the kitchen. It was like she knew what she was going to find, the pressure building in her brain, her pulse hammering in her ears.

'Mary!' she shouted and dropped to the ground.

Her neighbour was lying on the floor, her left leg bent at an odd angle, a trickle of blood at her temple. Her eyes were ghostly still.

'Mary!' she shouted again. A pulse—she needed to check for a pulse. She put her fingers to the old woman's wrist. *Yes.*

SPECIAL DELIVERY

It was as faint as a butterfly's touch, but her pulse was there. Mary was still alive.

Poppy grabbed frantically at her pockets for her phone, but they were empty. She sprang up, still holding Maeve tight to her side, and ran back to the pram. Jolted by the whiplash, Maeve began to wail.

Where was her bloody phone? She found it in the cup holder, yanked it out and ran back to Mary. *Please be okay*, she prayed as she dialled triple zero. Maeve was still screaming.

The call was answered on the first ring. 'Fire, police or ambulance?'

'Ambulance,' Poppy gasped. 'Quickly!' Forcing herself to form coherent sentences, she relayed the address and nodded furiously at the lady's instructions: check Mary's airways, observe her for spinal injuries, move her into the recovery position—and above all, don't leave her.

An ambulance arrived seven harrowing minutes later. A paramedic with a blonde ponytail strode in purposefully, not bothering to knock, and without greeting Poppy put a ventilator over Mary's face. With the help of her partner, she rolled the old woman onto a stretcher and wheeled it outside.

Poppy watched numbly as the back door of the ambulance was opened and the stretcher was rolled inside, just like that. She felt winded, as if a semitrailer had just knocked her clean off her feet. Maeve was still on her hip, her wailing having settled to a low whimper. Poppy squeezed her in what she hoped translated as comfort.

'Can we travel in the ambulance?' she heard herself ask the blonde paramedic, surprised she still had words, could still make sounds.

The paramedic shook her head. There were no child restraints, she explained. She'd have to follow them to the emergency department in her own car.

The paramedics got in the van—one in the front and one in the back with Mary.

'Please,' Poppy called, her voice cracking with the effort. 'Hold her hand.'

CHAPTER 42

'I came as soon as I got the message,' said James, running through the doors to the waiting room. 'I was in the delivery suite, phone on silent. Mum and Kate are on their way . . .' He trailed off, running his hands through his hair. 'How is she?'

Poppy sat with Maeve on her knee in one of the grey vinyl chairs, a pile of dusty magazines on the table to her left. The smells of antiseptic and hospital food mingled in the air.

'She's in surgery.' Poppy's knees felt so weak it was a miracle Maeve could sit on them.

'Shit, so . . .' James's eyes searched the room, her face, for answers.

'I'm so sorry,' gasped Poppy, trying to catch a breath before the terror constricted her airways, curling around her like a snake. Words and letters were scrambled in her mind, shooting out in fits and starts, spluttering like a leaking faucet. The magpies. The blood. The tiles. Mary's leg in a cubist V. All playing on a relentless loop in her mind.

The doctors had said she'd most likely fallen and broken her leg then passed out from the pain. The blood at her temple seemed to be circumstantial, but they'd scanned her for brain injuries just to be sure. At the very least Mary would need a steel pin in her leg to replace the shattered femur, and any recovery would be slow and painful, especially for someone her age. Technically speaking, though, a full recovery was possible.

'She's eighty-nine,' James muttered to himself, staring out the window to the atrium garden below. Poppy knew what he meant. Mary wouldn't be starting from a level playing field. Everything would be slower and harder, the gains so much smaller, the setbacks more severe. Normally they spoke of her age with reverence and incredulity. *Eighty-nine and acing the crossword! Eighty-nine and using an iPad!* And, most frequently, *Eighty-nine, can you believe it?* But they all believed it, profoundly, because they couldn't imagine life without her.

'I'm so sorry,' squeaked Poppy. Her arms were wrapped tight around her daughter's chest.

'Poppy,' said James, closing the space between them to stand in front of her. He put his hands to her jaw and gently tipped her face up, his eyes locking on to hers. 'It's not your fault.'

Poppy pulled her head away and buried her face in the crook of her daughter's neck, her tears falling onto Maeve's soft skin. 'It is,' she choked. 'If it wasn't for me, she wouldn't have been in the kitchen.'

James crouched beside them, bringing his hand onto her back. 'Poppy, you know Mary. She was always pottering around. No-one made her fall, especially not you.'

SPECIAL DELIVERY

'But the tea . . .'

'It wasn't your fault,' James repeated, his hand still resting on her back.

Poppy wondered what would happen if she leaned towards him and put her head on his shoulder like she wanted to. She wanted to let the pain seep out; she was exhausted, she was scared. She wished she could cry in his arms and they could share the pain, but she couldn't feel sorry for herself, not now, not in this grey room with its plastic chairs and scuffed floors. That would be the ultimate self-indulgence. It would be pathetic and selfish, and everything she was trying not to be. But she did feel sorry and she did feel scared and she hated herself for it and that made it worse.

Poppy lifted her eyes. 'James, I want to say something. I *need* to say something.'

He stood up and turned away from her. 'Not now, Poppy,' he said wearily. 'Mary's in surgery, my head is a mess. We'll talk. But not now.'

Poppy's stomach coiled. 'When?' she asked him quietly.

He sighed. 'Soon.'

Maeve whimpered and reached for James. He looked at Poppy for permission then scooped Maeve off her lap.

'She's miserable cooped up here,' said Poppy. 'She's been whining since we arrived.'

'I can take her for a walk to the ward,' he said. 'I'll only be five minutes and there are toys there. I need to pack up anyway and'—he paused, swallowing—'I need to hug someone.'

Poppy nodded. As she let him walk off with her daughter in his arms, she stifled a sob. She really needed a hug too.

CHAPTER 43

Mary died during surgery. The news hit like an earthquake. According to the doctor, there were complications from the anaesthesia. Terms like 'circulatory collapse', 'hypovolaemia' and 'benzodiazepines' swam past her, her brain refusing to latch on to them, her denial receptors working in overdrive. Mary had to wake up. They were supposed to have tea and jam drops.

Next door, the blinds were closed, the lights were off and the junk mail was piling up. Poppy left it in a neat pile at Mary's door because she knew how much her neighbour loved the catalogues. It was stupid, no-one would read them, but every day she added another catalogue to the pile. She couldn't do anything else, so she did this.

The funeral was horrible in the way they always were: the worst-timed celebration of someone's life. Why couldn't it have been held two weeks ago, when Mary could have sat up the front and marvelled at the slideshow, pointing out her favourite hairstyles and the cake she'd baked for her daughter's wedding? It was a sickening irony; everyone Mary loved was there but she wasn't. Poppy sat at the back, Maeve in the pram, both wearing navy because the only black clothes Poppy owned were leggings. By the time the service finished, Maeve was crying and ready for her morning sleep, so Poppy drove straight home and put her to bed. James wouldn't have known she was there.

As she pushed the pram out of the driveway, down the road and past the oak tree, everything reminded her of James and Mary. Poppy had offered the family her help, but no-one needed it. They had each other. She'd texted James and heard nothing back. Kate had responded to her message with a heart emoji. It was like she was on the edge of their vortex and no-one would let her jump in and feel the grief with them. She wanted to be useful, she wanted to cry with them, she wanted to tell them how much Mary had meant to her, but what right did she have? She hadn't even known Mary a year. They might be blaming her for all she knew. Poppy cursed herself again. What selfish idiot expects an eighty-nine-year-old woman to wait on them? *She* should have boiled the kettle, *she* should have made the tea, *she* should have baked the fucking jam drops!

To make matters worse, she really missed James. She wanted to comfort him, but she couldn't get close—he was keeping her at arms' length. She wanted to give him space but she didn't know how much he needed. Would it be weird to keep texting? The unanswered calls and messages were banking up and yes, there were mitigating circumstances, but at some point she'd have to ease up on the one-sided texting or be forever known as a psycho.

She took a deep breath and focused on the footpath ahead. The air smelled of wisteria. The Bustle, her walks, the unmown garden next door; everything reminded her of him. She wished they still hated each other so she wouldn't care, but as soon as that thought surfaced she knew it was a lie. She'd loved hating him almost as much as she'd loved liking him.

More blossoms were appearing each day; pompoms of pink and white and ruby had brought the cul-de-sac back to life. She was living in a pastel pink paradise and she'd never been more miserable. Maeve wasn't crawling yet, which was another thing to feel anxious about. Yesterday her daughter had almost managed a forward-shuffle and the elation Poppy felt was quickly matched by her dejection at realising no-one else but her mother would care. Dani and April would pretend to be excited but only because they were good people. Their kids were already walking and everyone knew that as soon as your child moved on to the next milestone you instantly forgot (and stopped caring) about any beforehand, because: brain space.

Mary would have been ecstatic. James would have been excited too. He would have high-fived her and told her it was proof Maeve was a genius. Mary would have said the same.

A ding in the cup holder interrupted her thoughts so Poppy stuck her hand in and pulled out her phone. The name on the screen made something heavy flip over in her rib cage. James. Equal parts eager and petrified, she opened the message.

Cleaning out some of Mary's stuff today. Will you be home?

Poppy began typing immediately. *Yes!! How are you? I've left all the junk mail at the doorstep, should I get rid of it? Hope*

SPECIAL DELIVERY

you're ok. Would love to see you. I can help if you need anything. Honestly.

Then she deleted everything. Maybe a thumbs-up emoji would suffice? But she had so much to say. She needed to tell him how much she was missing Mary and what had really happened with Henry. Hell, she needed to tell him she'd watched the Scott Cam interview on *60 Minutes*. More than anything, she wanted to see that smile spread across his face and his eyes light up and know it was because of her. There was no point in pretending.

Yes, will be home all day, she wrote. *Would love to see you xx.* She clicked send. No chance of him misunderstanding that.

Her footsteps lightened. She would be seeing him soon and even though it would be sad and awkward, she would apologise again and again until he understood how sorry she was, and maybe—hopefully—they could start again.

★

There was a quiet knock at the door and Poppy raced to open it.

'I didn't want to—' James was pointing at the doorbell. He was dressed in jeans, an old jumper and work boots.

Poppy smiled gratefully as she ushered him in. 'Thank you. Maeve's still asleep in the pram.'

They moved quietly to the kitchen. Her chest was a bubbling cauldron of feelings and words threatening to spit out. She wanted to jump up and fling her arms around his neck and wrap her legs around his waist. She wanted to say everything that had been running through her head on repeat since that night at the races. *Sorry sorry sorry, I miss you I miss you I miss you.* She was so profoundly happy to see him, she wanted to show him her real self—especially since he'd helped her find it—but she didn't know how to start. Eventually she whispered, 'I'm so glad to see you.'

James nodded, said nothing, and shoved his hands deeper in his pockets. His gaze darted to the pram, which was parked in the corner with Maeve hardly visible as she slept under a striped cotton blanket.

Poppy swallowed the scraping lump in her throat. It was now or never. She needed to look him in the eye and tell him how she felt.

'Hello-oooo!' boomed a voice in the distance.

Poppy's and James's eyes met. There was a moment of confusion. It wasn't her mum or her dad or Henry or April or Dani or anyone else who would or could or *should* be there. It was the sound of a war cannon, a crack of thunder that seems too close.

Then Poppy gasped. *What the hell?* Her heart lurched as she swept past James and ran to the window and—*oh god.* A giant SUV was parked on her driveway, its logo glinting in the sun. Poppy's stomach plummeted. No-one in this street drove a Tesla.

'Um, James—'

She heard the metallic clang of her front gate first, saw the shadow behind her front door. Her larynx compressed, her skin tightened around her whole body. *Oh no.* The door handle was turning; he was letting himself in.

'Babe!' exclaimed Patrick, striding through her front door and into the kitchen. 'It's been so long!' His long arms grabbed her in a crushing hug, his metallic watch band snagging on her hair. He still smelled exactly the same: of Burberry Hero, post-gym bodywash and his overpriced laundry service.

'Patrick, what . . . what are you doing here?' she stammered, recoiling. The white of his t-shirt was blinding and matched the whiteness of his socks and sneakers.

'I came to see my daughter,' he said as his gaze roamed over her kitchen-living area before landing squarely on James. She saw Patrick assess his outfit—from the threadbare jumper to the well-worn work boots—then he turned to Poppy and jerked his thumb over his shoulder. 'Who is this?' he asked, as if James wasn't there.

'Shhh,' hissed Poppy, tilting her head to where Maeve was still asleep in the pram.

James stepped forward and stuck out his hand. 'I'm James, a friend of Poppy's,' he said.

Patrick turned, his expression bemused, and gripped the proffered hand so tightly a vein pulsed in his neck. 'Patrick.' The handshake seemed to last longer than it should and there was zero shake.

'You okay, Poppy?' James asked quietly.

'What's that supposed to mean, bro?'

'It means I know who you are,' replied James, not looking at Patrick.

'And what's *that* supposed to mean?' Patrick demanded.

'Can we please keep it down?' begged Poppy. 'Maeve's not due to wake up for another fifty minutes.'

Patrick turned back to her and smirked. 'Never picked you as a routine type, babe.'

'What's that supposed to mean?' she hissed.

James cleared his throat. 'Uh, Poppy, I think I'll give you two some privacy. I'll be next door if you need me.'

Poppy spun towards him. 'James,' she began, but he was already moving towards the door. She wanted to cry, *Stay, I need you, I can't do this alone*—but she knew with an exhausting inevitability that she had to.

'Does he clean your gutters or something?' asked Patrick, not waiting for a reply as he began walking to the pram.

Poppy moved to intercept him. 'Patrick, what are you doing?'

'I'm waking up my daughter,' he replied, as though that should be self-evident. 'This is a big moment for her.'

'No, no, no!' whispered Poppy. 'You can't wake her up. She's not due to wake up now, and I'm the one who will have to deal with an overtired baby.'

'Babe, relax.'

'NO!' Poppy whispered more forcefully. 'You are one thousand per cent *not* waking her up. Sleep is actually pretty important for nine-month-old babies—not that you'd know, given that you've never taken the slightest interest in any child, let alone your own daughter.'

'Whoa, babe, where's my chill girl?' asked Patrick, his mouth quirking. 'Where's my girl who was up for anything?'

Poppy felt every muscle in her body become tense. 'You think it's stupid to care about what my daughter needs?' she hissed. 'What am I supposed to do, Patrick? Pretend I'm still twenty-two and get hammered every night?! Every single kid in the entire world has a routine, which you might actually know if you cared even one iota about your daughter. Seriously why are you even here?'

'I'm here to be a dad,' he said, spreading his arms wide, his palms to the sky. It was one of his favourite poses.

'Patrick, you didn't even text.'

'I know, babe, but I knew you wouldn't mind.'

Poppy pressed her fingertips to her temples. Her gut was a writhing mess of confusion and rage and sadness. She'd longed for this for nine months, and now that he was finally here, everything felt off. The bleached white of his t-shirt, the Bondi tan, the weirdly perfect beach body achieved through an obsessive gym regime. Against the backdrop of her 1980s suburban rental, nothing about Patrick felt real.

'But why today?' she sighed. 'Why now?'

Patrick shrugged. 'I thought it was time.'

Poppy felt the air seep from her lungs like deflating balloons. She recognised that expression. He was Maeve's dad. Maeve was half him. Maybe underneath that shiny Eastern Suburbs veneer, he was just a guy who'd taken nine months to realise he'd been an absolute dickhead.

Patrick continued. 'I want to get to know my daughter. Learn about her. I want her to run into my arms and call me Daddy.'

Poppy stifled a grimace. 'She's only nine months old. She can't walk and talk yet.'

'Really?' Patrick scratched his neck. 'She's not, like, slow or anything, is she?'

'No, Patrick.' He didn't need to know Maeve wasn't crawling yet.

'I'm so glad I came.' His eyes were dancing now, his pupils dilated and glossy. 'I've had the biggest few days. Massive work conference, and then last night we all ended up at the casino until four am and I woke up this morning and I was so bummed you weren't there. Remember how you used to buy me blueberry Gatorade when I was hungover? And then I thought about the fact that you had a kid now, and I was like, man, I should be there. Like, I should be with you and this kid—'

'She's not some *kid*,' Poppy interrupted. 'She's your *daughter*. Her name is Maeve.'

Patrick waved her quiet. 'Yeah, totally, babe, I know—but what I'm saying is, I just knew I needed to be here. Like, I just woke up and I was like, imagine if I could just wake up with you and this kid, who just loves me and wants to give me all these cute cuddles. Like, wouldn't that be the best thing ever? To wake up after a massive bender and just have all this love surrounding you? Like, isn't that the dream?'

Poppy blinked. Were these words actually coming out of his mouth?

'And then, like, I realised it didn't have to be a dream,' Patrick continued. 'I could literally just have that as my life. So I just got up and jumped in the car and started driving. Like, man, maybe I was still drunk, but I needed to get here and see you guys. And now I'm here, and'—he paused dramatically as if readying himself for the finale—'we can be a family.'

'I . . .' Poppy hesitated, taking a rare second to consider exactly what she wanted to say. She needed these words to match her feelings. This was not a time for word vomit. She

SPECIAL DELIVERY

needed to be thoughtful, deliberate. Her eyes landed on the door where James had walked out moments before.

'What?' asked Patrick, sensing her hesitation, his gaze following hers to the door. Poppy flinched slightly and a blush swarmed up her cheeks. Patrick's eyes were narrowed in confusion and then, slowly, they widened and he began to laugh. It was a low and menacing sound. 'No. *Fucking.* Way. That guy that was here—the gutter boy. You're *fucking* him?'

'Patrick!' cried Poppy.

Maeve suddenly wailed from the corner, woken by the noise.

Poppy rushed to her, tears forming in her eyes. 'How dare you storm in here and speak to me like that!'

'So you're not?'

Poppy glared at him as she lifted her daughter to her chest.

Patrick snorted. 'After me, I thought you could do better than him, babe.'

'STOP CALLING ME BABE!' she cried, her daughter still bawling in her arms. 'You lost that privilege a long time ago, Patrick. I do not answer to you. I answer to no-one but Maeve, and that's only because I *choose* to. You had a chance to be involved in her life but you ignored me. You ignored *us!* Do you not even understand how one *single* call in those early days would have helped me when I was drowning in loneliness, trying to parent by myself? And now you rock up here saying you're ready to be a dad. Do you even understand what that means, Patrick? It's more than a bloody Instagram post. It's cleaning shit off everything, it's waking up a million times in the middle of the night because she's lost her dummy, it's rewiring your whole brain to work according to her schedule, it's giving yourself to someone completely because their happiness matters more to you than anything else in the world. Do you think your ego could cope with that, Patrick?'

Patrick had hardly glanced at his daughter. 'Babe, you need to calm down.'

'Patrick!'

'I mean *Poppy*, not babe.' He spread his arms wide again in his *so sue me* pose. 'You know I'm a creature of habit.'

Every bone in her body was almost vibrating. Maeve was still crying on her chest. Patrick still hadn't asked to hold his child.

Poppy turned and walked to the lounge room. She placed Maeve on the play mat with some cushions behind her in case she fell, then spread a collection of her favourite toys in front of her, watching her daughter's tears subside as she picked up her favourite rattle. This would keep Maeve amused for a little while, and Poppy only needed five minutes, max.

She strode back to Patrick, tilted her chin and looked him straight in the eye. All those months she'd spent waiting for this moment and it had finally come. All those mornings and nights when she'd wished for an extra pair of hands or fretted about Maeve not having a father. Every unanswered text that had wrecked her with anxiety. Every minute she'd spent worrying that she wouldn't be enough for her daughter, that she couldn't do it by herself, that she was condemning her daughter to a subpar life, and the solution had landed in her kitchen, just like this.

'Get out,' she said.

SPECIAL DELIVERY

'What?'

'You heard me, Patrick. I said get out.'

'But, babe—I mean, Poppy!—didn't you hear me? I said I'm ready to be a dad. I'm ready for us to be a family. The whole shebang!'

Every word he said only strengthened her resolve. She didn't need him to complete their family. He wasn't the missing link. There *was* no missing link. Maeve and Poppy, they were a family by themselves, just the two of them. They didn't need each other for Instagram likes; they needed each other in a visceral way, like atoms need electrons. They were the same matter, the same blood, extensions of each other. Patrick had played a role in Maeve's conception, but he wasn't needed now, and he sure as hell wasn't going to walk in here and blow up everything that she'd worked so hard for.

'Maeve and I are more than a hangover cure, Patrick. We're not just here to pep you up when you're feeling sorry for yourself. If you can't see that, then you don't deserve us.'

'Poppy, seriously, stop being so hectic.' His eyes were darting wildly around the room as though looking for someone to back him up. 'You're talking like some whingeing bitch on *Dr Phil*. Just listen to me—'

'No, you listen to me,' blazed Poppy. 'You come into our home, disrespect me, practically ignore Maeve and then have the gall to confess you want me back because I buy you fucking Gatorade when you're coming down off god-knows-what. You show no inclination at all to interact with your child or call her by her name and assume with all your characteristic bloody egotism that she will automatically adore you. You offer zero apologies for ghosting me—and Maeve, your own flesh and blood—for the last nine months. I am well within my rights to kick you out of my house, but I am asking you nicely, for the sake of Maeve in the other room, to get out.'

Patrick looked murderous. 'And what happens then? You never hear from me again?'

'Ideally yes.'

'So, what? You're going to raise this kid by yourself?'

'That's exactly what I have been doing, Patrick, so yes, I think that's a safe assumption.'

'And what happens when she goes to school and realises all the other kids have dads and she wants to find hers?'

'Then I will tell her that her father and I have not spoken since that time he rocked up to my house and called me a whingeing bitch.'

'You know that's not what I meant.'

'I actually don't care what you meant, Patrick. I just want you to leave.'

Patrick slammed his hand on the kitchen bench. 'Jesus, Poppy! You're being an idiot!'

'Get out, Patrick.'

'Fine!' He balled his hands into fists and walked to the door. As he turned the handle, he spun back to face her. 'You'll regret this Poppy. Your daughter will hate you for doing this.'

'Her name is Maeve, Patrick. And somehow I don't think she will.'

'Don't come crying to me when everything turns to shit and you need help.'

'Trust me, I won't.'

SPECIAL DELIVERY

He yanked the door open and Poppy watched him stomp back to his Tesla. At her front gate he turned to look at her again, his features contorted in an ugly rage. 'And another thing,' he spat. 'Blueberry Gatorade tastes like shit.'

Poppy smiled with grim satisfaction. 'I know, Patrick.'

She closed the door.

In the lounge room, Maeve was still sitting on her play mat, passing the rattle between her chubby hands. At the sight of her mother, Maeve's face broke into a wide smile and Poppy's heart lifted. She would never know for sure if she'd made the right decision, but at this moment, her gut told her she had. Patrick didn't belong here. He was too impetuous, too self-centred, too frenetic and too vain. He needed everything to be orbiting him, as though he was the star and everyone else a member of the supporting cast.

Poppy's life now was not uncomplicated, but it was slower and more predictable in a way that nourished her. And that was what she and Maeve needed at the moment: predictability.

Poppy sat down opposite her daughter. Afternoons like this, sitting on a play mat watching her daughter's eyes sparkle as she tinkered with her dollar-shop rattle, were what she wanted. She picked up the rattle and shook it at Maeve. Her daughter reached her arms towards it happily. With a tumbling motion, she fell forward and raised herself on her hands and knees. With a giggle, she lurched herself forward and crawled straight into Poppy's lap, seizing the rattle between her chubby fingers.

Poppy gasped. 'Maevey, you crawled!' She picked up her daughter and laughed into her neck, smothering her with kisses. 'My clever, clever girl! I am so proud of you, Maevey!'

She scooped Maeve up and ran outside with the timid hope of the morning blossoming again in her chest. James would be so happy to hear the news. 'James!' she called across the hedge. 'James! You'll never guess what just happened!'

Mary's front door opened and James came outside quickly. 'What's wrong?'

'I'm fine! Everything's good!' Poppy rounded the fence and walked up Mary's front path. He was so close now she could almost reach out and touch him. They were together again—geographically, if nothing else. She could apologise properly and things could go back to how they were before. She beamed at him, radiant with hope.

James turned to look at the closed door, his forehead creased. 'Mum's inside packing up. She's pretty distraught.'

'Oh . . .' Poppy faltered. Fuck.

James gazed back at her, expressionless, and a tiny bead of fear crept into Poppy's stomach. She wanted to reach for him but it was as though he was standing purposely just out of her grasp.

'I wanted to tell you . . .' It seemed so stupid now. Why would he care about this when his grandma had just died? What sociopath would think a crawling baby trumped that? Poppy looked at the ground. 'Nothing, it's just, um . . . Maeve crawled for the first time.'

The corners of James's mouth tilted ever so slightly upwards for a second and then straightened. 'That's great, Poppy.' He sounded tired and, worse than that, he sounded sad.

'I'm sorry, James,' Poppy said abruptly. She needed to get this out before he could stop her or get away. 'I'm so sorry for that night after the races. I shouldn't have let Henry come home with me but I promise it wasn't what you think, and nothing happened. And I would never want it to, because'—she swallowed—'I only want to be with you.'

There, she'd said it. He couldn't unhear it now. She may as well have offered herself up naked on a sushi platter.

James looked at her intently, his black eyes penetrating hers. She searched him for clues—a smile, a glimmer in his eyes, a twitch of the lips—but his face was a mask.

'Poppy, we can't.'

'We can!' she insisted. 'I know this is a hard time for you, but I've realised whatever comes will come, and we can just enjoy being with each other now. We've wasted so much time already, why waste another minute?'

James grabbed the back of his head and sighed. The tiny bead of fear in her abdomen swelled.

'Poppy, it's too late. This whole thing with Mary . . . it's been another massive reminder that life doesn't go to plan. I have to go to Melbourne. I can't stay here and let life pass me by.'

'But you got accepted into the med program at CSU Orange too,' stammered Poppy. 'What if it's a sign you don't need to go to Melbourne?'

'What if getting into Melbourne is a sign I should go there, Poppy? Life isn't some secret code from the universe that we have to decipher. I can't trust fate to sort my life out for me. I have to make my own decisions. That's why I'm going to Melbourne.' He didn't need to add *without you*.

Poppy shook her head. She needed to jolt him out of this and make him laugh and remember who they were together but it was like trying to cup water in her hands. The more he spoke, the further away he slipped, sliding through her fingers like liquid.

'But you asked if I was okay,' she said quietly.

'What?'

'Back at my place, you asked if I was okay. I thought it meant you cared.'

The mask on James's face flickered for a millisecond and was back just as quickly. 'It doesn't matter if I do, Poppy. You have an ex-boyfriend who wants to get back together with you and another ex-boyfriend who hits on you when he's drunk. There's too much standing in our way.'

'This is stupid!' cried Poppy. 'Of every relationship I've been in, this is the one that feels like it could be . . . I dunno, good. Awesome, even. It feels real. Don't you feel it too? We just match.'

'You make it sound so simple Poppy, but it's not.'

'We can make it simple,' Poppy argued. 'This doesn't have to be anything more than what it is right now. We can be happy *right now*.'

A beat passed between them and Poppy wished she could read his mind like he could read hers. On her hip, Maeve shifted to lay her head against Poppy's chest and a horrible thought occurred to her.

'It is because I'm a single mum? Is it because of Maeve?'

The hurt in his eyes was instant. 'Of course not,' he said. 'You know I think Maeve is amazing. It's just—I'm moving to Melbourne. And you . . . you're not going anywhere, are you?'

For a moment Poppy imagined herself in Melbourne. Shushing Maeve at cool cafes in graffitied laneways, ending up in the hook turn lane, the pram getting stuck in the tram tracks. Sure, there would be good coffee, designer baby shops, the pleasant anonymity that came with city life, but she'd have to hustle and grind and always pay for parking and, at this point in her life, that was a giant negative.

In Orange, she had her parents, she had April and the mothers' group girls, the baristas at The Bustle knew her coffee order. Every member of the golf club mafia knew her life story, but she knew they'd protect her and Maeve like their own. When people said it took a village to raise a child, they forgot to mention it took a village to raise a mother, too. This town with its wide streets and colourful seasons had sheltered her when she needed it. Orange had become home again. 'You're right,' said Poppy quietly. 'I'm not going anywhere.'

James shifted on the balls of his feet. 'You and I are in different lanes, Poppy, and that's a fact we can't change, no matter how we feel.'

'How *do* you feel?' she asked softly. There was something underneath that mask. He was hiding something and she knew it.

'Poppy, at this point, how I feel won't change anything. It's not as though this is a Netflix special and all you need is love.'

'Love?' whispered Poppy.

James's face flickered again. 'Figure of speech,' he said weakly.

Poppy was suddenly furious. *Love?!* He drops the L-word and then insists they can't be together?! He was so bloody infuriating! Couldn't he see he was making the wrong decision? 'So that's it?' she asked. 'We're done?'

'We could be friends?'

'We tried that,' said Poppy hotly, her body livid at the memory of James undressing her in a stable.

'What do you want me to say?' asked James. 'That we should never speak again?'

'I want you to admit you're being stupid!' If he was going to outright reject her, he was going to have to try harder. She didn't care if she seemed psycho or needy or pathetic. James made her shameless. He was her kryptonite.

'I'm not being stupid!' James protested. 'It's easier this way, Poppy. I'm leaving next month. Why start something now? It'll be easier on both of us if we stop this now.'

'Before it's even begun? You talk about wanting to live your life and here I am, trying to be part of it, and you're running away.'

'We've never even been on a date!' cried James, losing his patience. 'I'm making it easier for you.'

'Oh my god,' fumed Poppy. 'If you think you're going to break my heart because we go on a couple of measly dates then you have a grossly overinflated sense of your own charisma.'

James threw his hands in the air. 'Do you even want to go out with me, Poppy?! Because I'm picking up on a lot of negative energy!'

Poppy glared at him. James glared back, and then, infuriatingly, he began to smile. It was small at first, creeping from the corners of his lips to his cheeks—and then a triumphant grin enveloped his whole face. He started to laugh. And damn it, now she was laughing too. She hadn't laughed since before Mary's accident and it was like the pressure of the past weeks was exploding from her like water from a fire hydrant. They were laughing so hard tears were streaming down their faces. James was doubled over and Poppy's abs were aching. Every time they made eye contact they'd convulse again. Maeve looked between them, delighted and confused.

'I honestly think this is dumb,' said Poppy when she'd recovered her breath.

'Agree to disagree,' said James, wiping his eyes.

Poppy stuck out her lower lip. 'I'll miss you.'

'Same,' said James. He was serious now.

'I don't think I can do the friends thing with you,' admitted Poppy. 'At least not for a little bit.'

James nodded. 'So what do we do?'

'Nothing.' Poppy sighed. 'Go to Melbourne. Buy a trendy Akubra. Start drinking oat milk piccolos. Don't worry about us. We'll be fine. We don't need anything—no texts, no calls. At least not for a while, until my head descrambles.'

James's lips were clamped shut. 'Okay,' he said eventually.

'Okay,' replied Poppy. She wanted to reach out to him for one last hug but that would delay the inevitable. It turned out their story had ended weeks ago, and she hadn't even realised.

CHAPTER 44

Poppy tucked her shirt into the waistband of her cropped jeans and reviewed herself in the mirror. Her hair was clean and hung loose on her shoulders, and her skin was lightly bronzed from the sun. Maeve crawled in circles at her feet wearing a striped jumpsuit. She hoped as a duo they'd give off a cool-but-not-trying-too-hard vibe. She wanted to look like a lovely but forgettable kindergarten teacher. Agreeable and, crucially, harmless.

Henry and Willa were back together. It had been indirectly confirmed by her mother who had called yesterday with the details of the long-awaited group dinner. 'Peggy said to arrive at six, darling. She said you can bring the portacot and put it in the spare room for Maeve. I asked what we could bring and she said nothing, but I'm going to make a date slice, so if you were thinking of making one don't. You should take something, though, darling, because it's good manners. Maybe you could make a soup and we could pour it into paper cups and

SPECIAL DELIVERY

pass them around as little appetisers? I saw that once on *Better Homes and Gardens* and it looked so fancy! I have a divine recipe for a potato and leek soup, if you want it? Or if you wanted to do something sweet, you could make a lemon slice and we could make a little dessert platter, which could be fun. I could buy those little toothpicks that have the flags on them so it's easy for people to pick them up. I saw some in the party section at Big W. Do you want me to pick some up on my way home from golf? I'll be finished at three so can whiz past there very easily.'

'I've already bought some wine, Mum.'

'Oh, right. That's a good idea, but you're sure you don't want the little flags? I might just pop in and grab some anyway, just in case. We can always keep them for a rainy day if you don't end up making the lemon slice.'

'Mum, I'm not making a lemon slice.'

'Okay, but I might get some anyway, just in case you end up baking. Just don't make a date slice, though, because that's what I'm doing, remember? But I suppose if you *really* wanted to, you *could* make a date slice and I could make a lemon slice because I've got so many lemons on the tree at the moment . . .'

'Whatever you reckon, Mum.'

'Okay, so I should buy the little flags?'

'Mum, I'm bringing wine.'

'Great, and that will be lovely. And I'll grab the little flags in case we do the dessert platter.'

Poppy wondered if it was possible to be more explicit about not making dessert.

'Darling, I must go, but I'll see you at six tomorrow.'

After her mother had hung up, Poppy had spent the rest of the day avoiding thinking about the impending dinner.

Now, at twenty minutes to six, it was proving impossible to not overthink everything. Should she have baked the lemon slice? Should she have trimmed Maeve's almost-mullet? Poppy picked up her daughter and did a final outfit check. No spew on her shoulder or sneaky mashed banana on her butt cheek, so she already looked at least thirty per cent better than usual.

She buckled Maeve into her car seat and put the nappy bag on the passenger seat, the neck of a shiraz bottle peeking out of it. As she turned the key, she spoke into the windscreen. 'Siri, call Dani.'

Her phone in the centre console spoke back to her. 'Calling Dar Nee.'

Her best friend answered on the first ring. 'PARPEE!'

'DARNEE! Mate, how are you?'

'Same old, girlfriend. Watching Nella eat sand while I try to paint my toenails. What are you up to?'

'Heading to dinner with Henry and Willa.'

'Stop it! No! Why would you do that?!'

'Our mums organised it.'

Dani made a hooting sound. 'And are you okay with that?'

Poppy sighed. 'I think I need it, for closure. I built up Willa so much in my mind. I was scared of her because she'd made it final that Henry and I would never be together again. I mean, I knew logically that was probably going to be the case, but she made it real. And god, now I realise how much I built up Henry in my mind too. Over those nine years with Patrick I had way too much distance to make the heart grow fonder.

Now I've got my head sorted a bit, I think I can handle it. In fact, I need to handle it.'

Dani cackled.

'What?'

'Pops, we will piss ourselves laughing about this one day! It's even a bit hilarious now. Your mums are setting you up on a play date.'

'Oh god,' yelped Poppy. 'Am I the kid who needs a momager to make friends? This is so embarrassing!'

Dani chuckled. 'Relax, Pops. I'm teasing. It's great that you and Henry are back to being friends. You need to call me immediately after dinner for a full recap. Extra points if it's Willa-related information. I want to know all. Even if she tells you about her bowel movements, you tell me that shit! Pun intended, obviously.'

'I am making no promises to ask about her bowel movements, but if she volunteers that information, I solemnly swear to pass it on.'

'Legend. That's why I love you, Pops.'

'Love you too, Dan.'

Poppy hung up as she pulled into a tree-lined street. The Marshalls' house was bordered by an expertly pruned garden, with spheres of ornamental roses sitting behind laser-level hedges. An eggshell-white gravel path led visitors to the front door, which refracted blues, reds and yellows through its leadlight windows.

Poppy hoisted Maeve onto her hip and walked towards it. The lion's head brass knocker clanged with an ear-splitting resonance and the door swung open. A tall girl in a white slip dress with a tiny diamond nose ring stood before her. 'You must be Poppy!' she said, and then a slow wave of recognition dawned across her blemish-free face. 'Oh, heyyyy!'

'What?!' spluttered Poppy. *The Woolworths Angel?! The woman who'd paid for her groceries?* 'You're Willa?'

'Guilty.'

'How old are you?!' cried Poppy.

'Er, twenty-nine. And a half, I guess, if we're being specific.'

'Oh my gosh, sorry. I didn't mean to ask that. It's just that, wow, you look nineteen or something. I thought you were a student.'

'I technically *am* still studying,' Willa said with a laugh. 'Eleven years and counting. Who'd do medicine, hey? At least I'm past the phase when people mistook me for that K-Pop man-child.'

Poppy laughed too, stunned. Willa spoke in the same gentle voice Poppy remembered from their previous encounter but delivered lines like a stand-up comedian. It was so disconcerting.

'Come in,' Willa said, and Poppy followed her into the hallway. It was adorned with the same pictures Poppy remembered from years ago: framed nineties photo shoots, beach holiday snaps and Madonna-esque wedding photos. The ceramic dish on the hallway table was still cluttered with keyrings.

'Hey, Poppy,' said Henry, not looking up as they walked into the kitchen. He had a tea towel over his shoulder and was carving the roast lamb. Poppy could guess the reason for the pink tinge on his ears. 'I see you've met Willa.'

'We've actually met before,' announced Willa.

SPECIAL DELIVERY

Henry jerked his head up. 'What?'

Willa waved airily. 'Tech issues, a passive-aggressive checkout chick . . . don't worry, we sorted it.'

Henry's laugh was stilted. 'Do I want to know more?'

'Nope,' said Willa. 'We're going to get along great, so you can stop directing your nervous energy into your knife skills. You look like Uma Thurman from *Kill Bill* and your ears are so red they're about to combust.' She tugged on his earlobe playfully as she walked past to open the fridge. 'Wine, Poppy?'

Poppy smiled. 'Love one.' If these first minutes were anything to go by, the giant elephant thundering in her chest could take a nap. No stampeding anxiousness required here.

In the living room, Poppy greeted Henry's parents and her own. Both mothers stood up immediately to fawn over Maeve and the fathers raised their beer bottles in a silent welcome. It was jarring to see Henry's parents looking so much older than she remembered, but that was life, she guessed. They were probably thinking the same about her.

Poppy, Henry and Willa sat down to dinner at the kids' end (as they all automatically called it) with Maeve in a highchair. As they passed the salads across the table, Poppy learned that Willa was a natural conversationalist. She was captivating, self-deprecating, she asked about motherhood and Taylor Swift's back catalogue, she had opinions on RAM drivers and regional healthcare, and segued seamlessly from Kanye West to European politics with an easy charm. Poppy was enthralled.

Henry was too. Poppy could tell by the way he caught Willa's eye to emphasise a point and knocked his head gently against hers when she teased him. He kept one arm slung over the back of her chair the whole night, and Poppy had the impression of witnessing something intensely intimate as they recounted the story of his proposal, and she noticed his fingers slide reflexively across her shoulder and settle there casually, like they'd apparently done countless times before.

The night after the races was an aeon ago. Who had they even been pretending to be that night? This table in front of them—with roast potatoes, tossed salads, homemade mint jelly and lamb from the butcher down the road—this was real life. Eating a meal with old friends and new ones, her parents and daughter, this was a tableau she wanted to recreate again and again.

Her mind drifted to James, how easily he'd fit in here with his knee against hers, laughing at their jokes, telling his own, picking up the rattle Maeve insisted on throwing to the floor, catching her eye and winking when no-one else was looking. The tiny keyhole inside her was still empty. It wasn't depression or sadness; it was just a hollow. But there was nothing more she could do. He'd made his decision, she'd made hers and they didn't align. Maybe one day their two paths would converge, but—and this was the thing she had to remind herself every day when she woke up and longed for his body next to hers— that was un-bloody-likely. He was a wonderful guy moving to a city of five million people, half of them female. People didn't find the love of their life in dusty hospital car parks. They found them in cool speakeasy bars with dim lighting and sexy playlists. They found them in lecture halls and libraries and after-work-drinks haunts, where common interests drew them

SPECIAL DELIVERY

together like magnets. Big cities were where big love stories were made. James would meet a model in a dive bar or a megababe in surgical scrubs. The odds were unspeakably strong.

Dinner passed quickly, and before she knew it Poppy was waking Maeve from the portacot in the spare room and carrying her daughter, heavy with sleep, to the car. Henry walked her out while inside the others put the wineglasses in the dishwasher and cling-wrapped the leftovers.

'Thanks for coming, Pops. I appreciate you being so—'

'Least I could do,' interrupted Poppy, knowing exactly what Henry wanted to say. 'Willa is awesome,' she added. 'I'm so happy for you, Hen.'

'Thanks, Pops. That means a lot.'

They looked at each other and smiled. There was so much in their smiles—joy, pain, sadness, understanding. Poppy knew it, and she knew Henry knew it. They were growing up. They weren't teenagers anymore and they were doing their best to grab adulthood with both hands. It would never be simple but they were both getting better at it. It helped that they had each other's back.

Poppy pulled her key out of her pocket and clicked the button to unlock the car. Henry pulled the back door open and Poppy slid her daughter into her car seat. Maeve grunted contentedly, her eyelids weighed down with sleep.

'You okay getting her home by yourself?' asked Henry.

Poppy smiled. 'I'm used to it.'

She climbed into the car, put the key in the ignition and waved goodbye. It wasn't the last time she'd do this by herself and she was learning to be okay with that.

CHAPTER 45

A television droned in the background with tiny men in cricket whites dotting the screen. It was thirty-two degrees and Maeve had taken her first steps, stumbling the forty or so centimetres from the floral sofa to the arms of Poppy, sitting cross-legged on the carpet of her parents' living room.

As Paul whooped, Chrissie had cried, 'You go, girl!' while Poppy dissolved into giggles and kissed her daughter's head where a blonde crown of curls was starting to form. Her daughter would be one—*one!*—in less than a week. She couldn't believe it. After the slog of those early days, when every hour had almost killed her, it now felt like it had been the most fulfilling year of her life. Sure, there had been some horrible lows—the sight of Mary's empty house still brought tears to her eyes every day—but the highs of the last twelve months had been sky-scraping. It was like motherhood had a way of magnifying and amplifying everything. Tasks she would have done a thousand times pre-kids—brunch, shopping, exercising—were now the highlights of her days, things to be pored over in minute detail with Dani and her mum, dissected and unpacked so every last mote of enjoyment could be fully squeezed out. Even the crap things could become beautiful moments. It only took a giggle from Maeve to turn a nappy change into the most wondrous bonding experience. It was as if Maeve made everything phosphorescent.

Poppy twisted her daughter around to sit on her lap and picked up a slice of leftover Christmas cake from the plate on the coffee table. December 25 had come and gone in a flurry of ham and turkey and cranberry sauce, rounded out with her dad snoring on the couch after too many eggnogs. (He didn't actually drink eggnog, but for some reason on Christmas Day he'd always declare he'd had too many.) It had just been the four of them, not a giant family-filled event like she knew James would be having at Burrendong, but it was the first Christmas the three generations of McKellars had spent together. They would make new family traditions with Maeve and—who knew?—maybe one day there would be another man joining her Dad for eggnog. Who knew how her family would grow in the future? Whatever happened, she was grateful for now.

In less than twenty-four hours, it would be a new year. April had invited her to come over and watch the fireworks on television, but in the end they'd both agreed they couldn't be bothered staying up until midnight. Everyone knew New Year's Eve was overrated unless you had someone to kiss, and this year she was glad of the excuse for an early night. She would get into her pyjamas and drift off to sleep and wake up with a clear head and a day full of potential.

Maeve was only having one nap a day now, so their schedule had changed again. Poppy hadn't walked the golf course loop in a while, but that was okay—she was trying to create new habits to distract from the pain of not being able to rely on a kind word and a cup of tea from Mary. Instead, Poppy had filled their mornings with music lessons, kinder gym and coffees with the other mothers' group girls. A new wholefoods cafe had opened with outdoor tables and giant shade cloths, so they'd been spending many mornings there to savour the vitamin D. With Maeve crawling, visits to The Bustle had become too difficult (the art and expensive homewares seemed to magnetically attract sticky-fingered babies). It meant she didn't see Henry as much anymore, but that was okay too. She'd had brunch with him and Willa and April last Sunday, which had been surprisingly lovely. The ratio of four adults to two babies was a particular game-changer. Privately, April had asked Poppy if they could all hang out more often. When Poppy had needed to go to the bathroom, Willa had settled Maeve on her knee and played a game of peekaboo, this arrangement being infinitely preferable to balancing a wriggly baby on your lap while trying to pee. Henry had looked more like himself than Poppy had seen him in months. Willa was so calm and gentle but so bitingly witty, Poppy was in awe of her. They were planning to go to a yoga class together the following week.

The shadow of James was constant. Every time she passed the oak tree, she automatically checked to see if he was there. She wanted to know how he was doing but they'd agreed there would be no contact. She wondered if he was finding it as

SPECIAL DELIVERY

difficult as she was. She wasn't miserable—there was so much to be thankful for—but there was room in her heart for him. He just wasn't here.

Most days she was tempted to text him, but so far she'd stayed strong. She knew distance and time would heal her, so she needed to keep up her end of the bargain. Once they emerged from the weird void between Christmas and New Year, there would be lots to distract her.

The golf club mafia had found Maeve a spot in a lovely day care centre run by the daughter of a second cousin of a friend—or something like that. It wasn't the newest or shiniest facility, but when Poppy and Maeve visited, the staff had been warm and engaged, and that was what Poppy needed: people to love her daughter while she was at work, loving her from a distance. She was already terrified at how the first drop-off would go but she figured she'd survive. (You couldn't literally die from mum guilt, could you?) It would be gut-wrenching, but she needed to get a job to support her family, and she *wanted* to work, so this was another hurdle to add to the list—and after a year of hurdling like an Olympian, she knew she'd make it.

Maeve would start at day care in three weeks' time. Poppy had ordered personalised labels for Maeve's teeny clothes and had been carefully ironing them on, neatly parallel to the seam. It felt simultaneously both completely over-the-top and yet somehow completely appropriate. How else did you commemorate the start of day care if not with the religious labelling of soon-to-be lost or trashed clothing?

'Any plans for tomorrow?' asked Poppy's dad.

'None,' replied Poppy. 'Though you're going to pop over, aren't you, Mum? And I'm going to try to build Maeve a sandpit, so I'll have to go to Bunnings, and then depending on how I go with the sandpit, April and her son might come around for a play.'

She'd been targeted on Instagram endlessly by a new flat-pack sandpit company, and it had got her thinking it would probably be good for Maeve to have a few more outdoor activities. It would be great for entertaining, too, which was one of her New Year's resolutions: to make the most of her new friends by inviting them over. She didn't fancy spending five hundred dollars on the Instagram version of a sandpit, but she reckoned with a few timber sleepers from Bunnings, a tarp and some bags of sand, she could rig up a passable version.

'Maeve will enjoy that,' said her mum. 'I remember you loved the sandpit—mainly to eat the sand. You never got sick so I let you get on with it. Kids know what's good for them.'

As if in agreement, Maeve plucked a leaf from the vase of flowers on the coffee table, inspected it thoughtfully then shoved it into her mouth.

'See?' said Chrissie. 'She eats her greens like a good girl.'

Poppy smiled and tugged the leaf from her daughter's lips. 'It'll be my first DIY project of the year.'

'Setting the tone for another year of self-sufficiency,' said her dad.

'Exactly,' agreed Poppy, an image of James in a tool belt flashing through her mind. She was waiting for time to fade her memories of him but it was as though her brain had carefully bottled and preserved every detail of him; his eyes,

SPECIAL DELIVERY

his smile, his warmth, how his hands felt on her skin. The distance and the silence were conspiring to make her miss him even more, but she knew this would pass. She just had to wait it out, focus on what was in front of her, keep making plans, keep ploughing ahead, and slowly, inexorably, James would fade to a hazy broad-shouldered silhouette on a horizon she'd long since left behind.

Poppy passed a slice of apple to Maeve, who was now licking the leg of the coffee table.

'Do you want me to give you a hand?' asked her dad.

'Nah,' replied Poppy. 'It shouldn't be too hard, according to the videos.'

'Are you sure?' pressed her mother. 'If you break your arm carrying the timber around you won't be able to start the new job, and that would be such a shame when I've just downloaded that app for Maeve's day care on my phone. I'm already getting notifications.'

Poppy caught her dad's eye. 'Mum, I'll be fine.'

'Oh, I know, darling, but you young girls race around like busyness is a competitive sport, so just be careful. I've always said channelling the tortoise, not the hare, is the surest path to victory.'

Poppy smiled. 'And what's victory?'

Poppy's parents glanced at each other and Poppy had the sense this was a conversation they'd had many times before. 'Peace,' her dad said simply.

'That's all we want, isn't it?' added her mum.

Peace. Her parents were right. That was all she wanted. She wasn't a complicated girl. She just needed reassurance, love and a pat on the back occasionally. It was simple really. Her love language was cups of tea and punny jokes. She might never find someone to share those knowing looks with, but that was fine. There were other ways she could fill her cup. Family time was one of them.

She turned back to her parents and smiled. 'How did you two get so wise?'

Her mum opened her mouth but her dad cut in before she could speak. 'Maeve and I have been watching a lot of *Judge Judy*,' he said.

CHAPTER 46

Poppy swatted uselessly at a blowfly that was buzzing angrily at her windscreen. The windows were all open in an attempt to suction it out, but the bastard was too dumb to notice. The buzzing sound was becoming exponentially more frustrating with every second. Maeve was crying in the car seat as the hot air outside pummelled her face but the stupid fly was determinedly not flying out. Groaning, Poppy lunged at it as she slowed for the roundabout. The fly, as if in response, lazily swerved left and landed on her dash.

Maeve wailed again, increasing her volume this time, so Poppy reluctantly pressed the windows-up button. The fly had won this round, but the joke was on it; she'd trapped it now, so it better think twice if it thought it was getting out alive.

Maeve's cry declined to an irritating grumble. It was a shudderingly hot day, and the fabric of the seatbelt was sticky against her skin. The streets were empty, the black tar reflecting the heat back onto the few cars that were bothering to go anywhere on the scorching public holiday.

Her mother, who'd called her this morning to wish her a Happy New Year, had no idea why she was so determined to build this sandpit.

'It's going to reach thirty-eight degrees, darling. Karl Stefanovic said it was the hottest start to the year in a thousand years. Or maybe it was a hundred? Actually, it could have been a million. It was something like that. If you ask me, I think you'd be better off putting on the sprinkler.'

'Mum, there are water restrictions. I can't.'

'I know, darling, I wasn't suggesting you break the law, but I thought if you just did it quickly—just for Maeve—no-one would really mind.'

'It's fine, Mum. I need a project.'

'I know, darling, but do you need to do it today? It's not as though there's any deadline.'

Poppy couldn't explain it but there was a deadline. She'd made the decision to build it today and now she needed to execute the plan. If she didn't, she feared that would imply something significant. She wanted to be a woman—a mother—who kicked goals and got shit done. As her dad had said, she was setting the tone for the year. For some reason, this sandpit had become emblematic of so much more than a box of imported sand.

'Mum, it's totally fine. After being pregnant last summer, I can hardly feel the heat this time around, and this is the first New Year's Day in about fifteen years that I haven't been hungover . . . or pregnant. I need to capitalise on my good health.'

SPECIAL DELIVERY

'*Bon santé*, then,' said her mother. 'And before I forget, I just found out *Better Homes and Gardens* is filming me two weeks from Friday. I got a last-minute hair appointment on the Thursday, which is outrageously lucky. I'm going to hit the sales tomorrow to find an outfit, if you want to join? Rockmans has some lovely colours at the mo—'

'Wait, what? Why are you going to be on *Better Homes and Gardens*?'

'Didn't I tell you, darling? Martha's garden has been selected for one of those whizz-bang garden features! The ones where Johanna Griggs and that Graham fellow walk around and tell jokes while they look at the flowerbeds. Their angle is "the neighbourhood garden", so I'm being interviewed as one of the friendly neighbours! Imagine that! Your mum on prime-time TV! I'm going to get your dad to film me on the iPad tonight so I can work out my best angles. It's all so thrilling!'

'I thought you weren't speaking to Martha?'

'Oh no, darling, don't be ridiculous. We've both just been a bit busy, that's all, and then there was that little miscommunication over the magnolia. And actually, the jasmine has grown on me. There are apparently lots of jasmine notes in the Dior perfumes—the ones with Charlize Theron in the ads. Anyhow, you be careful at Bunnings and remember to get a nice shop person to help you carry the timber. You don't want to hurt yourself in this heat. I've got to pop over to Martha's. We're going to do a little run-through of the garden and practise some good comments. I was thinking we should make a point of mentioning the birdhouse because then I can make some funny jokes about us being a pair of old birds too. I think Johanna would really have a giggle at that one. Better go, darling, bye!'

Poppy stared at the road and blinked three times to check it wasn't a dream. The backflips her mother could perform were incredible.

Maeve was still grumbling in the back when she arrived at the Bunnings car park. Poppy glanced at her phone and suddenly Dani's name appeared on the screen before she'd even heard it ring. Funny how often that happened. She scooped it up and pressed the green button.

'DARNEE!'

'PARPEE! Happy New Year, my dear. How are you?'

'It's too hot. I feel like a gelatinous lobster. My hairline is so sweaty I look like I'm trying for that wet-look style that J.Lo used to do—though in my case it stinks of BO.'

'Wow, there's a lot to unpack there.'

'Yeah, and Maeve has the shits too,' Poppy said, getting out of the car to open Maeve's door. 'Not gastro. Just the figurative shits. It's too hot.'

'Where are you?'

'Just arrived at Bunnings, why?'

'Why are you at Bunnings?'

Poppy explained her plans for the sandpit while Dani made unimpressed grunting sounds to convey her distaste for hardware stores. That was a luxury she could afford, living in an already-renovated terrace.

'I'll leave you to it then, my dear,' said Dani. 'Enjoy yourself and then go have a shower. I can smell you from here.'

'Did you call just to annoy me?'

SPECIAL DELIVERY

'Just to hear your voice, my lovely.'

Poppy walked into the store and smiled. 'Love you too, dickhead.'

She slid the phone into the pocket of her denim shorts and grabbed a trolley, funnelling Maeve's legs into the front seat.

'Can I help you?' asked a teenage boy wearing a Bunnings polo. He had a magnificent mullet that cascaded onto his shoulders. He must have been growing it since his tweens.

'I'm looking for sand,' said Poppy. 'And tarps. And timber. I'm making a sandpit.'

'You're doing it yourself?' he asked.

'Yep.'

'Cool,' he said, impressed, and Poppy felt herself swell with pride.

'The sand is in the outdoor section and the timber is at the opposite end, down there.' He pointed to his left. 'Tarps are in aisle twenty-three. Good luck.'

'Thanks,' replied Poppy. She set off towards aisle twenty-three, coming to an abrupt stop when she reached it. Wow, there were lots of tarps. And Jesus, so many specifications she'd not considered: fabric type, grams per square metre, hem quality, denier density. She needed help.

'Excuse me,' she called lamely, looking left and right for a polo-shirted staff member.

Predictably, no-one came. She lifted up her t-shirt to wipe the sweat off her face, squinting at the packaging in front of her. Maeve whined more loudly.

'Far out,' Poppy muttered under her breath. What was the difference between 'extreme heavy duty' and 'industrial strength'? They sounded the same but the price difference was huge. Was this some secret code designed to confuse her?

She scanned the shelves for the second-cheapest brand. It was flimsy logic but hopefully it would do the job. She chucked a dark green tarp into the trolley and Maeve grumbled at the jolt. Poppy patted her head. 'It'll be over soon,' she promised, steering the trolley back towards the central aisle.

Playing a half-hearted one-handed game of peekaboo to distract Maeve, she made her way to the outdoor section, which was a giant steel greenhouse tightly packed with plants, cubby houses and acrid-smelling potting mix. Poppy took a half-breath in shock when they entered. It was so stiflingly hot she could taste the heat on her tongue. Maeve began to wail, so Poppy pulled her out of the trolley and onto her hip, steering the trolley with her spare hand. She needed this sand and she needed it fast.

She finally found the aisle with bags of sand piled up in towers. She plonked Maeve on the concrete floor at her feet and went to grab a bag from the top of the pile. Jeez, they were heavy. She looked left and right for help. Again, there was no-one in sight. This was becoming a common theme.

She turned back to the sand tower and tugged at one of the bags. She yanked again and the bag shifted two inches towards her. Progress. She gave another almighty yank and the bag came with her as she fell to the floor, her tailbone hitting hot concrete.

A pain tingled up her spine and Poppy felt tears of helplessness prick her eyes as she heaved the sandbag into the trolley and hoisted her daughter onto her hip. Deep down she'd known it was ridiculous to build a sandpit, but that stupid, stubborn part of her had wanted to impress everyone with how capable she was. *Look at me, just casually building a sandpit. Don't mind me, just single-mothering like a boss.* God, if this past year had taught her anything it should have been to lower her standards to the lowest possible degree, not try to be a hero.

She moved Maeve from her hip, lowered her into the trolley and began pushing it towards her last stop: the timber section.

'Okay,' breathed Poppy, more to herself than to her daughter. The walls of timber were threateningly high and the lengths were preposterously long. Maeve banged her hands against the trolley handle. Poppy looked up and down the empty aisle, feeling a familiar sinking feeling, when suddenly—like the sun peeping through the clouds—a red polo shirt appeared.

'Need some help, ma'am?' asked another teenager with a mullet.

'I need four pieces of timber, please—about a metre long each.'

'I can give you one four-metre length for you to cut into one-metre lengths,' suggested the kid.

Poppy found his assumption that she would own some kind of woodcutting implement both fortifying and irritating. Kids these days knew nothing about how people actually lived.

'No, thank you, I'll just take four one-metre lengths.'

'I can't do that,' replied the kid.

'Excuse me?' asked Poppy, raising an eyebrow.

'The tradies all prefer four metres, so we only stock those. We don't get many lady customers up here in the timber section.' He paused as if to remind her of her own femaleness. 'Can't you get your husband to cut it up for you?'

Poppy stared at the kid, a fire igniting in her belly that had nothing to do with the heatwave. Was this really happening on the first of January? Was she going to have another whole year of this assumed husband crap? She hadn't even made it to Australia Day. Wasn't this generation supposed to be woke? Oh, the things she could teach this mullet head.

She was about to give him an education in heteronormative stereotypes when she heard a voice behind her, say, 'I can help.'

Poppy turned, knowing in some part of her body what she was about to see. Thoughts of strangling the mullet kid faded. It was as though every bad decision had led her here. As she spun, it was as though her brain had retired. She was muscle and energy, a beating heart and a clueless soul.

'James?' she squeaked.

'Poppy.' He said it like an incantation, his eyes on her, unwavering.

'Budda ludda budda baaa!' cried Maeve happily, reaching towards James. He picked her up and kissed her forehead, letting her tiny legs wrap around his torso.

'What are you doing here?' Poppy asked.

He cleared his throat. 'I was—'

'Awesome,' interrupted the teenager. 'Your husband can cut the timber for you.' He turned to James now. 'Mate, grab any piece you want and take it through the checkout at the back. Saves carrying it through the whole shop.'

Poppy watched him lope off, oblivious to the mess he'd left behind.

'He's not my husband!' she yelled at his back.

The teenager just shrugged as if to say, *Whatever, lady.*

SPECIAL DELIVERY

'Can you believe that kid?' she fumed. 'Did he grow up with the Amish or something? Does he think women are still milking cows and churning butter like the suffragettes never existed? I mean, do I look like I can't handle myself with a chainsaw?' She glanced down at herself. 'Actually don't answer that.'

She looked back up at James. The corners of his mouth were struggling to stay neutral.

'What?' she demanded.

James's face relented and a wide grin appeared, blinding like the sun. 'Nothing's changed, I see.'

Poppy glared. 'Are you patronising me?'

'By definition, no,' replied James. 'I never feel any inch of control when you're around, hence the lack of condescension.'

Poppy narrowed her eyes. Maeve was still in his arms.

'I was admiring your commitment to exposing unconscious biases and'—James paused—'your commitment to DIY projects.'

Now he was definitely making fun of her. It was already too hot in this godforsaken town; she did not need James swanning in being so handsome and distracting when she knew he'd moved to Melbourne six weeks ago.

'Why are you here?'

'I would have thought that was obvious.'

'You're buying timber?'

'I came to see you.' He was serious now. Maeve's head was on his shoulder.

'How did you know I was here?'

'I can't tell you that,' replied James.

'Why?'

'Because it's kind of stalker-ish.'

Poppy pulled her daughter out of his arms, her fingertips buzzing as they brushed his skin. She wondered if he felt it too—a pull in the stomach, an attraction she couldn't control. She couldn't look at him holding Maeve anymore. It was too confusing.

'Tell me,' she ordered.

James raked a hand through his hair. 'To cut a long story short, I rang Kate, who rang April, who messaged Dani, who rang you and then called April, who rang Kate, who rang me, and now here we are. Though I'm glossing over the bits where each of them independently reached out to lecture me about the broken heart.'

Poppy bristled. 'I never told any of them I had a broken heart.'

'I never said it was yours,' James said quietly.

Poppy swallowed. There was fear in her throat but there was a flicker of hope too.

'Why are you here?' she asked again. 'You live in Melbourne.'

'I did move to Melbourne,' James agreed, nodding slowly.

Poppy felt a pent-up tension in her chest deflate. He *had* moved to Melbourne; it hadn't been a bad dream.

Maeve reached for James and he stuck his finger out for her to latch on to. They were linked now. Poppy holding Maeve, Maeve holding James.

'It was all going perfectly,' James continued. 'I was meeting great people, I had this shiny apartment, I was walking distance to the MCG and twenty-seven cafes or something. But then

SPECIAL DELIVERY

I realised nothing actually felt real. It was easy, it was okay, it was good even, but it wasn't me. I was doing what I thought I *should* want but I hadn't considered what I actually wanted.'

His voice was soft now, like a breeze. The sounds of nearby shoppers had faded to silence. Maeve was uncharacteristically silent.

'I was trying to kickstart my life by forcing a big change but I realised I didn't need to manufacture an artificial turning point to push me forward. My turning point came twelve months ago and it led me to exactly where I wanted to be and I was too dumb to realise.' He shook his head. 'I didn't need to move to a big city to find myself. I know who I am already. I'm a boring loser who loves his mum and family and dog, and I love my cricket team and I fucking love country music, and I realised I actually hate hipster cafes where the music is too loud and the coffee comes in weird cups without handles, and sometimes I like watching TV on a Saturday night and not socialising, and sometimes I go to the gym just to see people and belong somewhere, and sometimes I smile and nod because I can't be bothered with conflict, and sometimes I do get angry and that's okay, because I've realised I don't have to be perfect and no-one is.' James paused and took a deep breath. 'So, when I realised I didn't even like the coffee down there, I had to ask myself the obvious question.'

'Which was?' asked Poppy, her voice timid.

'There were lots of questions, actually, but the first question was: could I transfer universities?'

Okay, that had not been as significant as the lead-up suggested, but practical was fine. She could deal with practical.

'There were other questions,' he continued. 'Big things I needed to consider and face up to.'

He shifted on the balls of his feet, rocking towards Poppy. 'After I broke up with Adelaide, I wasn't so much sad as I was angry with myself. I knew she wasn't right for me, but I stuck around because I didn't want to be like my dad and just leave. So instead I stayed and was miserable, and then when we broke up I resolved never to waste my time being the nice guy again. Life's too short to be a boyfriend of Instagram. And then I met you, and here was this beautiful, intelligent, confident woman, and I literally didn't care what you thought of me, and you were the same, and it was perfect: I could be myself because there was nothing at stake.

'And then somehow, a year goes by and suddenly everything is at stake, and I wish I could take back all the times I've upset you and made you mad, but at the same time I'm so glad I did that because you *know* me now. I've never been so honest with anyone, I've never been so vulnerable and so real. You know the cracks and flaws and, somehow, you still don't hate me.'

'I could never hate you,' said Poppy, her heart beating thunderously against her rib cage.

James raised his eyebrow. 'Really?'

'Okay, but in my defence, I was chock-full of hormones when we first met.'

James smiled now, his eyes sparkling. 'The more I saw you, the happier I became. All this resentment I'd been carrying just kind of . . . faded. I was so confused, because I didn't know if I was happier because of something in me, or if I was happier because of you, and then I worked it out. It wasn't just about me and it wasn't just about you; it was about us together. We were two negatives making a positive.'

Poppy's throat felt thick. The movement of oxygen to her brain was slowing. All she could taste was sawdust and sand.

'I was so sick of pretending,' said James. 'I was so scared of settling. But with you, I never pretended. We were both so real. I understand now that I don't need to be the nice guy all the time. Sometimes people piss me off, sometimes I want to yell at Eileen for eating my shoes, sometimes I want to troll people on social media.'

'You'd never!' cried Poppy.

'I might. Did you hear they might stop producing Cornflakes? I actually considered trolling the CEO.'

'Well, that's fair enough.'

'Completely. But more to the point, while I was sitting in Melbourne drinking my piccolos, I realised if this last year has taught me anything it's that life can change in an instant, and that when you find something that makes you happy, you have to grab it and hold on to it. And then I realised I'm the luckiest guy in the world because I found two somethings that make me happy. I found you and I found Maeve.'

Poppy stood rooted to the spot. She couldn't definitively confirm it but she suspected she had stopped breathing. 'Back to the original question,' she whispered. 'Could you swap universities?'

'Yes.' The light in James's eyes began to dance.

'And?'

'I start Monday week.' He paused. 'And I get free parking.'

'For the love of god,' cried Poppy. 'Tell me where!'

James grinned. 'You're looking at the newest obstetrician-in-training at CSU Orange.'

Poppy's body reacted before her brain did. Her spare arm flung around James's neck, and she pressed herself against his warmth. Tears were forming in the corners of her eyes and she blinked them away. This was so embarrassing, but she was so *happy* he was back. She didn't need any labels or any commitment or anything more than this. She just needed this moment, this three-person hug.

She didn't care she was covering him with sweat and grime, because if he complained she knew she could tell him he was ruining the moment, and he'd laugh and say she was right but she was still gross, then she would laugh and agree. She didn't need to bite her tongue or tiptoe around anything. She didn't need to pretend. She'd found someone with whom she could be her truest self, and she was going to keep her body pressed against his for as long as she could.

'I was really hoping you'd react like this,' James murmured into her hair, one arm wrapped around her back as Maeve gripped the other. 'Otherwise, that stalking would have seemed so much creepier.'

Poppy laughed and pulled back slightly. She put Maeve in the trolley and they both handed her their keys. Maeve's eyes widened, delighted. Double keys! Jackpot!

James took Poppy's hands and wove his fingers through hers. 'Poppy McKellar, sometimes I get angry and sometimes things piss me off, but when I'm with you, even the bad stuff feels easier. You make me happier than I've ever been before, and if you'll accept that my intentions are completely dishonourable and I am extremely committed to getting you into bed again, I would love to take you out to dinner.'

Poppy's heart thundered in her chest. 'Like a date?'

'It would one thousand per cent be a date, and I want many more dates after that. We can go to every restaurant in town, then we can try every pub, we can try every barbecue station in every park, and then maybe we can branch out to Millthorpe and Molong. By the time I've courted you properly, you'll know every eatery in the Central West.'

Poppy's head was swimming with stars. This was everything she'd been dreaming of for months and it was here, a real chance at a life with James in it, but she couldn't walk into this blind. She had Maeve to think about. They were a package deal.

'Are you sure, James?' she asked. 'I'm a single mum, remember. There are so many single women out there who are much cooler than I am and heaps more organised too. I mean, there are probably girls out there who like cricket—and I have to be upfront about this: I don't think I'll *ever* like cricket. Are you sure you want to go out with me?'

James smiled. 'Poppy,' he said, his hands sliding up her arms, 'I've never been more sure of anything in my life.'

'But what if—'

'Poppy,' James interrupted, 'please shut up. I'm in love with you.'

Poppy felt it then: a tectonic plate shifting deep within her. She didn't know if she was breathing or her heart was beating, but something inside her suddenly unravelled.

'I love you too,' she breathed. The words slipped out like blossoms on a breeze. She hadn't even formed the words in her head before she said them, but a part of her had known for ages. *Yes, I love him.* It seemed so obvious now.

James pulled her towards him and kissed her. His lips were just as she remembered, warm and tender and giving, and Poppy felt herself melt. If she could have this for forever, or even just a little while, the last twelve months would be worth it.

They wrapped their arms around one another and fell into a hug, breathing into each other's skin.

'Is this fate?' asked James, his lips against her neck.

Poppy considered this. If the universe had a plan for her, she was eternally grateful it had brought her to Bunnings on this New Year's Day, but she knew with a deep confidence that she'd brought herself here. Poppy McKellar had been the person who decided to build a sandpit even when everyone else called her crazy. She'd made every decision leading to this point, and while there had been moments over the past year that had tested her and scared her, she had battled through them. She still wasn't a brave person, but she knew now that she was strong.

'I've decided I don't believe in fate anymore,' she said, picking Maeve back up. 'I think we're all just doing the best we can, and sometimes—call it fate if you want—the right person turns up at the right time.'

'Like now?' asked James.

'Like now,' Poppy agreed. There would always be decisions to make, chaos to overcome and a daughter to decode, but for now, she felt at peace with that.

In her arms, Maeve shook the keys like a pair of maracas and around them oblivious shoppers searched for skirting

SPECIAL DELIVERY

boards and pedestal fans while mullet-haired kids in red polo shirts pretended to be useful.

James squeezed her tight and kissed her forehead. Poppy's heart was as full as it had ever been.

'Want to get out of here?' she asked, her eyes giddy with possibility.

James nodded. 'You lead the way.'

And then, whether it was the universe's plan or not, he carried the timber to the checkout and then on to her car.

ACKNOWLEDGEMENTS

Writing this book was such a joyous exercise because I wrote exactly what I wanted to read. I filled my story with big, colourful, loving characters, then took them to my favourite places and let them have as much fun as I could imagine. I wrote on the couch, in bed, at the kitchen bench and wherever and whenever I could find the time. There wasn't much of a game plan other than: rom + com + mumming + Orange. I'm so grateful that the team at Allen & Unwin enjoyed the story and helped me polish it into the novel it is today. Thanks to Annette Barlow, Cate Paterson, Greer Gamble, Sam Mansell, Ali Hampton and Shannon Edwards for your unending patience and wisdom. Having you all in my corner is such a privilege. Thanks also to my razor-sharp copyeditor Ali Lavau who I would like to permanently transplant into my brain and to Christa Moffit for bringing such an incredible cover to life. To extend a metaphor, it really does take a village . . .

My late dad spun the greatest of yarns and lucky for him, he married my mum who's a wonderful audience because she'll laugh at anything, even if it's not that funny. Both of them taught me the joy of storytelling and encouraged me to write, so thanks Mum and Dad—for everything. Rounding out the family acknowledgements, shout-out to my sister, who was my trusted first reader (sorry if she stuffed up anyone's payroll while she was reading this at work; according to some very biased sources it was '*unputdownable!*') and to my brother—thanks for letting us watch all those rom-coms growing up. You're a very a good man.

I'm lucky to have many friends across the world who are absolute legends and who've embraced my foray into novel writing with their usual level of awesomeness. Thanks to my beta-reader, Hayley, without whom I would never have been inspired to try and pursue a book deal, and to Soph and Beauy who conspired to connect me with Allen & Unwin. Ally, Lizzie and Anna, thanks for the early feedback, and Andie, thanks for the covert hospital-ward pics that you *definitely did not take* while in labour. To everyone else who's giggled with me through the journey—over coffees, lunches, sneaky NYC trips and Saturday run sessions—you know who you are, and I value your friendship so, so much.

My friend Torie Finnane will never get to read this book, but I thought of her often during the writing process. Not only was she an amazing midwife, she was an incredible mum and source of support as I navigated early parenthood. If I hadn't met Torie, I'm not sure if I would have ever had the idea for this book. Her legacy lives on through the

Torie Finnane Foundation, so please look it up and donate if you can.

I was a bundle of self-doubt as I tip-toed into the online writing world, but I was immediately blown away by the generosity and encouragement of the Australian writing community. It's like a live Oprah audience permanently ready to hype you up. Thank you to everyone I've connected with online and in real life—your support continually amazes and humbles me. Kelly Rimmer, in particular, has been an incredible sounding board and cheerleader. I feel so lucky that you responded to my cold call after I got the book offer, and while it may have seemed a bit creepy, *je ne regrette rien*.

There is no big enough way to adequately thank my husband. If I was a more organised and culinarily gifted person I would bake some kind of Bruce Bogtrotter–style cake and let him have it all to himself. He deserves it! Throughout this adventure he has been my most valued confidante and supporter. I'm eternally grateful that I tricked such a clever, funny, handsome man into marrying me.

To my kids: if you ever read this book I will have to staple a few pages together before you get started, however I hope the story helps you understand how much you mean to me. The love I have for you is cellular and crazy and it makes me laugh every day.

Last but not least, I think I should acknowledge myself. It was a bit of a random, crazy idea to write a book, but I got there in the end. Well done, me!